"Fast-paced, suspenseful."

—*Publishers Weekly* on *Breakthrough*

PRAISE FOR *EXPOSURE*

"*Exposure,* Pineiro's fifth book, is suspenseful and exciting."
—*The Baton Rouge Morning Advocate*

"Grisham fans will enjoy this well-written version of *The Pelican Brief* meets *The Net*."
—*Austin American Statesman*

PRAISE FOR *RETRIBUTION*

"Pineiro scrunches you into an ejection seat and sends you rocketing aloft. . . . Thank God for a realist in the ranks."
—Dean Ing

"A story as frighteningly real as tomorrow's headlines."
—Richard Henrick, bestselling author of *Crimson Tide*

"A scary scenario. . . . First rate."
—*Texas Monthly*

"A tightly plotted, fast-paced thriller that reads like future history. . . . Pineiro's vision of what might be evokes visceral fear."
—Mark Berent, *New York Times* bestselling author of *Storm Flight*

PRAISE FOR *ULTIMATUM*

"*Ultimatum* is the purest techno-thriller I've seen in years. This book may define the genre."
—Stephen Coonts

"The action has a dramatic, urgent flair that has entertained readers and audiences since the days of Errol Flynn. All in all, if you like books that you almost can't put down and that keep you on the edge of your seat, you won't regret reading *Ultimatum*."
—*Austin Chronicle*

BOOKS BY R. J. PINEIRO

BREAKTHROUGH

R. J. PINEIRO

TOR®

A TOM DOHERTY ASSOCIATES BOOK
NEW YORK

This is a work of fiction. All the characters and events portrayed in this book are either products of the author's imagination or are used fictitiously.

BREAKTHROUGH

Copyright © 1997 by Rogelio J. Pineiro

A Tor Book
Published by Tom Doherty Associates, Inc.
175 Fifth Avenue
New York, NY 10010

Tor Books on the World Wide Web:
http://www.tor.com

Tor® is a registered trademark of Tom Doherty Associates, Inc.

ISBN: 0-812-54390-4
Library of Congress Card Catalog Number: 97-11946

First edition: September 1997
First mass market edition: February 1999

Printed in the United States of America

0 9 8 7 6 5 4 3 2 1

For my son, Cameron, age eight. Your daddy is very proud of the fine young man you're very quickly turning out to be. Your good heart, Christian values, positive outlook, and awesome school grades will carry you very far in life.

AND

Once again, for St. Jude, Saint of the Impossible, for continuing to make it possible.

ACKNOWLEDGMENTS

As always, there are many wonderful individuals to thank for their valuable contribution throughout the process.

For being there for me every day and night of my life, during the good times and the few bad ones, I thank Lory Anne, my wife, my friend, my soulmate. It's impossible for me to imagine life without you.

My good friend Dave, for an ongoing education in firearms, the Russian language, and other subjects. Also, very special thanks for the *Scientific American* article on protein transistors, which became the basis for this story.

Thanks go to Alicia Vidaurreta for her assistance with the French and German languages, and also for her feedback on Paris geography.

Deep gratitude goes to my editor, Andy Zack, who continues to set a standard for excellence in this business. It's been a genuine pleasure and honor to have worked with you on all five of my novels. I'm looking forward to the next five.

For selecting my query letter and sample chapters from a stack of unsolicited mail eight years ago, I thank Matt Bialer of the William Morris Agency. Your continued support and confidence in a business as unstable and unpredictable as the publishing industry is very much appreciated. Special thanks also go to Matt's top-notch assistant, Maya Perez, for looking after my interests.

Tom Doherty and the entire staff at Tor/Forge for supporting each of my works and for publishing the finest books in the business. Thanks go to Steve de las Heras for his solid efforts during the production process.

The hero of this book is an engineer. Very special thanks go to the brightest and most innovative engineer I know: my father, Rogelio de los Angeles Pineiro.

Thanks also go to the rest of my family:

My mother, Dora, for always believing in me.

Mike and Linda Wiltz, who are not just my in-laws, but also two of the most loving and caring people I know.

Michael Wiltz, my brother-in-law, for teaching me a thing or two about standing up for the right to life of the unborn.

My sister Irene del Carmen, her husband, Julio, and all of the kids, Julito, Paola, Eddie, Rogelin, and Juan Pablo, for many wonderful memories.

My sister Dora Maria and her husband, Lorenzo, for all of the good times. May life bring you nothing but happiness.

Bill, Maureen, Bobby, and Kevin Moser, for being there for me.

During my fourteen-year engineering career at Advanced Micro Devices I've been quite fortunate to have met and worked with many brilliant, disciplined, and creative engineers. My deepest gratitude goes to all of them for helping me shape my views of the most challenging discipline of all. It's been one hell of a ride, gentlemen, but we still have a long way to go.

Thank you.

R. J. PINEIRO
Austin, Texas, 1997

Science is the attempt to make the chaotic diversity of our sense-experience correspond to a logical uniformity of thought.

—Einstein

It is a profound and necessary truth that the deep things in science are not found because they are useful; they are found because it was possible to find them.

—Robert Oppenheimer

BREAKTHROUGH

PROLOGUE

They moved swiftly, quietly, with purpose, under a moonless sky in southern Japan. Dark clothing and hoods blended their muscular figures with the night as they raced through a meadow that led to the back of the building housing the digital-TV division of Mitsubishi Electric Corporation in Kyoto. At this late hour the building, home to a large and well-funded Research & Development program charged with the development of the world's most advanced DTV computer chips, was nearly deserted.

Wearing night-vision goggles, which changed the night into palettes of green, the team of four advanced with practiced ease, reaching the chain-link fence guarding the building's rear moments later. The leader whispered into his voice-activated headset, *"Wir haben Stellung eingenommen."* We are in position.

A mile away, near the Kyoto Imperial Palace, a man sat in the rear of a van, his eyes glued to the information displayed on his laptop while his fingers pounded the keyboard.

"Halt. Warten Sie." Hold. Wait. Using his wireless modem, he dialed into the network of the large corporation. In seconds he was in and immediately accessed the main system, using the root password provided to him just two hours ago by the building's systems administrator, who now rested at the bottom of the Katsuragawa River with both feet chained to a cement block. Only two other people knew the password. The administrator's assistant, who had been run over by a car as he'd left the Ashiya Steak House in eastern Kyoto an hour ago, and the director of opera-

tions, currently traveling abroad. With the password, the hacker could bypass every one of the network's security points.

Now he focused on the *kanji* characters displayed on the small screen. Fingering the laptop's trackball, the hacker navigated down several directories, until he reached the main control page of the fully computerized building. In less than a minute he switched off the entire lighting system, surveillance cameras, most phones, and closed the security gates at all eight entrances to the colossal building, cutting it off from the outside world. In addition, he lowered dozens of steel plates designed to isolate sections of the building in case of fire or a security breach.

Darkness suddenly enshrouded the building when the lights went out. Through his goggles, the leader watched it change to a darker hue of green.

"Gehen Sie." Proceed, the hacker said in a monotone.

Reaching for the Omega chronometer hugging his left wrist, the leader started the countdown, *"Fünf, vier, drei, zwei, eins, null,"* and pressed the timer. His men, wearing identical watches, did likewise.

The team jumped over the fence and moved quickly toward one of two entrances on the north side of the building, just as they had rehearsed during the last four weeks. They cruised past a few parked vehicles, across a manicured lawn, over a line of waist-high bushes, and finally stopped by an entrance used only for equipment deliveries.

In German, the leader said, "Phase one complete. Forty-seven seconds."

Inside the van, the hacker selected the equipment entrance and clicked on it.

The gate slowly began to rise. The leader rolled under it, followed by his men.

"We're in. Commence phase two. Time, one minute, ten seconds."

The gate lowered and the team proceeded down a wide corridor flanked by walls of floor-to-ceiling glass separating the access hallway from one of several clean rooms on the first floor, where Mitsubishi technicians manufactured the prototypes of a revolutionary set of digital-TV computer chips.

The fabrication area was empty.

The team moved past it and reached a security gate blocking access to the other side of the corridor. The steel plate had been lowered from the ceiling by the same hacker who now raised it at the request of the team leader.

Two minutes into the mission they proceeded up a flight of stairs, through three more security gates, and finally reached the heart of the building: the design area, where the final version of the chip set that Mitsubishi planned to start sampling in one year was being designed.

The leader spotted a security guard feeling his way down the pitch-black hallway, totally unaware of the intruders about to steal the crown jewels of the Japanese corporation. He raised a fist, and his team silently stepped aside, letting the leader move closer to the guard, a man much shorter than he. Pointing his stun gun at the unsuspecting figure, the leader pressed the trigger.

Two probes shot out of the gun, attached to the ends of microwires. A moment later the probes pierced through the guard's uniform and delivered a shocking voltage that knocked him unconscious.

The leader checked his chronometer. Four minutes and twenty seconds. They were thirty seconds behind schedule, thanks to the guard.

Turning his attention back to the security door separating the hallway from the design area, he made another radio request, and the door unlocked, letting him in. His subordinates remained outside.

Tables cluttered with workstations and schematics surrounded the leader as he walked toward the rear of the room, where his sources had informed him that the design team kept the archive tapes.

He reached another security door, which opened upon request, as if by magic, exposing a room filled with the daily back-up tapes storing the coveted designs of the computer chips required to demodulate, decode, and process video and audio signals to support the new digital-TV standards, which had been set six months earlier by an international steering committee controlled primarily by Mitsubishi, the world's leading developer of DTV technology. Mitsubishi had used its phenomenal market influence to strong-arm the committee to vote for the standard that the Japanese company had already spent five years and billions of yen developing. In doing so, the committee had practically handed Mitsubishi the digital-TV market on a silver platter, shutting out the competition, which now found itself five years behind the Japanese giant.

But that edge ends now, thought the leader as he selected the archive tapes for each of the computer chips and stored them in a nylon backpack. His country needed the technology in order to compete in this lucrative market, and his government had sent him here to get it. His country's scientists planned not to copy the Japanese design, for that would violate many international copyright laws. His people would simply learn from the Japanese. They would leverage from the time and capital already spent by Mitsubishi, and use that technology as a platform from which to launch their own.

And we shall teach them a lesson they will never forget, thought the leader, who reached into a pouch strapped to his left calf and produced a powerful magnet. For the next few minutes he ran the magnet over the surface of each of nearly a hundred older back-up tapes inside the secured room, turning the highly technical data they contained into gibberish.

"Back-ups destroyed," he whispered into his headset. "Time, eleven minutes, forty seconds. Commence final phase."

The leader had the hacker shut the door to the archive room as he walked back into the hallway, also having the hacker close the door to the design area behind him. One of his subordinates knelt by the unconscious security guard and removed the probes. There could not be any physical evidence left behind of their work. Another one of his men had already poured half of a pint of *shochu,* a Japanese liquor distilled from potatoes, into the guard's mouth. He then placed the bottle in the guard's left hand.

As the team retraced their steps and left the building, the hacker in the van injected an electronic worm into Mitsubishi's network. Armed with root privilege, the worm started at the very top of the main directory and began to release a mutating virus throughout the entire system. The virus caused the files it touched to change very slightly, not enough for anyone to notice for some time. The worm crawled through every path in every directory in the complex system, eventually reaching the primary databases housing the current versions of the DTV chips and also the secret disk partitions where Mitsubishi scientists had hidden back-ups to some databases under fake names in an effort to fool a hacker. But nothing escaped the root-privileged worm, which penetrated every last byte of stored information in every one of the networked drives of the system. The mutating virus altered the functionality of the DTV chips ever so slightly to fool engineers into thinking that their work in these secret directories had not been affected. After altering the files, the virus erased itself, eliminating all evidence of ever being there.

As the team jumped over the perimeter fence and proceeded up the meadow exactly fifteen minutes after they had started the mission, the hacker in the van restored all systems to normal and exited the network, but not before releasing a small algorithm that remained behind for thirty seconds after the hacker had logged off. The small program altered the electronic log of the remote dial-in system, erasing all evidence of the hacker's phone call.

In the morning, employees returned to their work areas and continued their tasks. Over lunch, many discussed the mysterious power glitch the night before and speculated on its cause. Their work, luckily, had not been affected, sparing them from having to resort to the seldomly used archive tapes. Some joked about the guard who had gotten himself fired for drinking on the job. Others talked about the unfortunate accident outside the Ashiya Steak House. No one knew why the systems administrator had failed to show up for work that morning.

Three months later, the new revision of the DTV chips would reach the prototype stage, but it would not work as expected, puzzling engineers and technicians with its nondeterministic behavior, leading to random glitches across the television screen. While the main design team focused their efforts on debugging this new observation, another team went off to perform a comparison of the schematics of the current version with those of the previous revision, which had been stored in the archive room three months before. The data in all of the old back-up tapes, however, was corrupted. The team also noticed that the tapes for one week were missing. The investigation that followed led nowhere.

Mitsubishi eventually fixed the logic bugs and came up with a new revision enabling the company to launch its product into the market, but just barely in time to compete with the products offered by its German competitors, who had managed to develop a similar chip set in record time.

1 PROTEIN TRANSISTORS

*Applied science is a conjurer, whose bottomless hat
yields impartially the softest of Angora rabbits and
the most petrifying of Medusas.*

—Aldous Huxley

SANTA CLARA COUNTY, CALIFORNIA
Friday, July 14, 2:45 A.M.

Yellowish light diffused through the hissing rain as a burgundy
Ford Bronco turned a corner, sending a three-foot-high wave of
puddled water splashing onto the sidewalk. Even on high speed
the wipers could barely keep up.

Through the thick rain pounding the windshield, Jake Thomas
Fischer spotted his company's one-story brick building, a small
structure lost in the ocean of opulent corporate headquarters in
Silicon Valley.

Small but all mine, he thought as he turned into his reserved
parking slot by the building's main entrance. Fischer Technologies represented Jake's lifework, the culmination of a dream that
had come dangerously close to an end almost a decade ago at Los
Alamos National Laboratory, when his proposal for the next gen-
eration of computer chips failed to receive federal funding. Out
of options, the young Ph.D. from Berkeley had sought—and
found—financial backing for his idea in the private sector.

Jake briefly shook his head at how fast time had passed as he
scanned the nearly deserted parking lot. Three figures huddled
by the double glass doors leading into the small reception area.

One of them, a large man, dressed in khaki slacks, sneakers, and a white long-sleeved shirt and holding a blue umbrella, left the protection of the building and ventured down the walkway, carefully balancing himself against the high wind. The other two turned around and headed back inside.

"You have arrived just in time, my friend!" the man clutching the umbrella shouted over the whistling wind in a heavy Slavic accent as the president and CEO of Fischer Technologies, Inc., stepped out of the Bronco. Jake smelled a hint of vodka on the large man's breath.

"Hi, Sergei. Have you tested it yet?" Jake asked, squinting through the rain as they splashed their way to the building.

"The beautiful Katherina is setting up the test," said Sergei Konstantinovich Iyevenski, FTI's chief technical officer, as the pair reached the glass doors and stepped inside the carpeted lobby, shutting out the storm. The room had plain white walls on the left side and a small guard station crowded with nine-inch black-and-white monitors. A pair of plain chairs flanking a glass side table gave silent testimony to the infrequency of customers or visitors at the four-year-old venture. No one but those working at FTI could go beyond the reception room.

No one. Except, of course, for selected members of the board at the venture capital firm Preston, Colton & Associates. And even then, PCA executives had to make arrangements with Jake Fischer a week in advance before showing up on his doorstep.

Jake Fischer ran a hand through his damp black hair and wiped it on his Levi's. He turned to Iyevenski. "When did the disks come out of the helifurnace?" he asked.

"Thirty minutes ago," responded the Russian biochemist. A fork of lightning illuminated the parking lot and flashed inside the lobby, followed a few seconds later by thunder. "Right when I telephoned you."

FTI's graveyard-shift security guard left his station and brought them a pair of extra-large white lab coats, the initials FTI stenciled in blue across the breast pocket.

"Here you go, gentlemen," said Raul Martinez, the short and muscular guard. Like the two other guards handling the day and swing shifts, he had been carefully interviewed before he was hired, and Jake had run a background check on him.

"Thanks, Raul," Jake responded while Iyevenski donned the lab coat and tried to button it. Even an extra-large barely fit the powerfully built Russian.

Jake also put on his coat as the pair approached a heavy metal door in the rear of the reception room. Jake pressed the palm of his right hand against a square foot of smoked glass on the wall next to the door and said, "Fischer, Jake."

A laser scanner took a snapshot of his handprint, instantly projecting it onto a focal plane made of an array of three million optical transistors, which translated the image into a file. At the same time a voice digitizer converted his words into a second file. In a fraction of a second, the security system compared the digitized handprint against the approved list of images until it found a match. Then it did the same for the digitized voice file. If both matched files were for the same name—if the voice matched the handprint—the system would release the magnetic locking mechanism separating the outside world from the secret research of Fischer Technologies, Inc.

The lock snapped and the door automatically swung open.

They headed for the test area, halfway down the long, dimly lit corridor.

"I'm amazed that lightning hasn't crashed the system," Jake commented. He glanced up at the two dozen sets of fluorescent lights. Every other set was off, following one of his cost-cutting measures, which also included keeping the air conditioning at seventy-eight degrees everywhere in the building, except for the R&D floor, where FTI's largest investment in equipment required a steady sixty-eight degrees and 40 percent humidity.

"Tap on wood, friend," Iyevenski said. On his pale, lined face, under the unkempt salt-and-pepper hair, a smile of crooked, yellowish teeth flashed at Jake.

"It's *knock*, Sergei. *Knock* on wood. Nobody says *tap* on wood."

"Ah . . . knock, yes?" Iyevenski said with a slight grunt. Born in Serpukhov, a city south of Moscow, he spoke, in addition to Russian, fluent French, German, and English, but couldn't seem to get a handle on the slang.

"Probecards arrived in time?" asked Jake, referring to custom-designed printed circuit boards with an array of built-in microscopic needles. They were vital for testing the protein-based random access memory (RAM) FTI's president had designed with the assistance of Sergei.

"Katherina drove to Probe Technology this afternoon and picked them up. We have three ready. Relax, friend. I have it all within control."

Jake took a deep breath and also smiled, deciding to let that one go. He rubbed a hand over the stubble he usually allowed himself unless it was time to make a progress report to the PCA board up in San Francisco. Only then did FTI's twenty-two full-time employees see their founder wear a tie. Preston, Colton & Associates had financed Jake's venture in the high-tech industry after the whiz kid from Berkeley and Los Alamos had dazzled PCA executives four years before with an idea to design a revolutionary RAM so advanced that it would leapfrog all existing designs by three generations. The protein memory design had one hundred times the capacity of today's best RAM chips. But what had finally sold his pitch to the venture capital firm, resulting in the transfer of twenty-seven million dollars to FTI's general account at the Bank of San Francisco, was more than the mere fact that Jake Fischer's design took advantage of the unusual properties of bacteriorhodopsin. This bacterial protein, commonly found in salt marshes, included a segment known as a chromophore, which changed its properties when exposed to light. What made FTI so attractive among all the other corporations and private laboratories doing research on the future applications of light-sensitive bacterial proteins was that Jake Thomas Fischer had found Sergei Iyevenski.

The man walking by his side, absently murmuring something in Russian, was the last surviving disciple of the late Yuri A. Ovchinnikov, who had spent the last twenty years of his life developing a non-silicon-based computer to help his decaying motherland catch up with the West. The secrets of those twenty years—secrets Russia lost during the collapse of Communism—were locked in Iyevenski's head. The F1 RAM chip was the fruit of Iyevenski's bioorganic chemistry genius and Jake's expertise in bioscience and state-of-the-art memory designs.

"I would be more relaxed if the bean counters at PCA stopped bothering us," said Jake. PCA had called every day this week requesting an update.

"The board is worried that the new revision of the F1 will not operate like we designed it, yes?"

Jake raised a brow, which almost touched a lock of wet hair falling over his forehead. "Can't say I blame them, though. Los Alamos wouldn't give me five million to fund the project for two years. PCA's in for *twenty-seven* million. They want a return on their investment. Four years is a long time."

"If this revision works, we will achieve production in less than four months, my friend."

"I know, Sergei. That'll put us two quarters away from reporting any revenue. PCA isn't too happy about that. In fact, the board disliked it so much that the two big men have invited me to a breakfast meeting tomorrow morning to discuss it."

PCA's owners, William Preston and Jacob Colton, were famous in Silicon Valley for their "breakfast meetings" with the CEOs of failing ventures.

Sergei stopped cold, well aware of what the meeting could mean to FTI. "You never told me about—"

"Didn't want to worry you, or anyone else," said Jake, patting the Russian's broad shoulders.

"How long have you known about this meeting?"

Jake shrugged. "Since last week. Look, I've handled PCA in the past. That's my job. I'll handle them again tomorrow. I just need some ammo to fight back and show them that it's in their best interest to let us keep going until the end of our contract."

Iyevenski's wrinkled face tilted to the side. "Ammo?"

Jake smiled. "Ammunition, Sergei."

"Oh, I see. Like a functional design?" he said, and began to walk again.

"That's right. Otherwise they'll close us down for good and liquefy our assets—including our intellectual property, our patents, which we signed off to PCA as collateral for their dough four years ago."

"Dough?"

"Money, Sergei. Cash, dollars. We fail and FTI takes the equipment and the patents and tries to sell them in the open market."

"But the patents," Iyevenski said. "So much has changed since we started."

Jake nodded his head at the Russian, who was dead on the money with that comment. The biotech recipes that had gone into the original patents released to PCA no longer reflected the technology used by FTI today. Through a long and painful trial-and-error process, FTI had completely redefined the biotechnology required to manufacture computer chips. As CTO, it fell to Sergei Iyevenski to write up the new patents and send them to the legal department at PCA for filing, but the neck-breaking schedules

Jake had imposed on his team to meet their deadline left little time for such "bookkeeping" tasks.

"Don't worry about that, Sergei. We'll get to them soon enough. Right now we have to concentrate on *executing* our plan, or PCA will take everything away. It won't matter that we failed to write new patents to describe the technology we're using today. We need their funding to turn our ideas into realities. We lose the funding and we're dead in the water."

"Ah . . . but we are so close," murmured the Russian. "Just like in 1985."

As they reached the doors leading to the development area, Jake gave Iyevenski a furtive glance. Twenty years of research in bioelectronics had evaporated after the death of Yuri Ovchinnikov. The Politburo, which had kept the project alive only because of Ovchinnikov's prestige, began to lose faith in the potential of biotechnology and cut back funds the week after his death in 1985, nearly halting the projects of Iyevenski and a few other surviving Ovchinnikov disciples at the Shemyakin Institute of Bioorganic Chemistry in Moscow.

Iyevenski pressed his right palm against the reader by the double doors and spoke his name. The doors opened a second later, exposing the largest room in the building. The R&D area, divided into two sections by a floor-to-ceiling wall of glass, represented a significant portion of FTI's budget. One half, the test area, included a state-of-the-art Teradyne tester, the best in the industry, to test high-speed RAM chips. This half provided Jake Fischer with the best return on investment. On the other side of the glass partition was the process area, Iyevenski's domain of dangerous chemicals and complex furnaces.

Jake felt a rush of cold air escaping the environmentally controlled room as the two FTI executives walked across the raised floor of the test area, in the center of which stood the Teradyne tester and prober system. The Teradyne looked like five refrigerators connected side by side. The prober resembled a small storage freezer with its lid up.

"Ah, Katherina!" exclaimed Sergei Iyevenski. "Are we ready?"

"Almost, Sergei," said Kathy Bennett, a petite UCLA Ph.D. graduate in electrical engineering. She wore her long black hair in a bun, and a pair of designer glasses rested on her fine nose. As she pounded her keyboard her brown eyes took in the data peppering the nineteen-inch color screen of the SUN workstation that drove the Teradyne tester. She glanced up at Jake Fischer.

"Hello, Jake. How have *you* been?" she said.

"Sorry, Kathy," responded Jake, feeling embarrassed that he'd forgotten their lunch date earlier that day. "Didn't mean to—"

"Forget it," she said curtly, her stare returning to the screen. "I'm used to it."

Jake frowned as Iyevenski slowly shook his head and murmured something in Russian. Maybe he should stop dating her altogether. Starting a relationship with one of his employees had not been Jake's smartest move, but at the time, eight months ago, when Kathy and Jake had been spending countless hours planning the test methodology for the F1, it had almost been natural. Long working hours, no personal lives, no way to release stress, no one to talk to outside work, a few drinks at midnight at her place—Jake remembered it all too well. Now each had a key to each other's place, but after five months of planning the test program, he had started devoting his attention to other problems while she had gone off to write and debug thousands of lines of code. They'd seen little of each other since.

"Katherina, watching you work makes me wish I was ten years younger!" said Iyevenski, filling the silence with a loud laugh, showing his large yellow teeth. He stepped behind Kathy and began massaging her shoulders with his large, hairy hands. "Only a fool would let you out of his sight!"

Jake frowned again, not only at the comment, but also because he failed to understand how his Russian colleague could seem so relaxed at this moment. Jake's entire life was on the line if the F1 didn't work as designed. William Preston and Jacob Colton were ready to nail Jake to a cross if the protein RAM didn't produce the promised return on their investment.

A spark of devilish amusement in Kathy's brown eyes accompanied the smile that came to her lips. "Only *ten* years younger, Sergei?"

Iyevenski threw his hands up in the air. "Fifteen? Yes?"

"Try *twenty*, Sergei," Kathy replied, winking at Jake. She broke the seals on each side of a pink plastic container next to the workstation and removed the top, exposing ten round disks six inches in diameter and a quarter-inch thick, each holding seventy F1 memory cubes in a gridlike pattern. Conventional silicon disks had a thickness of approximately twenty-thousandths of an inch—twenty mils—but the molecular lattice of bacteriorhodopsin required a thicker medium.

Using a pair of special tweezers, Iyevenski extracted one of the disks from the plastic container and held it up to the light. "Twenty years? Maybe for an *amerikanets,* my lovely Katherina," said Iyevenski, pointing at Jake with his free hand before extending a thumb toward his massive chest. "But us Russians . . . we are vigorous, like a bear."

Iyevenski slowly set the disk on a metal chuck controlled by the automatic prober. The chuck, slightly larger in diameter than the hybrid disk, had over a hundred tiny holes on its surface. The holes were the ends of microtubes connected to the prober's vacuum system. The moment the perfectly flat underside of the disk came in contact with the chuck, a vacuum sucked it into place. The chuck rested on a cushion of air in the middle of the prober, and it could move in any horizontal direction via a magnetic-driven servomotor.

Iyevenski lowered the prober's lid over the disk-chuck assembly. A round hole in the center of the lid held one of the probecards, its array of microneedles matching the connections at the periphery of each F1 cube on the disk. When the Russian scientist locked the lid in place, it left the end of the microneedles just over ten mils above the surface of the hybrid disk; the space between the sharp needles and the highly polished disks could not be seen with the naked eye. This was one of the reasons for the powerful microscope that Iyevenski pivoted over the probecard. A tiny camera connected to the microscope sent a clear color image to a nine-inch Sony monitor built into the side of the prober and tilted in the Russian's direction.

Jake's dark blue eyes focused on the screen, which showed the array of needles not aligned with the landing pads on the surface of one F1 RAM chip in the center of the disk.

Iyevenski reached for a joysticklike control on the prober and positioned the chuck so that the F1 chip lined up perfectly with the probecard's needles. The moment he reached the desired alignment, he thumbed a red button at the top of the joystick, and the chuck moved up eleven mils, bringing the F1 up to the stationary needles of the probecard and applying a mil of vertical pressure to ensure a solid contact. Another push of the same button and the chuck lowered again.

"Pretty good scrub marks," commented Jake as the screen displayed an image of the needle imprints on the square landing pads in the periphery of the square RAM chip.

"Let's go, Katherina," said Iyevenski.

Kathy Bennett checked her display one final time and gave Iyevenski the nod. The Russian pressed the red button on the prober's joystick, elevating the chuck until the microneedles once again came in contact with the F1 landing pads.

Kathy Bennett typed a few more commands and pressed the Enter key. Forty billion bytes of data were sequentially driven out of the Teradyne tester, through an array of woven cables, into the back of the probecard, through the microneedles, and into the F1 chip under test.

Inside the F1, the tiny pulses of electricity arriving from the Teradyne flowed through a complex maze of microscopic aluminum lines deposited on the surface of the silicon section of the RAM. The aluminum lines connected the outside world to the array of microscopic optical transistors surrounding the cube of bacterial protein. In an instant, tens of thousands of optical transistors came alive, achieving a frequency of operation large enough to begin shooting red laserlike strobes of light one millionth the thickness of a human hair into the tridimensional bacterio-rhodopsin lattice, triggering multiple photocycles—series of structural changes that forced the billions of light-sensitive chromophores in the cube to specific states. The moment the last byte of data was written into the RAM cube, the reverse process took place. The optical transistors switched their frequency of operation to the green-laser range and once again began to fire into the cube, reversing the process and forcing the stored data into a "detector" plane, which translated the light pulses into the electrical signals that returned to the Teradyne tester in the programmed time.

"It works!" shouted Iyevenski, raising both hands above his head, closing his eyes, and shuffling a few steps of some Russian dance while humming a tune Jake couldn't make out.

Jake just stood still, his eyes glued to the green light above the prober, indicating a passing hybrid chip, a fully functional F1 molecular memory.

"Hit it again, Kathy," Jake said, still skeptical. After a barely functional rev A and a partially functional rev B, this just seemed too good to be true. Over seventy design changes had been made between revisions B and C of the F1, including a drastic change in the way Iyevenski formed the protein cubes to improve their uniformity. Ideally, the cubes needed to be formed in zero gravity, making this endeavor too expensive to manufacture commercially. To "simulate" zero gravity, Iyevenski, using a technique he had developed while working under Ovchinnikov, modified a conventional furnace, where porous carbon disks, after going through a chemical purification process, were "thickened" by adding multiple planes of bacterial protein. The Russian scientist had modified the floor of the furnace with a grid pattern of five hundred tiny gas nozzles, all connected to a pressurized helium tank. As the protein lattice formed over the carbon disks, the nozzles sprayed helium upward, through the forming cubes, at a speed of thirty-two feet per second, balancing the gravitational force on the molecules. Since helium was a stable, inert gas, its molecules ran cleanly through the forming lattice without disturbing the protein molecules while maintaining them at a virtual zero gravity. During the first two tries, the upward flow didn't compensate for the unusually thick hybrid disks, almost ten times the thickness of those Iyevenski had successfully developed in Russia. The imperfections in the molecular lattice of those earlier revisions had caused most of the problems that this revision was intended to fix.

Kathy typed a few commands to initiate another test. The result was the same: a pass.

A smile reached Jake's stunned face, softening his sharp features. He felt Sergei patting him on the shoulder. "We did it, friend! Seventy changes!"

A questioning look replaced the brief smile as Jake's logical side swept away his burgeoning emotions. The time for celebration would come later. Right now he had to keep his engineering hat on. "What's the max frequency?" he asked, referring to the maximum frequency at which the F1 would operate. The original target had been 350 MHz, over three times the speed of the competition's fastest RAM chip. Not only did the F1 have the capacity to store a hundred times as much data as any existing RAM, but it should also run three times as fast. Unfortunately, revision A had only worked up to 180 MHz and revision B up to 270 MHz. Part of the seventy design changes between revision B and C were targeted at improving the F1's performance.

"It stops functioning at three hundred and ninety megahertz," responded Kathy as she read the information off the screen.

Three hundred ninety megahertz!

Staring at the screen with a combination of skepticism and euphoria, Jake took a long, deep breath while shifting his eyes from the Teradyne to the single most expensive piece of equipment owned by Fischer Technologies: a HyperCray supercomputer worth four and a half million dollars and as powerful as ten of the older Cray systems still in use at various universities and government agencies. It had been inside the HyperCray that Jake and his team of memory architects ran simulations of the F1 during the design phase, ensuring the proper functionality and speed of the revolutionary design before committing it to silicon and bacterial protein. It had been inside the HyperCray that Sergei Iyevenski and his team of bioorganic chemists simulated the process of growing a perfect molecular lattice prior to spending precious investment dollars running hybrid disks through the helifurnaces in the process area. While everyone else in the industry preferred to purchase Hewlett Packard workstations at $75,000 each and then link them together, Jake had taken a radically different approach, blowing a significant portion of his R&D budget on a single HyperCray, shared by all of his engineers. His approach had worked, not only enabling him to get fully functional F1s after three revisions, but also chopping the development schedule in half. To get a project of this magnitude to this stage would have taken IBM fifty times the number of engineers, six or seven revisions, and over ten years.

"Let's test the whole disk," Jake said. "Let's see how many

good RAMs are on it." Now that the F1 design was fully functional, the next question was the yield they would get out of each disk.

"What's the stepping distance?" asked Kathy Bennett as she left the keyboard and approached the prober.

"Zero point six three by zero point four inches," answered Jake, providing Kathy with the exact distance that the chuck would have to move to bring the next F1 on the disk up to the microneedles.

Kathy nodded and entered the stepping distance into the small keypad beneath the monitor. Using the joystick, she moved the chuck so that the first chip in the array patterned on the disk would be right under the microneedles.

"Ready, Sergei?" she asked without looking at the Russian.

"Da!"

Kathy pressed a button on the side of the keypad labeled AUTOTEST.

The chuck immediately rose to bring the first F1 to the microneedles. For the next three seconds the Teradyne tested its functionality. A red light flashed above the prober. A bad F1.

The tip of a special inker, strapped to the side of the microneedles, automatically extended and placed a small drop of red ink in the center of the bad memory chip. The chuck then automatically lowered and moved by the preprogrammed distance in the X-direction, bringing the adjacent RAM in the array under the microneedles and lifting it up to test. This time a green light flashed.

One by one the F1s from the first disk were tested. At just over three seconds each, plus the time it took the chuck to lower the disk, step over to the next cube, and raise the disk up to the needles, six minutes elapsed before the entire disk completed testing.

"Fifty-one good ones," commented Kathy.

Jake quickly did the math in his head. With a potential yield of seventy F1s, this wafer gave him a 67 percent yield. With a projected selling price of just over $1,300 per chip, the wafer Kathy removed from the prober represented $66,300 in sales.

"Not bad for our third rev, friend," said the large Iyevenski, wrapping a log of an arm around Jake's shoulders. "Not bad at all."

"So," Kathy said, a smile on her light brown face. She gave Iyevenski a kiss on the cheek, then went to Jake and gave him one on the lips. "Where's the Dom?"

"Sergei," Jake said, removing the Russian's heavy arm, "go to my office and check the box next to my filing cabinet. There's a—"

Kathy reached down next to the prober and pulled a bottle of Dom Pérignon from an ice bucket.

"Everyone in the office knew about the booze," said Kathy, a wide smile painted on her oval face as she passed the bottle to Iyevenski, who began to remove the foil over the cork. A loud pop and the cork flew across the test area, bounced against the glass partition, and landed next to the HyperCray. The rest of the company would celebrate in the morning but these three would do it now.

"Okay," Jake said, taking a filled glass and downing it. "Let's test the entire lot."

Two hours later, alone in his office at the front of the building, Jake Fischer sat behind his desk and turned his computer on.

Leaning back in his chair, he waited for the PC to boot, his eyes on the floor-to-ceiling metal bookcases lining opposite walls of the room. The double doors at one end faced a small window overlooking the parking lot, where the storm had turned into a light drizzle. A single door between two overfull bookcases led to a small private bathroom, which included the shower Jake had used more in the past four years than the one in his modest house just outside of San Jose.

Jake checked his watch. Almost four o'clock in the morning. His breakfast meeting was at nine-thirty. He eyed the army cot folded next to the small weight set in front of the bookcases, shaking his head at the items he had used more than his own bed at home and the equipment at his health club. The weights he had pumped for the past half hour, right before sitting down. Even though this year he would reach forty, Jake Fischer worked out often enough to keep some semblance of the lean and solid body of his UC Berkeley wrestling days.

Jake knew he would not be able to use the army cot tonight. Not after sorting all ten disks in the lot and getting a total yield of 510 fully functional F1 memories, or an average of fifty-one good RAM chips per hybrid disk. He wanted to generate a few financial projections for the morning meeting with the top bean counters at PCA.

In his mind, however, Jake Fischer already knew his team had made history today. Unlike past technical breakthroughs, such as CD-ROMs, videophones, and even personal computers, all of which were created for a society lacking the infrastructure to make immediate use of them, the F1 had been designed to take *immediate* advantage of the booming personal computer and workstation market. It had taken nearly a decade for CDs to re-place LPs. It had taken almost another decade for personal com-puters to really make it in the consumer marketplace. It would take the F1 only a few months to establish itself in a market ready to accept it. The massive storage capacity of the F1 chip would enable computer users worldwide to store and run all of their programs directly from very fast RAM, obsoleting slow hard drives and other sluggish storage devices. The F1 would kick off a new age in computing, promising all users true real-time interaction without the burden of waiting for a slow hard drive to catch up to their speed. And that was just the beginning. Fast, high-capacity, and relatively cheap RAM had many applications in an industry starving for computer memory. From the Internet and multimedia to robotics, aviation, and the military, the F1 RAM promised to set a new technological standard. Such a timely breakthrough, of course, also brought huge financial rewards.

His fingers reached for the keyboard, and he pulled up a file containing one of many financial spreadsheets on his operation. This particular spreadsheet calculated the total manufacturing cost of an F1 RAM chip based on a specific yield per disk. The higher the yield, the cheaper the manufacturing cost of each F1, since the total wafer cost would be spread out among more F1s. Cheaper manufacturing cost, of course, resulted in bigger profits per F1.

The screen displayed:

> Fischer Technologies, Inc.
> Manufacturing Cost per F1 Chip
> Enter estimated yield _____

Jake entered "51."
The screen changed to:

> Fischer Technologies, Inc.
> Manufacturing Cost per F1 Chip

F1 yield per disk	51
Processing cost per F1 (incl. depreciation)	$ 58.50
Probe test cost per F1	$ 7.60
Assembly cost	$ 28.00
Postassembly test cost	$ 10.35
Mark and pack	$ 1.55

| Shipping | $ 0.75 |
| Total manufacturing cost per F1 | $ 106.75 |

Jake looked at the last line, which showed him the manufacturing cost after the F1 was tested in disk form, assembled in a specially designed ceramic package, tested again after assembly, marked, packed in its shipping box, and sent off to the customer. The assembly process, which was not done by FTI but by a subcontractor in nearby Milpitas, consisted of sawing out the individual F1 chips from the hybrid disk and setting them into custom-built packages, which would then be sealed to look like the silicon chips advertised in newspapers and magazines—with the exception that the F1s would be thicker.

He printed that spreadsheet and opened up another one, which showed him the potential revenue of the F1 per month, assuming Iyevenski's processing equipment, which Jake planned to double in the next year, could keep up the agreed-upon volume of 120,000 F1s per month after initial production ramp.

Fischer Technologies, Inc.
Projected Monthly Revenue

F1 manufacturing cost	$ 106.75
Estimated selling price	$ 1300.00
Estimated profit margin	$ 1193.25
Projected monthly volume (initial)	120,000 units
Estimated monthly profit (unadjusted)	$ 143,190,000
Monthly lease	$ 83,000
Loan interest due PCA	$ 410,000
Headcount expense (salaries)	$ 175,000
Advertising	$ 950,000
Legal	$ 1,500,000
Adjusted monthly profit	$ 140,072,000

Jake Thomas Fischer stared at the last figure long and hard with his bloodshot eyes. That was the beauty of high-tech industry. If a company could create the right device for the right market at the right time, the profits were almost obscene. In the case of Fischer Technologies, the start-up company would be in a position to repay its investors plus generate a significant profit only one month after initial production.

Of course, that level of profits could not be maintained for more than a year. Then the selling price would most likely decline as FTI saturated the market with F1 memory chips.

But what a year that would be.

At an average of $140 million per month, FTI could easily exceed the one-billion-dollar profit mark after just one year in volume production, collecting the kind of cash required to fund the design of the next-generation memory chip, the F2. It would also mean a new building, more equipment, more engineers, better advertising in industry journals and trade magazines, and of course a large sales force to expand market share. Jake was even toying with the idea of reducing the manufacturing cost next year by moving the labor-intensive test-and-assembly operations to Singapore, leaving the design and high-tech process manufacturing in Palo Alto. And memory, of course, was just the initial application of biotechnology in the computer field. The massive injection of capital would allow Jake Fischer to hire the best architects and designers in other fields, like microprocessors, CD-ROM drivers, and video drivers, enabling FTI to gain control of those markets just as it was about to dominate the memory industry.

This is the kind of ammo I was talking about, Sergei, Jake thought as he printed the second spreadsheet and launched his e-mail software, hoping this news would be good enough to keep PCA from prematurely shutting down FTI.

As his e-mail software came up on the screen, Jake was reminded of Kathy, who had disguised FTI's cyber address as a bike tour agency's. She had also written the scrambler that Jake now enabled. Even if an unwanted cyberspace user wanted to intercept a message being generated by a bike tour agency, all the hacker would get was a meaningless soup of letter and numbers.

Confident of his electronic privacy, Jake began to type a short report to give Preston, Colton, & Associates a heads-up on the events of this night. Revision C of the F1 was a blistering success. Jake just hoped the figures in the spreadsheets would be sufficient to satisfy the money-hungry PCA. He shivered at the thought of FTI's following in the footsteps of so many other Silicon Valley start-ups, killed prematurely by nearsighted venture capital firms in sudden need of currency.

As he finished the message, he heard a noise behind him.

"I see you've already had a workout," Kathy Bennett said, stepping around the stainless-steel weights and approaching his desk.

Jake turned on the swivel chair and watched the lithe figure of the only woman he had ever gotten personally involved with in his entire adult life. Sure, he'd had his share of sexual encounters during college, particularly during his Berkeley wrestling days. His boyish looks, combined with his muscular body and the vitality with which he forced adversaries from three dozen schools flat on their backs, had certainly gotten Jake his share of one-nighter female fans. But Kathy was different. She shared his entrepreneurial spirit and had turned down job offers from Intel, IBM, and Texas Instruments to work at FTI. But unlike Jake, who had a difficult time separating his personal life from his business, Kathy always seemed to find the time to devote to Jake. Jake, on the other hand, was always, without meaning to, making Kathy feel she came in second place to FTI.

"True," he responded, pushing himself away from his computer. "But only a *small* workout. I still have plenty of energy in me."

"Buy me breakfast?" she said invitingly.

Jake stood, walked around his desk, and wrapped his firm arms around her slim waist, pulling her closer to him. "Let's work up an appetite first. Then I'll *make* you breakfast."

"Hmm . . . lucky me."

He smiled, removed her glasses, set them on the desk, and gave her a long kiss.

He whispered, "Let's go to my place instead of yours. It's much closer." Kathy owned a small condominium in San Francisco, an hour away.

"Deal," she said. "Let's go have a head start on our victory celebration."

From his window office, fifty-five-year-old Sergei Iyevenski watched Jake and Kathy leave the building. The bearlike man grunted, blue eyes gravitating back to the half-drunk glass of vodka in his right hand and the printed results from the test floor in his left, a sense of accomplishment filling his large frame just as the warm vodka drowned his senses.

The Bronco's headlights came alive as Jake backed out of his parking spot and drove across the parking lot, under a blanket of clouds billowing up under a smudged orange moon in its last quarter.

This is too perfect, thought the rugged man. After twenty years working under a regime that did not reward innovation, Sergei Iyevenski had found that his love for his country had taken second place to his obsession with biotechnology. When he was finally ordered to halt his research, Iyevenski had done the only thing he could do: defect. He had met Jake Thomas Fischer three years before he defected, in the summer of 1987, when the large Russian had participated in a worldwide biotechnology forum hosted by France at the Bibliothèque Nationale in Paris. To the disappointment of the multilingual Russian, the forum had concentrated on the applications of biotechnology in the rapidly emerging field of genetics. Not one discussion had mentioned the possibility of using biotechnology as the next platform for computing.

Iyevenski remembered Fischer, then a Ph.D. candidate from Berkeley, part of the American envoy, sitting by the refreshment bar following a long—and quite boring—talk on genetic cloning given by some German professor. While everyone in the large reception hall discussed genetics, Jake and Iyevenski—under the distant but watchful eye of the two political officers accompanying the Russian group—struck up a conversation on the world's failure to appreciate the potential of biotechnology as a replacement for semiconductors. Even the Soviet Union had lost faith in biotechnology, especially after the death of Yuri Ovchinnikov. Constantly adjusting to budget cuts had slowed research at the Russian institute almost to a halt, forcing Iyevenski to consider other avenues to continue his work.

A friendship formed almost instantly. It was one of those instances when enthusiasm for technological advancement overcame political barriers. For the remainder of the week, the two scientists met whenever they could, sometimes while under surveillance, other times managing to get away for a few minutes before KGB agents caught up with them. But Iyevenski knew how to fool those KGB agents. He'd been one himself during most of his twenties and thirties, when his engineering skills required him to become a scientific officer in the KGB, which had forced him to go through the basic training required for all officers. While in the KGB, he became a high-tech spymaster, using his skills to run surveillance on German, French, and Italian industries for the benefit of the Rodina, the motherland.

It was during this two-decade-long assignment that it became evident to him that Russia had been left behind in the silicon-based computing age.

He also realized that semiconductor technology was approaching a molecular barrier to miniaturization. His estimates indicated that silicon transistors, the switches making up a computer chip, would reach their smallest size somewhere around the year 2015, when further size reduction would not only be extremely difficult because of the molecular limitations of the silicon lattice, but also too expensive. Silicon chips had been consistently shrunk to achieve the current levels of integration. Unfortunately, each factor of two in miniaturization increased the cost of manufacturing by a factor of five or more. Each "shrink cycle," therefore, became more expensive than the previous cycle, turning highly exponential as the size of the individual silicon transistors approached their molecular size.

The next-generation technology, Iyevenski and his Russian colleagues believed, was the protein transistor, the molecular structure of which allowed it to be a thousandth the size and a hundred times faster than the silicon transistor. Iyevenski's presentation on the matter to his KGB superiors in 1980 had gotten him immediate release from his KGB duties and an assignment to work with Dr. Ovchinnikov at the Shemyakin Institute of Bioorganic Chemistry in Moscow.

By the end of the conference in Paris an agreement had been reached: Iyevenski would return to Moscow and figure a way out while Jake returned to America to find an avenue to develop their biotechnology. Jake had originally hoped to conduct the research at Los Alamos, but the legendary lab had refused him funding. Determined, Jake turned to the private sector and began to lay the groundwork for what would eventually become FTI.

In the fall of 1990, Iyevenski had used his old espionage talents to make his escape during another international conference on genetics, again held in Paris. Jake Fischer had arranged for a taxi to wait in the rear of the hotel hosting the Russian delegation. The taxi delivered Iyevenski to the American embassy before his KGB escorts, whom Iyevenski had tricked into thinking he was sleeping in his room, realized he was gone. Political asylum was granted within days, and a month later Jake and Iyevenski were hard at work developing the business plan that became Fischer Technologies, Inc., three years later.

"And here we are, my friend," Iyevenski said, a smile cracking his broad face as he raised his glass at the taillights of the Bronco exiting the parking lot. "Today we proved them all wrong. Today we made history."

Propping his feet up on the desk, he drank the last of his vodka. Then, leaning his head against the wall behind him, Sergei Konstantinovich Iyevenski fell asleep in seconds.

The e-mail Jake Fischer had sent traveled through his modem, up a dedicated ISDN line, and to the backbone, or digital highway, feeding the local Internet service provider. The ISP software and hardware, optimized to handle thousands of such messages every second, verified the account number before relaying the message to another backbone linked to an ISP in San Francisco, where the message was relayed to the offices of Preston, Colton & Associates.

While the message transitioned from FTI to the local ISP, a secret FBI tap into the backbone made an exact replica of the transmission and relayed it to another ISP in nearby Milpitas, where it was routed to a three-month-old CompuServe account.

A half hour later, at a first-floor apartment in Sunnyvale, FBI Special Agent Sonya Wüttenberg woke up the moment the alarm in her Compaq notebook went off, informing her it had received a new e-mail message from FTI.

Half asleep, dressed in a denim skirt and a black T-shirt, no bra, Sonya sat up in bed and verified that her Sig Sauer 9mm automatic lay next to the Compaq notebook on the nightstand.

At forty-one, with cropped blond hair and pearl-white skin, she retained a firm figure through daily workouts. Her calf muscles, visible below the knee-high skirt, pumped under her ghostly skin when she stood and stretched. A touch of lipstick adorned a mouth a bit too generous for her narrow face. But combined with her exotic eyes, high cheekbones, and delicate nose, it made the seasoned Fed the target of hungry stares from the male population at FBI headquarters in Washington, D.C.

Her mouth dry and pasty, Sonya grimaced when she checked her watch. Not quite five o'clock in the morning. A brief glance around the room, and she reached for the portable computer system, currently programmed to dial automatically into the local CompuServe node via cellular phone every thirty minutes, check for new messages, and log off.

Because FTI didn't have an e-mail address or Web page, intercepting e-mails from FTI hadn't been simple for Sonya and her high-tech surveillance team. First she had to find the ISPs servicing Silicon Valley, break into the backbone that connected that area of Santa Clara County with the local ISP, and write a program that eliminated all legitimate Web sites within the area serviced by the ISP, such as corporations, banks, restaurants, and department stores. That had narrowed down the search to about a hundred sites. Another handy little program written by one of Sonya's subordinates had compared each Web site address with its physical address in the on-line Palo Alto phone book. The program had come up with matches for all but one site: the Palo Alto Bike Tour Agency, the physical address of which turned out to be the location of FTI's leased building in Palo Alto. Sonya then began to monitor all e-mail activity initiating from that site and intercepted scrambled messages going back and forth between the fake tour agency and Preston, Colton & Associates, a San Francisco venture capital firm, which IRS records revealed to be the company financing FTI. Sonya had her team decipher the first message in about three days, wrote a descrambler in another two, and now could intercept any message to or from FTI and have it deciphered within seconds.

Sudden gloom shadowed her face and her full lips compressed as she read the words written by Jake Fischer, the mysterious entrepreneur Sonya felt she already knew quite well from all the background research she had done in the past months. The FBI surveillance of Jake Fischer and Sergei Iyevenski had been very thorough. In addition to the e-mail surveillance, she had planted eavesdropping devices in their homes. And she had fed all collected intelligence back to FBI Director Roman Palenski in Washington, her superior, and also to CIA Deputy Director for Operations Donald Bane in Langley. The two American intelligence agencies, under direct order from the president, were working together on this and a dozen other special cases requiring their mutual cooperation.

It had been the CIA, through one of its German agents, that learned about an increased level of activity in the Bundesnachrichtendienst, Germany's federal intelligence service. The eyes of the BND apparently had landed on a small start-up in Silicon Valley. Germany apparently had a fierce interest in biotechnology breakthroughs.

Since the merging of East and West Germany, the German government had shown an increasing level of activity in the area of industrial espionage. This surprised no one, as the East Germans had had a long history of stealing other countries' technology, as did the French and the Israelis. But the newly united Germany posed a greater threat than either of those countries, as its position at the center of the European Economic Community gave its theft of technology greater impact. Germany, after all, was the economic powerhouse of Western Europe. Markets rose and fell on the deutsche mark's performance, and Germany desperately needed new industries to fuel its economic growth.

But more than the Germans' sudden interest had the CIA and

FBI directors concerned. In fact, they were both ready to *thank* the Germans for bringing FTI to their attention, because, as their economic and technological analysts had shown them, FTI had the potential to cripple the economies of almost every major country in the world. If FTI's biotechnology made it into today's marketplace, it would destroy high-tech industries not just in the United States but in Europe and Asia, crashing Wall Street in a manner far worse than 1987 or 1929.

Although biotechnology was the way to the future, it had to be phased into the commercial, industrial, and military markets slowly, starting a decade from now, not right away, when it would erase the thriving semiconductor industry, which was still at its peak. The world had invested trillions of dollars in semiconductor technology. It required a return on its investment before the next technological breakthrough. From corporations and R&D labs to university curriculums, and everything in between, such colossal infrastructure could not change overnight. Just as the government had concealed the existence of cheap petroleum alternatives, and thereby prevented the collapse of the automotive and oil industries, so would it conceal the existence of the F1, if indeed it worked. Biotechnology was simply too dangerous to exist anywhere outside the protection of a place like Los Alamos or Sandia Labs, where it could be properly managed and protected.

Sonya's job was to gather intelligence on FTI's secret activities and either confirm or deny the suspicion that the small start-up was well on its way to developing the first protein-based RAM.

Sonya frowned. Uncle Sam intended to acquire this technology from FTI by whatever means possible to protect the U.S. economy. This brought back memories of her Cold War days, when Sonya Wüttenberg worked not for America, her adoptive country, but for the East Germans. Sonya's initial clandestine training came from the Staatssicherheit, the East German ministry of state security, commonly known as the Stasi. The Stasi had been among the finest and most feared intelligence networks in the world during the Cold War, until its dissolution after the breakup of the Soviet Union.

Sonya had joined the CIA and become an expert in industrial counterespionage, her objective to protect the technology vital to the continued economic success and global domination of the United States. Later, when the Federal Bureau of Investigation began to take on a larger role in industrial counterespionage not just inside the United States but also abroad, Sonya switched agencies to maximize her level of contribution to her adopted country. At the FBI, she quickly worked her way up the ranks, until she reached her current position as head of the Office of Liaison and International Affairs (OLIA), operating out of FBI headquarters in Washington. In this capacity, Sonya controlled the activities of twenty foreign offices, known as legal attachés, or legats, chartered with the coordination of FBI activities with foreign police, security services, and other intelligence services. The legats worked out of American embassies and focused on the FBI's expanding role in fighting international crime.

So, when the CIA secretly funneled the information it had gathered from its mole inside the BND to the FBI legat office in Berlin, Sonya began to investigate the small California start-up. The investigation, which quickly revealed the powerful economic weapon in biotechnology, led to a full surveillance operation, which Director Palenski had approved and placed under Sonya's management. Although based in Washington, Sonya spent the majority of her time traveling to follow her top cases. Because of the incredibly high stakes in the FTI case, Sonya had spent most of the past week in Sunnyvale. Her surveillance was so secret that aside from her team, only Roman Palenski and CIA DDO Donald Bane knew of her work.

Pallid hands resting on her lap, her disciplined mind focused on the message still flashing on the color screen, Sonya picked up the phone, activated a scrambler, and dialed Roman Palenski's private number. Fischer Technologies, Inc., claimed that it had just created the first marketable RAM using protein technology. If this was true, the U.S. government had to take immediate action to prevent the irresponsible introduction of this technology into the high-tech marketplace.

Jake Fischer slowly got out of bed, careful not to wake up Kathy Bennett. It was six o'clock in the morning and he had dozed off for about thirty minutes after he and Kathy had made love. The success of the F1 had brought a giddiness and playfulness to their lovemaking. The F1 worked and they were all going to be *rich!*

Putting on a robe, Jake quietly picked up the empty bottle of zinfandel and glasses next to the bed, slowly tiptoed out of the bedroom, and went into the kitchen. Without turning on the overhead, guided only by the dim orange light filtering through the living-room windows, he deposited the bottle and glasses in the sink, opened the almond-colored refrigerator, and found a bottle of apple juice on the top shelf. Little else rested on the glass shelves. Jake Fischer seldom cooked.

Pouring himself a glass of juice, Jake walked over to the double glass doors facing the back and stared at the sunrise, at the fading stars on the deep sapphire sky over the Sierra Moreno, the mountain range separating Silicon Valley from the Pacific Ocean and running all the way down to Los Angeles.

The City of Angels.

Jake Fischer grimaced, his mind flashing visions of street gangs, of graffiti-filled walls, of metal detectors at the entrances and exits of his high school in L.A. Most of his classmates were now probably in jail or dead. But Jake Fischer had remained in school, kept up his grades, and stayed off the streets after school by joining the wrestling team. His father, an LAPD officer killed in the line of duty, had left Jake and his mother with little else besides a monthly pension, barely enough to make ends meet while Jake attended high school. There was no money for college. Jake needed straight A's and a high SAT score, the weapons that his school principal could take to the California Board of Education to support Jake's application for an academic scholarship to the University of California. Two months before his graduation, Jake learned that he had received a scholarship to UC Berkeley.

Jake Fischer had managed to escape Los Angeles. College away from home, however, presented a problem for Jake Fischer: money. His scholarship took care of tuition and books. Jake had to pay for everything else. While going to high school, he had been able to live at home. Room and board had been free. At Berkeley, the legendary university northeast of San Francisco, Jake was forced to get a full-time job to cover living expenses while also pulling eighteen semester hours. He struggled for a few months, until he decided to try out for the Berkeley wrestling team. To his surprise, he made the cut and received a minor scholarship that took care of dorm and cafeteria fees. Jake had prevailed at Berkeley, and several years later received his Ph.D. in electrical engineering. His only regret was that his mother had not been alive to see him graduate. She had died during his senior year in college. His mother had taught Jake Fischer not only the moral values that had carried him this far in life, but also a sense of independence that kept him pushing forward in the face of adversity.

"Are you all right?"

Jake almost spilled his juice, his thoughts interrupted by the arms of Kathy Bennett embracing him from behind.

"You sure are jumpy," she said, pressing her breasts against his back. "You want to come back to bed, tiger? Maybe show me some of those old wrestling moves?"

Jake chuckled, turned around, and said, "With pleasure. I happen to know this great takedown."

She smiled lewdly. Undoing his robe, letting it fall to his feet, and taking him by the hand, Kathy said, "Follow me, wrestling boy, and I'll show you a few moves you haven't seen yet."

Giving the mountains a final glance and discreetly checking his watch, Jake followed her back into the bedroom.

"Stop checking your watch, Jake," she said without turning around. Her black hair reached the middle of her back. "I'll cut you loose with plenty of time to make your breakfast meeting."

Jake stopped and gently pulled her toward him. "You know?"

She gave him a devilish smile, eyes filled with dark amusement. "Sergei told me," she said. Her taut brown nipples grazed his chest as she stood in front of him. "I'm disappointed that you didn't tell me about something so important. I thought you trusted me."

"Kathy, I do—I just didn't want you to—"

"Do I *look* or *behave* like an innocent little girl, Jake?"

The taste of her still alive in his mouth, Jake simply shook his head.

"Then stop treating me like one. I'm a grown woman who happens to be madly in love with a tender and compassionate man—who also happens to be ambitious and hardworking.

"Now, tell me," she said, "how do you think this meeting's going to go?"

Feeling a bit strange discussing business completely naked standing in the middle of the living room, Jake motioned her into the bedroom, where they lay side by side under the covers.

"I mean . . . it can't be all *that* bad," Kathy said, noticing the concern on his face as he rested his head on a pillow. "Especially after last night."

"They're getting restless," he said. "Four years is a very long time."

"But you were quite up-front with them back then. They knew what they were getting into before they signed up for it."

Jake chuckled. "I wish it were that simple. I know they know what they signed up for, but they were also hoping we would be able to pull in our schedule by at least six months, maybe get there with rev B instead of rev C."

"But at least we *did* get there, and still within the time stipulated by our contract," she said, planting an elbow on the pillow and resting the side of her head on her palm. "Shouldn't the news of rev C be enough to calm them now?"

"In theory, yes. But they'll never be satisfied until their investment has paid off."

"Like when we're shipping product for revenue?"

Jake smiled. "Nothing else matters. William Preston and Jacob Colton don't share our enthusiasm about biotechnology. They see it strictly as a business deal, nothing more, nothing less. I worry that tomorrow they might see it just like that and might want to shut us down, maybe sell the equipment and the patents to recoup their investment."

"Shut us down? That's crazy!" she cried, slapping the bed.

"Not in their eyes, and I've seen them do it to other start-ups without a second thought."

"But . . . but can they do that before the end of our legal contract?"

"Under the dismemberment clause, yes."

Kathy sat up in bed, the sheet falling to her lap, firm, round breasts pointing straight at Jake Fischer. "I was never involved in the contract negotiations," she said. "Educate me on what the dismemberment clause really means. Just the name implies trouble."

Jake exhaled heavily and rolled on his back, hands behind his head, eyes on the slow-turning ceiling fan. "It means PCA can cancel the contract if it has reason to believe that selling the pieces of FTI might bring PCA more revenue than the value of the company as a whole, including any projected near-term profits from initial sales."

"But . . . they wouldn't really be getting much for the used HyperCray, the Teradyne tester, and the other equipment. Maybe twenty million at the most. They'd still be plenty short from—"

Jake shook his head. "No, Kathy. Right now, FTI is worth *much* more than that to PCA under the dismemberment clause, and *that's* why I'm worried."

Kathy Bennett lifted a palm. "I'm lost. I don't see how."

"Let me explain. Four years ago, when we first approached PCA with our proposal, nobody cared about biotechnology replacing the silicon chip. Now things are different. Intel, Motorola, IBM, and even Los Alamos are all pursuing an alternative to the silicon transistor. We just happen to be way ahead because we were visionaries and jumped on the wagon first. The value of FTI is *not* the HyperCray, or that old Teradyne tester, or the helifurnaces that Sergei built. The *real* value is up here," Jake said, bringing an index finger to Kathy's temple and gently tapping it.

Kathy looked at Jake from under her fine eyebrows, pursing her mouth before saying, "Intellectual property."

"Yep. The biotech patents they currently control if they shut us down are probably worth a hundred times their original investment," Jake said, deciding not to complicate the explanation with the minor technicality that those particular patents weren't worth anything until Iyevenski updated them. "I know it, and I know Preston and the rest of the vultures at PCA know it. *That's* why they've summoned me for breakfast today."

Jake put a hand to his flat stomach. Although the ripples of his wrestling days were long gone, he hadn't picked up any excess fat. "And *that's* why I think I'm going to be sick."

Kathy looked at Jake, brown eyes shimmering in sudden anger. "Don't you *let* them get to you, Jake Fischer. You hear me? You—*we*—have worked out butts off for the past four years while William Preston and Jacob Colton spent their days at Pebble Beach riding in their golf carts. You go to them and make your case with all the facts in hand. You explain to them where we are, what we have seen . . . and yes, how much *money* they stand to make if they let us keep moving forward. And whatever their answer, you come back to me and I'll be here for you. I love you with or without your CEO title. You just don't let those . . . those *assholes* get you down. You're too good for them."

"Thanks," Jake said, turning to her and resting a hand on her delicate shoulder.

"I'm serious, Jake." Kathy took his hand in hers and kissed it. "Just remember, none of those vultures up in San Francisco really cares about you. If you died today, they wouldn't even go to your funeral. They'd all be at their exclusive golf course."

Jake's angular face settled into a stony, tired, and somewhat sardonic look. "Executioners usually *don't* attend the funerals of their victims, Kathy."

"Oh, stop it!" she barked, pushing his hand away and crossing her arms. "You know what I mean."

"I've gone over this a million times, Kathy. I saw it coming two years ago, when IBM announced its biotechnology division up in Poughkeepsie. Then Intel executives began talking about the end of the silicon transistor around the year 2017. The clock started ticking for FTI. We either had to get a major breakthrough, bring in some revenue, and quickly position ourselves as a major competitor, moving up the high-tech food chain . . . or risk getting swallowed by a larger fish."

"So that's why you kept pushing us so hard, even when we were still ahead of our business plan?"

"That *was* my job, to do everything I could to protect my team, to prevent it from being absorbed by a large company."

"And that's *still* your job, Jake. You're still president and CEO of Fischer Technologies, and you have a meeting to attend. So stop talking nonsense about shutdowns. I think the best is yet to come."

Jake nodded. "You're right."

"I *know* I am," she said, an inviting smile parting her lips. "Now, I want you to make love to me again, then go shower, and I'll help you get dressed. You have a breakfast meeting to attend."

At seven o'clock in the morning, Raul Martinez left FTI's building security in the capable hands of the day-shift guard. Instead of going straight home to get some sleep, however, Martinez drove his seven-year-old Accord to a nearby convenience store.

He deposited a quarter in the slot of the public phone and dialed a number he had committed to memory six months before. Every time he called in to report, Martinez wondered how long it would be before he would be allowed to spend some of the dough he had stashed under his bed at his apartment in Milpitas. He wouldn't mind dumping the Honda and getting himself new wheels, perhaps one of those new convertible—

Not yet, Raul!

The phone rang three times, and an answering machine came on. Closing his eyes, Martinez spoke slowly after the beep for about a minute. Then he hung up and headed home.

Ever since the initial meeting, he had spoken to no live persons, only machines. But the cash kept coming, and as long as it did, Martinez would continue to report. Soon his stash would reach the critical level that would allow him to quit his job and vanish. Until then, he had to be patient and keep on doing what he had been doing.

2

BREAKFAST OF CHAMPIONS

*There is no need to fear the strong. All one needs
is to know the method of overcoming them.*
—Yevgeny Yevtushenko

SANTA CLARA COUNTY, CALIFORNIA

Friday, July 14, 9:40 A.M.

Jake Fischer, wearing the best business suit he owned, walked up to the revolving doors at the front of the Fairmont Hotel. Catching his reflection in the glass, he noticed the tie hanging like a gray-and-maroon pendulum from the collar of his heavily starched white shirt and smiled at the memory of a naked Kathy Bennett slowly tying the knot.

The smile, however, quickly vanished as he entered the lavishly decorated lobby and walked across the gray-and-white marble floors to the golden elevator doors in the rear. Soft piano music flowed out of unseen speakers; neatly dressed clerks behind the long front desk served elegant guests under the brilliant crystal chandeliers hanging by thick brass chains from the twenty-foot ceiling. An exclusive restaurant enclosed in smoked glass and partially shielded from the lobby by rows of potted palm trees to his immediate left served breakfast to many of Silicon Valley's executives.

The popular restaurant, however, was not good enough for William Preston and Jacob Colton, who routinely rented the best suite at the Fairmont, thanks to the money earned by PCA from the blood and sweat of promising start-ups like Fischer Technologies, Inc.

Pressing the UP button, Jake waited, hands behind his back, eyes closed as he mentally went through the information contained in the folded sheets of paper in his coat's inside pocket.

The elevator bell rang and the doors slid into the wall. Jake opened his eyes and waited for an elderly couple to leave the elevator, then walked in and pressed the top-floor button.

Alone, he once again closed his eyes and felt the gentle upward acceleration that took him to the top floor, where the large suites were, each with a stunning view of Silicon Valley.

Jake Fischer's anxiety built as he walked down the burgundy-carpeted corridor toward a pair of large wooden doors. He briefly inspected the dark, glossy wood and the gleaming brass handles that led to the two-thousand-dollar-a-day suite.

A deep breath and Jake buttoned his gray suit coat, adjusted the knot of his tie, ran a hand through his thick black hair, and mumbled to himself, "Show time."

He knocked twice, gently but firmly, a little signal to the PCA executives that he respected them but was not intimidated by them. One thing Jake had learned very quickly in this business relationship was that William Preston and Jacob Colton respected arrogant men like themselves. That arrogance, of course, had to be accompanied by good business sense . . . and guts. *Plenty* of guts. Jake reminded himself to check his watch at least twice during the meeting to let them know he also had other appointments to keep.

The door inched open. A man about Jake's height but much thinner and older, with mostly gray hair, a broad, veiny nose from too many cocktails at the golf course, and a dark blue double-breasted suit flapping loosely on him, appeared in the doorway. He smiled an empty smile and extended his hand.

Jake pumped it and said, "Good morning, Mr. Colton."

"Phew!" Jacob Colton said. "Market's down seventeen points.

There's *nothing* good about *that!*" He abruptly waved Jake in and led the way.

Jake shrugged and closed the door. Colton was a legend in the valley. A self-made billionaire, he had made his fortune by taking risks and investing heavily in companies like Apple Computers, Intel, Sun Microsystems, and Microsoft. The old man had a nose for business and always seemed to know when to buy and when to bail out. He could smell a good deal a mile away and a rotten one a hundred miles away. To him there was nothing personal in ventures like FTI. There was no passion, no emotion, only opportunities and risks. The same business sense that had made Jacob Colton dish out $27 million to create FTI was now telling him to use the dismemberment clause to collect ten times his original investment.

Jake followed the older man to a small conference table in the rear of the spacious, well-decorated suite. A stunning view of downtown San Jose and the mountains momentarily stole Jake's attention from the lavish suite, which he estimated was probably larger than his home.

Colton pointed to a tray of fresh fruit, coffee, and bagels at one end of the mahogany table, opposite where another man sat, at the head of the table, his eyes on a report spread in front of him. Reading spectacles hung from the edge of his aristocratic nose as William Preston ignored Jake Fischer just long enough to let him know who was in charge. Then he gathered the loose sheets, set down the spectacles, and turned his attention to the unimpressed CEO of FTI. Jake had dealt with these characters long enough to know how the game was played.

The handsome William Preston, fifty-five years old, with an athletic body that looked youthful in either tailored suits at work or golf outfits at Pebble Beach, rose fluidly from the chair, not to be polite, but to stretch. Unlike Colton, Preston had been born to wealth. His father, co-owner of the Bank of San Francisco, had made his only son the full beneficiary of his estate. William Preston simply continued to carry on the investment tradition of his father.

Covering a yawn with a manicured hand, William Preston pointed to a chair to his immediate left.

"Get yourself some breakfast. Then come sit right here."

Jake simply nodded at another sign of power: the lack of polite words in Preston's or Colton's vocabularies. Their $27 million had essentially bought them the right to be first-class assholes to Jake Fischer and any other CEO of a PCA-financed, high-tech start-up.

Jake let all of that roll right off. As long as PCA left his team alone, he was willing to take the heat and abuse, shielding his team from the drudgery of dealing with venture capitalists.

Preston sat back down. Colton grabbed the chair to Preston's immediate right. The two instantly engaged in a whisper-level conversation designed to keep reminding Jake of his hired-hand status. Jake, annoyed but determined not to show an ounce of weakness—for he knew all too well that would spell disaster with these two—slowly picked up a china plate and served himself a modest portion of sliced cantaloupe and apples. He also poured himself a cup of black coffee.

Taking his assigned seat—which had no effect on the ongoing whispering—Jake forced himself to eat his breakfast, his back to the windows and the spectacular view behind him, his cobalt-blue eyes flicking between his breakfast, the muttering executives, and the extravagant suite.

"We got your e-mail this morning," said Preston in a patrician tone. His full head of silver hair framed a well-tanned face and intelligent light blue eyes, and his wide mouth smiled slightly, seeming to express satisfaction at knowing that he controlled Fischer's life. "Most impressive," he said.

"But a bit *late*," hissed Jacob Colton under his breath, briefly eyeing Jake before shifting his gaze to the clear skies of northern California beyond him.

Jake, who had anticipated the possibility of being addressed while chewing a mouthful of fresh fruit, had opted for small bites and was able to swallow quickly and say, "It is indeed a great breakthrough, *and* right on time per our business plan."

"We know it is, Jake," continued Preston. Colton, his ramshackle frame slouched on the chair, kept his sunken, hazel eyes on the scenery outside. "My associate here is just sharing the concern expressed by our board. Three and a half years is a very long time not to see any return on our investment."

"I realize that," Jake said, carefully measuring his words. "And your patience and confidence are about to pay off in a manner far larger than anticipated."

Colton turned a face wrinkled and flecked with age to the distinguished Preston, a bony thumb pointed at Jake as he said in a rheumy voice, "I thought you were going to tell him about our decision, Bill. He doesn't know yet, does he?"

Jake's ears tuned to that comment like a hunting dog. Preston, raising his palm toward the older man, slowly shook his head before turning back to Jake Fischer. It had taken Jake about three meetings with the PCA executives to catch on to the borderline-amusing good-guy-bad-guy routine they went through.

Probably something they picked up from some cop show, he thought.

"What my associate meant," Preston said in a serene, controlled tone, "is that the board has been seriously questioning—as of recently—the ability of FTI to actually *deliver* according to the business plan. We all held high hopes for revision B last Christmas and were utterly disappointed to see it come short of our expectations."

"And we just can't wait any longer," said Colton. "We must get a return on our investment immediately."

"We've been doing some homework, Jake," said Preston, using another tactic Jake Fischer was only too familiar with: sudden nonstop talk to keep Jake from interrupting, to keep his mind always trying to catch up with the conversation. "And our analysts feel that, given the current condition of the high-tech market and the recent shift by some corporations to develop an alternative to the silicon chip, the biotechnology intellectual property of FTI is worth today far more than our original investment."

"Therefore," said Colton, talking right over Preston's last sentence, "we strongly feel that the best way to maximize our return on the investment we made three and a half years ago is to license that knowledge, those patents, to corporations with far more resources than what FTI has today."

"FTI has done a remarkable job in accelerating the development of this technology, Jake," continued Preston, reaching for Jake and planting a hand on his shoulder, his tone becoming grandfatherly. "But we all know that you're still a ways from generating substantial revenue. Let's not kid ourselves here. You simply don't have the muscle, the capacity, or the sales force to bring a product like that to market within the next two to five years."

"Like IBM or Motorola," said Colton, a finger pointing at a document sporting Motorola's letterhead. "We already have offers to the tune of half a billion dollars for the rights to FTI's works. That's five hundred big ones, and all we have to do is release the technology."

"Look, Jake," said Preston, the hand off Jake's shoulder and back on the table. "The F1 RAM was a wonderful idea, but revision B didn't work as expected, and I don't get the feeling we're sure this revision C is as good as it seems. There's simply *too much risk* in the program, too many unknowns, too many unresolved issues. For example, your process involves too many dangerous chemicals. You've apparently managed to manipulate them safely in a research and development mode. But in production an accident could be disastrous."

"Look at the number of fires at processing plants last year alone!" exclaimed Colton. "Over six billion dollars in damages! Six billion bucks! That just adds more risk to the program."

"Jake," said Preston in a soft and slower tone, carefully articulating each word, "we frankly see no choice but to exercise the dismemberment clause in our contract. We don't have a good feeling that waiting until the end of the four years is a good business decision at this moment."

"Not when we have a number of companies knocking down our doors with mountains of cash to sell out."

Both sets of eyes on him, Jake took the opportunity to check his watch before pushing his chair back a few inches, unbuttoning his coat, crossing his legs, and responding in an amazingly calm voice tinged with condescension, "Gentlemen, revision B of the F1 did *exactly* what was expected of it: create a platform from which we could tune up the design and achieve the required memory capacity and speed while also tweaking the manufacturing process. The effort has paid off. Our new revision C has not only achieved its goals, but in many ways exceeded them, providing us with an excellent vehicle to penetrate the lucrative memory market *today,* not in six months. Revenue will start flowing in as soon as we open the books and start taking orders."

"And how do we know this time is for real? How do we know we're not going to get ourselves in trouble, perhaps even get sued for false advertising?" blurted Colton, his wiry lips shaking not from anger but from old age.

"Because we have *working prototypes,* gentlemen," Jake responded in a polite but matter-of-fact tone.

Colton uttered an indrawn gasp as Preston said, "You mean . . . real, working RAMs?"

"I thought you gentlemen read my e-mail."

"Well . . . yes, we did," admitted Preston, an unusual embarrassment straining his otherwise commanding voice. "But we weren't sure what to make of it. We thought it was maybe just a computer model of the real thing."

In spite of the multiple meetings Jake had had with these two, it never ceased to amaze him how differently they viewed engineering reports. He had clearly stated that revision C of the F1 was fully functional. Yet that message had not made it through to the financial minds of William Preston and Jacob Colton. But Jake also knew the value of not showing an ounce of frustration at the sheer inability of his venture capitalists to grasp reality. He had to indulge them.

Keeping a cool head, he calmly said, "No, sir. I'm not talking about some computer model, or a schedule, or a business plan. I'm talking about *working* biomemories. By this afternoon we'll have some of those F1s plugged into our fastest Pentium systems at FTI. Imagine a world where memory capacity was unlimited, where hard disks existed only as backups, and everything else—everything from operating systems like Windows and OS/2 to word processors, spreadsheets, graphics, and all other applications—resided in memory all the time. There would be no more waiting for a program to load to memory, no slowing down to the speed of the machine while working with three-D graphics.

"Imagine full-motion video on your entire screen with a quality and sound that challenged a movie theater. Imagine enough memory to handle video conferencing with multiple sites, each covering a portion of your screen, and each with perfect video and audio clarity. Imagine a world no longer limited by the classic sixteen or thirty-two megabytes of expensive memory but freed by one hundred *gigabytes*—one hundred *thousand* megabytes—of relatively inexpensive memory on the same space currently taken by the low-density memory chips of today.

"The applications beyond the personal computer are equally mind-numbing. Imagine robots, for example, capable, because of their F1 neuronlike memories, to learn, to see, to hear, and to act and move based on human inputs without the burden of keyboards or giant control systems. I'm talking robots that are mobile, battery-operated, portable units. Or imagine the Internet speeding up to real time thanks to massive banks of biomemory handling communications at the speed of its users, all of whom use modems and workstations with more memory capacity than what's onboard the space shuttle while communicating through the fiber-optics networks that already exist in many cities. FTI has the technology today.

"We also have the manufacturing muscle to get started and quickly grow into a computer giant, one that will bring not just a *one-time* five-hundred-million-dollar profit, but several *billions* every year. Selling out to a large firm now would be the equivalent of Bill Gates selling out to IBM after coming up with the first version of his PC operating system back in the early eighties—an enormous mistake considering where Microsoft is today. We could become *the* company of the twenty-first century, gentlemen. We have a ten-year head start on our competition and are uniquely positioned to maintain that gap. You don't have to sell out to Intel or IBM or Motorola. FTI is going to be *larger* than Intel and IBM and Motorola . . . *combined.*"

Jake paused to let his words sink in. Preston's jaw had dropped about an inch. A mix of curiosity and the sheer possibility of stunning success had softened Colton's defiant stare. And all because Jake Fischer had kept the explanation fairly nontechnical and had thrown in ballpark financial figures.

"*That,* gentlemen," Jake added, "is the promise of FTI and of *our* biotechnology."

With that, Jake shoved his right hand inside his coat pocket and pulled out the two spreadsheets he had printed just six hours before. "Now let's go over financial details," he added, and went on to discuss the profits of the first year in business. He spent the next twenty minutes covering production yields, manufacturing costs, expenses, salaries, new constructions, headcount expansions, offshore plants, increasing market share, and everything else that the venture capitalists wanted to hear. Their eyes suddenly filmed with greed, their half-opened mouths wanting to gobble up the two printouts.

Fucking vultures, Jake thought as he watched them salivate at the magnitude of the projected income.

"Can you expand this fast and still keep control of the company?" asked Preston, a finger tapping the spreadsheets.

"Absolutely. The expansion plans were defined six months ago, sir. With our current facility we can generate over a billion dollars in revenue in the first year, but we don't want to stop there. If we start building after only three months' worth of revenue, we could triple our capacity—and our revenue—within a year, at the same time expanding in the United States and setting up plants in Singapore and Malaysia. I've already made all of the necessary arrangements and obtained all of the required import-export licenses and permits to break ground in those two countries within three months. In terms of staffing, I have the required core team in place. We're talking about increasing the number of technicians and junior engineers. With schools like Stanford, UC Berkeley, and UCLA, there's no reason we can't make the required headcount numbers."

The capitalists nodded and looked at each other and agreed it was a good answer.

"What about just hiring from the pool of available experienced engineers in the Valley?" asked Preston, his country-club tan gleaming in the sunshine streaming through the panoramic window. "There's at least a couple hundred thousand electrical engineers available for the right price."

Jake checked his watch for the second time, smoothed his tie, and flashed the financial pair a frown. "That's a good suggestion, but I'm afraid it won't work. Current electrical and computer engineers don't have the biochemical background vital for understanding our technology. I need a special breed of people, mostly bio or chemistry majors that we can then mold into our hybrid discipline. We still might choose to pick a select few computer engineers, especially to work in the design of new chips, but they'll still have to be retrained to forget semiconductors and start thinking biotech."

"That's interesting," observed Colton. "You're really creating a new breed of engineers."

Jake nodded. "That's why FTI is so special. No company, regardless of size or capital, has the accumulated knowledge and training that we possess now, and in a few years we would be truly untouchable, even by the likes of IBM and Intel."

"What about the press, Jake?" asked Colton, calling Jake Fischer by his first name, his tone of voice warmed by the dollar bills cascading behind his sunken eyes. "Shouldn't we be planning some kind of press release about this?"

Jake smiled. "I've already set up a press conference for the twentieth of this month. I've gotten RSVPs from seven trade journals and six major newspapers."

More nods as Preston and Colton exchanged pleased glances. Jake continued to smile cordially.

"What about setting up the infrastructure to handle chemicals in a volume production environment?" asked Preston.

This time Jake's approving nod was genuine. That was indeed a good question, especially from someone with limited exposure in the technical field. Everyone at FTI knew the danger involved in working with so many chemicals stored in portable containers kept inside the main building, instead of an adjacent building. But FTI had grown beyond the physical dimensions of the building,

and there was no more leased space available in the business park—
not that Jake Fischer had the budget to lease more floor space.

"That's an excellent question, sir. My CTO, Sergei Iyevenski,
is already hard at work hammering out the final details of the manufacturing plan. I expect to have an entire production ramp and
expansion proposal ready for your review within two weeks."

The questions and the approving nods continued up to the
point when Jake, flanked by the smiling executives, walked to the
front door of the suite, where the back-patting and handshakes
almost overwhelmed even the seasoned CEO. But he played
along, thanking them for their confidence and inviting them to
the press conference. They both agreed to be there and help field
any questions the skeptical media might have.

The moment the doors closed behind him, Jake dropped to a
deep crouch and pulled in his right elbow, hand in a tight fist.
"Yes!" he hissed under his breath before he straightened, buttoned
his coat, ran a hand through his hair, and respectably walked toward the elevators.

Two hours later, Jake Fischer felt the electricity inside the test area,
where all twenty-three employees of FTI had gathered for a group
communications meeting. Lacking a conference room large
enough to accommodate his team, Jake used the extra space on
the test floor to hold these periodic meetings, targeted at keeping every member of his team well informed on company issues.
Soon—very soon—Jake hoped to have a proper room and fill the
cavernous test area with Teradyne testers and probers.

Today there was reason for celebration, and Jake could see it
in his team's glinting eyes. They were all there, Sergei to his right,
Kathy to his left, and the rest of the crew, wearing their lab coats,
in front of the trio. Everyone held a plastic cup of Dom Pérignon.

"Last night we made history, my friends," Jake began. "Last
night FTI joined the ranks of companies like IBM, Intel, Mi-

crosoft, and Apple in terms of technological breakthrough. Soon we will also join them in terms of the revenues and profits associated with such scientific innovations."

Everyone howled and cheered. Kathy leaned over and kissed him on the cheek. Iyevenski raised both hands above his head and joined in the howling.

Jake paused a moment and then said, "Three and a half years ago we set off to create a technology that everyone else felt could not be achieved for another fifteen years, perhaps even longer. Last night, thanks to the incredible effort of each and every one of you, we proved them all wrong. The F1 RAM is a real product, probably the most notable technological breakthrough since the invention of the silicon transistor. Last night *we* made a difference, *we* went against conventional wisdom and succeeded beyond our expectations. Last night we prevailed in a business where most fail. And for that, I thank you."

More cheering. Jake waited until they had calmed down.

"The challenge ahead is that of healthy growth and diligent execution of our business plan. We're about to transition from an R&D facility to a manufacturing giant, and that will bring along new challenges, new roadblocks, new difficulties. But I'm fully confident that we *will* overcome them and succeed. We can do it . . .*you* can do it."

Jake raised his cup at the small crowd. "To you, the finest engineering team in the world."

The applause that followed was longer than Jake's speech.

"What happens to our stock options now?" one of test engineers in Kathy's team asked, a young kid from the Rochester Institute of Technology.

Jake smiled at the RIT grad. Like many Silicon Valley start-ups, FTI offered stock options to compensate employees for the high risk they took by working at a small company instead of accepting safer jobs at large corporations. Stock options awards were based on salary level and position, but even the lowest employee in the crowd stood to make a few hundred thousand dollars the moment FTI went public.

"The plan is still the same," Jake said. "As soon as we complete two profitable quarters and revenues exceed one hundred million dollars, FTI goes public and you are free to cash in your stock or watch it climb through the roof."

Everyone cheered. Kathy had tears in her eyes. Iyevenski had already downed one cup of champagne and was pouring himself another one.

One of the process engineers in Iyevenski's team, a former professor of chemistry at Stanford, asked, "Can we get drunk now?"

Jake smiled and nodded. Heck, they deserved it. They had worked too hard for a very long time to get here. They had ignored their families and friends. They had put their personal lives on hold for the past three and a half years. Now it was time to harvest the fruits of their arduous labor. It was time to let the entire world know about FTI's breakthrough.

3

THE KARDINAL

Men loved darkness rather than light, because their deeds were evil.

—John 3:19

A crimson sunrise broke the darkness covering the city, splashing a blood-red hue over the Detlev-Rohwedder-Haus, a bureaucratic-looking hulk filling an entire city block. The grim stone building, originally designed as the headquarters for the Third Reich, overlooked what once had been called "no-man's-land," the desolate and very dangerous stretch separating the two barriers of the nearly vanished Berlin Wall. This former death zone, ranging in width from a few yards to a few thousand, and patrolled in the not-so-distant past by hundreds of Soviet-bloc troops, now ranked among the most prized real estate in Europe.

A light fog began to lift off the multiple construction projects rising on this land that still bore the memory of those who had dared cross it to reach the West. Motorists now raced past the few remaining sections of the Wall—relics of a dead era, silent reminders of the Cold War.

The intersection of Zimmerstrasse and Charlottenstrasse marked the spot where, in 1962, eighteen-year-old Peter Fechter was shot dead while attempting to climb over the Wall, in plain view of a large crowd of international journalists and American soldiers. The single cross at the street corner, a prime tourist attraction, was largely ignored by the bumper-to-bumper early-morning traffic cruising past the five-story building, stalling three

blocks later as a peaceful demonstration of people bearing signs
of the National Trade Union Federation (DGB) partially blocked
the street at the Potsdamer Platz. The square, once a legendary
bastion of the privileged and chic with its first-class hotels and
cafés, was now one of the most depressing and controversial lo-
cales in Germany. And on this cool and breezy morning, over two
thousand members of the DGB, most of them former East Germans, were demanding a more balanced distribution among German corporations of the financial burden of job training.

Forming a safety cordon around the relatively calm DGB
group, two hundred members of the Berlin police wearily kept
watch over the poorly dressed and unshaved East Germans demanding the free training promised to them during the early days
of the reunification process—promises the German industry
found hard to meet without some relief from the federal government. But the government, encumbered with rising unemployment, inflation, and a falling deutsche mark, had recommended
a "training fee" that, in theory, could be reduced by the companies through the incurred cost of in-house job training. German
industrialists, however, struggling to cope with increased manufacturing costs, tough global competition, and softer markets,
had refused the training fee reduction proposal, claiming that un-
trained workers—mostly East Germans—had to pay for most of
the cost of their training. As a result, for the past month there had
been DGB demonstrations across Berlin. Today the protesters directed their anger at Telekom, Germany's largest communications company, headquartered across the street.

The police captain, a hand on the black sidearm inside his
shiny leather holster, slowly moved his gaze up and down the long
row of police officers shielding the demonstrators from the slow-
flowing morning traffic, which a dozen of his men helped direct.
The captain was almost fifty-five years old, due for retirement in
another three years. He had a son inside the crowd, the one he'd

thought he had lost forever in 1961, when the East Germans erected the Berlin Wall, trapping his pregnant wife, who died in childbirth. The captain, however, had been fortunate not only that his older brother had remained behind and was able to raise his son, but that he was allowed enough visits into East Berlin to see him grow up. Father and son were finally reunited the day the Wall fell in 1989.

The captain turned his attention to a group of uniformed teenagers on their way to a nearby school. They had stopped to point and laugh at the ragged-looking demonstrators from across the busy street.

"Achtung!" the captain bellowed over the four lanes of traffic. "Keep going! This is not a street show!"

The teens, books in hand, kept walking toward their private school, totally unaware of the realities the men and women in the crowd faced every day in the reunified Germany: layoffs, hunger, mockery, humiliation. The police captain heard the pain in his son's voice and saw the abuse in his son's melancholic stare every morning as he fixed him breakfast, before each went their separate ways—the captain to protect the people denying his son the training he needed to regain his self-respect, his son to seek employment, which he would sometimes find, but never a job using his skills as a telephone repair operator. The outdated telephone systems in East Germany were nothing like the computerized communications systems in the West. His son needed the training that Telekom was unwilling to provide without a hefty training fee.

That was another aspect of the fallacy of the "training fee." The higher-paying the job, the higher the training fee. For his son to bring his telecommunications skills up to date would require the captain not only to spend his life's savings but also to take out a "training loan," which the German government offered at low interest for East German men and women under thirty years of age.

His son was now thirty-seven and unofficially deemed "untrainable" by the current system, which would not even offer a regular, high-interest personal loan because his father lacked adequate collateral.

The captain's attention returned to the crowd, to the faces, to the silent stares of envy shot across the police barrier at the groomed businessmen inside shiny Mercedes-Benzes, BMWs, and Audis.

Two blocks down and across from the Potsdamer Platz, a man in his early forties, dressed in a pair of black leather pants, a white shirt, and a black leather jacket, watched the DGB crowd from behind small round sunglasses. His shaved head glistening in the sunshine, the man checked his watch and smiled when his beeper went off. The message on his alpha pager made his smile widen. His superior had sent the signal, the order to deliver another message to the East Germans from the people of West Germany.

The skinhead shoved a tattooed hand inside his leather jacket, curling his fingers around a hand grenade. The iron object felt cold, rugged, powerful. It gave him a sense of control, a feeling of worthiness, of pride, of honor, to know that he had been selected, along with three others, for this glorious assignment.

The skinhead felt nothing but contempt for the protesters, the leeches who continued to rob his Germany of its true future, of its precious deutsche marks. Little had he known that the fall of the Wall, which he himself had cheered, would bring such misery, unemployment, and inflation to his country. Fifty years of progress had come to a crashing halt for the West Germans while they tried to absorb a nation with Third World status.

And, in many ways, *below* Third World status. At least countries in South America and Asia had the infrastructure in place—mostly thanks to heavy foreign investment—to access most of their natural resources: oil, iron, sugar, cotton. East Germany lacked such foreign help. The Russians had abused the land and its people through fifty years of Communism. And after squeezing the population clean of their self-worth, of their pride, of their future, they had left it behind for the affluent West Germans to come to its rescue.

But financial help to the East Germans wasn't the skinhead's problem. The East Germans simply *had* to find a way to build a country for themselves from the ashes of the old, just as West Germany had after the war. Maybe then, reunification could occur. But not now, when it put such a massive burden on the West German government that it could no longer afford to employ former border patrol guards like himself, who had been laid off three years before. For six months the former officer had tried to find new employment. He tried the local police, the army, and security firms without luck. His resentment for the people who had caused him to lose a job in which he had already invested twenty years of his life grew with every rejection letter, with every failed job interview.

The skinhead walked toward the Potsdamer Platz, slowly, calmly, controlled by the unyielding determination to carry out his mission with icy efficiency, to deliver his message with utter resolve.

The police captain saw the man in black as his eyes swept over the slow-flowing morning traffic. The group of uniformed teens moved to the side as they crossed paths with the lonely pedestrian, continuing up the street and disappearing around the corner. But the captain's trained eyes followed the bald man in black as he casually strolled down the opposite sidewalk without glancing at the crowd, his dark sunglasses pointed straight ahead.

Then he stopped and faced the protesters on the square.

"Move!" the captain screamed from across the street, pointing at the neo-Nazi and then pointing at the end of the block. "You! Keep walking! This is not a show!"

The man remained motionless, expressionless, a hand hidden inside his black jacket, the sun reflecting off his sunglasses.

Then he grinned.

His pulse racing, adrenaline boiling through him, the captain brought his walkie-talkie to his lips and shouted to three of his officers directing traffic to use extreme caution and escort the bald man in black away from the protesters. Twenty-five years of law enforcement had given him a sixth sense, and that sense right now blared at him. The man was hiding something under his coat, and the captain would have bet his life savings that it was a gun.

One of his officers, a kid from Munich, began to walk across the barely moving traffic, snaking his way in between bumpers, a hand reaching for his sidearm. Two other officers followed him, using hand signals to halt traffic as they trailed the first officer.

Then it happened. The neo-Nazi revealed the object he had been hiding under the coat. At the sight of the black, pear-shaped grenade the captain grasped for his revolver. But it was too late. Howling like a madman, the skinhead removed the pin and threw the grenade at the crowd with all his might.

"Granate! Achtung! Granate!" the captain screamed at the top of his lungs as the rookie police officers jumped on the skinhead and pinned him to the concrete sidewalk, just as the grenade landed in the middle of the crowd.

In a single, ear-piercing shriek of terror, the protesters broke through the police cordon and raced across the street, over the hoods and trunks of luxury automobiles and their honking owners. Sheet metal bent and windshields cracked as the wave of people stomped right over the stalled traffic.

The blast came. Inky smoke rose in the middle of the stampeding crowd, their shouts mixing with the blaring horns and the cries from wounded protesters.

Going against the current of people leaving the Potsdamer Platz, the police captain shoved his way through the thick, acrid smoke. He reached the victims and had to control his urge to vomit. Three men were unconscious, their chests and necks torn open by the shrapnel, dark blood staining their shirts, pooling around them. Two more screamed for help, one bleeding from his leg, the other bracing his abdomen, holding on to his exposed viscera from a huge, blackened wound above his groin.

And it was his son!

"Fa—Father . . . please, help me . . . cold . . ."

His heart shrinking, his hands trembling, tears of anger streaming down his wrinkled face, the captain knelt by his dying son and took him in his arms, cradling him, pressing the trembling body against him as three more explosions thundered across the Potsdamer Platz. More screams and cries filled the square, more smoke rose up to the clear skies above Berlin. His son stopped moving. His dead, filmy eyes stared at the tall granite-and-glass building headquartering the telecommunications company that had refused to train him. Now he was dead, killed by Telekom, by Germany, by a nation that refused to accept its own people.

The police captain, confused, furious, blood-chilling anger tearing his insides just as the shrapnel had raked his son's intestines, set his son's limp body back on the concrete and defiantly stared at the Telekom employees walking out to the balconies to see the commotion.

"See what you have done!" the captain screamed at the top of his lungs. "This is all your fault! You are responsible! You have done this to me, to us, to our Deutschland!"

A demon had come alive inside the captain, a force he could not control, a beast released by the loss of his only son, murdered by people who called themselves Germans.

The people at Telekom remained motionless on the balconies. All perfectly groomed, elegantly dressed in their business suits or expensive dresses. All enjoying the madness below from the safety of their building, without the smallest realization that they had caused it.

"You hear me?" the captain screamed as he paced around his dead son, mourning, crying, hating. "You did this! You!" he shouted, pointing at the people on the balconies. "You bastards! You miserable bastards!"

Unholstering his weapon, possessed by an unrestrainable urge to release his bottled-up anger, his son's blood pooling by his boots, the police captain lifted his weapon and began to fire at the Telekom building. Two men in business suits fell over the railing, and the rest of the employees fled inside the building. But the captain did not stop firing, in spite of the shouts from his subordinate officers, who ran toward him from the street. His index finger kept pulling the trigger. His anger had taken total control.

The captain released the empty magazine and inserted a fresh one. Cocking the weapon, he again pointed the weapon at the building, but did not get to fire another round. A piercing pain in his chest, carrying the power of a thousand knuckle punches, propelled him backward, over his son. He landed on his back, suddenly feeling cold, nauseated. He realized he had been shot by one of his men. He had left them no choice.

Eyelids twitching, mouth quivering, the dying captain gave his son a final glance before his vision darkened.

A mile away, on the top floor of the Detlev-Rohwedder-Haus, German Minister of Industry and Commerce Johann von Hunsinger, wearing a tailored Italian suit, a hand-painted tie adorning his starched shirt, held a cup of hot tea in his right hand and watched a blaring ambulance maneuvering through the congested streets.

His steady gaze shifted to the Hedwigskirche, the Roman Catholic cathedral of the Berlin diocese, its copper-sheathed dome stained in hues of orange and yellow. Minister von Hunsinger took a deep breath and nodded as he heard the two aides he'd sent to meet with representatives of the ministries of economy and finance walking into the room. The savvy von Hunsinger already knew most of the answers his subordinates would bring, but he was a thorough man and wanted to do his homework, wanted to get final confirmation of the true state of the German economy before his upcoming secret meeting with his country's intelligence service.

"Sit down, please," von Hunsinger said, taking a sip of hot tea. He still faced the beautiful sunrise, which he could enjoy every morning not because he arrived at the office early, but because part of the floor below was actually his private suite, where the bachelor minister, one of the most important figures in German politics, spent most weeknights, often in the company of one of the department's secretaries.

Turning around and walking to the head of the conference table, von Hunsinger set his cup of tea on the smooth rosewood surface and sat down, leaned back, and crossed his legs. "I only have ten minutes before my next meeting. . . . What is the situation?"

His two aides, a woman in her early forties and a man in his mid-thirties, both dressed according to von Hunsinger's strict standards, looked at each other and then at the silver-haired minister.

Olga Rittner, a slim brunette with sharp brown eyes behind rimless glasses and a soft mouth painted a bit too orange, peered at her notes and then at her superior. "Our figures show an additional twenty billion deutsche marks in tax revenue losses for this year, Herr Minister."

Von Hunsinger stared at the woman's bony face and then closed his eyes in disgust. That brought the total tax revenue loss to sixty-two billion deutsche marks more than last year. Waving a hand in the air, the minister said, "And?"

Olga Rittner added, "The additional loss is due to five percent fewer goods produced and services rendered in the past three months."

"Which were the worst markets?"

"Automotive was the worst," said Olga Rittner, consulting her notes. "We've experienced large market-share losses in sales in America, Asia, and even Europe to the Japanese. The aerospace, industrial, chemical, and even electronics industries have experienced similar setbacks. The lower exports, combined with higher agricultural imports required to feed our nation until the farmlands of East Germany achieve the required levels of production, have inflated our trade deficit."

"In addition," added his second subordinate, Klaus Scharping, a slightly overweight man with a huge brown mustache and a heavy square face, "the ministry of economy has reported that it seems certain that this year Germany will not be able to meet its criteria for membership in the European Currency Union."

Now *that* was unexpected. "Why not?" von Hunsinger asked, dreading the answer.

"First is unemployment, Herr Minister," continued the large Scharping, his double chin almost hanging over the knot of the maroon tie on his dress shirt. "The ministry of economy and the ministry of finance both agree that unemployment will rise by half a million people, bringing the total to five million unemployed Germans, two-thirds former East Germans."

"Five million . . ." von Hunsinger repeated to himself, setting both elbows on the table. He cursed the day West Germany began the reunification process. "What about the new workplaces we were planning to create?" Two days ago von Hunsinger had approached several German industries with a proposal to increase job openings by lowering overtime hours.

"The metals, electrical, and chemical industries rejected the idea yesterday, Herr Minister. Telekom is still reviewing the proposal."

"Very well," von Hunsinger said in a frustrated tone of voice. "What else?"

"Aside from the unemployment figures," said Olga Rittner, her fine hands holding loose sheets of yellow paper with red ink scribbles, "the ECU is quite concerned about our public debt, which, at one point nine trillion deutsche marks, is softening the position of our currency against the dollar and the yen."

Von Hunsinger stood and returned to the windows, where, to his surprise, he saw two more ambulances, their lights and alarms clearing their way through traffic as they rushed in the same direction as the first one he had spotted a few minutes ago.

"Did they confirm the amount?" he asked, his eyes on the blue and red lights flashing down the street. His question referred to a national campaign underway to spread the legend that Germany was quickly becoming truly unified.

"Yes, Herr Minister," responded Klaus Scharping. "This year so far, our government has spent eight billion deutsche marks in taxpayers' funds to sell the reunified slogan not just to the German people, but to foreigners."

Von Hunsinger shook his head. He'd heard about the plan but never known exactly how much capital the German chancellor and the parliament had approved for the implementation of the reunification propaganda machine. The economic situation was so bad that his country had to spend money telling its citizens that they didn't have a bad economic situation and that the reunification process continued at a steady pace.

The minister exhaled and shoved both hands into his side pockets. Unemployment was up, inflation was on the rise, the public debt was terrifyingly high, and the German government was now wasting *billions* of precious deutsche marks contradicting truths that the people of Germany lived through every day.

Another ambulance rushed by. Von Hunsinger reached for the phone and dialed his new secretary, a blonde from Düsseldorf with a body that had instantly landed her a job in spite of her mediocre typing skills.

"Yes, Herr Minister?" came the soft voice.

"I have seen six ambulances in the past few minutes."

"A terrible thing just happened," she said, her voice a bit broken with emotion. "The radio says bombs went off at a DMG demonstration at Potsdamer Platz. Several people are dead and many were injured."

Having heard everything he cared to hear about the chaotic state of the German economy, von Hunsinger dismissed his two aides and ordered his secretary to let in the chief of the BND, Germany's federal intelligence service.

Germany's top spy walked into the spacious office.

"A tragedy," von Hunsinger said, clenching his jaw, his eyes serious and remote as he sat back at the head of the conference table.

Hans Bölling, a general in the MIS, Germany's military intelligence service until his appointment as director of the BND two years before by Chancellor Helmut Kohl—after the personal endorsement of Johann von Hunsinger—gave the elegant minister a slight nod as he also sat. "A terrible thing, Herr Minister. Simply a terrible thing."

His voice carrying an edge he usually could disguise when addressing the press or his superiors, von Hunsinger said, "I thought you had the situation under control, Hans. I thought we had them watched."

Hans Bölling, in his mid-sixties, with thinning white hair, a white mustache, a face flecked and wrinkled with age, and clothes that looked a few sizes too big for his skinny frame, simply said, "They are always recruiting new soldiers. And with our current economic situation there is a large pool of dissatisfied Germans willing to take matters into their own hands. I am afraid there will be more attacks."

"How many so far this year?" asked the minister.

The seasoned intelligence officer said, "Since January there have been more than seventy-four hundred racist, anti-Semitic, right-wing-extremist, and neo-Nazi attacks in Germany. These include attacks against persons and property, theft and robbery, firebombings, and cemetery desecrations."

Johann von Hunsinger pinched the bridge of his nose as he felt a headache nearing. So much death and injury. So much destruction. So much hatred consuming his country.

But as minister of industry and commerce, Johann von Hunsinger had to look beyond these problems and focus on the main issue facing his country: cash flow. Germany needed hard currency to solve the social problems of the reunification process.

Peering into the tired eyes of the chief of the BND, von Hunsinger said, "The reason I summoned you here today is to get an update on the situation in California."

"Our source inside Fischer Technologies has informed us that the company has finally succeeded in creating a working memory device."

Von Hunsinger froze. He hadn't expected a breakthrough so soon in the process. "A working RAM?"

"Yes, sir. Apparently plug-in-compatible with existing RAMs, but much denser and faster."

"What kind of capacity? What speeds?"

The spy shook his head. "Our source is not that sophisticated, sir."

Putting a hand to his forehead, von Hunsinger inhaled deeply, his eyes closed. "All right. How are *our* teams progressing in this quest?"

"Our sources tell us that the team at Wannsee-Brecht Biochemical in Munich has been unsuccessful in controlling even the most basic electrochemical responses from bacterial proteins. They believe WBB's method of extracting rhodopsin from salt marshes is introducing impurities into the lattice structure, destroying its ability to react to light. The team is also experiencing difficulties zeroing in on the right wavelength of the lasers. The trial-and-error process of going through the billions of possible laser frequencies and the uncertainties of the contaminated protein lattice are discouraging even our most experienced scientists at WBB."

Johann von Hunsinger shook his head, wishing the BND had not lost use of the Russian biochemists after the end of the Cold War. "What about Siemens?" he asked.

"It is just as bad as any of the other R&D centers. . . . What I still do not understand is how a small American company with such limited resources has accomplished what our scientists could not do with a thousand times the capital and employees," Bölling said, even though he already knew why.

"Der Russisch . . ." von Hunsinger said, letting his words trail off, silently chastising himself again for having let the top Russian scientist slip through his hands. Among its many responsibilities, the BND assessed the foreign availability of high-tech products in dozens of countries, including the former Soviet bloc, where, during the Cold War years, the minister of industry and commerce, with help from the BND, had tracked the activities taking place at the Shemyakin Institute of Bioorganic Chemistry in Moscow. During the early eighties, Dr. Yuri Ovchinnikov had successfully developed a crude memory device using bacterial protein and chemical lasers. After the collapse of the Soviet Union in 1989, BND operatives had lost track of the surviving disciples of the late Ovchinnikov and, under direction from Chancellor Kohl, abandoned all efforts in that field, redirecting energies to

assist the government during the critical transition period into a unified Germany—an effort that was still far from over.

Von Hunsinger rubbed his chin as his gaze traversed to the blue skies beyond the huge glass panes. Biotechnology was the way of the future. Those economies that possessed it would prosper. Those that didn't would languish. It was that simple. The power of biotechnology would dwarf the billions of deutsche marks generated by the German digital-TV business that von Hunsinger himself orchestrated. Ownership of such technology would translate into the *trillions* of deutsche marks required to truly unite the German people, to solve the thousands of problems inherent to the reunification process. Hard currency would go a long way toward alleviating the psychic and emotional differences still separating the two sides of Germany.

How ironic, von Hunsinger thought, his eyes on a large crane lowering a beam onto a future skyscraper. The world sighed in relief at the nearly bloodless revolution that led to the unification of Germany. Yet, far more blood had been spilled since unification than during the months prior to the breaching of the Berlin Wall. The constant tension, the unemployment, the physical assaults, the public protests, the marches, and the demonstrations kept a veil of depression over Germany, a shroud that could be easily removed with the astronomical influx of capital that biotechnology could create.

International competition for technology had become so fierce in recent years that over half of the BND's annual budget had been diverted to not only steal others' technological advances, but also to protect Germany's own intellectual property. A good offense had to be combined with a solid defense to win the game; otherwise, scientific secrets would leave as fast as they came. The Japanese were among the worst, and most recently the Koreans had also moved up the industrial espionage ladder, probing countries like the United States and Germany and taking whatever they could get back to their homeland.

Offense and defense. Von Hunsinger had to play both tactics and play them better than anyone else in order to win. And today the game was offense.

Johann von Hunsinger, a man who had not reached his current position and status among the German people by accident, intended to do everything within his power to dig Germany out of the reunification hole and propel it to be the great nation it had once been. It was up to visionaries like himself to make the difficult decisions that would guide his nation to greatness.

His eyes on the opulent Hedwigskirche three blocks away, von Hunsinger remembered the day his country lost that greatness, the day Germany lost the war. An eight-year-old orphan, the boy had faced an uphill battle. Success in his career had required the perseverance to push ahead in the face of adversity, to succeed at all costs.

The early-morning light reflected off the copper-sheathed dome of the Hedwigskirche, casting a yellowish hue over the surrounding blocks. Johann von Hunsinger, minister of industry and commerce, would not rest until he had given Germany the edge it would need to become the most powerful nation in the world in the twenty-first century.

At exactly ten minutes before noon, Hans Bölling walked up the steps to the main entrance of the Hedwigskirche.

Removing his sunglasses and casually slipping them into a coat pocket, the seasoned intelligence officer glanced at a dozen Japanese tourists to his left, posing in front of a large stained-glass window for a group picture. To his right, three couples casually read the bronze plaque next to the entrance, which provided a brief history of the cathedral. Construction had begun in 1747; the dome had been designed after the Roman Pantheon. Slowly, with a discretion that came naturally to him after decades of clandestine work, Bölling looked for signs of interest or recognition from anyone in the crowd.

Satisfied, he pulled open one of the four ten-foot-tall wooden doors, thick enough to stop a tank. Surprised at the ease with which the heavy but well-balanced door swung on its hinges, Bölling waited a moment for his eyes to adjust to the murky interior, shivering slightly at the ten-degree drop in temperature inside the cavernous room, naturally illuminated by the midday sun streaming through the windows lining both sides of the nave.

The BND chief unconsciously adjusted the knot in his bow tie as he walked down the far-right aisle, the clicking of his Italian shoes over the marble floors echoing through the cathedral, his eyes sweeping across the endless rows of pews. The building was mostly empty at this hour, save for the usual tourists inspecting marble sculptures, wooden carvings, or the endless rows of stained-glass windows, each vividly displaying a different Biblical scene and coming eerily alive in the blazing sunlight.

He checked his watch before turning his attention to a hooded man walking in the opposite direction and watching as he went into one of the confessional booths against the right-hand wall. The time was noon. The cloaked figure was the Kardinal.

His pulse quickening, his mouth turning dry, his hands developing a slight tremble in spite of his many years of field service, Hans Bölling controlled his pace, not wishing to look like an amateur in the presence of this man, this legend. He reached the booth, parted the curtain, stepped inside, and knelt next to the one-foot-square translucent window separating the priest from the sinner, or in this case the contract assassin from the employer.

"Angelus Domini," whispered the Kardinal.

His hooded head turned to Bölling, who quickly dropped his

gaze, not wishing to know what this man looked like, but unable to avoid a brief glance into a pair of iron-gray eyes studying him from inside the darkness of the hood.

No one knew the real identity of the Kardinal, not even Hans Bölling, who had many contacts inside the top intelligence agencies in the world, including the American CIA, the Israeli Mossad, the British MI6, and France's DST. The Kardinal had first surfaced in the European intelligence community three years after the collapse of the Soviet Union, providing the BND with detailed information on the plans of a neo-Nazi terrorist group to detonate a bomb in the basement of the Reichstag, the new parliament building in Berlin. The information not only prevented the deaths of many German government officials but also guided the BND to a terrorist safe house outside Berlin, resulting in the arrest of seven terrorists. A month later, a message from the Kardinal made its way to the office of the chief of police in Munich, revealing an Iraqi plot to detonate a large bomb in an office building. Again, the information from the mysterious informer paid off. German officers stormed a house several blocks from the targeted structure, arresting five Iraqi students and confiscating fifty pounds of Semtex, a Czech-made explosive. The Kardinal had since become a highly regarded, and highly paid, independent contractor.

Although the Kardinal performed services for several countries, he always put Germany first on his list—which led the BND to believe that this man was of German origin, or at least sympathetic to the German cause, although no one knew for certain. So far, Bölling was not aware of any services the Kardinal had performed for the Americans.

"Angelus Domini," Bölling replied, struggling to keep his voice from cracking. "Forgive me, father, for I have sinned. My last confession was three years and three months ago," he added, completing the code.

"Someone sent the signal," the assassin said, exposing a hand holding a newspaper clipping. "What can this humble servant do for the BND?"

Bölling took a deep breath. The legendary assassin was anything but humble in his work, although he did manage to display some humility in the simplicity of his meetings. The newspaper ad in yesterday's international edition of the *New York Times* had described a fictitious job opening at the German consulate in Washington, D.C.

"You could do our German nation a great service," he began, slipping a dossier under the screen and taking ten full minutes to explain the situation to the assassin.

"And what is the time frame of this noble but highly dangerous cause?" the Kardinal asked.

Keeping his eyes down, Bölling said, "Immediately. We're prepared to compensate you far better than before. This is the most critical request we've ever made. Above all, we don't want the technology lost. My government needs the biotech recipes as well as the Russian scientist. Everyone else is expendable."

"I understand. Have your agency make the appropriate donations, and I will begin my journey."

Five hours after the meeting, twenty-five million deutsche marks were transferred from a secret BND account at the Dresden Bank in Frankfurt, Germany, to a numbered account at Crédit Suisse in Zurich, Switzerland. From there, a third of the funds made it to another account at the Suisse Bank Corp. in Balse, Switzerland, and another third to the Sanwa Bank Ltd. branch in the Cayman Islands.

SANTA CLARA COUNTY, CALIFORNIA
Wednesday, July 19, 7:45 P.M.

FBI Special Agent Sonya Wüttenberg could barely control her breathing. Her green, catlike eyes read the flash report from the Zurich legat with appalled speed.

Twenty-five million deutsche marks had found their way to one of hundreds of bank accounts monitored by the FBI in conjunction with police and security agencies of seven European countries. This particular account at Crédit Suisse had received deposits in the past from front companies laundering money for the Sicilian Mafia, the Libyans, French criminal networks, the Iraqis, the Russian Mafia, the Nigerians, the Omanians, the Serbs, and now the BND. And each transfer of funds had been followed by an unresolved, high-profile international crime or terrorist act that benefited the party making the deposit. The crimes, which ranged from car bombs to disappearances, followed no obvious pattern. The timing of the deposits and the lack of any credible claim of responsibility for the acts strongly indicated the possibility that they had all been committed by the same terrorist, or team of terrorists. But there was another clue in the style of the hits, something no one at the FBI but Sonya could have picked up. The crimes resembled Stasi assassinations—they employed techniques she had learned nearly two decades before. This led her to believe that the BND, which had been showing such interest in FTI, had contracted a former Stasi officer to steal FTI's biotechnology.

The implications of this finding made her pulse rush, her throat clamp. Most Stasi officers, including the legendary Markus Wolf, who'd headed the secretive ministry for almost thirty-five years, had been arrested during the days of the fall of the Berlin Wall. One officer, Vladimir Titov-Escobar, Markus Wolf's right-hand man and deputy minister of the foreign espionage service, the largest division in the Stasi, had managed to escape to southern Germany. While dozens of Stasi officers, including Markus Wolf, underwent prosecution for crimes committed against the people of Germany during the Cold War, Vladimir Titov-Escobar escaped.

Remembering an encounter with Titov-Escobar and Karla, his pregnant wife, in the woods of southern Germany, Sonya Wüttenberg turned off her system and reached for the phone on the nightstand of the rented apartment, dialing a Washington number. After three rings and the light static hum of Roman Palenski's security system, the director of the FBI got on the line.

"Yes," came the raspy voice from the other end, almost a whisper.

"I believe the BND has contracted the services of an old acquaintance of mine to steal technology from FTI," she said matter-of-factly, her professional side forcing any trace of emotion out of her voice.

Silence, followed by: "Old acquaintance?"

Sonya cleared her throat of rumbling phlegm and said, "Titov-Escobar."

More silence. Then, "Are you certain?"

"I'm absolutely certain it is a former Stasi officer, sir. By process of elimination, most of them are now either in jail or too old to do this," Sonya said, also explaining the Swiss bank account connection.

"All right," said Palenski after a further moment of silence. "We'll assume that either he or someone else quite capable has been contracted. How long ago did this happen?"

"The report arrived ten minutes ago," Sonya said. "The transaction took place on Monday, two days ago."

"Two days ago? *Damn!*" Palenski said in frustration. "Why so . . . so fucking long before you were notified?"

Sonya shrugged. "Our electronic queries take place once a day, usually at the end of the bank's closing time, when it can be disguised as part of its shutdown routines. Remember, this tap is not sanctioned by the Swiss. We have to do it without their knowledge. So it was not until Tuesday morning that the message reached the Zurich legat, but my people couldn't read it until Tuesday night because the network at the embassy went down because of a power glitch, and—"

"Fine, fine," Palenski interrupted. "Assuming that he is indeed the Kardinal, how long do we have?"

Sonya Wüttenberg tapped a scarlet fingernail against her chin. "Not long at all. We must act immediately, sir. I recommend doubling the number of operatives. I also recommend a strike team nearby, ready to move the moment Titov is spotted."

"You'll get more agents within twenty-four hours, but a strike team might take a little longer."

Sonya closed her eyes, her heart thumping against her rib cage. "Sooner is better. FTI is *extremely* vulnerable to someone like Titov, sir. I know how he operates. He'll strike fast, hard, and effectively, and when we least expect it. And then he will vanish. He will disappear as suddenly as he came. The only way to catch him is by ambushing him at FTI. But we must move fast—set up a perimeter of operations around the company without being seen. To do so with the proper coordination will take at least twenty-four hours after the strike team arrives, and Titov already has a two-day head start.".

"We'll move as fast as possible," came the hoarse reply. "In the meantime, you'll have to cover with what you have."

A whisper of terror ran through her at the possibility of having to face Vladimir Titov-Escobar alone. "I don't want to sound paranoid, sir, but I've worked with Titov, and I know how he operates. This whole thing could be *over* in less than twenty-four hours, and all my team will be able to do is watch him perform—if we're alive. We need firepower, sir. I cannot do it with my current team."

"Hang in there. The cavalry's heading your way."

The line went dead, and Sonya Wüttenberg replaced the phone on its cradle, her normally pale face pink with anxiety. Her team was perfect for surveillance but abysmally inadequate for anything else. Trying to stop Titov and the guns he would surely bring along with him would be suicidal. All she could do was continue her surveillance, wait, and hope like hell that Titov-Escobar would not strike within the next forty-eight hours.

LANGLEY, VIRGINIA
Wednesday, July 19, 6:30 P.M.

CIA Deputy Director for Operations Donald Bane was an old hand, an experienced dinosaur, in the clandestine world. He had been around the block more times than he could count. He had pounded the streets as a field agent with the FBI starting in the late sixties, put in twenty years of hard labor as a Fed, transferred to the CIA in the late eighties, and served another ten years as a spook. In the process he had been double-crossed, kidnapped, interrogated, kicked, punched, stabbed, and shot. He had traveled through more countries than he could remember, seen too many people he cared for die terrible deaths, and sworn many times that he would leave the damn intelligence business after completing his current mission. His wife had left him because of the job. His body looked and felt ten years older than his age because of the job. His nights were filled with nightmares because of the job. His heart had long ago been squeezed clean of all emotion because of the job.

Donald Bane sighed as he ran a hand through his thinning, mostly white hair, neatly combed straight back, which framed a square, weathered face that could have belonged to a retired boxer.

He had certainly been around the block. He had met with three presidents in the Oval Office, had been personally labeled for termination by Saddam Hussein while on a mission in Iraq, had been one of the rare survivors of an Iraqi interrogation session, and had nearly frozen to death north of Moscow while being pursued by the Russian Mafia. After thirty years of clandestine operations, Bane was not easily surprised. He had seen, heard, and lived through the worst of situations, in the process developing a shell hard enough to withstand events or news of any kind.

But even the experienced dinosaur in him could not dispel the apprehension cramping his stomach at the mention of Vladimir Titov-Escobar, the Stasi's finest and most feared assassin, responsible for the deaths of many fine CIA, MI6, Mossad, and BND officers during the final years of the Cold War. Although Bane had never confronted Titov during Bane's six-year assignment as chief of the CIA's Moscow station, before transferring to Langley, he'd heard enough stories and read enough reports from his counterpart in the West Berlin office to take Roman Palenski's comments quite seriously.

"One of the problems with intercepting him before he makes it into the country is that he probably won't be using a conventional port of entry," Bane said to Palenski over the phone, gazing around his seventh-floor office without looking at anything in particular. "We'll have people posted at every major airport in Europe within twelve hours. . . . Can I use some of your folks?" asked Bane, who just five short years before would not have dreamed of working so closely with the FBI. But with the FBI legats deployed to so many countries, and most of them occupying offices just a few doors down from the CIA's at numerous embassies, the level of cooperation between the two agencies had greatly risen in the past years, an allegiance that had served the United States well in fighting exactly this type of international conspiracy.

"That's what I was going to suggest," replied Palenski. "I think I can give you close to four or five agents in each country."

"I'll take them . . . although I really doubt we'll get a breakthrough overseas, especially with the Kardinal's two-day head start. For all we know he could already be in California," said

Bane. He stood and stretched his large frame, his sunken, blood-shot eyes peering out the window. The parking lot was quickly emptying at this time of the day. But Bane's day was only half over. With everyone gone, this was the time when he could actually get some uninterrupted work done. Besides his DDO responsibilities, Bane was acting director of central intelligence while the real DCI recovered from a quadruple bypass.

A heavy sigh came through the line. "I guess anything's possible. Sonya's already warned me about the swiftness of this guy. Our records show that some operations were carried out within a day or less from the time the funds reached the Swiss account."

"I'm not surprised. How soon before she gets help?"

"No more than twenty-four hours. I've got several agents on the way now, but to mount a reasonably controlled operation will take at least a day or two after they arrive. We could just surround the place with Feds, but that's just going to tip the assassin. We not only want to prevent him from stealing the technology, we want to *nail* the bastard."

"Agreed . . . which also means we can't notify FTI of this, right?"

"For the time being," said Palenski. "We can't afford for them to deviate from their normal routine. If the place has the slightest smell of an ambush, all bets are off and this guy's gone. If Sonya's data is accurate, the Kardinal is responsible for nineteen terrorist strikes in the past five years, resulting in the deaths of sixty-seven people and over eight billion dollars in damages. He's right up there with Abu Nidal and Carlos the Jackal. This is a great opportunity to stop him for good."

Bane, the phone jammed against his right ear and an index finger slowly rubbing his left temple, said, "I'm right behind you, but I'm also concerned that we're using one hell of a bait to trap the Kardinal. From what I understand from Sonya's reports, this stuff could easily replace silicon chips. I bet my next paycheck that half the countries in Europe and Asia will be dying to get their hands on it. Germany's just the first. It will be an economic blow to many American corporations if this technology makes it into the market right now, but it would be a massive disaster if another country gets it and uses it as an economic weapon against us."

"Protection," said Palenski.

"Exactly. We have to transfer it to Los Alamos."

"That was our plan as soon as we verified that they indeed had the technology. But we don't want to create waves between the government and the private industry until we really have to. But this business with the Kardinal is throwing a monkey wrench into everything."

"All right, then," Bane said. "We rush agents to California, fend off the Kardinal, and then move the technology to Los Alamos."

"Agreed. We already had a financial compensation plan in place for the board of directors at PCA. I'm quite certain we can persuade them to give up the technology when we explain it's a matter of national security."

"Yes, but for all of that to work, we first have to make sure that no one steals it."

"We're on it."

Bane hung up the phone and prayed that they were not too late.

Turning on his swivel chair to face his computer terminal, he accessed the next day's President's Daily Brief, a CIA-generated intelligence summary of all foreign operations for the eyes of the President of the United States. It was time to update his commander in chief.

4   FIRES IN THE NIGHT

He who bears the brand of Cain shall rule the earth.
—*George Bernard Shaw*

Kathy Bennett, dressed in jeans, a plain T-shirt, and sneakers, waved at Raul Martinez, the muscular guard sitting behind the dozen video terminals inside the small reception area of FTI's building.

"Night, ma'am," the guard responded as the petite UCLA engineering graduate pushed a glass door and stepped out into a warm but pleasant evening.

Breathing deeply, she scanned the parking lot and spotted her car in the last row, a six-month-old Ford Mustang. Red. She figured that if she had to work this hard, the least she could do was drive a decent car back and forth between her condo in San Francisco, an hour away, and FTI.

Kathy heard the familiar noise of the servomotor of one of the security cameras turning to keep her in view as she left the glass doors behind and strolled across the walkway, past Jake's Bronco, always parked in the front row, and toward her car.

She had grown accustomed to the tight level of security Jake demanded around the building, including FTI's most coveted asset—its people. She only wished Jake would take their relationship as seriously as he did the security of FTI. Tonight he had done it again. They were supposed to go out to dinner after work, but Jake, Iyevenski, and the process team had a long technical review of the latest changes in the bacterial-protein-growing process. She had waited for him to get out of the meeting for two hours, and finally given up ten minutes ago.

The hell with him. I'm going home.

She reached her car and glanced at her personalized license plate, a gift from Jake, who'd helped her pick out the car at a Palo Alto dealership.

BIOTECH.

Jake had suggested the name. She now wished she had gotten something a little more hip. Pulling out her key chain, Kathy pressed a button on the keyless-entry remote control. She gave the camera on the roof a final glance and a wave before getting in, starting the engine, and taking off, leaving the parking lot behind, one hand on the steering wheel and the other on the stereo, which she tuned to an easy-listening station.

As she turned into the on-ramp for Highway 101, Kathy Bennett felt a cold, round object pressed against the back of her neck.

"Do not look back. It is not my wish to hurt you," a male voice with a heavy foreign accent said from behind. "Get on the highway and drive normally."

Kathy's throat constricted as her hands clasped the steering wheel. Her right foot froze over the gas, keeping the Mustang at a steady forty miles an hour as she entered the highway.

"Harm will not come to you," the voice said. "But you must choose to obey me, as all others do. Accelerate to sixty, do not draw attention, and do not look behind you. We shall travel to San Francisco."

Trying to steady her trembling limbs, Kathy slowly pressed her right foot on the gas and watched the speedometer inch up to fifty-five.

"You've chosen wisely," the voice said in an eerily relaxed tone. Kathy managed to swallow before taking a sobbing breath through her mouth. Her gaze shifted from the road to the rearview mirror, where she saw a pair of charcoal eyes studying her from the darkness of the backseat.

A gloved hand reached over her right shoulder and angled the mirror away from her. "The flesh is weak," the voice said. "Blessed are those who resist the temptations of the flesh. Watch the road and *pray* that you do not yield to temptation again."

SANTA CLARA COUNTY, CALIFORNIA
Thursday, July 20, 9:45 A.M.

The crowd inside the small lobby grew anxious as the scheduled time for Fischer Technologies' first press conference neared. Three rows of neatly spaced folding chairs faced a small podium, which backed against the heavy door separating the old world of semiconductors from the new world of the protein transistor.

A middle-aged man with dark hair and an unkempt beard hiding his Slavic features sat in the third row and read the sign above the security door: WELCOME TO THE NEW WORLD. His name tag identified him as Kirk Schlosser, a reporter from the *Wisconsin Electronic Monthly,* a small trade journal. But this man had never worked a single day of his life at *WEM*. The real Kirk Schlosser lay dead at the bottom of San Francisco Bay, fifty pounds of chains wrapped around his chest.

Unlike the other reporters in the room, who'd spent the last half hour reviewing their questions and reading the color brochures provided by the security guard, Vladimir Titov-Escobar, the man known simply as the Kardinal by the international intelligence community, carefully observed the cameras mounted on the ceiling of the reception room. He had seen at least two similar cameras on the roof.

Before sitting down, Titov-Escobar, wearing the carefully applied wig and beard, hazel-colored contact lenses, and the body pillows that made him look three sizes larger than his athletic body, had strolled casually by the podium and had checked the palm reader. Unlike many American corporations, this one had spared no expense protecting its assets, matching the top security systems at several European corporations.

Checking his watch, the Kardinal stood and walked over to the guard station, where a blond, muscular man in his early forties sat behind a dozen monitors.

"May I help you?" the guard asked politely, his eyes never leaving the black-and-white images flashing on the array of nine-inch Sony monitors.

Hazel eyes absorbing the images on the screen, Titov-Escobar responded in a sepulchral voice, "I apologize for disturbing you."

That got the guard's attention. "That's . . . that's no problem. What can I do for you?"

"I was just wondering how long before the press conference begins. We were told nine forty-five sharp."

The guard shrugged. "It should be any time now."

Nodding while giving the lobby a quick scan, the Kardinal spotted a burgundy Bronco parked by the building's entrance. "What a beautiful truck," said Titov-Escobar, a finger extended toward the shiny utility vehicle. "Are you the fortunate one?"

The guard narrowed his eyes at the Kardinal and slowly shook his head. "Ah . . . no, no. It's Mr. Fischer's."

Titov-Escobar thanked him before returning to his seat. Only two of the twelve monitors covered the parking lot. The rest had shown images of the interior of the building. This observation matched the two cameras he had spotted on the roof the night before, as he had surveyed the area prior to breaking into Kathy Bennett's car.

Checking his watch one more time, the Kardinal sat and waited for the press conference to begin, his hand reaching inside his jacket, fingers groping inside a pocket and pulling forth a small rosary. Keeping his hand hidden in the jacket, the Kardinal closed his eyes and silently began to pray. *Our Father who art in Heaven . . .*

"Where is she?" Jake Fischer asked a puzzled Sergei Iyevenski as the two of them walked down the corridor leading to the front of the building.

"She left at almost eleven o'clock last night, yes?" said the large Russian scientist, who, for a change, was dressed in a suit, as was Jake. "She was waiting for you, yes?"

"Yeah. I totally forgot about our dinner date."

"Maybe she is pissed on you?"

Jake couldn't help a brief smile. "It's pissed *at* you, Sergei. Not pissed *on* you. And even though I'm sure she wouldn't mind pissing *on* me for forgetting about last night, I hope she knows better than to get even by refusing to show up today. Not only the press but also Preston and Colton are expecting all three of us. Even the fucking brochures we printed say so." Jake drove a fist into his palm and continued, "I need my two lead scientists with me today, dammit!"

Not only was Kathy Bennett the software guru at FTI, but she was also the system administrator for the Teradyne and the HyperCray, where the jewels of FTI resided. And, in that capacity, she managed the tape archive system, where she kept copies of test programs, biotechnology process recipes, and design databases—all locked in a custom-built fireproof vault inside a secure room in the rear of the building. Over half of FTI's employees reported to Kathy. The rest worked for either Iyevenski or Jake, who doubled as design manager.

"I called her earlier today," said Iyevenski, "and her answering machine said she was not home."

Swell.

"We'll just have to do this without her, I guess. I'm going to look for her as soon as this thing is over, and we're going to have a little chat about mixing business with pleasure."

"She could be sick, yes?"

"All I gotta say is that she'd better be half *dead* to have missed this. Blood or a broken leg is the only excuse, and even then I would have expected a courtesy phone call," responded Jake as they reached the door to the reception area. "We'll deal with her later. Right now it's show time, Sergei. Don't forget to smile. The PCA execs are supposed to be out there too."

The automatic door opened, showing a room full of reporters. But no sign of Preston or Colton.

Jake walked right up to the podium. Iyevenski stood by his side. Reaching into his pocket while inspecting the crowd of two dozen men and women, Jake decided not to mention Kathy's absence. Pulling out a prepared speech and spreading it on the podium, he began to read it.

"Good morning, ladies and gentlemen," Jake said, reaching under the podium and grabbing two glass containers, each roughly the size of a beer can. He set them both over his notes and opened the lid of the first.

"This . . . is the *past*," he said, pouring the contents next to him. "Sand, the basic ingredient of silicon technology—which industry experts believe will reach a wall in terms of miniaturization and manufacturability in fifteen years."

Next, he showed everyone the contents of the second jar. "This is a little bit of salt marsh, the basic ingredient of the technology of the future." And he spent the next five minutes outlining what it was that FTI had been doing for the past four years. He talked about the potential FTI had unleashed in biotechnology, and how the F1 benefited from that potential. William Preston and Jacob Colton, dressed in their fine suits, arrived halfway through the speech and just remained standing in the rear, quietly observing the show. The moment Jake finished, a dozen hands went up.

"Yes?" Jake said, pointing to a brunette in a gray business suit sitting in the front row, her intelligent brown eyes skeptical.

"Linda Michaels, *San Jose Mercury News*," she said, standing up. "I thought that Dr. Bennett would also be here today."

Jake met the comment with a prepared response. "She's currently unavailable. We're in the final stages of shipping our initial production samples, and, given our limited staff, we can't afford for any of our employees to get distracted. Dr. Iyevenski and I are more than qualified to answer any questions you or the rest of the audience may have."

Crossing her arms, the attractive reporter gave Iyevenski a glance, then looked back at Jake. "Can you comment on your customer base?"

Jake knew he would be hit with that one almost right away. Smiling, he said, "We currently have four strategic customers under nondisclosure agreements. They're scheduled to receive initial samples this coming Monday."

Remaining standing, Linda Michaels asked, "Who are they?"

Jake shook his head. "Sorry. The nondisclosure agreement prevents me from revealing their names. I can tell you, however, that all of them are major players in the computer market. . . . Next question, please."

Again the hands went up. He pointed to a man next to Linda Michaels.

"Yes, Frank Jorden, the *Memory Report*. Can you give us some specifics on the storage capacity and speed targets of the F1 RAM?"

Jake nodded. "Certainly. The initial version of the F1 has a storage capacity of fifteen billion bytes running at a frequency of three hundred and fifty megahertz."

That drew laughs from several reporters, one of whom shouted through the laughter, "That's one hundred times the storage capacity and many times the speed of any memory device that exists today, Dr. Fischer! Please! Do you truly expects us to believe *that?*"

"That's the beauty of biotechnology," replied Jake after the crowd quieted down, flashing an easy grin at the group, his eyes briefly glancing at William Preston and Jacob Colton, both of whom gave him a thumbs-up. "Biotech gives you a freedom impossible to achieve with semiconductors. . . . Next question, please." Jake pointed to an elderly woman in the second row.

For the next thirty minutes, Jake answered as many questions as he could. Some were directed at Sergei Iyevenski, who responded candidly in his heavy accent and unusual grammar. A few Jake was not able to answer because of their confidential nature. The rest, however, he had fully answered, in the hope of generating enough articles to raise just enough industry awareness about FTI, but not too much to maintain the right level of suspense.

"I'll take one more question. . . . Yes, Miss Michaels," said Jake, pointing again at the attractive brunette.

"Dr. Fischer, we've spent the last hour discussing a memory device that, according to industry experts, exists only in the imagination of dreamers. Yet you claim to be in possession of this 'dream.' How about a demo? Furthermore, how about a tour of the facility? I think I speak for everyone here when I ask to see the type of equipment that can turn salt marshes into an advanced memory device."

Jake set both hands on the podium and leaned forward over the mike. "I'm going to have to beg off for now, Miss Michaels. The first public demo of the F1 will occur this coming September, at the Bay Area Computer Show in San Francisco, where all four of our customers will have working systems with F1 RAMs. I'm bound by my legal contracts not to show or demonstrate an F1 until then. As far as a tour, I will have to ask you to contact the offices of Preston, Colton, and Associates. Its board of directors has the final say on who can and can't enter this facility. . . . Now, I thank you all for coming here to—"

"Let me get this straight," said Linda Michaels from the front row. "You called a press conference today to announce the F1. You tell us all these marvels about a revolutionary technology that's not supposed to exist for many years. But you refuse to show us a working prototype. How do you expect the press to react to that?"

"Mr. Fischer cannot control your reaction, Miss Michaels," said William Preston from the rear of the room before Jake could answer.

Almost in unison all heads turned around to look at the two venture capitalists, legends in Silicon Valley.

"Mr. Fischer also can't control the reaction of anyone else in this room. My partner and I feel it would be appropriate to inch back the curtains on FTI by a notch, now that we're about to ramp production, and let everyone know what we're all about. We did this not to manipulate any stock or attract Wall Street investors. We're simply officially announcing our plans. Back to you, Jake."

"Thank you, Mr. Preston," Jake said, glad that the high-profile investor had jumped in at the perfect time to diffuse the bomb the attractive reporter had thrown. "I would like to thank all of you for coming here this morning to learn about the wonderful product we have created, and I hope to see you in San Francisco this coming September. We'll have exciting joint demos with our customers. My business card is attached to the color brochure. Please don't hesitate to call if you have any further questions."

Jake stepped down from the podium as Iyevenski leaned over to him.

"I would not mind a woman like that asking me questions all day long, yes?" the Russian whispered as the reporters stood and headed for the exit.

"You can keep her. I have enough problems trying to deal with just one woman, Sergei. I won't even entertain the thought of two," Jake responded, watching several reporters surround the PCA executives, who were all smiles while they boasted about the great achievement of the F1 biomemory.

Jake shook his head at the vulture capitalists, who less than a week ago had wanted to shut him down and sell the technology to some corporate giant, where the bio inventions would probably have gotten lost at some bureaucratic level. *Now look at them,* he thought.

"Are you going to look for her, yes?" asked the bearlike Iyevenski.

Jake checked his watch. Almost eleven o'clock and still no sign of Kathy, who'd never missed a day of work in the three and a half years FTI had been in business.

Damn, Kathy! Where are you?

"Hey, Jake!" screamed Preston over the heads of the departing reporters and waved him over. "Let's go outside. This lovely lady from the *Mercury News* has agreed to put us on the front page, and she wants a picture. You too, Sergei!"

Swell. "I guess Kathy's going to have to wait," Jake said as he walked around the chairs and followed his investors out into the parking lot.

At nine o'clock that evening, while all of FTI's employees worked overtime to make the Monday deadline of getting F1 prototypes into customers' hands, Jake Thomas Fischer, after changing from his suit to a comfortable pair of jeans, a shirt, and sneakers, finally left the building and headed for Kathy's condo in San Francisco.

After the press release, Preston and Colton had wanted a private tour of the place, and they'd specifically requested that Jake play tour guide. That had burned up almost three hours. Then the Teradyne had decided to act up and one of the helifurnaces had overheated. Although Jake felt fortunate that the equipment malfunctions had occurred after the executives had left the building, the problems had kept him tied up until fifteen minutes ago.

Jake had tried calling and beeping Kathy all day long, in between crises, but had gotten no response. He floored the Bronco as he reached the highway entrance.

Thirty feet below Highway 101, the Kardinal moved through the darkness in the knee-deep water of a pipe. His Bausch & Lomb night-vision goggles painted the curved concrete walls in shades of green. He turned into the tunnel connecting to FTI's rainwater drainage.

Water rats swam across his path, furry heads followed by the wake created by their little legs. The Kardinal gently moved them aside. A gloved hand reached down and softly rubbed the hairy back of one of the creatures. Rodents had been his only companions during his post–Cold War years, which he'd spent in isolation and reflection at a mountaintop monastery in Croatia, a place that now lived only in memory.

For the earth and all of its creatures belong to the Lord. . . .

The Kardinal adjusted the goggles as he reached a Y in the sewer. The right tunnel, according to the small laminated map strapped to his right thigh, would take him directly to the rear of the FTI building. His sandy hair and Slavic features hidden below a black hood, the former Stasi operative inspected the long pipe curving up to the surface.

Slowly now, with the same caution with which he had stalked CIA operatives during the glorious days of the Cold War, Titov-Escobar covered the last few hundred feet of the tunnel, until his ears discerned the noise of the air-conditioning compressors he had spotted earlier that day, behind the one-story building. Above, through the square steel grid, moonlight diffused into the drainage pipe, reaching his night-vision goggles, which instantly shut off to avoid blinding him.

The Kardinal removed them and strapped them to the black utility belt looped around his black nylon jumpsuit. Gloved hands reached for the rusted ladder built into the side of the vertical tunnel, which led him to the grid fifty feet above. Connected to the concrete opening by a pair of hinges on one side and a padlocked latch on the other, the cover didn't appear to have been opened for years.

His right hand gripping the large padlock, he kicked off his rubber boots, letting them fall to the bottom, where the slow current would carry them out to the main drainpipe. Anchoring the black leather sneakers he'd worn beneath the boots against the sides of the ladder, he pulled out a black penlike object. Keeping the padlock at an arm's length, the Kardinal pressed a button on the top of the pen while pressing the tip against the lock. Several drops of sulfuric acid fell onto the lock and began to sizzle. He kept his face away from the smoking padlock as the harmful fumes rose through the openings in the cover and into the night.

After some seconds the acid did its magical work, eating through the padlock's latching mechanism. He silently thanked God for the wisdom to devise such instruments, which allowed him to carry out his noble mission against the Americans.

He forced the padlock open and let it fall to the bottom of the tunnel; it made a distant splashing sound. Replacing the acid dispenser in its Velcro-secured container on his utility belt, he curled the fingers of both hands against the yellow-painted metal cover and took a deep breath. Hinges creaking in silent protest, the heavy cover inched upward.

A minute later he lay still over the cool grass, relaxing his muscles, hidden from view by the bushes surrounding the building. At fifty years of age, he was not quite the strong man of his youth. But what little Vladimir Titov-Escobar had lost in physical strength, he had made up in spiritual power, in the inner faith and strength he had gained through the years of isolation following the fall of the Berlin Wall, after the death of his beloved Karla and his unborn son at the hands of the Central Intelligence Agency . . . at the hands of the evil Americans.

For by grace are ye saved through faith; and that not of yourselves; it is the gift of God.

The Kardinal breathed deeply, forcing his mind to concentrate on his noble mission, on his opportunity to strike at the country that had taken so much from him.

Oh, Lord, make me your instrument of justice against the infidels.

He rose from the cool grass to a deep crouch, remaining behind the waist-high bushes shielding him from the rooftop camera that automatically swept his area once every thirty seconds, and from any possible surveillance coming from the woods across the parking lot.

To his left, the compressors hummed steadily, keeping the employees and the equipment inside the building within the comfort zone. His iron-gray eyes looked beyond the compressors, at the large metal door on the side of the building. He had learned earlier in the day that, for security reasons, the mechanical room beyond that door didn't connect to the interior of the building. But that didn't matter to the former Stasi operative, who began to crawl in that direction while the lone security camera swept other areas of the grounds on this side of the building. The Kardinal knew that the guard watching that monitor was on the BND's payroll, but he wasn't on his. Titov-Escobar would not trust such an infidel. And besides, part of his contract called for the elimination of the guard to remove all links to the BND.

Reaching the door, Titov carefully looked for an alarm sensor on the door and was pleasantly surprised to see none. Just a padlock separated him from the mechanical room where, according to the plans he had memorized at the county courthouse in Palo Alto, a set of large fans forced cold air into a maze of AC ducts feeding the building.

Studying the parking lot and then the camera as it made its next pass, the Kardinal once again reached for the dispenser of concentrated acid. The security camera, the noise from its servomotor drowned by the sound of the compressors, slowly moved past his position exactly every thirty seconds.

Titov quickly reached for the lock and let the acid do its magical work. On the next pass, he pried it open. And thirty seconds later, he quickly opened the door, went inside, and closed it behind him.

The deafening sound of a dozen fans, muffled by the thick door, now drilled his eardrums. The Kardinal endured it for the two minutes it took him to remove the cover of the main AC duct and empty the contents of another dispenser—concentrated sleeping gas—into it.

The return air sucked in the last of the gas, and the Kardinal checked his watch. He waited a full ten minutes before opening the door and crawling back outside with plenty of time before the camera made another sweep over the area—not that it mattered any longer. He knew there would be no one looking at those monitors now.

Twenty years ago, when he had been just a teenager growing up in Moscow, this type of mission would have sickened him. But not now. Not after the training that had started at a Directorio General de Inteligencia camp in Pinar del Río, a town in central Cuba. The atrocities he had been forced to commit before he was deemed tough enough to fight for the DGI, the Cuban version of the KGB, had deadened the human compassion his Cuban mother had tried to instill in him before he was taken away from her by the Russian soldier and turned to the Cuban military system.

His first-rate work with Cuban intelligence had earned him a reassignment to East Germany, where he had met the legendary Markus Wolf, chief of the East German ministry of state security, the Stasi, in East Berlin, during a celebration to commemorate the golden anniversary of the Cheka, the forerunner of the KGB. Vladimir Titov-Escobar had been impressed by the elegant, highly personable Markus Wolf, who became the center of attention at the party when he delivered a gift from the Stasi to the head of the KGB *rezidentura* in Berlin. The assembled officers cheered when the local KGB chief opened a flat red box containing a copy of the BND's secret annual intelligence report. Stolen by Stasi operatives in West Germany, the report provided the KGB with mounds of information regarding one of its adversary networks. Markus Wolf had listened intently to Titov-Escobar's life story as they sat near the bar drinking French wine. Wolf not only recruited Titov but became his close friend. A month later, Vladimir Titov-Escobar obtained Castro's personal permission to leave the DGI to join the East German Staatssicherheit.

The Kardinal slipped on an Israeli-made gas mask and made sure that the slim acid dispenser was still in his jumpsuit's side pocket before crawling slowly toward the only entrance to the building, hidden from view by the shrubbery. He instinctively ran a gloved hand over his left thigh, fingers feeling for the holstered automatic he didn't expect to use on this star-filled night.

Keeping an eye on the overhead camera, he approached the building's entrance from the side, crawling behind the line of bushes and peeking into the small lobby.

Satisfied, Titov pressed a button on the side of his wristwatch. Thirty seconds later a large United Parcel Service delivery truck pulled up to the front of the building, shielding him from any onlookers. Two men dressed in UPS uniforms, with nylon stockings over their heads to disfigure their features, got out of the truck with packages in hand, and flanking a visibly shaken Kathy Bennett, also dressed as a UPS worker. Her day-old mascara marked the tracks of tears she had shed during the past twenty-four hours while the Kardinal had extracted all of the information he would need to carry out his contract.

Titov-Escobar, following tactics he had learned long ago in the Stasi, had actually performed two interrogations on Kathy. The first he had carried out immediately following her abduction, when she was conscious. After he explained the situation and told her he meant no harm as long as she cooperated, Kathy had readily answered all of his questions. But that alone had not been enough for the seasoned operative. Titov-Escobar needed that vital second session, the one he had started after injecting Kathy with Pentothal. The truth serum brought Kathy to a state of semi-consciousness that allowed the Kardinal to confirm all of the information that Kathy had given him. She had no recollection that she had divulged so much more while she "slept," providing the Kardinal with a powerful tool, which he intended to use on the naive female scientist as he had used it on so many people during the Cold War.

Spotting Raul Martinez unconscious on the floor of the small lobby, Titov-Escobar checked his watch and led the way inside. He disabled the monitoring system in the guard station, and removed the keys strapped to Martinez's belt.

May God have mercy on your soul, infidel, he thought, making the sign of the cross on the guard's forehead with a gloved thumb. Titov checked his watch once more, removed his gas mask, and took a deep breath. The gas became inert after about ten minutes, though those exposed to it would remain in a deep sleep for at least two hours, giving him more than ample time to execute his plan.

"Come," the Kardinal said, turning his hooded face to Kathy Bennett and her two escorts. He reached for her pale hand.

As he said this, a third man pulled up in Kathy's Mustang. He was dressed in a guard's uniform and was accompanied by a homeless man they'd picked up an hour ago in nearby Santa Cruz with promises of food and shelter, plus some new clothes, in exchange for some janitorial work. The homeless man was dressed in blue coveralls and carried a small toolbox. An observer would have noticed nothing out of the ordinary. A late UPS delivery followed by a guard shift change, and someone dressed like a repairman, toolbox and all.

"Please . . . I've told you everything . . ." Kathy began to say, her lips trembling, her round brown eyes filling with tears, her mouth feeling unusually dry and pasty after her sedative-induced sleep.

"Shhh. . . . You have, you certainly have, and as promised, I shall in turn show you the mercy reserved for all of God's creatures, the benevolence usually absent in my world."

Kathy's bloodshot eyes spotted the guard on the floor. "Oh, my God!" Her wet stare turned to the Kardinal. "You promised me . . . you told me that no one would be—"

"Fear not a broken promise. He is just sleeping," the Kardinal said. "Do you remember our agreement?"

"Yes, but—"

"Has anyone harmed you in any way?"

She shook her head and crossed her thin arms, bracing herself.

"Even during our interrogation?"

Another slight shake.

"I shall stand by my word. This too shall pass, and you and your friends will be once again reunited. Isn't that our agreement?"

Kathy gave him a slight nod, eyes still on the carpeted floor. She found it difficult to look him in the eye. The man carried a powerful presence that continued to overwhelm her self-control.

"I swore to you that not a single one of my men will raise his hand against you or any of your colleagues. I intend to keep that promise," the hooded figure said before tossing the keys to the fake guard.

"One got away," said one of the UPS men to his superior. "A man in a burgundy Ford Bronco. Ten minutes ago."

Glancing at the empty parking spot, where he had noticed Jake Fischer's truck parked before the press conference, the Kardinal simply nodded. "It's Fischer. It doesn't matter. I mean no harm to him either."

Kathy tried to remember if she had told this hooded man that Jake drove a Bronco. She quickly decided that she had not. He had gotten this information from someone else. *But whom?*

"Hey, man," said the homeless man, letting go of the toolbox and pointing at the guard on the floor. "I thought you said—"

The fake guard struck the base of the homeless man's neck. He dropped to the ground a corpse as the leader led a horrified Kathy to the heavy metal door. The Kardinal inspected the palm scanner on the wall and eyed the red light above the door.

"Do not mind him," he said. "He was not one of yours. Now, the door. Please open it." His polite voice carried a power far stronger than the weapon strapped to his belt.

Slowly, briefly glancing at the homeless man and wondering if he was dead, Kathy Bennett walked up to the door, pressed the palm of her right hand against the scanner, thought about her next action quite carefully, and decided to take advantage of her current emotional state, saying with a forced trembling voice, "Be— Bennett, Katherine."

Nothing happened. The door remained closed. The light above the door remained red.

She turned to her captor. "I . . . I don't know what's wrong," she lied, well aware that the security system had a built-in stress analyzer to prevent someone who was being forced from opening the door.

"My dear, *dear* Katherine," the mysterious man whispered from underneath the dark hood, placing his hands on her slight shoulders and gently turning her to face him.

Kathy braced herself once again, her gaze quickly yielding to the armor-piercing glare of the hooded man. "You must regain control of your *voice*. The Lord is our shepherd, Katherine. You shall not fear, for He is at your side. You must speak *without* fear or the system will not give you access . . . and all will be lost."

Kathy was momentarily stunned and prayed that it didn't show. How did this man know about the stress analyzer? She had made no mention of it during the interrogation session following her abduction. She had left that and many other details out of her explanations, hoping she could lessen the impact of this man on FTI by not volunteering any information aside from that required to answer his questions.

"For your friends," the Kardinal whispered once more, his hands softly massaging her shoulders before gently but firmly turning her around to face the access door again. "For your friends sleeping inside, and for *your life,* I beg you to concentrate and relax your voice."

For your friends and for your life. Kathy Bennett heard the words from this stranger, who so far had not harmed her except for the sedative that had knocked her out for several hours. She had not been abused, physically or verbally. No one had insulted her. No one had raped her. The man with the iron-gray eyes and the commanding German-accented voice had kept his word so far.

Kathy stared at the door, trying to decide what to do. Refuse to cooperate and end up dead? Maybe even push this stranger, who already appeared to be on the edge, to kill the entire team, as he had just threatened? Somehow Kathy Bennett didn't think the man would spare her life or those of her coworkers if she didn't cooperate.

She spoke once again, keeping her voice steady and calm.

The red light above the door turned green and the automatic door inched open, revealing a long corridor that ended in a brick wall at the rear of the building. A dozen doors on either side of the corridor had similar palm readers.

Kathy breathed heavily once, twice, putting a palm to her forehead, closing her eyes, not believing that she had actually let these people inside the building.

"Well done, Katherine. We're almost through," the hooded stranger said, taking Kathy by the hand and motioning his team inside as he inspected the long corridor.

The man ordered his subordinates to drag the body of the homeless man to the door leading into the R&D area, then said to Kathy, "Take me to the archive vault."

Kathy nodded and guided him to the rear of the building, where once again he used her to get inside.

Facing a seven-foot-high stainless-steel vault protected by a palm reader, a voice-recognition system, and an old-fashion combination lock, Kathy smiled inwardly. This is where it got tricky. First the voice, then the combination lock, and last the palm reader—information Kathy had purposefully withheld during the interrogation session. Any other order and a silent alarm would sound at the Palo Alto police station, three minutes away. This was her chance, her opportunity to nail these criminals.

"Remember, Katherine," the stranger ordered. "Everything in this world has an order, a sequence, including this archive vault. Remember our agreement. Remember your friends."

Kathy froze at the comment, at how much this stranger knew about FTI's operations. Did he kidnap others and question them separately? Nothing else made sense. And if that was indeed the case, what else did this stranger know? When was Kathy's loyalty being tested and when could she get away with a lie, with a trick that might tip the police about the high-tech robbery under way?

Since it was impossible for Kathy to know for certain, she decided not to risk her own life or those of the team. Technology could be replaced, lives could not. Those priorities had been clear in her mind the moment she understood what was expected of her by her captors, and those priorities were clear now, as she followed proper procedures and opened the vault.

"I need the most recent backup," the stranger said.

Kathy nodded and roamed through hundreds of archive tapes, finding the one that held the most recent backup, the one she herself had done the night before.

"Here," Kathy said, handing the man in black a tape slightly larger than an 8mm Sony videotape.

"Just one tape?" the hooded stranger said.

Hesitating for a moment, she once again opted for the truth. "Yes . . . it contains the recipes for manufacturing protein transistors . . . along with the software to test it and the blueprints of the equipment required to manufacture it.

The stranger grinned and said, "Well done. You have lived up to your word."

Kathy was about to close the vault when he stopped her. "There will be time for that later. Right now there is one more thing I need before I set you and your team free."

Crossing her arms and slightly raising her shoulders as she walked back into the main hallway, Kathy decided to take a chance. She said, "You have the tape. . . . It represents years—*many years*—of research and development. You promised that no one would be harmed if—"

"Patience is a virtue," the man interrupted. He pulled out an airtight freezer bag, put the tape in it, and shoved it in a pocket of his jumpsuit. "It is the companion of wisdom."

He took Kathy's hand and drew her back up the hallway, where his team stood by the door leading to the R&D area, their disfigured faces underneath the stockings turning to her.

The leader checked his watch and pointed at the secured door. "One more favor and we will be gone."

Kathy's saucerlike eyes slowly traveled from the hooded leader to his muscular companions, to the unconscious homeless man, and back to the gray stare waiting a response. "And then you will leave us alone?"

"My word is all I have. No one will raise a hand to you or your team if you cooperate. Those are the terms of our agreement. I have not raised my hand against you or any of your colleagues, and I will not, as long as you also keep your word."

Figuring that if she'd already gone this far, she might as well finish it and get these people out of FTI, Kathy nodded and opened the door leading to the R&D area.

"There," she said, remaining in the hallway as the heavy door automatically opened. "I've opened the door and—"

She stopped when she noticed one of the two men holding the homeless man reaching for a tiny canister. The man abruptly brought it up to her face and sprayed its contents.

Kathy instinctively jerked away, but not before taking a shallow breath. The potent gas attacked her nostrils and was quickly absorbed by her bloodstream, and it reached the brain within seconds.

Kathy collapsed on the floor, the mysterious man's words reverberating in her mind as darkness engulfed her: *Not a single one of my men will raise his hand against you or any of your colleagues.*

The Kardinal made the sign of the cross on her forehead, then ordered his team to drag the bodies inside. He stopped briefly to glance at the men and women in lab coats sprawled across the raised floors, at the Teradyne system, and at the HyperCray, his eyes finally landing on the processing equipment on the other side of the glass wall dividing the large R&D floor. The process area was by far the most dangerous place in the entire facility. Chemicals such as sulfuric acid, nitric acid, hydrochloric acid, and phosphorus—which would ignite in the presence of oxygen—were used to process the hybrid disks as they made their way through the manufacturing line.

One man put a laboratory coat on Kathy Bennett. Titov-Escobar caught his black reflection on the glass wall as he approached it followed by his second subordinate, who dragged the homeless man. The process area on the other side resembled a long assembly line; the hybrid disks went in at one end, moved through a series of chemical baths and furnaces, and came out at the other end. The baths varied according to the type of process step required. Disks had to be immersed in twenty-second baths of hydrochloric acid to remove all impurities from the outer layer of the bacterial protein prior to starting the purification and growth process in a helifurnace.

The first operative joined the second, and the two of them picked up the homeless man and followed their leader, who reached the sliding glass door and went into the process area, his eyes searching for Sergei Iyevenski.

"Him!" he hissed at his men the moment he spotted the large Russian. "Set the body next to him and exchange their clothes. Then take the Russian to the truck immediately."

The figures in UPS uniforms finished in just under two minutes. Hefting the large, limp body of the Russian scientist, they headed back to the hallway.

"Get the truck started," the Kardinal commanded them. "Wait for me by the front entrance."

The Kardinal walked up to several carts supporting tanks of hydrochloric acid, each roughly the size of a keg of beer. He counted six carts. Twenty feet away, next to the same wall, he spotted another cluster of carts and chemical tanks, their shiny metallic finish reflecting the grayish glare of the fluorescent overheads. Those held the volatile phosphorus used to support a high-temperature nitric-acid chemical bath.

One by one, Titov slowly pushed all of the hydrochloric acid carts next to the group of phosphorus carts.

Removing his small dispenser of concentrated acid, he emptied the last of it over the top of a phosphorus tank. The chemical began to sizzle, eating away the metal.

Titov-Escobar had only a minute, perhaps two. He raced out of the R&D area, through the lobby, and out the building's front entrance, where his team already waited inside the truck.

The hydrochloric acid etched through the layer of steel housing the phosphorus, which ignited the moment it came in contact with oxygen. The burning phosphorus began to pressurize the metal casing. The tiny hole created by the acid could not release the building pressure fast enough, and in another forty-five seconds the tank detonated with metal-ripping force, blasting shrapnel in a radial pattern across the entire R&D area. The shrapnel killed all the technicians and pierced adjacent phosphorous tanks. Alarms blared and overhead fire extinguishers began to fill the room with foam.

The blast that followed a few minutes later dwarfed the initial explosion, as severed gas lines erupted in a cloud of yellow and orange flames that quickly spread across the entire building in spite of the fire-extinguishing system, which ceased to operate when water mains burst from the pressure and the heat.

The Kardinal, already heading north on Highway 101, heard the thunder of the explosion and saw a column of crimson flames in his rearview mirror reaching up to the night sky, staining it red, before a mushroom cloud formed right over the rubble.

The Kardinal rejoiced in the sight.

The hammer of God has fallen to destroy the wicked, the infidels! I am his instrument of justice. The Lord God Jehovah has blessed me to carry on His name, to complete His work, to remind the infidels of His power!

At the edge of the parking lot, her back to the narrow stretch of woods separating FTI's parking lot from the access road of Highway 101, Sonya Wüttenberg shielded her eyes as the blast ripped through the building, turning it into a living inferno. The scorching shock wave threw nearby vehicles end over end through the air like toys, setting them ablaze. Debris whistled through the air as the building's roof lifted off in sections on cushions of fire before collapsing onto itself. Burning bricks, like whirling meteorites, punched through the windows of the vehicles parked farther away, some crashing against roofs, grilles, doors.

Smoke spewed out of broken windows, out of cracks in the roof and the walls, mixing with swelling flames erupting through a dozens places at once, rapidly enveloping the brick and glass structure. Alarms wailed as the hot wind made the hazy cloud swirl above the building, before it joined the skies of northern California.

Momentarily frozen, transfixed by the sudden blast, by the billowing fires, by the rumbling explosions of parked vehicles as the flames reached their gas tanks, Sonya felt the immense heat from her surveillance spot. She had seen a UPS truck and a red Mustang arrive fifteen minutes ago. She'd noticed nothing out of the ordinary up until the moment when the two UPS workers rushed out of the building carrying a limp body. Her instincts had told her then that the contract assassin had penetrated the company.

Raising an arm to shield her face, anger filling her gut, hands shaking and heart hammering at the unexpected blast, Sonya brought her walkie-talkie to her lips.

"They are leaving the parking lot in a UPS truck. Do not let them get away!" she barked to four members of her team waiting in an unmarked sedan parked two blocks away, her professional side controlling her tone of voice in spite of the exasperation sweeping through her. *He did it right in front of me, dammit!*

Sonya had received the first wave of help only six hours before in the form of eight agents to relieve her team of three. More agents were due in the morning, along with a ten-man strike team. With her exhausted subordinates sleeping at a nearby hotel and the relief team split in half—four operatives following Jake

Fischer from the moment he left the building and the other four on standby—Sonya had been all alone when she'd realized that the Kardinal was in the process of fulfilling his contract.

It had taken only minutes. Vladimir Titov-Escobar certainly continued to live up to his Stasi reputation.

"Christ! What happened in there?" the voice of one of the new arrivals hissed through the static.

"They blew up the place," came Sonya's monotone trained response, her logical side ignoring the panic ravaging the rest of her system, the frustration eating her stomach.

"What about the one who got out before—"

"I will relieve the team that's following him. You just make sure that you do not lose the truck. They have the Russian scientist with them," Sonya said, common sense telling her that if Titov's intentions were to steal biotechnology secrets from the United States, the former Stasi operative would have kidnapped the lead scientist, namely Sergei Konstantinovich Iyevenski—the limp figure she had seen through the binoculars as he was being carried into the delivery truck.

"We got them . . . they're headed for the San Jose airport. Should we intercept?"

Sonya thought about it for a moment. Four FBI agents against Titov and three of his subordinates, and there were probably more she had not seen.

"No . . . just observe and report unless they try to get on a plane. Then open fire and disable their craft."

"Got it."

Blood rising, jaws clenched, cheek muscles pulsating, Sonya turned off the two-way radio and raced back to her car, hearing the distant alarms of an approaching fire engine mixing with the rumble of multiple explosions.

Yellowish flashes cast dancing shadows through the woods where Sonya ran, fading away as she reached the other side of the strip of woods. A strong wind carried the smoke past the trees, bringing tears to her eyes. For a moment she wasn't sure if the tears were from the smoke, from the anger swelling up inside of her, or from the deep sorrow she felt for Jake Fischer.

She unlocked the door and collapsed on the seat, panting, laboring to control her breathing, furious at her inability to prevent this disaster, disappointed in herself for failing to see the operation in progress, and in her boss for not acting fast enough. Even now, as they tracked the assassin, the FBI didn't have a strike team in place to intercept him.

Sonya started the engine. The rented sedan rumbled to life. She put it in gear and reached the highway a minute later, merging with the traffic flowing north, toward San Francisco, where she knew Jake now headed, as unaware of the destruction that had taken place at his corporation as of the team tailing him, the team that Sonya would reach through her mobile phone.

But first she had to report.

Tears filled her burning eyes even after she'd left the cloud of smoke behind, even with the cool evening air streaming into the car through the dash vents. Anger, frustration, and grief devoured her. She wished had never joined this world of deceit, of betrayal, of impossible choices.

Grabbing the mobile phone, Sonya dialed Roman Palenski's secure line.

SANTA CLARA COUNTY, CALIFORNIA
Friday, July 21, 1:23 A.M.

From the safety of the front seat of a police patrol car, Jake Thomas Fischer, in utter shock, watched the flames licking the skies over Palo Alto. Even three hours after the blast, the flames lashed out at the streams of high-pressure water and foam.

FTI continued to burn, continued to consume Jake Fischer's team, his lifework, his dream. Flames burst through the white dust

boiling up to the heavens as brick walls collapsed, igniting the
night with clouds of sparks that hung in midair like an army of
lightning bugs. Swelling flames kept forking through the demolished structure, brightening the hazy parking lot, backlighting the
firefighters trying to minimize the volume of toxic gas released
into the atmosphere by spraying foam. Dark clouds created by the
chemical fire continued to block the stars of what had once been
a crystalline night. Fortunately, the winds, in favor of the local
population, blew the toxic fumes away over the mountains.

Jake could barely move. He had been in shock for the past
ninety minutes, since the cops had let him through the police barricades and into the outer edge of the parking lot of his burning
company. Only his eyes moved, and in a way he wished he could
also stop them from feeding him the nightmare images. Firefighters, their black-and-yellow coats stained red by the pulsating flames, slowly dragged sizzling corpses one by one into the
parking lot, where the body count continued to rise.

Through tears, Jake watched the line of the dead, all members
of the FTI family, all killed by what appeared to be a chemical fire
that had started in the process area, according to initial reports
from the firefighters.

Even the executives at PCA had questioned storing the chemical carts in the same building.

*It's not your fault, Jake! You had no budget to expand, no allo-
cation to purchase a storage building!*

Jake began to feel nauseated, felt hot vomit reaching his gorge,
burning his throat, and he fought it, just as he had done for the
past hour and a half, since he'd returned from San Francisco and
found his team, his company, his family, turned into charred flesh.

They had all perished. All of them, except for Kathy and him.
Iyevenski and his team had been the first to die as the chemical
explosion ripped them apart. Next had been the test team, who
had been fine-tuning the production program in preparation for

testing the samples Iyevenski was in the process of generating. The last to die had probably been Raul Martinez, the security guard.

And where was Kathy?

Her disappearance was the only reason Jake was still alive. Jake had worked with Iyevenski's team inside the process area up to the moment when he'd decided to take a break and go looking for—

A knock on the window made him jump on the seat.

Jake turned and saw the familiar face of Officer Patrick Larson, one of the two Palo Alto officers who had kept him informed since he arrived at the scene.

Jake got out. "Yes, Officer?"

"Just wanted to make sure you're doing okay, Dr. Fischer."

Jake nodded. "Better than they are," he said, pointing to the row of body bags. "Although not by much."

Officer Larson, a large blond Californian in his early thirties with bulging biceps straining his dark shirt, put a hand to his square chin and, looking away, said, "Just let me know if you need anything, sir. Our lieutenant wants to talk to you later on. We'll take you downtown in a couple of hours to meet with him. Then we'll take you home."

Jake gave him a slight nod.

The officer jogged back to a group of policemen standing by the barricades. Jake sighed and sat back in the cruiser, leaving the door wide open.

What a fucking mess, he thought, shaking his head, staring at the ever-growing line of corpses. Twenty at the last count. There were twenty-three employees at FTI, including himself and Kathy, meaning there should still be one inside. Flickering orange flames reflected on the windshield. His mind filled with guilt. If he hadn't made his team work this late, they would still be alive, perhaps watching the fire at home on CNN. If he had insisted that Iyevenski use safer procedures for the handling of the chemicals, maybe pushed harder to build that off-site storage facility for chemicals not in immediate use, perhaps the initial fire could have been contained. Or maybe if he had purchased a better sprinkler system . . .

Don't do it, Jake! Don't think about it!

But the images before his watering eyes prevented him from thinking about anything else.

He saw the firefighters hauling a long, black smoking figure and quickly shoving it into a body bag for later identification. He tightened his fists and prayed for death. How could he go on living when his dream—his obsession—had caused this tragedy? After all, he was ultimately responsible for the safety of his employees. All twenty-two of them, minus Kathy.

His eyes passed over the body bags.

Twenty-one dead.

At that moment, two firefighters, pursued by a gushing arm of flame, lurched out of the blaze carrying another body, its charred flesh smoking.

Another one?

Impossible!

Leaping out of the vehicle and running toward the bodies—an action that caused Officer Patrick Larson to shout Jake's name—the president and CEO of FTI quickly recounted the body bags. Twenty-one plus the body two young firefighters now zipped up and laid next to the rest.

"Dr. Fischer. Please, you must return to the—"

"There's twenty-two," Jake said, confused, the possibility of what that could mean beginning to shatter the last remnants of sanity left in him. "There *can't* be twenty-two. Kathy Bennett wasn't at work! She—"

"We don't know who they are, sir," said Officer Larson. "We'll determine identities later. But now you must return to the vehicle, and remain there. Please, sir. It's for your own safety."

"You don't understand! There can't be twenty-two! There simply can't—"

At that moment, as Officer Larson reached for Jake's shoulder and gently pulled him back, as his mind crazily searched for a reasonable explanation, as his soul prayed that his gut feeling was wrong, Jake's wild stare landed on the license plate of one of the vehicles that had been flipped upside down by the initial blast and had caught fire. Foam covered its charred underside, but not the personalized license plate.

BIOTECH.

"NO! It . . . it *can't* . . . Oh, God, No . . . *no!*" Jake felt dizzy, light-headed, his mind refusing to accept the savage reality of the moment, the chilling fact that Kathy had returned to FTI, and had perished with the rest of the team.

The stench of burned flesh and singed hair sickening him, tears now streaming freely, Jake dropped to his knees and stretched his arms to the smoky night sky, wrenching out of his lungs a crazed howl, an agonizing cry, the desperate scream of a desperate man.

Everything around him began to spin. Black body bags, scarlet sheets of fire in the dark, yellow-uniformed firemen hauling air tanks and Plexiglas breathing masks. His body gave and he collapsed, exhausted, drained, his core emptied from all emotions, his mind surrendering.

5

PERCEPTIONS

*We perceive an image of truth, and possess only a
lie.*

—Pascal

Jake Thomas Fischer had always wanted to be an engineer. He'd
always wanted to be a high-tech pioneer, a visionary. He had the
talent, the desire, and the patience to create, to build, to invent.
He had always admired the entrepreneurial spirit of people like
William Shockley, who established his semiconductor laboratory
in Palo Alto in 1955, in the process baptizing the region Silicon
Valley. At the time, Shockley had gone against the conventional
wisdom, against the corporate giants manufacturing vacuum
tubes. And he had prevailed. He had proved that technological
innovation could burst through any barrier, political or corporate,
and move the world forward.

Jake thought about all of the underdogs who, like him, had
taken a stand against the giants with the slingshot of technical innovation. He thought about Intel when it was first founded in
1968 by Gordon Moore and Robert Noyce, and how little they
knew at the time of the phenomenal market force it would become
one day. Jake thought about Bill Gates's founding of Microsoft
in 1975. He thought of Steve Jobs's Apple Computer, a garage
start-up that nearly broke IBM's back in the personal computer
market. He thought of Compaq Computer, another start-up that
grabbed huge market share from the colossal IBM.

He thought about FTI, about the biomemory and what it could

have meant to the personal computer industry, to Internet users, to the robotics industry, the avionics industry, the space program, the world. He thought about his team, true heroes in a time when corporate greed and market share ruled the day. When technical innovation was measured more by its near-term revenue than by its long-term potential, and it was up to people like Shockley, Jobs, and Gates to go against the current, to take a risk, to take a stand for what they believed, and hope that the rest of the world would catch up eventually.

Jake Fischer thought about his commitment to join that elite group of cyberpioneers, to make his mark in this world. To make a difference, regardless of the obstacles he would have to surmount, regardless of the defeats, the criticisms, the multiple failures. That was all a part of the engineering game, all a part of the high-tech marathon race run and won by determined scientists willing to go the distance to see their dreams become reality, to see their visions become the future.

Jake Fischer gazed at the nearby mountains as he rode in the passenger seat of the police cruiser down Highway 101. The sun high overhead washed the color from the rimrock, on the sparsely forested inclines. He spotted a lonely hawk riding the hot updrafts on four-foot wings, facing the wind, searching for prey. There was no compromise for that raptor, only the options of winning or losing, of eating or dying. It was just a sense of survival, of living to see another sunrise, of earning the right to hunt again.

Jake Fischer remembered the day he lost his funding at Los Alamos, when his technical dream fell victim to his lack of experience, to his lack of knowledge of how to play the political game, how to defend his ideas, his dreams, his passion to invent, to design, to create. He had promised to himself then that he would prevail, regardless of the headwind, of the storms, of the downdrafts that would threaten his flight to greatness. He would endure adversity because he would also learn how to take advantage of opportunities, often as unexpected and powerful as the thermals supporting that rising hawk.

Updrafts and downdrafts, forces that Jake Fischer had used for the past four years to keep FTI alive, to keep it moving forward. Until last night, when a totally unexpected storm had reached down from nowhere and crushed his dream with savage force, leaving nothing but charred bodies and a pile of smoldering rubble.

Jake thought about his team, about Sergei Iyevenski.

He thought about Kathy.

He sighed as the cruiser turned off Highway 101, down the service road, and into his tree-lined neighborhood, passing a bus hugging the curve while loading and unloading passengers.

He felt calmer now, his eyes staring at the white cumulus momentarily blocking the sun, dotting the blue skies over Silicon Valley. He breathed in the aroma of the scalding-hot 7-Eleven coffee in his hands while vaguely listening to the coded messages of a female police dispatcher flowing out of a single speaker under the dash.

A group of teenage boys crowded the neighborhood street playing tag football, shed T-shirts shoved into the backs of their shorts, like multicolored tails, flapping as they ran. A smaller group of teen girls sat on the front lawn of a red-brick house and watched their boyfriends' testosterone display.

The police officer bumped the horn. The teens quickly moved off to the sidewalk and joined the girls, who stood as the cruiser inched forward, their young eyes staring at Jake as he sipped his coffee. Some wore sunglasses. Several were barefoot. A large kid held a football under his left arm.

Jake envied them, young, tanned, and carefree, enjoying a beautiful summer day in northern California.

Without a worry in the world.

Without a worry . . .

At that moment, sunlight forked through the cumulus. As the

cruiser slowly drove by, a petite brunette wearing cutoffs and a white T-shirt stood in front of the group, her young eyes on Jake. Sunlight splashed her face, changing it, transforming it. Like an apparition, like a luminous ghost, Jake saw Kathy's shining face, saw her auburn hair, her brown eyes glinting in the moonlight, taking him in with a greedy glance. He felt her embrace, breasts pressed against his back as she lured him back to bed. Jake remembered her smile, her laugh, her tears, her eyes filled with anger every time he'd broken a date, every time he'd broken her heart.

Broken heart.

Jake turned away from her, away from the kids, away from the bare-chested, sweaty teens in shorts and sneakers, his bloodshot eyes filling once more with the cotton clouds visible through the windshield.

He struggled to get the victims out of his mind, the scorched, smoking corpses, charred beyond recognition, removed of their identity, of their dignity, reduced to a smoldering mass of human refuse in a whirling haze of flames and death that had taken so much from him.

Last night he had been unable to control his feelings. Now Jake felt strong enough to start thinking logically, to face the consequences of the fire, which apparently had destroyed everything—including the archive tapes. Somehow the vault had been left open, in clear violation of one of Jake's cardinal safety rules.

The initial verbal report from the fire marshal an hour before indicated the possibility of an industrial accident. Although firefighters could find no signs of arson, there were strange observations made by the rescuing crew. Raul Martinez, FTI's security guard, for example, had been found incinerated next to his desk. Certainly he should have heard the alarms and either gone inside to help the others or gotten the hell out of the building. Yet the guard had done neither, almost as if he had been asleep—something Jake didn't think likely with the blaring fire alarms probably heard as far as a mile away. He had expressed his concerns to Lieutenant Francisco Miranda of the Santa Clara County district attorney's high-tech crime unit, with whom Jake had spent the past five hours. The security tape, which could have helped the investigation, was missing. The electronic log, however, kept in a small vault under the guard's desk, and resembling the black boxes aboard airliners, had kept a record of the last eight hours' accesses to each secured door in the building. Jake was logged as leaving exactly when he had claimed he had the night before. But fifteen minutes later, Kathy Bennett was recorded going inside the building, directly to the vault room, and into the vault itself. A few minutes later, she had gone inside the R&D area, and three minutes after that the fire had started.

But she was not there when I left. Why the sudden arrival? And why did she go straight to the vault after being gone for so long? And why did she leave it open?

While there were still a number of unanswered questions, Lieutenant Miranda released Jake to go home, requesting that he remain in town for the next few days.

Jake had wanted to drive himself, but the officers had talked him out of it. "You're still shaken and also pretty drugged up, pal," had said the police officer currently driving Jake's Bronco twenty feet behind the cruiser. A medic had given Jake a strong sedative following his collapse. "We'll take you home, where you can get some sleep."

Sleep?

Right.

If there was one thing Jake would not be able to do, it was sleep. *Especially after I drink this coffee.*

Jake took a sip through the tiny opening in the plastic lid and burned the roof of his mouth. The pain, however, didn't seem to bother him, and he took another sip, letting the black coffee revitalize him.

"Is this your block?" asked Officer Larson.

"Yeah," Jake responded, pointing with his left hand while holding the coffee with his right. "Second-to-last house on the right."

"Got it," Officer Larson said. "Now, remember, don't leave town without checking with us first." The officer handed Jake a business card. "The lieutenant might have more questions for you."

Jake shook his head, a hand running through the side of his short black hair. "I'm sure there are a lot of people who want to question me, including your detective, my investors, my customers, my insurance company, the lawyers representing the victims, and probably the entire fucking media. I'm sure the phone and the doorbell won't stop ringing today. Anyway I look at it, I'm fucked. Lost my girl, my team, my dream, and I'm just about to lose my marbles."

"I'm really sorry, Dr. Fischer. We should get the results from the autopsies in another day or so. That at least might help shed some light on this mess."

Jake shrugged and took another sip. "It doesn't really matter, does it? My team's dead. No autopsy will bring them back."

Officer Larson didn't respond as he pulled up to the curb and the other officer steered the Bronco into the driveway of the small two-bedroom house that Jake leased for sixteen hundred dollars a month, a bargain, considering it was only fifteen minutes from work.

Not anymore. FTI is gone.

Jake got his truck's key from the police officer, thanked them both, and walked away.

"You sure you're going to be all right? Would you like us to come in for a while?"

Jake shook his head. "I'll be fine. Thanks for everything," he said, reaching into his jeans as he approached the front entrance. He produced a set of keys, slipped his truck's key onto the ring, and unlocked the door, also grabbing the mail shoved into the small mailbox by the front door and tucking it under his arm.

Before going inside he watched the cruiser slowly drive down the block and turn at the corner. The moment he shut the door behind him, he closed his eyes and took a deep breath.

And froze.

"What the *hell?*" he mumbled, sniffing as he quickly scanned the foyer, living room, and kitchen, before dropping the coffee, the keys, and the mail on the white laminate counter next to the stainless-steel sink.

The smell . . . urine . . . it smells like . . . shit!

He looked in the sink, but found nothing out of the ordinary, just an empty bottle of white zinfandel and dirty glasses from the last time he had been with . . .

The nauseating smell pressed at him.

Jake looked in the brown plastic garbage can next to the dishwasher, but saw nothing that could generate the stench.

Rubbing a hand over his darkening stubble, he followed the smell out of the kitchen, across the carpeted foyer, and into the other side of the house, where two bedrooms shared a small bathroom in the middle.

Jake peeked inside the bathroom. Although he didn't find a toilet that needed flushing, he did notice small round, dark stains on the white tile floor.

Blood? Kneeling, he smeared a tissue in one of the stains and brought it up to his nose. Coppery. Definitely blood.

But whose? And that still doesn't explain the stench.

Jake went into his bedroom and instant paralysis overcame him. A man was sitting up in his bed, his back resting against the headboard, hands fallen to the sides, a weapon with a bulky cylinder attached to the barrel still held in his left hand. The man stared at the slow-moving ceiling fan with dead eyes. A small hole between the eyes explained the red spray on the headboard and pillows. The stains on his pants showed Jake the origin of the stench: the dead man had urinated and voided his bowels after getting shot.

"Mother of *God!*" he hissed, taking a step back, the sight slapping him across the face. Pressing his back against the wall, he breathed in short gasps, felt as if he'd just swallowed ice cubes, his throat numbing.

Panting in terror, his stomach cramped from tension, from fear, from the shocking sight inside his own bedroom, Jake Fischer trembled, a chill surging through him.

What's he doing dead in my bed? Was he waiting to kill me? And why? And who killed him first?

Jake thought about running out of the house, and actually took a step in that direction, his heart hammering. He had to get out of there, call the police, seek help!

But then he stopped, focused on a sheet of paper hanging from the man's neck. *A note?*

For reasons he could not explain, Jake looked to either side of him before returning his gaze to the dead man, almost as if he needed permission to step forward and grab the note.

Slowly, overcoming the paralysis, Jake took one step, then another, swallowing hard when he reached the side of the bed. He leaned over the man and snatched the sheet of paper, tearing the thread looped around the man's neck.

YOU ARE IN GRAVE DANGER. EXPLOSION NOT AN ACCIDENT. DRIVE AROUND THE CITY. TALK TO NO ONE. MEET WITH NO ONE. TRUST NO ONE. I WILL CONTACT YOU AT 7:00 P.M. WITH INSTRUCTIONS.
A FRIEND

Grave danger? The explosion not an accident? A friend?

"What in the *hell?*"

Dropping his lids halfway, Jake reread the sheet of paper in his trembling hands, his mind struggling to understand what was happening to him, trying to make some sense of this insane turn of events, of the spiraling madness that threatened once again to push him over the edge.

Focus! Concentrate!

Folding the note and shoving it in a side pocket, Jake Fischer gave the dead man a final glance before leaving the room. He noticed that the small bloodstains on the champagne carpet made a trail running out of the bedroom, into the bathroom, back into the bedroom, and all the way to the living room, pooling again by a window onto the unfenced backyard. Jake noticed a few drops of blood on the windowsill, and only then did he also realize that the window was closed but not locked.

Jesus!

Looking back at the inky trail over the carpet, Jake recalled the words on the message.

You are in grave danger.

Trust no one.

His self-control slowly winning the battle against insanity, Jake walked into the kitchen, grabbed his keys, and eyed the answering machine, which showed he had thirteen messages. He couldn't run through them all now. He ran back into his room and, without giving the dead stranger another glance, turned on his desktop personal computer. He shouldered his laptop carrying case, which housed a Toshiba notebook and a number of accessories. Jake's analytical mind had already begun to kick into gear. He could use his portable to log in remotely to his home system and retrieve the only surviving backup of the biorecipes, the backup Kathy made once a week onto Jake's hard drive at home to keep a copy of the files at an offsite location.

Where are you going, Jake? You have a dead man in your bed! You can't just leave! You have to call the police!

Jake briefly closed his eyes.

You are in grave danger. Trust no one.

Standing in the entrance doorway, one foot on the concrete walk and another on the tiled foyer, Jake, apprehensive, confused, unsure of the right thing to do, slowly shook his head.

What if I leave? Won't it look suspicious? I'm the only one who survived, by leaving just before the blast to go look for someone who returned to the building minutes later. Does that make me a suspect? Is that why Lieutenant Miranda wants me in town?

But another voice, far more powerful, reverberated through him.

You are in grave danger! Trust no one!

The words kept running in his head, over and over. He had to believe them, had to trust whoever had written them, whoever had saved his life.

Leave, you imbecile! That guy in the bedroom was a killer! He was going to shoot you! Screw the cops! Listen to this friend who's just saved your miserable life! Call the cops from the car phone if you want, but leave! Leave now!

Closing and locking the door, Jake jogged over the narrow walk and got into the Bronco. A minute later he merged with the light afternoon traffic on Highway 101, heading for downtown San Jose.

He checked his watch. It was only two-thirty. He had plenty of time before whoever had saved his life would contact him.

Rolling down the window to feel the cool breeze, Jake forced himself to listen to the reasoning part of his anguished mind. It told him to use his mobile phone to check his messages, even though he had a pretty good idea who had left them. The first message was from Kathy Bennett, thanking him for not even bothering to come out of the meeting to cancel their date.

Jake listened to it three times, tears welling in his dark eyes. Her voice, cold, eerie, and also precious now that she was gone, cut through his layers of pride and self-control, piercing his heart. The last words from the woman he loved were a scolding.

Anger swelling up inside him, Jake sighed in frustration, a sharp pain jabbing his temples. He forced Kathy out of his mind for the moment and checked the rest of his messages.

Jacob Colton was next in line. The old venture capitalist was simply enraged, but not at the loss of Jake's team—just at the loss of his money.

Jake shook his head at the nerve and total lack of human emotion of this man, who remained on the line to tell him that even if the insurance company replaced the lost equipment, PCA would still come short by a long way because a large portion of the twenty-seven million dollars had already been spent in salaries for three and a half years.

Jake deleted the message, only to have to endure another speech from William Preston, who at least had the decency to express his condolences before also getting down to finances.

Jake's own lawyer followed, encouraging him to call immediately and advising him not to discuss anything with anyone, especially the police.

In spite of the wave of gloom sweeping through him, Jake almost chuckled at that one.

The rest were either from the press or from the families of some of the victims.

Jake let the breeze from the open window caress his face, hoping it would take away the brooding hurt as he aimlessly drove through the streets of San Jose until they became Palo Alto, or Milpitas, or Mountain View, or Sunnyvale, and back to Palo Alto. The tears came to his eyes as he drove down Highway 101 and glanced at the demolished building, smoke still curling up into skies far brighter than his life would ever be.

* * *

At an apartment complex in Sunnyvale, surrounded by towering pines and recently laid asphalt, FBI Special Agent Sonya Wüttenberg pulled up to the parking spot in front of her unit.

Sonya grimaced as she twisted her torso to unbuckle her safety belt, her lower left abdomen burning from the knife thrust that had nearly ended her life an hour ago, when she had neutralized one of Titov's assassins. Sonya's swift reaction, turning sideways and almost missing the blade while she palm-struck the man's elbow, had caught the man entirely by surprise, granting Sonya the precious seconds she had needed to throw a sidekick to his solar plexus, sending the assassin flying toward the bed. As he landed on the comforter, the man had pulled out a silencer-fitted weapon, but Sonya already had him in the sights of her Glock 19 automatic pistol and fired off a single round.

Victory, unfortunately, had not come free for the forty-year-old agent. She ripped her blouse off, not bothering to fumble for buttons, raced for the small bathroom between the two bedrooms, and shoved a white hand towel hard against the open wound, stanching the blood flow. Briefly removing it after a few seconds, she verified, to her relief, that the blade had sliced horizontally, cutting roughly four inches above her waistline, and just a quarter inch into the barely noticeable layer of fat she had developed in the past five years. In spite of the pain, Sonya grinned at the irony. The same fat that she had cursed for refusing to disappear in spite of her rigorous exercise program had now taken the cut that could have damaged a muscle or internal organ.

Searching through the small cabinet above the sink in Jake Fischer's bathroom, she had found some peroxide, which she poured over the towel before folding it and placing it over the wound. She wrapped her torn blouse around her torso to hold the towel in place.

In the closet she found a black T-shirt and put it on. Then she wrote the note, hung it from the assassin's neck, and made her escape through a rear window, reaching her car a few minutes later.

Now, as she struggled to get out of the vehicle while hauling a small backpack and a leather attaché case—without bringing any attention to herself—Sonya kept her upper body from twisting.

Her mobile phone rang.

Sonya sighed and reached for it. "Yes?"

"Fischer just left his house. I'm tailing him," one of the new FBI guns said.

"Make sure you don't lose him too!" she snapped, angry at the relief team for having lost track of the men in the van when it reached San Jose International Airport. To the team's surprise, the UPS truck had pulled up into a cargo ramp cluttered with other UPS trucks and two UPS cargo jets. Before they could get to him, the Kardinal, his team, and his special cargo had escaped in a twin-engine Cessna headed southeast, toward Nevada. Sonya had quickly called Palenski, who had immediately requested support from nearby Moffet Field Naval Air station. Unfortunately, by the time the Navy jets arrived, the plane had long dropped from radar. Guessing that the fleeing Cessna would most likely head for Mexico, Bane and Palenski had alerted border authorities on both sides of the Rio Grande, from Tijuana, by the Pacific shore, to Matamoros by the Gulf of Mexico. In an matter of hours, Lockheed U-2R high-altitude reconnaissance jets had left three Air Force bases and begun to perform high-altitude surveillance of the twelve hundred miles of desert separating the countries.

She hung up the mobile phone and turned her attention to her current predicament. The makeshift bandage was already soaked in her blood, and so was the black T-shirt, which she had selected to make her bleeding less noticeable to any bystander.

The stench of fresh asphalt in her nostrils, Sonya briefly inspected the small parking lot. A few cars, mostly older models, marked the leased units of the run-down one-story complex. The ceaseless hum of traffic on 101 mixed with the distant whine of an ambulance and the chirping of a flock of birds gathered on the overhead power lines. Sonya painfully walked up to the old building, its warped brown siding and flapping shingles matching the fading letters of the weathered sign by the roadway.

But regardless of its appearance, the place had one great advantage: the manager had no interest in Sonya after she had given him three months' rent in cash before moving in. It was the perfect FBI hideout during a surveillance operation.

She reached her unit, unlocked the door, and went inside, dropping the red backpack and the attaché case on the double bed of the dimly lit room. Dried-up wallpaper curled from the yellow plaster above the bed and by the splintered door, and the lumpy furniture was faded and dusty.

Staring at the dull flower design peeling off the walls, Sonya took a deep breath of mildew and leftover pizza. The place reminded her of her old apartment in East Berlin, before the Stasi assigned her to work at the American embassy in West Berlin. Sonya had used this unit as her base of operations during her visits over the past weeks, while her team running the surveillance of the lead FTI scientists worked out of an apartment in Milpitas. The drawn red-velour curtains provided the privacy her mission demanded.

In silent resignation, Sonya dropped her jade-green eyes to a wound she would have to treat alone. She had deployed every one of her agents—the number of which continued climbing—to cover Fischer, to look for clues at the demolished factory, and to run a full investigation at the airport's UPS shipping and receiving center. Sixteen FBI agents were busily trying to pick up the pieces, trying to limit the damage. Even her director, whom Sonya had tried to reach on the way to the apartment, had been too busy to come to the phone. Palenski and Donald Bane were hard at work at the National Photographic Interpretation Center in Washington studying the results from the high-altitude surveillance. She would try Palenski again later. Right now she had a wound to tend.

She considered going to an emergency room and getting her wound taken care of there, but she couldn't afford to be stuck in an ER if she had to spring into action. She was running an operation that had gone haywire, and she had to be instantly available for her team.

And besides, Sonya had not come unprepared.

Kicking off her shoes, she sat on the edge of the bed, her burgundy skirt rising halfway up her firm thighs, the left one stained with inky tracks of dried blood. Pulling the cotton fabric farther up, revealing a nylon holster attached to her upper right thigh by a Velcro strap, Sonya unholstered the Glock 19 pistol and released the magazine. One round was missing—the one imbedded in the wooden headboard in Jake Fischer's bedroom, behind the blown cranium of the bastard who had inflicted the wound. She shoved the magazine back into the Glock and used a tiny dagger, also strapped to her right thigh, to slice through the T-shirt.

Sonya controlled her tears of pain as she cut off the blouse securing the towel to her torso, finally cringing, feeling as if a white-hot claw raked her side, when she tried to lift the towel and realized that it had stuck to her wound.

Her face twisted. This was going to hurt. Teeth clenched, eyes mere slits of agonizing anticipation, she gave the towel a quick, firm tug, producing the sound of ripping fabric and a scourging pain that nearly made her lose control of her bladder.

"Verflucht!" she shouted, staring at the four-inch-long reopened cut, fresh blood oozing over coagulated blood. She would definitely need stitches to keep the wound closed. Reaching for the nylon backpack, she extracted a small field medical kit, which included a long curved needle with a couple of feet of black surgical thread dangling from the end.

Naked from the waist up, her china-white skin glistening in the yellow light from the lamp on the nightstand, Sonya rubbed her tongue against the back of her teeth, remembering the first and only time she had done this: West Berlin, 1986, after fending off two thugs late one evening on her way home from her "secretarial" work at the American embassy. To avoid going to a hospital and drawing unnecessary attention, Sonya had sought help at the closest Stasi safe house in the capitalist section of Berlin, and she had received help—in the form of a bottle of disinfectant and a surgical needle and sutures. Her Stasi superior, Vladimir Titov-Escobar, who was spending the month in West Berlin to check on his agents, saw the wound as an opportunity for Sonya to learn how to perform basic surgery on herself if she ever got hurt and could not reach a safe house.

And it hurt, she thought, running a finger over her left forearm, where a six-inch scar ran from her elbow halfway to her thin wrist.

Every nerve in her body on edge, Sonya tensed as she poured peroxide on the wound, feeling light-headed from the pain as the disinfectant bubbled up. Sobbing, breathing in gasps through her mouth, she used the fingers of her right hand to hold the sliced flesh together while pressing a long Band-Aid along the wound to keep it tightly closed. Next, she used peroxide to sterilize the curved needle and the black thread.

Tightening her face and abdominal muscles, the FBI agent inserted the needle into the pinkish flesh right below the plastic Band-Aid, ran it up just under the skin, and out above the Band-Aid, which she peeled back slightly before bringing the needle back down, sealing the gap with a neat stitch. She painfully repeated the process eight times, her jaws welded shut, her hand trembling, her dark lips quivering, her eyes blinking rapidly to keep her tears from clouding her view.

The job took just under three minutes—an eternity for Sonya

Wüttenberg. She gave her work an approving nod, deciding that the stitches should hold.

It took her five minutes lying in bed, staring at the dusty, slow-turning ceiling fan hanging from a water-stained ceiling, before she could muster the strength to unzip her skirt, remove her black panties, and walk to the bathroom. Shivering as her feet came in contact with the cold tile of the floor, Sonya pressed her forearms against her uptilted breasts, fine hands tucked under her chin.

She turned on the water, adjusted the jets by spinning the dial of the shower, and let it run for a minute before stepping in, careful not to let the water hit the wound directly. Sonya wished she could have taken a bath instead, but the small bathroom had only a shower.

A silent scream clamped her throat and colors exploded in her brain as warm water streamed over her wound before she could move to the side. She wished she'd never joined the damn intelligence business. The water burned her like acid, but she endured it while carefully cleaning not only the area around the wound, but also her blood-stained abdomen and legs. After five minutes, she turned up the heat, breathing in the steam fogging the mirrors and clouding the ceiling. The wound no longer burned. It also no longer bled. The pink flesh, swollen into welts, was forced together by the short, dark, vertical stitches.

She towel-dried her short blond hair before drying the rest of her slim body, softly swabbing the wound.

"You are getting too old for this," she told her pale reflection on the foggy mirror. "Too *fucking* old." High cheekbones met the lines of age under her green eyes. Fine lines, but nevertheless lines missing ten years ago, when one of her jobs had been seducing lonely Marines at the American embassy in West Berlin. Sonya had never had sex with any of them, but she'd slow-danced with most and kissed some. She had listened to their problems, heard about their cheating wives or girlfriends back home, encouraged conversation that sometimes resulted in snippets of American intelligence. Sonya had been one of Titov's Juliet agents, a high-level penetration mole planted in West Berlin to spy for the Stasi by seducing her victims.

But after three short years in the field, Sonya turned. She had grown to enjoy the naiveté and tenderness of those American men, sharp contrasts with the abusive Russians and East Germans, who never stopped to ask permission before trying to get their hands inside her skirt. During those years operating in West Berlin, Sonya became accustomed to grocery stores packed with produce, fresh meat, poultry, canned goods, and every dairy product imaginable. She grew attached to her two-year-old Volkswagen coupe, the automatic ice maker of her Whirlpool refrigerator, and her brand-new remote-control nineteen-inch Sony television—all purchased on her handsome salary at the embassy.

Sonya dried her blond hair, almost shaved at the back and sides but long in the front. She brushed it and parted it on the side, letting it run diagonally across her forehead, a lock covering the corner of her right eye.

After laying a non-stick pad over the wound and securing it with long strips of medical tape, Sonya Wüttenberg began to dress, slowly, with the care of a mother dressing a newborn.

Testing the extent of her lateral movement, she put on a clean black T-shirt, no bra. Growing up in a country where brassieres were a luxury, Sonya had never put one on until the age of nineteen, and the experience had lasted only a few seconds. She'd never worn once since.

Next came a fresh pair of black panties and a pair of Levi's, which she was able to pull up with surprising ease. The sutures were holding and the wound didn't burn as much as it had. But in spite of the care with which she had cleaned the shallow cut, Sonya could not ignore the possibility of an infection. From the first-aid kit she took a pack of four 500mg capsules of amoxicillin, a general antibiotic. She put one between her lips, went to the bathroom, swallowed it with a handful of water, and returned to the bedroom.

Leaning down to put on her sneakers caused her to tense from the pain, which she shivered away while completing the task. Managing pain had been another trait her Stasi superiors had instilled in her from the day she'd walked into the Staatssicherheit training camp at the age of seventeen, shortly after her German mother, a single parent, perished in an auto accident while returning to their East Berlin apartment one evening in 1975. Sonya had to work to support her young brother, ten at the time of the accident.

Ludwig.

The painful memory of her brother made her throat ache with regret, but she pushed it aside and checked her watch, a stainless-steel Seiko. Time to report again.

Dialing Washington, Sonya heard the hoarse voice of Roman Palenski after the light hum of the voice scrambler kicked in. Every word of Sonya's was scrambled in the mobile unit, sent via dedicated satellite link to FBI headquarters, and reassembled by the matching descrambler in Palenski's office. Anyone listening in would get nothing but noise.

"Sonya, I'm going to put you on the box," said Palenski. "I have Donald Bane with me."

"Hello, Sonya," Bane said in a booming voice that rivaled Palenski's.

"Hello, sir." Sonya was no stranger to the CIA's deputy director for operations. Bane and Sonya essentially managed the interaction of FBI legats with CIA stations, which fell under the control of the Directorate of Operations.

Briefly she told Palenski and Bane about her encounter at Jake Fischer's apartment and her wound. Then she asked, before they could order her to come in for medical treatment, "Any news on Titov?"

"Nothing yet," responded Palenski. "We're still trying to find them. Any leads from your team over there?"

"Nothing so far. Nobody at the UPS center seems to know what we're talking about. As far as they're concerned, every truck was accounted for. The same story at the demolished building. No clues. This unfortunately tends to confirm even more that we're dealing with Titov and not some other international assassin. This job has his signature. He strikes and then vanishes, leaving nothing behind but ashes and bodies."

Silence, followed by Bane asking, "Any ideas?"

"Titov has been paid to deliver stolen goods, and if I know him well, he will collect some kind of balance of his payment upon delivery. I believe our best chance to apprehend him now is to figure out where the exchange will take place."

"How are you going to find that out?" asked Palenski.

Sonya smiled and proceeded to explain her plan, taking a full minute to do so.

"Does Fischer know about this?" asked Palenski when Sonya was through.

"No. For this to work, it's imperative that he react normally."

"Fine," said Palenski. "Just keep in mind that if Iyevenski is killed, Fischer's the only one left with any knowledge of this technology. We can't afford to lose him."

"He's under heavy surveillance. Nothing's going to happen to him. I protected him once already. I'll guarantee his safety."

"Very well. Call me after the meeting."

"Yes, sir." Sonya hung up the phone and verified she still had plenty of time before having to meet Jake Fischer. With some luck, her team would leave her alone for a few hours. She was exhausted, and not just physically. Sonya was tired of playing the game, dissatisfied with herself for having to rely on a plan that involved using Jake Fischer as bait.

Maybe it was the recent explosion, resulting in so many deaths. Maybe it was the fine wrinkles around her eyes, or maybe it was her near-death just over an hour ago, but a voice told the seasoned operative that she'd better slow down.

You're not thirty years old anymore.

Sonya suddenly felt the urge to call it quits, to call Palenski once more and request her immediate release.

But would she miss it? Could she handle life on the outside? Clandestine operations had been her way of life since the age of seventeen. In fact, she had a difficult time remembering when she had *not* been in the espionage business, which for her had peaked in complexity when she began to spy for the CIA in 1988 but remained with the Stasi until its dissolution, carefully feeding Titov-Escobar and Markus Wolf disinformation. Those eighteen months had been the most difficult of her life, acting as a double agent, crossing the people who had trained her, given her every skill she possessed.

But the slim woman with the pale skin, lips a bit too full for her narrow face, and golden blond hair always covering a corner of her forehead had succumbed to capitalism, had rejected her old system for one that held the promise of a better life.

Sonya shook her head. The abdominal wound had begun to throb.

Better life?

Not only was she forty, single, and recently stabbed, but she had to patch herself back up without anesthetic inside a crummy, filthy motel room to avoid wasting time in what she considered the most important case of her career. This was definitely not her idea of a comfortable life in America.

Sonya decided to sleep. She set the alarm of the clock-radio on

the nightstand to wake her up in four hours. Although she had
minimized the blood loss, she estimated that she'd still lost at least
a pint. She had to give her system time to recover, time to rest.

  Rest is a weapon. Vladimir Titov-Escobar had taught her that
during her advanced training at the academy. *An operative with
a clear mind and rested body will always have the advantage over
a tired enemy.*

  Sonya Wüttenberg, former Stasi officer, closed her eyes and,
lying sideways in a fetal position, hands cupped under her chin
but less than six inches away from her Glock, drifted into sleep.

6 PAST AND PRESENT

Time ripens all things. No man is born wise.
— *Cervantes*

SOUTH TEXAS

Friday, July 21, 5:30 P.M.

Luminous shafts of yellow blazed at the edge of the nearing dark clouds, touching a cluster of cacti and boulders sheltering scorpions, spiders, millipedes, rodents, and other desert creatures from the relentless heat wave. Overhead, a hawk scrolling the hot updrafts in wide, lazy circles kept a hungry eye on the blistering terrain below. Shrieking the moment its telescopic vision detected movement in the pattern of rocks and fissures, the hawk folded its wings and plunged groundward, its sharp eyes focused on a rattler sidewinding toward the shade offered by a yucca. Senses honed to perfection by thousands of years of evolution kept the hunter in a perfect dive. Another screech, and the raptor reached its prey, caught it, and winged back up toward the gray clouds quickly extending over the desert, the dying reptile dangling in its talons.

Temperatures slowly dropped into the upper nineties as the storm, which had originated over west Texas, brought the first sign of relief from a month-long dry spell. The initial drops of rain evaporated a hundred feet from the ground, victims of the rising heat wave released by a soil fit for only the toughest vegetation. The storm eventually won, though, pouring down almost three inches of water in less than an hour. In a matter of minutes, dry creeks turned into torrential rivers, uprooting trees and everything else that stood in their way. Water momentarily ruled the dry land, changing it, scarring it, before vanishing as suddenly as it had appeared.

As the last raindrops fell, sixty miles south of San Antonio, in the middle of the desert that served as a natural shield between Mexico and the United States, a twin-engine Cessna slowly taxied out of an old wooden hangar. The abandoned airstrip, cracked by the relentless heat and overgrown with weeds, was occasionally used by Mexican drug lords for night drops—which held an average 70 percent success rate. This particular plane had participated in many such runs, had been confiscated twice by U.S. federal agents, and had been bought back during public auctions by law firms representing foreign clients, many of them south of the Rio Grande.

The pilot, a former crop duster by the name of José García, taxied the ten-year-old plane to one end of the short airstrip, turned it around, and pressed his feet against the brakes above the rudder pedals while throttling up to full power and adding fifteen degrees of flaps. He had flown this route many times before for his bosses in Monterrey. He'd even been caught by the DEA at this airstrip six months ago and sentenced to ten years at the correctional institute in Bastrop, Texas, where he'd served three months before being transferred to Mexican authorities to finish his term at a prison outside Monterrey. He'd spent less than a week there before the right palm was greased. He'd made eleven of these trips since.

Tumbleweeds rolled across the narrow runway as García waited for both engines to reach full RPM before releasing the brakes. The Cessna sprinted down the uneven strip, its aluminum frame rattling, the analog instrumentation of the vibrating control panel momentarily blurring. Thirty seconds later he was airborne, keeping the plane at exactly twenty feet from the flat, rugged terrain while pushing 230 knots. The twin-engine plane should be lost in the ground clutter, making it nearly invisible to the Americans, who by now were probably sweeping the airspace above the border between the two countries.

"*Muy bien, José,*" commended Vladimir Titov-Escobar, sitting behind the pilot in the middle row of the nine-seat plane. It was a bit weathered by the Kardinal's standards, with cracks in the Plexiglas windows, frayed upholstery, and the rancid smell of grease coming from the open toolbox on the rear seat.

"*Gracias, señor,*" responded the short and skinny native of Monterrey, a former underpaid AeroMexico pilot who had decided to make a better life for himself by offering his services to anyone who wanted to cross the border clandestinely. During the thirteen years since he had left the Mexican airline, José García had carried out many smuggling jobs for clients throughout Central and South America and the Caribbean, including special jobs for Raúl Castro, Fidel's brother. His business transactions with the Cuban government had required García to visit the island frequently. It was during one of those visits to Havana many years before that he'd met Vladimir Titov-Escobar, almost instantly striking up a friendship that would span nearly a decade.

Dressed in a pair of black slacks and a navy-blue nylon windbreaker with an oversized hood he used to hide his face, the Kardinal eased back into his seat while giving his Russian hostage a sideways glance of his narrowed iron-gray eyes. Titov's Slavic features were further concealed beneath the same beard he'd worn for the FTI press conference. In his business he could not be too careful.

Sergei Iyevenski had remained quiet since awakening from his drug-induced sleep, and that had suited Titov-Escobar just fine. He had been chosen to kidnap the Russian and deliver him—and the tape inside the briefcase at his feet—to the German people, not to entertain the bastard. If he succeeded, a grateful Germany would donate another DM 25 million, mostly in bonds and stock certificates, to his cause in a meeting in Paris in several hours, bringing the rolling total to fifty million.

The Kardinal sighed. He would have done this job for free. Money could not match the satisfaction he received from serving his Lord in the fight against the American infidels.

Iyevenski, hands tied behind his back, turned his large, bear-like face to the Kardinal, his blue eyes, encased in small rolls of flesh below the unkempt salt-and-pepper hair, looking at the assassin with contempt.

"Shto Vam Nuzhna?" the Russian scientist asked sternly, his wrinkled face turning into a mask of anger while his eyes burned Titov-Escobar with a stare as harsh as his insult.

"Even the most foolish of men fears the unknown," the Kardinal warned in flawless Russian, his voice low and steady. Titov took in the beefy Russian with a mix of curiosity and condescension. "But he who insults his captors holds the greatest fear of all."

"You are wasting your time," responded Iyevenski, eyes locked with Titov's in open warfare.

Slowly shaking his head, the Kardinal said, "Such disappointing words I hear, for I know who you are, where you came from. Has it been that long? Don't you remember the most basic tactic of the Komitet Gosudarstvennoi Bezopasnosti? If you don't cooperate, not I, but *you* will be dooming your *kallegi* at FTI."

Iyevenski's face, wrinkled but toughened like dry hide, turned red, his strong jaw trembling as his anger spiraled nearly out of control at the mention of his friends.

"The Komitet?" barked Iyevenski. "The Komitet is dead! I watched it die!" The Russian suddenly grinned, but the smile didn't reach his eyes, the sleeping KGB demon in him awakening as he defiantly added, "All that remains of the KGB is poor fools, like *you,* who can't let it go."

"We all carry our pasts in our hearts, in our words, in our souls.

I haven't forgotten mine . . . Sergei Konstantinovich," said the Kardinal, unmoved by the Russian's surprisingly strong response. "You, however, have forgotten who you are, where you came from. You have forgotten our ways. Agencies will always perish, Sergei Konstantinovich, but the ways of the men who ran them remain very much alive. Soon you will meet a destiny which will present you with two choices. The unwise choice will bring death to those whom you left behind in California."

Shouting, unable to restrain the fury swelling inside him, Sergei began tugging on the rope binding his wrists, large, hairy hands trembling in anger, old but hard muscles straining beneath the leathery skin. He attempted to stand and charge the man hiding behind the dark hood, but the seat belt hugging his thick waist held him back.

One of the two bodyguards sitting in the rear seat banged the barrel of his handgun against the back of Russian's neck. *"Molchi tye!" Shut up, old fool!*

The Kardinal raised a palm and slowly shook his hand at the guards. "I have a promise to keep. Not a single one of my men shall raise his hand to you or any of our colleagues as long as you obey me."

Mumbling something Titov could not make out, Iyevenski turned his attention back to the rapidly changing scenery.

For a moment the Kardinal kept his gaze on this incorrigible Russian who refused to be broken, who was living up to the reputation he had earned during his KGB years. Turning his cloaked face to the vast dry lands, Titov narrowed his iron-gray eyes, as he always did when he encountered a man who matched his own strength of character—which was quite seldom. According to what he'd read about Sergei Iyevenski, and also based on the way the Russian had behaved since awakening from the sleeping gas, Titov-Escobar's logical side told him to treat this massive man with the respect he deserved. Those arms, old but still as thick as Titov's own thighs, would have no problem crushing any of his guards.

The Kardinal thrust a hand inside a pocket and clasped his rosary. He pushed the Russian scientist from his mind, but found him replaced by thoughts of Karla Valentinovna Naidenova, his best long-term penetration agent in West Berlin. He remembered the missions, the risks, the results, the rewards. He recalled the short wedding in Moscow, her reassignment as executive secretary at the BND, her shocking report about a possible mole inside the Stasi. Further probing had found the source of the Stasi intelligence reports making their way into the BND: the American embassy in West Berlin. It was then that Titov-Escobar realized that his agent Sonya Wüttenberg had been turned. Using Sonya's younger brother, Ludwig, as bait, Titov-Escobar had drawn the traitorous operative into a trap. Ludwig had managed to warn her just in time, losing his life in the process but saving Sonya's. She managed to fight her way out of the ambush and return to West Berlin.

"We're almost there," shouted the pilot, ending Titov's musing.

His breath escaping slowly as his eyes shifted from his tight fist holding the rosary to the horizon, he saw the Rio Grande in the distance, beyond the hot, featureless land.

They came in from the north, fast, hugging the terrain as the pilot slightly dropped the nose, giving Titov the impression that they would run into the ground. The ocean of cracked soil and tumbleweeds, just ten feet beneath the aluminum belly of the plane, rushed past at a hypnotic speed.

The Cessna crossed the gleaming river, a moving oasis snaking its way through vast expanses of infernal land, separating prosperity from poverty, two societies kept apart by river and desert, a death zone engineered by the imperialists to isolate themselves from the disease and famine to the south. The plane entered Mexican airspace, a tiny object in the inhospitable desert, where rattlers and coyotes ruled.

Mexico.

Titov-Escobar peered wearily at the deeply fissured land, empty, dry, dead, just as his heart had become after Karla's death, after the death of his unborn child, alive in her womb at the time of her cold-blooded murder at the hand of Sonya Wüttenberg.

The rosary still in hand, the Kardinal winced in pain, felt transported back to a remote mountaintop monastery in Croatia. He remembered the view of tree-studded hills leading to the forested plains that met the Adriatic Sea, as seen through the stone-framed windows of the isolated room he had been granted after making a large cash donation and giving his word to abide by the strict rules of the holy place. In the seclusion of his room, Vladimir Titov-Escobar had struggled to cope with the changes in his life— changes for which he had not been trained, physically, emotionally, or spiritually.

Communism had taught him that God did not exist except in the hearts of the weak, of the sentimental, of the foolish. Communism had taught him that the government, the system, would always take care of all his needs. And when that system crumbled, Titov found himself empty, abandoned, alone. But at least he'd had Karla, someone to cling to so that he could survive the winds of change sweeping through his life. But Karla had been taken away by the same Westerners who had pushed Communism into extinction. Half mad, considering the suicide route taken by so many of his former associates, Titov-Escobar listened to the last remnants of logic left in him. He needed a place to hide, to rest, to reflect on his life and on his future. He sought an inner peace that would not come unless he vanished, broke all links to his past, reached a place where he could start over again. He thought of his youth in Cuba, and the religious teachings of his Roman Catholic mother. At one point in his life he had been a believer, before Communism erased the word of God from his young mind. Memories of his belief rushed to the forefront of his thoughts after Karla's death.

He had reached the monastery a month later; had reached an oasis in a stormy world. Solitude, prayer, calisthenics, jump rope, and weekly fasting quickly became his new way of life, providing him with the strength to survive the terrible loss of his family, of his network, of his world.

Titov-Escobar remembered the cold and drizzly nights, hugging himself and weeping while trying to sleep on a two-inch-thick mattress on the gray slate floor. His only companion was a lonely mouse that came through a small crack in the mortar at a corner every night to feed on scraps of the bread, cheese, and vegetables brought to his doorstep every day by an old monk.

For years the wind swept through the Croatian countryside and up the steep mountains, whistling through every crack and crevice in Titov's rustic room. He would shut his eyes and pray for the strength to go on, to resist the daily temptation to use his jump rope and end his life. *Whom the Lord loveth he chasteneth.* The words of the Holy Book would carry him through sleepless nights, restless days, through anxiety attacks, through the daily agony of having lost everything. But the feeling of hopelessness slowly became a liberation. Through prayer, exercise, and fasting he purged the pain, the anger, the temptations, the past. His body purged itself from a life of excess. His lean torso and limbs became one in harmony with his purified mind, his purified soul. His spirit grew in strength during the four years he spent in near-solitude, praying, learning how to live and love all over again, learning to respect his fellow monks, to volunteer some of his time to the vegetable garden in the center of the monastery, to integrate himself with his adopted family.

But then the incessant shelling started in the hills surrounding the monastery. Artillery units from one faction shelled defenseless civilians belonging to another faction. Titov-Escobar had heard an American fighter-bomber one morning before dawn, as he knelt before the small wooden crucifix next to his mattress. He'd heard it and known that it was targeting the nearby artillery units. He had jumped out of the window, landing on a cushion of pine needles as he rolled downhill. The destruction was sudden and total, with sheets of orange flames lighting the pine forest, consuming the entire monastery. It was over as suddenly as it had started, and once again Titov had found himself alone, walking with faltering steps through the rubble of another destroyed world.

But the Lord had spoken to Titov-Escobar. He had been spared, had been saved from the flames consuming the other monks. The Lord had kept him alive for a reason, and this reason was for Titov to become His instrument of justice against a world dominated by the evil West, by the capitalists, by the oligarchs. Titov-Escobar had been allowed to live so that he could prevent the further expansion of Western pornography and decadence.

The Kardinal was born that day.

Like the crusaders of times past, who fought the pagans to free the world, the Kardinal was absolved of all sins incurred while acting as God's hammer of justice. He was a holy warrior, free from the burden of sin—and so were all of his disciples, his righteous angels.

The Kardinal leaned forward and asked, "How much longer, José?"

José García glanced over his left shoulder, an action that made Titov-Escobar uncomfortable, since the cocky Mexican pilot still had the Cessna caressing the tumbleweeds.

"Almost there, señor."

To Titov's alarm, García kept looking over his shoulder.

"It is not wise to tempt fate, José," the Kardinal said, turning his bearded face, darkened by the large hood, away from the Mexican pilot.

García quickly went back to flying the plane, climbing to two hundred feet once they were fifteen miles inside Mexico, and finally landing at a private airstrip in the middle of a cotton plantation seventy miles from the border.

The twin-engine plane came to a stop by the small terminal, a one-story brown stucco building at one end of the recently paved runway. This plantation belonged to a local drug lord, who allowed García to use the airstrip for an inflated fee in dollars. Three other planes crowded the small ramp—another twin-engine Cessna, a single-engine crop duster, and a shiny Grumman Gulfstream IV. The first two belonged to the renegade pilot. The Gulfstream jet, capable of crossing the Atlantic without refueling, belonged to an import-export firm in Munich, a front company for the Kardinal's clandestine operations.

"Get him out," Titov ordered his two subordinates, "and strap him to a seat in the rear of the jet." Grabbing the leather attaché case, the Kardinal unbuckled his safety belt and unlocked the side door, which swung downward to form a stair.

Keeping the hood on to shield his eyes from the sun, which was still hours above the horizon, Titov pocketed the rosary and walked toward his craft. The blue and green stripes running from the nose to the tail contrasted sharply with its white skin, glistening under the shimmering sun. A lean but muscular woman with long black hair and skin as dark as the half-Cuban Titov's, and dressed in black jeans, a plain T-shirt, and boots, stood in the doorway, a red backpack in her hands.

"Hola, mi amor. Cómo fue todo?"

"Bien," responded the Kardinal, putting a hand to her face, softly touching the smooth skin of his second-in-command, Yolanda Vasquez, a former Cuban air force pilot.

Putting a hand over his and raising fine eyebrows over her onyx-black eyes, Yolanda said, "I'm afraid we have *un problema.*"

The Kardinal did not like *problemas.*

"Jürgen?"

The tall native of Havana, her smooth, golden skin gleaming in the sunlight, nodded once.

Whom the Lord loveth He chasteneth.

The Kardinal closed his eyes and tightened the grip on the attaché case's handle. He had ordered Jürgen Brautingam—one of the operatives accompanying him to California while Yolanda remained behind guarding the jet—to track down and kill Jake Fischer.

"He called in once on the cellular phone to report that Fischer was still alive," Yolanda added. "Jürgen also told me he would go to Fischer's house and wait for him to show. He never called again. *I* should have been allowed to come with you and do this right, instead of relying on those rookies."

The Kardinal raised a brow at Yolanda's rebuke, softly clamping his hand around her fine neck and slowly forcing her smooth face toward him. "Jürgen is a good man, my dear child. I do not regret my decision," he said slowly. Yolanda was as spoiled as she was beautiful, but he indulged her as a husband indulges a young, beautiful wife.

Freeing herself from the Kardinal's relaxing grip and taking a step back, she retorted while pointing at the guards escorting Iyevenski out of the Cessna, "Those *pendejos* would never have gotten past Stasi, KGB, or GRU examination boards, and you know it."

"Your sudden bursts of hostility disturb me greatly, Yolanda. You must learn to accept my wishes, and I in turn shall help you release your anger."

Reluctantly, she nodded, a hand rubbing her neck. "I try . . . but it's difficult."

Titov continued, "Carrying out the word of the Lord *is* difficult, my beautiful Yolanda, and I admire you for your efforts. Did you try contacting Jürgen after he failed to report?"

Yolanda began to speak. The Kardinal calmly listened to how Jürgen had never returned Yolanda's repeated pages, how he'd failed to answer his mobile phone when she'd called a dozen times. Something had gone terribly wrong. The seasoned Jürgen, a veteran from the Cold War days, a master spy capable of escaping numerous CIA and MI6 traps, would have found a way to report, even if he'd had to kill to reach a phone. This fact alone left little doubt in Titov's mind that his operative had been neutralized.

"We shall depart immediately," said the Kardinal, with the control that came from knowing that no one could take away from him anything worth more than what he had already lost in the past.

"How can you be so calm?" the Cuban asked. "One of our best operatives has been compro—"

"I have lost one of my crusaders, but his soul has been saved, for he perished while carrying out the will of our Lord."

"What about Fischer?" she asked.

"The hammer of our Lord shall fall upon any infidel who dares challenge my crusade. I'll send the order. There will be many takers."

"What about the plan, the delivery, the *money?*" asked Yolanda, as two of Titov's guards escorted a visibly unwilling Iyevenski up the steps and into the Gulfstream.

"Money is just a necessary evil, my dear child. But you must not live for money. Live for the joy that comes from knowing that you are making a difference, that you are fighting for a just cause. Have faith in my judgment, for it's the will of our Lord." He handed her the attaché case and took the red backpack. "Are we ready to depart?"

Yolanda, a MiG pilot until the fall of Communism, when the Soviet Union could no longer support Cuba's large air force, headed toward the Gulfstream. "Fueled and ready," she said, her back to him, her long black hair swinging just above the belt of her tight jeans.

He watched her lithe figure disappear inside the Gulfstream. Yolanda lacked faith, was tough, hard, merciless, and in a seemingly endless bad mood. But she was also a terrific pilot, highly proficient with a variety of weapons and in hand-to-hand combat, and unusually skilled at breaking any man to extract information. She was a precious asset which the Kardinal used to execute his mission on this earth.

Already perspiring from the scorching sun, Vladimir Titov-Escobar wiped his forehead before walking over to José García, who was tying down the Cessna.

"Gracias," Titov-Escobar said, setting the backpack next to him and patting it. "It's all in here."

The Mexican pilot, kneeling by the nose gear as he looped a tie-down rope through a metal hook in the fuselage, eyed the red backpack before looking up, grinning. "It's always a pleasure doing business with you, *señor.*"

"Vaya con Dios, José," said the Kardinal.

"Gracias, señor."

A firm handshake, and the Kardinal returned to his jet. In the rearmost seat, alone, out of sight of the Russian strapped to one of the seats at the front of the cabin, he removed his hood and beard and massaged his face, silently thanking God for the refreshing pleasure of the overhead vents streaming cold air across his sharp Slavic features.

As Yolanda taxied the jet to the runway, the Kardinal pulled out his rosary and once more began to pray.

Our Father who art in Heaven . . .

The Gulfstream's takeoff was witnessed not only by José García, as he unzipped the bag and dipped his hands into fifty thousand dollars in unmarked twenties and fifties, but also by Donald Bane and Roman Palenski, sitting in an observation room at the National Photographic Interpretation Center (NPIC) in Washington, D.C.

From inside the seven-story concrete complex, the CIA's deputy director for operations and the FBI director watched the real-time images displayed on the large color screen covering one end of the observation room. The images were collected by one of several surveillance cameras aboard a Lockheed U-2R high-altitude reconnaissance aircraft, flying at sixty-eight thousand feet above the region of interest. For the past twelve hours, since the Cessna had left the San Jose airport and headed southeast, Palenski and Bane had remained patiently seated at the small conference table, now layered with paper cups of coffee, a large ashtray containing three half-smoked cigars, white boxes of Chinese takeout food, notepads with red and blue scribbles, and dozens of digitized color images.

The twin-engine Cessna had been spotted while refueling at an airstrip near Amarillo, up in the Texas panhandle. By the time authorities arrived, the plane had vanished from the field, but not from the sharp lenses of the telescopic cameras aboard a U-2R diverted from the border to north Texas. The U-2R had tracked it since, losing it briefly during an hour-long storm south of San Antonio but quickly reacquiring it after the dark clouds blew east.

Bane turned his face from the multicolored screen to the bald-headed director, who was as large as Bane and wore gray slacks, a white shirt, a loosened maroon tie, and matching suspenders. A cigar hung from the corner of his mouth.

"What do you think, Don?" asked Palenski, rolling the sleeves of his starched shirt up to his elbows and gnawing the cigar. "Central Europe?"

"Looks like it. Let's see if this thing can predict where." Bane, dressed like Palenski but without the suspenders, typed a few commands on the keyboard that slid from under the table, and the screen split in two. One half still showed the tiny silvery shape of the Gulfstream as it climbed to its cruising altitude. The second half displayed a map of the world. A few more keystrokes and the map zoomed in to cover only the region between northern Mexico and central Europe. A green dot marked the current location of the fleeing jet. Red dotted lines projecting from the plane marked the computer estimates of possible flight paths, based on current heading and speed and assuming full fuel tanks. Calculating a range of 4,123 miles plus a thirty-minute reserve, the NPIC computers estimated destinations from Madrid to Moscow, from Olso to Athens.

"Great," grunted Palenski, cigar in hand as he pointed at the screen. "Millions of taxpayers' bucks in high-tech hardware plus tens of thousands of dollars an hour in jet fuel only to find out that the plane could land just about any-fucking-where. I could have told you that."

"You gotta love this job," Bane said, yawning and nodding, and rubbing a finger under the depression below his right eye, courtesy of the boot of an Iraqi soldier a few years ago during a mission in northern Iraq. Back then Bane had been concerned with stopping the proliferation of nuclear weapons. Now he was trying to prevent the loss of the technology of the twenty-first century to the Germans.

"Do you want to risk an interception?" asked Palenski. "The carrier *America*'s coming home from the Mediterranean. We could get the Navy to send a couple of F-14s and force them to land in Spain . . . or elsewhere."

Bane shook his head. "Then we turn this thing into a hostage situation, with the Kardinal holding the best cards. Face it, Roman, the bastard's got the tape and the world's best scientist in the field. If a couple of Tomcats show up out of the blue and order him to turn to Texas, he'll probably just laugh at them, because he knows we can't shoot him down. We'd just be telegraphing our intentions . . . giving him time to come up with a plan. And if Sonya's take on this guy's anywhere close to the truth, he would most likely find a way to evade us."

Palenski shoved the cigar back in his mouth and grunted. "Bastard."

"I'd much rather catch Titov by surprise," added Bane. "We keep monitoring him, and get our people to nail him either shortly before, during, or after the exchange."

The director ran a hand over his shiny cranium. "That's if we ever find out where in the hell they're headed. . . . Shit, I gotta take a leak."

Bane grimaced as Roman Palenski left the observation room. Ten years ago he had worried about the threat of Armageddon, then about nuclear proliferation. It seemed that every other country wanted to become the next nuclear nation, and it had been his job to prevent that from happening, regardless of the consequences. Now he faced a different kind of demon: the violent growth of international competition, and not just in the field of computer chips. The Japanese sought American technological breakthroughs that they could copy, perfect, and call their own, just like flat-screen televisions. The Koreans, in turn, spied on the Japanese with an eye toward cheaper manufacturing of anything made in Japan. The Europeans spied on the Americans to enhance their aerospace programs, triggering wars between companies like Boeing and Airbus. The once-mighty NASA had lost most of the commercial satellite-deployment business to the European Space Agency and the Japanese. Now even China was getting into the space business.

On the automotive front, everyone was at war with everyone else. The security systems protecting the design centers at Ford, GMC, and Chrysler rivaled those of a defense contractor. Mercedes, BMW, and Porsche were ready to launch ballistic missiles at Lexus, Accura, and Infinity for styling their vehicles like the German models and penetrating the luxury markets. In the work-station world, Sun Microsystems and Hewlett-Packard were under constant attack by Japanese and Europeans wanting to participate in their lucrative niche market.

And now the Germans were in the process of stealing a tech-nology so valuable that it had merited deploying a team to steal it.

And they had not only stolen the archive tapes, which Bane felt certain had been taken from that vault, but kidnapped a scientist and destroyed the rest of the employees and their equipment. Now those high-tech bandits were on the run, and it was Donald Bane's job to intercept them.

To succeed against the legendary Kardinal, Bane would need much more than just high-level surveillance and intercept teams. He would need his experience, his innate ability to make the right calls during critical situations. He would have to follow his in-stinct.

Instinct.

Returning his attention to the screen, Bane began to pound the keyboard again, hoping the millions of dollars in computer hard-ware and software at his fingertips would give him a clue to the destination of that Gulfstream. He could only pray that it was close to one of the teams on standby at several major European cities.

Across the country, at dusk, another man also pounded a key-board with matching intensity. But unlike Donald Bane's, Jake Fis-cher's system was worth only three thousand dollars: a Toshiba Portégé notebook computer with a built-in fax-modem.

Jake sat in the front seat of his burgundy Bronco, which idled at the edge of the parking lot of a computer superstore on the out-skirts of San Jose, where the former CEO of FTI had purchased a PCMCIA one-hundred-megabyte hard-drive card, slightly thicker than a regular credit card and designed to plug into one of the slots on the side of the Portégé. Jake kept the engine on to power not only the notebook computer through the cigarette lighter, but also the car phone, which Jake had connected to the notebook's modem.

His eyes scanned the parking lot and the terrific view of Silicon Valley under a sky stained with hues of yellow, orange, and red-gold, save for the distant storm clouds slowly drifting in from the northeast.

The first stars sprang forth in the twilight as the crimson sun disappeared below the western rimrock in a dazzling display of colors, bathing the early-evening shoppers in pools of flattering yellow and orange.

Jake had selected this spot not because of the view, but because it gave him the best signal strength on the car phone.

His eyes swung back to the notebook. Time was also of the essence. The active-matrix color screen flashed a phone number in the middle of a red square as the modem dialed in to Jake's home computer, which he had turned on when he was at his house several hours ago.

His eyes nervously returned to the parking lot when the mercury lights flickered and began to glow, breaking the dimming yellowish glow with gray light. He searched for someone who might be following him, but wasn't certain what to look for. He forced his concentration back to the screen, which now displayed the Explorer menu of his system at home.

I'm in.

Jake used the built-in pointer to guide the cursor to the largest directory in his home system's hard drive: an off-site backup of FTI's files and recipes. The time stamp showed July 14.

Seven days ago.

Jake quickly selected all of the files in the directory, occupying close to thirty megabytes of disk space, and moved them to the virtual directory created by the dial-in system—meaning the files would be transferred to the Portégé via the wireless link.

He hit Enter, and the screen displayed two manila folders, with sheets of paper moving from one to the other. Beneath it, a percentage scale slowly began to increase from zero percent. The data on his hard drive at home began to transfer to the desktop's modem, where the digital signal got converted to analog electrical pulses similar to those made by fax machines. In an instant, hundreds of data files began to move through the modem, down the telephone wire, and to the nearest mobile phone provider, where they were amplified and burst into the night sky.

Jake's lifework now cruised through the evening air like a cloud of invisible particles, each holding the precious bits of information that as a whole made up the most important technical innovation of the decade. The airborne data, riding along the crests and valleys of ultra-high-frequency radio waves, descended over the burgundy Bronco and reached the mobile unit, where they were once again translated into electrical pulses that traveled from the phone to the Toshiba Portégé's modem. The data underwent one final transformation from the analog world to the precise digital world as it entered the portable computer's main bus. The Portégé's operating system moved the arriving data into the PCMCIA hard drive, where it began to make an exact replica of the files at the other end of the wireless connection.

Jake watched closely as the download indicator changed from 5 percent to 6 percent. A decoding password had to be entered the moment the indicator reached 7 percent. For security reasons, no one else in the team—not even Kathy Bennett—had known that a decoding password was required. This was the ultimate security measure that Jake Fischer and Sergei Iyevenski had chosen four years ago, when the two scientists finalized the business plan for FTI and began the hiring process. For years Kathy had made back-ups using a program written by Jake that automatically inserted this safety feature without her knowing.

The system paused in the data transfer for a mere twenty seconds, allowing the user to enter a password, but without prompting the user for one. The user had to know that one had to be entered, otherwise the download algorithm would corrupt what had been downloaded so far and randomly scramble the rest of the data while downloading it without giving any indication that there was a problem.

It took almost twenty minutes to complete the transfer. Jake nodded approvingly when he received confirmation from the system that the data had been downloaded safely into the PCMCIA hard drive. As a safety check, he browsed through a dozen files and verified that they indeed were healthy.

Pulling up the Explorer program, Jake once again reached his root directory at home, selected all of the biotechnology files he had just duplicated in the PCMCIA hard drive, and pressed the Delete key.

The system responded with:

DELETE ALL FILES IN DIRECTORY.
ARE YOU SURE? Y/N

Jake pressed the Y key and then Enter. The system responded with a deleting message followed by rapidly changing file names, until all of the files were gone.

Jake stared at the empty directory of his home system and frowned. Although no files now existed in the biotechnology directory, the hard-drive sectors occupied by the files had not been altered. The delete function merely eliminated the links between the operating system and the hard-drive sectors. The sectors themselves would remain intact until another file overwrote them.

This meant that any skilled hacker armed with the right disk utilities could actually retrieve all of the biotechnology files from the hard drive of his home computer.

Surprised at himself for almost forgetting that, Jake shook his head and pulled down the menu to select the Disk Format command. Unlike Delete, Format would overwrite every sector of the hard drive, forever eliminating all information residing in the disk.

Jake Fischer clicked twice on the Format command and reformatted his entire hard drive at home, a process that took an additional twenty-five minutes.

Now he was the only one in possession of the files—aside from the bastards who'd robbed him.

But those assholes are in for a big surprise. All they'll get is thirty megabytes of trash.

In the event that an exceptionally talented hacker eventually managed to figure out the download password and enter it at the correct time, it would still require the experienced Jake Fischer or Sergei Iyevenski to turn the information in the files into something useful. Biotechnology was an innovative science slowly being developed at several labs, including, ironically, Los Alamos, but they were all many years behind FTI. It would take those scientists a good decade to interpret the files correctly, through a painful trial-and-error process, until they could organize them as FTI had.

Jake removed the PCMCIA hard-drive card and stared at it. He still had a chance to achieve his dream. Although his team had been killed and his company destroyed, Jake Fischer possessed the basic ingredients to start over.

But not before I find the bastards who did this to me, to Kathy, to Sergei, he thought, his sharp features hardening, his indigo-blue eyes under the thick black hair narrowing in an anger he knew he would have to control.

Discipline. Control. Logic.

Jake expanded his chest and slowly exhaled, repeating the words in his mind. He had to believe them, had to abide by them to make some sense of the deaths, the explosions, the trail of bodies, the mysterious friend.

He checked his watch. Almost seven o'clock—the time when his friend would make contact.

Jake turned off the Portégé and shut off the engine, letting the darkness here at the edge of the parking lot engulf him. Disconnecting the phone from the Toshiba's modem, he leaned his head against the headrest and took in the spectacular view of Silicon Valley at night. The long valley sandwiched between two mountain ranges snaked its way north, toward San Francisco. The valley had been home since Los Alamos, and he'd loved every minute of it until yesterday, when his life had come to a shocking halt.

And why?

The indigo sky over northern California was slowly losing ground to the incoming rain clouds. Jake's mind flashed images of a life crushed by the fist of corporate greed. Or was it politics? Or was it something else, something he could not yet imagine, that had come and destroyed his world?

Explosion not an accident.

Those simple words had given the blast an entirely different meaning. If his mysterious friend was right, then someone was responsible. And that someone Jake intended to find and expose, if it was the last thing he did. He owed it to Sergei, to his team . . . to Kathy.

He stared at the shrouding rain clouds, at the display of headlights cruising down Highway 101. The buzzing drone of a locust, the distant hum of evening traffic, and the growling jetliners landing at San Jose mixed with the sound of his own breathing.

Jake saw it all, heard it all, and thought of Kathy, of the precious moments they'd had together, moments that now didn't seem long enough. If he could only turn back the clock, have a second chance to be with her, make up for the lost time. . . .

And the rest of his team . . . *Sergei.* . . .

Jake thought about his Russian colleague as another jetliner made its final approach into the airport, its landing lights piercing the darkness, its distant silvery fuselage reflecting the vast sea of city lights below. Gripping the leather-wrapped steering wheel, he followed the plane all the way down as he remembered the gentle giant that was Sergei Iyevenski. Large but solid, with a head probably twice the size of Jake's, hands that would be the envy of any football player, and an intelligence that had made him one of the top scientists in the world, the Russian biochemist had reminded Jake of the father he barely remembered. Iyevenski had even been instrumental in Jake's relationship with Kathy. It was Iyevenski who'd helped the lovebirds get over some of their fights in ways that were uniquely his, like the time when—

Jake jerked as the phone rang. Picking up the unit and pressing it against the side of his head, he said testily, "Hello?"

"Mr. Fischer?" a young male voice asked. Jake could hear conversation in the background.

"Yes . . . that's me."

"Yes, sir. I'm calling from the Fish Market over in El Camino to confirm your reservations for two at eight o'clock tonight."

"Reservations?" he said aloud without really thinking, caught by surprise.

"Ah . . . yes, sir. Your wife made them earlier today. You *are* Jake Thomas Fischer, are you not?"

"Yes, yes," Jake responded, certain that he had made no reserva—

"Well, sir? Will you be joining us for dinner tonight?"

"Yes," he responded. "I'll be there."

"Thank you, sir. We'll see you at eight."

The line went dead. Jake hung up the phone and stared at the nearing storm clouds, his mind wondering if this was all some kind of setup.

Jake's hawkish face hardened as he sat back in the bucket seat of the Bronco.

Am I walking into a trap?

But what about the dead killer in the house?

A plant?

No, it can't be! Otherwise why the dinner reservation game? Why not just kill me when I go home?

Jake tried to convince himself that this "friend" had to be for real. Otherwise nothing made sense. But then again, nothing had really made any sense since Kathy's mysterious disappearance and even more enigmatic reappearance minutes after he'd left to go looking for her.

Smoke and mirrors.

He drummed his fingers against the steering wheel, the reality of his situation sinking in, his sensible side telling him this would be best handled by the police but definitely *not* by him.

The Fish Market.

Jake knew the restaurant well. It had been one of Iyevenski's favorites. The large Russian loved mussels, clams, oysters, and American beer.

Sergei.

Bastards!

Frowning while turning the ignition, silently swearing revenge against those who had taken so much from him, Jake Thomas Fischer put the Bronco in gear and slowly steered it out of the parking lot. He had a meeting in one hour at a restaurant that was only fifteen minutes away, giving him plenty of time to find a place to hide the PCMCIA hard-drive card housing the secrets of the F1 chip, secrets someone had deemed valuable enough to justify the termination of twenty-two people.

A mile away, Sonya Wüttenberg hung up the phone after leaving a short message on Jake Fischer's home answering machine, which the FBI agent suspected was being monitored not just by the FBI, but also by Titov's men.

7

GUARDIANS

Greater love hath no man than this, that a man lay down his life for his friends.

—John 15:13

Menu in hand as he sat at a corner booth in the crowded Fish Market, Jake Fischer was too jittery to read it. The scent of grilled fish and boiled shrimp failed to soothe his frayed nerves as his eyes swept the lively place. The steady hum of dinner conversation mixed with the incessant footsteps of waiters walking over hardwood floors, the clatter of silverware and plates as a busboy cleaned up an adjacent table, and the distant sound of a baseball game playing on three screens hanging over the bar at the front of the restaurant. Yellowish light came from a spotlight above his booth, and smooth jazz flowed out of the dark ceiling.

Jake remembered being here many times with Sergei Iyevenski. In fact, he remembered the very first time he'd brought the large scientist to the popular restaurant. Iyevenski's bulging eyes had nearly popped out of their sockets when he was served a huge plate of mussels followed by two dozen oysters—food Iyevenski had consumed in the time it'd taken Jake to eat a small shrimp cocktail.

His gaze quickly traveled from face to face, businessmen, college kids, couples, families. He looked for a pair of eyes that would show a trace of recognition. *An unfair advantage,* he thought. His "friend" knew what Jake looked like but the opposite, to Jake's growing displeasure, did not hold true, forcing him to inspect every man that walked through the French doors at the front of the restaurant.

But how do I know it's a man, this friend of mine?

As Jake considered the question, a tall, slender woman with porcelain skin, firm arms, breasts high and full under a plain black T-shirt, and short blond hair that fell at an angle across her forehead walked into the restaurant. The startlingly attractive woman paused, broadcasting a regal certainty, drawing the eyes of a small group of businessmen waiting for their table. She turned toward the bar, sat on a stool, and pulled a cigarette from her small purse, wedging it between two fingers as she leaned over the wooden bar. A bartender instantly approached her, a cheap plastic lighter leading the way as he reached across, lighted the flame, and held it steady under the cigarette. She took a drag and gave the bartender a slow female wink. Her mouth, a bit generous for her face, but highly provocative, parted as she raised her chin and exhaled the smoke into the wineglasses hanging upside down from an overhead rack. The blonde set the cigarette in an ashtray, opened her purse, and removed a compact. Ostensibly checking her makeup, she angled the small mirror to the left and then to the right, checking the crowd behind her, before putting it back in the purse and taking another drag of the cigarette.

Casually running a red fingernail over her cheek while sitting sideways on the bar stool, the woman inspected the other half of the restaurant, shapely legs inside her tight jeans crossed as she scanned the crowd with her catlike eyes, which displayed a curiosity that made Jake suspicious.

The light-colored eyes—green eyes—moved toward Jake, who quickly dropped his gaze to the menu, elbows planted on the table. He sensed her stare. She was studying him. He could feel that, somehow. Perhaps it was just his imagination, or maybe his situation had honed his senses to the point of near-madness.

His breath suspended, Jake's mind began to race. *Is that my friend? Was she really inspecting the crowd with that compact, or am I imagining—*

"Sir?"

Jake Fischer jerked at the female voice. A waitress. His menu dropped on the table, nearly tipping a glass of ice water next to the salt and pepper shakers.

"I'm sorry, sir. I didn't mean to—"

"It's okay," he said, raising his gaze to the bar, finding the woman gone. He leaned forward, quickly scanning the restaurant.

She's gone!

"Sir?"

Jake turned his attention back to the waitress, a brunette dressed in a khaki uniform and white apron and holding a small pad and pen, her brown eyes giving him a puzzled look. "I still need a few more minutes," he said, pointing to the open menu resting on the checkered tablecloth while laboring to control his breathing.

"A lady at the bar asked me to give you this," she said. A hand with long, unpainted fingernails held a small yellow envelope a foot from Jake's face.

Jake took it and thanked her, waiting until she had walked away before tearing it open with trembling hands, his heartbeat and rate of perspiration rocketing.

A handwritten note:

MEET ME BEHIND THE RESTAURANT IMMEDIATELY. CAREFUL. WE'RE IN EXTREME DANGER. A FRIEND.

Jake began to feel light-headed and realized he had stopped breathing. Expanding his lungs with stuffy, cigarette-stained air, however, didn't help. He needed fresh air, felt the urge to breathe in the cool California evening. But he could not move, felt a form of paralysis sweeping over him.

Careful. Extreme danger. Careful.

What does that mean? Is someone here going to try to kill me? And how do I be careful? What should I do? Slowly walk out? Run out?

Then Jake saw an Asian man walking into the restaurant. He was of medium height, stocky, with long black hair tied in a ponytail. He wore jeans and a tweed jacket over a white T-shirt; a large gold earring on his left ear reflected the dim overheads. Keeping his right hand inside his jacket, the Asian scanned the crowd, dark, angled eyes flashing instant recognition when they reached a terrified Jake Fischer, who felt his feet glued to the hardwood floors.

Jesus! I can't move!

Using the crowd well, excusing himself through the large group of businessmen waiting for their table by the hostess's station, the Asian moved in Jake's direction, his dark eyes fixed on Jake like a predator looking out from the bush, his intentions clear, his determination strong.

Jake heard a noise to his immediate left, large metal doors swinging open as a young waiter hefting a tray full of dinner plates left the kitchen and rushed toward a table of six halfway between the oncoming man and Jake.

The strategy came to the former wrestler in a flash, as the Asian, like a running back abruptly rushing through the line of scrimmage, shoved the waiter aside while gracefully moving around him, sending him crashing over his patrons in an ear-piercing noise of shattering glass and plates mixed with the blood-curdling scream of a woman. In the same fluid motion, the Asian pulled his hand from the coat, revealing a black pistol with a bulky cylindrical extension attached to the barrel.

"Everybody down!" shouted the Asian in unaccented English

as he swung the weapon in Jake's direction. At the same instant, two men in business suits sprang to their feet while drawing their weapons and turning them toward the incoming Asian.

"FBI! Freeze!"

Two muted spits from the Asian's weapon and both FBI agents arched back, disappearing beneath the sea of tables and frightened patrons.

Fortunately for Jake, havoc set in. The panicked crowd, instead of ducking for cover under tables, almost in unison stood and raced toward the exit, stampeding past the gunman, giving Jake the precious seconds he needed to make his escape.

He forced himself into action, overcame his paralysis, his self-preservation instincts overpowering his fear. He shot left, lurching between two tables of horrified patrons surging to their feet, getting ready to follow the mob crashing open the French doors.

His stomach cramped from fear, Jake scrambled toward the swinging doors leading to the kitchen, going against the river of humanity exiting the building through the front. His left shoulder bumped into a silver-haired businessman going in the opposite direction. Jake heard the sound of a bee buzzing in his left ear, felt air rushing past his cheek. In the same instant a bullet plowed up the businessman's nostrils, his face erupting as Jake Fischer jumped away in terror, crashing against the swinging doors, blood and gray fluid splattered on his face, his neck, his tanned arms, staining his shirt. Finding himself kneeling on the wooden floor, a dozen screams drilling his eardrums, Jake momentarily lost sight of his assassin, which meant the assassin couldn't see him either with the crowd in between. Staying low, his heart pounding so heavily that he feared he might become sick, the blood mixed with bits of human matter on his arms and hands nauseating him, Jake Fischer pawed at the metal doors, propelled by his thrusting knees.

The buzzing sound came again. Two bullets walloped the left

door as he pushed the right one open, punching dime-sized holes in the aluminum skin, the hammering sounds assaulting Jake's ears.

Jake squeezed into the opening between the swinging doors and scrambled inside the kitchen, temporarily leaving the commotion outside, but aware that in seconds the Asian killer would burst in and take another shot at him.

Jake's frantic eyes searched the large room. Under a ceiling of hanging pots and pans, a four-foot pathway to his immediate left separated a row of sinks from the smoking grill station and the sizzling stoves. The sucking sound of the extractors overhead further shut out the chaos beyond the metal doors. Three men in white aprons and hats, frozen and staring at him, stood behind the stoves. They were all Asians, all wearing the same mask of horror Jake had seen painted on the frenzied crowd. A pair of equally shocked busboys leaned against the sinks, hands still holding pans of greasy dishes.

His heartbeat pounded in his ears, rattled his mind, his soul. Jake had to move fast, find a place to hide, escape his assassin. But how?

No time to analyze! Just do! Escape!

Beyond the sinks and mops and push brooms, Jake spotted garbage cans.

Trash cans . . . an exit!

Moving away from the doors, his logical side partly eclipsed by terror, Jake managed to take a step toward the garbage cans, toward the red exit sign. Ignoring the stares of the cooks and busboys, Jake took another step . . . and suddenly stopped, glancing back at the swinging doors and then again at the black garbage cans. If the Asian made it to the doors before Jake could reach the exit, he would have a perfect shot.

Instinctively dropping to a crouch with the same grace with which he had helped take UC Berkeley to two consecutive wrestling championships, Jake moved closer to the swinging doors, his upper lip lifting, doglike, over his white teeth, which contrasted sharply with the blood splattered on his face. Pulse rushing, fear clawing his insides so hard that his bladder muscles nearly failed, he waited.

The Asian burst into the kitchen, the swinging door fanning air past Jake, briefly swirling his black hair as he remained still, crouched on the tile floor, eyes following the large black weapon and gloved hand leading the way, sweeping the area.

All thought drained from his mind, the former wrestler felt a spring snap deep within him, and he lunged, screaming in animal rage, striking his opponent with the left elbow hard between the waist and the rib cage.

As the Asian dropped the weapon and bent forward, gasping for air, Jake Fischer, operating entirely on instinct, reached around the killer's waist from behind, slightly lifting him while using his own forward momentum to spin viciously around. Letting go of the assassin after completing one full revolution, Jake threw him against a cart full of dirty dishes, which overturned with a shattering crash.

Dropping his gaze to the silenced weapon, Jake picked it up as he raced over the slippery tile, slipping and falling once, his right shoulder burning from the blow, but quickly getting up and reaching the garbage cans.

A backward glance showed him the assassin on all fours amid broken dishes, shaking his head. Everyone else in the room, the cooks, the busboys, remained frozen, like wax figures, their wide eyes reflecting the terror that returned to Jake's mind at the thought of what he had just done, at the weapon he now clutched in his bloody hand.

Jesus!

No time to think! Get out of here!

The door. The exit sign. He saw it, ran toward it, reached it.

Get out! Get out!

He pushed the door with his left shoulder and staggered into the dimly lit employee parking lot behind the building. The smell of drain water and old fish struck him like a moist breeze, somehow sharpening his senses, making him aware of his new surroundings.

Blinking rapidly to adjust his eyes to the night, Jake sensed motion to his left and—

He gasped, the pain streaking up his torso sudden and excruciating. The weapon dropped from his quivering hand as another blow, this one to his face, made his knees give, and he collapsed, his back crashing hard against the wet concrete. The blurry silhouette of a man in an overcoat slowly walked in front of him and pointed a weapon at the dazed scientist.

A second assassin.

Tears filling his eyes at the crippling pain from his side, nose, and back, Jake Fischer realized he had been tricked. The first assassin had flushed him into a trap.

Raising an open palm at his opponent, Jake tried to speak but couldn't. The kick to his solar plexus had taken the wind out of him, forcing him to breathe in short sobbing gasps, the words wedged in his throat.

Two muted spits broke the brief silence. The assassin jerked back as though an invisible hand had lifted him a foot off the ground and flipped him in midair. The smell of gunpowder reached Jake's nostrils.

Silence.

Confused, dazed, the cloudy night spinning over him, Jake tried to focus on a dark, slim silhouette approaching him.

"Quick! Get up!" a female voice hissed in a foreign accent.

Confused, events developing too fast for him, Jake, holding his abdomen while feeling warm liquid trickling down his face, again tried to speak but failed to produce anything but a garbled noise, his breath caught in his lungs.

His head on fire, his mind fiddling at the edge of consciousness from the sudden blows, Jake saw a hand reach down for him, pulling him up, helping him regain his footing. Rising to a deep crouch, tears turning the evening into a translucent nightmare from which he wished to awaken, Jake slowly raised his gaze while blinking, bringing a pale, narrow face into focus.

The blonde!

"What . . . is—"

"Come," she said, helping him walk. "You must come with me. There are more of them."

The accent. German?

"Who . . . who *are* you?"

"A friend," she responded, the voice steady but tinged with emotion. "I am a friend."

A friend. Jake dropped his eyes to the concrete parking lot, where his would-be assassin lay sprawled face up, arms bent at unnatural angles, dead brown eyes staring at the dark sky, blood gushing out of fist-size holes in his chest and pooling around him.

"Why . . . me . . . why?" he mumbled, feeling nauseated, an invisible fist jabbing his ribs every time he inhaled, every time he took a faltering step, reminding him of lost wrestling matches.

"It is not you they are trying to eliminate . . . but what you know," responded the woman, an arm around Jake's back as the two of them, like a drunk couple, staggered toward the rear of the parking lot. "We must hurry," she added in her German accent. "The police will be here soon."

Blood dripped from his nose, mixing with that already drying on his face, and trickled down his chin and onto the concrete. He struggled to keep his balance in spite of the agonizing pain. He said, "Another . . . there is another one inside."

"I know," she replied. "I tried to warn you. What took you so long?"

Slowly, Jake gave her a blank look, blinking in bafflement. Was she *serious?* Had she actually asked what had taken him so long? Jake felt at most one minute had passed from the time he read the note to the time he first spotted the stocky Asian. Maybe that was too long in this business. Maybe he should have gotten up immediately after getting the note. But how was he supposed to *know* this? *I'm a damned scientist, for crying out loud!*

They reached a red Mercury Sable. The blonde helped Jake into the front passenger seat, closed the door, walked around the car, and got in. Reaching into the backseat, she tossed him a white towel.

"Here," she said, her mouth twisting into a sour grin as she pressed a hand against her side, right above her waist.

"Are you hurt?" he asked, watching her wince in pain while turning the ignition and flipping on the headlights. The glow from the dash instruments revealed an expression tight with strain on her china-doll face.

"I'm fine," she responded.

"You don't look right," he added, looking at her almost enigmatically.

"Trust me," she said, her stern tone suddenly holding a note of mockery. "I look better than you do."

Jake shrugged as he noticed several drops of blood falling on the clean towel in his hands. "I won't argue with that. Who are you?" he asked again, wiping his face, neck, and arms and pressing the white towel to his bleeding nose while the blonde drove them out of the parking lot. Police sirens blared in the distance. His side stung, the pain flaring every time he inhaled and expanded his rib cage, bringing back memories of wrestling matches, of sweaty bodies in tights grounding him against padded gymnasium floors.

"Sonya Wüttenberg," she replied, flashing Jake an FBI ID and a badge. "I am the friend whom you *definitely* want to have on your side at this moment." She reached for a cigarette and punched the lighter on the dash before glancing at her rearview mirror. "One who has saved your life twice today already."

"And for that I'm grateful," Jake responded, a bit annoyed at the woman's throwing that in his face. But she *had* saved his life.

The throbbing of his nose moved to first place as the pain from his abdomen and back began to recede when he forced himself to take shallow breaths. A sudden exhaustion descended over him, perhaps a side effect of the excitement of the near-death encounter. As the adrenaline left his system and his heart rate dropped back to normal, Jake got the unexpected urge to lie down and rest. His analytical mind, however, would not allow that until he got some answers.

"What does the FBI want with me? And who is responsible for what happened to my company? You said the explosion was no accident. Who did it, then?"

Snatching the lighter the moment it popped, the woman aligned the red-hot end with the cigarette wedged between her lips, lighted up, and took a long drag, exhaling through her nostrils while brushing the blond hair off her forehead. With her slightly oversized mouth she reminded Jake of the actress Lauren Hutton.

"You ask too many questions, Dr. Fischer. You should just be grateful that you are alive."

His head leaning back as he tried to stop the nosebleed, Jake said, "Wouldn't you ask questions in my position?, And by the way, the name's Jake."

Jetting cigarette smoke at the windshield, the FBI agent didn't respond as she steered the Sable through the evening traffic on El Camino Real Boulevard. Instead, she asked, "Did it really work?"

His eyes shifting to the control buttons on the door, Jake Fischer lowered the window, letting the cool evening air soothe his throbbing nose, which felt the size of Alaska.

"Did *what* work?" he asked, leaning his head forward and releasing the pressure on the towel, but keeping it on his lap while attempting to breath through his nostrils. It worked. No more blood dripped from his aching nose. Jake finished wiping his hands and forearms before throwing the towel into the rear seat.

"The F1. Is it as good as your press release indicated?"

"It's even better. Or I should say, it *was* better." Lowering the visor, Jake inspected his nose in the vanity mirror. It was red at the base but appeared barely swollen.

Jake felt moisture in the cool air caressing his bruised face. Traffic headlights sliced through the mistlike rain, and Sonya had switched on the wipers, whose slow back-and-forth sweep seemed in rhythm with the throbbing of his nose.

"It will look like a plum by tomorrow morning," she said, a slim wrist resting on top of the wheel, the burning cigarette wedged in between her index and middle fingers. "But do not worry. You will not be having many visitors."

"Excuse me?"

"I have to get you off the streets, Dr. Fischer—Jake. You are obviously a very popular man these days, and we cannot afford to lose you as we lost the rest of your team. You are a target, Jake, and that puts everyone around you in terrible danger."

Jake closed his eyes, the scene in the restaurant fresh in his mind. "Two men in the restaurant identified themselves as FBI agents."

"I know. They worked for me. They were good men who died to protect you, Jake. That alone should give you an idea of how much we value you," Sonya responded, sudden gloom shadowing her features. She took a final drag before rolling down her window and throwing out the butt, her short hair brushing back in the breeze as they drove in the center lane of the wide boulevard.

After a few moments of silence Jake asked, "Why is Uncle Sam suddenly interested in biotech for the computer industry?"

"Times have changed, Jake. Everyone is interested in it, especially the folks at Los Alamos."

"They weren't that interested five years ago."

Sonya grimaced. "We know about what happened at Los Alamos."

"I'm sure you do," he said, grinding the words out between his teeth as he leaned away from her and crossed his arms.

"Look . . . Jake. The Los Alamos of today is very different from the one you left several years ago. Our scientists are actively pursuing a suitable replacement for the silicon transistor, but they are still at least a decade away from making a serious breakthrough. They need your help."

Jake swallowed hard and turned his eyes to the blurred orange reflection of streetlights on the wet asphalt. "If Uncle Sam's so damned interested in the technology developed at FTI," Jake said, rancor sharpening his voice, "why didn't Uncle Sam protect it from whoever it was that destroyed it? And, by the way, who did it? Who's responsible?"

They approached an intersection just as the light turned yellow, splintering its liquid glare through the drizzling night. She floored the Sable, sneaking through before it turned red, and rolled up the window as she cruised through the heavy traffic leaving Silicon Valley. Jake also rolled up his window as the light rain turned into a sudden downpour.

"We're running an investigation right now," she said, switching the wipers to high speed. "But it is too early to tell. You can rest assured, however, that those responsible will pay for what they've done."

Lightning flashed, the thunder that followed descending as heavily as the rain hammering the roof and hood of the Sable.

Jake slowly shook his head as the next bolt flashed. "I'm sure the FBI has at least *some* idea who did this."

She shook her head. "We are hoping for a breakthrough in another day or so. There are over twenty agents currently in Palo Alto working on this." Again the hand went to her lower left abdomen, and a mask of pain covered her fine features.

"You *are* hurt."

The windows began to fog. Jake reached for the air-conditioning controls and switched the selection lever to force outside air through the slots on top of the dash. Looking back at her, he added, "Maybe I should drive."

"I said I was *fine*," she responded, flushed with momentary indignation, the hand quickly moving from her side back to the wheel. "Now, tell me, how difficult would it be for you to re-create the technology lost by the fire?"

Jake shook his head not only at her feeble attempt to hide the obvious, but also at her assumption that he would reveal the secrets of FTI so easily. "Next to impossible," Jake said, opting to keep his PCMCIA backup—which he had hidden in a locker at the San Jose Amtrak station—a secret for now.

Seeming to withdraw into herself for consultation, Sonya remained quiet for several seconds, then said, "We are on the same side, Jake. We just want to protect you."

He looked up, making real eye contact for the first time, long enough for him to notice a flicker of honesty in her jade-green stare as they reached the next intersection and stopped behind a white truck waiting for the light to turn green, a fierce blaze of lightning turning the night into day. "Are you working in conjunction with Lieutenant Miranda from the DA's high-tech crime unit? I already gave them my deposition."

"They are ordinary cops, Jake. They have no idea how far this goes or what the long-term implications of losing this technology are."

Jake threw his hands up in the air. "I don't get it. You tell me that the technology is incredibly important, yet you failed to protect it. Why didn't the FBI park a dozen agents around my building? *Damn!* Why didn't you contact us and warn us? We could have done *something*."

"We never expected them to destroy the—" She stopped, briefly closing her eyes, obviously chastising herself for letting that one out. "Never mind."

"What did you just say?"

She blushed. "Don't worry about it."

A mix of surprise and anger brought blood to his tanned face. "Wait a moment. I thought you just said you didn't know who did this. Now you're telling me that you *knew?*" Jake seethed with mounting rage, turning sideways in the seat, his left hand stabbing the air between them as the storm blew rain at an angle, pounding the side windows. "You—you're telling me that the FBI actually *knew* someone was going to try to steal my company's invention?"

Soft red suffused her cheeks. "Jake, please try to understand . . . it was more complicated than that."

Crossing his arms, cocking his head at the slender FBI agent, Jake retorted, "Try me."

Sonya shifted uneasily, obviously apprehensive. She spoke slowly, feeling her way. "Some of our sources . . . well, we got an unconfirmed message about someone in Europe having an interest in the biotechnology FTI had developed."

"And?"

"And we get many of those unconfirmed reports every day. We are not prepared to follow up on every one of them, especially when they come from a single source."

"When did you receive the warning?"

"A few days ago."

Jake shook his head. Things just weren't adding up. "Hold on. Let me see if I've got this straight. First you told me that the FBI's currently running a full investigation, right?"

She nodded.

"With twenty agents in the area, right?"

"Look, Jake—"

"Just answer the question."

She gave him another nod.

"And now you just admitted to receiving an unconfirmed warning three days ago."

"Yes."

"Well, I may not be in the intelligence business, but I believe that you just contradicted yourself. If you received this warning only three days ago and you normally don't follow up on such information, then what are twenty FBI agents doing here?"

"We deployed them as soon as we got news of the fire."

"No way. The fire's less than a day old, and the initial report from the fire marshal doesn't mention arson. You knew, Sonya. The FBI knew but chose to do nothing about it," Jake said, his voice cold.

Biting her lip, Sonya awkwardly cleared her throat, increasingly uneasy under his scrutiny. "I . . . the FBI is here because we're concerned about the well-being of FTI, Jake."

"Please . . . you're insulting my intelligence." Jake chuckled bitterly and shook his head as lightning splashed the interior of the sedan with blinding white light.

"Look, Jake," she continued, her voice conciliatory. "By the time we got the report it was too late. We couldn't prevent this unfortunate tragedy. I wish it could be different, I really do, but we are where we are, and there is nothing you or anyone else can do to change that."

"C'mon, lady," Jake said, his impatience quickly mushrooming. "Who do you take me for?"

"I'm telling you the FBI did everything it could to prevent the explosion, Jake. But there just wasn't enough time to set up a proper defense before the explosion," she said, her voice carrying an edge.

"And I'm not convinced that you're being honest with me."

The silky face turned in Jake's direction, large green eyes shooting him an admonishing glance. "You don't understand, Jake," Sonya said. "This goes much deeper than just what happened here. There is—"

"A larger picture that I don't understand?" he interrupted as they approached a red light. "Well, let me tell you what I *do* understand. Less than twenty-four hours ago my team was murdered. Do you understand that? Murdered, Sonya! Killed! Butchered! Twenty-two people, some of them very close to me. Now they're all gone, dead, and so is my company, my invention— my fucking life! Can you understand that? Can you get that through your thick FBI skull?" Jake put a hand to his forehead and slowly shook his head.

Briefly closing her eyes as they reached the stoplight, Sonya put a hand to his shoulder, her eyes under the blond hair falling across her forehead taking in Jake Fischer. "I'm really sorry, Jake. There's nothing I can tell you that will change what has happened. But there's much we can do together to catch those who did this."

Jerking his shoulder away, Jake retorted, "Don't touch me, please. Right now I feel nothing but contempt toward your agency. You think I'm foolish enough to believe what you tell me? To think that you haven't known for some time about this and *chose* not to warn anyone! People *died,* Sonya! Do you understand that? Or is that not part of your *big picture?*"

"Jake . . . I don't know what—"

"I think I've heard all I care to hear from you!" Jake barked, unable to control himself any longer. "You let someone out there kill my team, destroy my plant, and now you're keeping me alive because you want to know if I can turn the secrets of my company over to you! How's that for grasping the *big picture?*"

Silence, broken by the crack of thunder as Sonya stopped at the next light. Without warning, Jake opened the door and bolted outside, the rain streaking his face.

"No! Wait!" Sonya screamed.

Jake shut the door on the FBI woman, splashed across two lanes of bumper-to-bumper traffic, earned a few horn blasts from angered drivers, and finally reached the sidewalk, his heart pounding, the cold rain drenching his shirt and jeans, soaking through to his skin.

Blinking through the storm, the wind stinging him as he charged through the rain-shrouded night, Jake felt the adrenaline sear his veins. He turned his face to the sky, letting the rain wash his eyes, his nose, his face. The cold air stinging his nostrils, his ribs aching, his mind screaming, Jake reached the next intersection and turned the corner, running parallel to a large business park, two-story steel-and-glass structures separated by well-kept lawns, colorful gardens, and recently groomed pines, all under the yellowish glow of floodlights piercing through the storm. He remembered the place. One of his equipment suppliers had a sales office here, in one of the buildings across the lush landscaping.

Ignoring the hammering of the rain, Jake kept running through the deserted streets, never once glancing back to see if the woman was following him. Only his splashing shoes and the natural sounds of the storm filled him, enveloped him, carried him away from this world of uncertainty, of betrayal.

The FBI knew! . . . Bastards!

He ran in spite of his burning lungs, his protesting ribs, his—

The grass by his feet suddenly erupted in a cloud of mud, the explosion preceded by what had sounded like rumbling thunder. But there had been no lightning before the thunder. It had to be . . .

Gunfire!

Another shot cracked through the night, through the rain coming down in slanted, layered sheets. Another explosion of grass and mud.

Perplexed, Jake shot into the narrow strip of trees between two buildings, losing himself in the waist-high bushes, the low branches of a pine brushing him as he rushed across, emerging on the deserted parking lot at the other end.

Jake Fischer felt exposed under the floodlights gleaming down on him like an actor on a stage. Could the shooter see him through the storm?

But who's shooting at me? Sonya? Is she trying to kill me because I wouldn't cooperate? Was that my only choice?

A blaze of lightning followed by shuddering thunder, and two bullets ricocheted off the wet pavement as the unseen killer adjusted his fire. Sensing that in seconds a bullet would find its mark, Jake raced back into the bushes, his sneakers sinking in the mud, his head turning in every direction, looking for his pursuer but seeing nothing through the rain.

How can the killer see me?

Puzzled, angry, cold, Jake dropped to a deep crouch and ran parallel to the line of bushes, using them as a shield against an enemy equipped with gear that magically enabled him to see through the torrential rain.

But who's shooting?

No time to analyze, Jake! Run!

And so he did, remaining in a crouch, running for several hundred feet along the strip of plantings until he reached the end of

the business park, which butted against an undeveloped area by
the foot of the mountains.

Trees, woods . . . protection.

His analytical mind told him to continue, to lose himself in the
woods, where he would be safe.

Lightning strobed, lighting him as his burning legs carried him
from unyielding asphalt to soft, muddy soil. He reached the trees
and immersed himself in the ocean of dark evergreens until the
shimmering lights from the business park faded out completely.

Pausing in the darkness, Jake waited, listening for footsteps,
looking for figures looming in the darkness, but only the whin-
ing shrieks of storm winds and the frequent lightning and thunder filled his senses, making him believe he had lost his pursuer.

Time.

Jake waited, cold, beginning to shiver as the rain beat down on
his immobile figure huddled among the trees. He had to wait, had
to be certain.

But how long was long enough? How long was that killer willing to wait it out? An hour? Two hours? Until daybreak?

Jake wasn't sure. He actually wasn't sure about anything anymore. Had he made a drastic error in running away from the FBI?
Was the Bureau his only friend?

But she told you she knew about the nearing threat! his analytical mind insisted. *The FBI knew and did nothing! NOTHING!*

Don't trust them, Jake! Don't trust the FBI!

Then who can I trust? Who can help me?

Jake would have to wait for the answers to come to him. In
the meantime, he had to find shelter, had to get off the streets
and regroup, to put his engineering mind to good use, to think
logically through this nightmare and come up with a plan of action.

Just like in engineering or business, he thought. A challenge was presented, options were discussed, a plan of action was generated, and a team was identified to execute the plan. If market conditions changed and the goal moved, new options were discussed, a new plan generated, and the team shifted direction and went after the new target.

A team. A team of one.

He began to move. Towering pines funneled streams of rainwater onto him as he ran through the California woods like a crazed animal, struggling to survive, willing to fight to earn the right to live, determined to exact revenge from those who had wronged him, who had wronged Kathy.

For a brief moment her face flashed in his mind. Hugging himself, Jake breathed deeply as he continued to run, remembering her warm embrace, her soothing words, the love she felt for him . . . the love that was gone forever.

Feeling terribly alone, tears assaulting his eyes, Jake knew then there was no turning back. He would seek help, he would learn the ways of this alien world, he would adjust, adapt, improvise, overcome any obstacles, just as he'd done in the cutthroat world of high-tech business, just as he'd done all his life. He'd just survived tonight—twice. He would survive again.

Jake Thomas Fischer would win, or he would die trying.

Drenched and nearly out of breath, her side wound screaming obscenities as she knelt before the man lying facedown in the bushes, Sonya Wüttenberg inspected the bullet hole in his lower back, the one blown by a hollow-point round from her Glock 19 automatic. Dark blood erupted from the inch-wide opening, staining his shirt, mixing with the rainwater streaming onto him from the redwood branches overhead.

Sonya shook away the alien sorrow filling her as she tucked her hands under the man's heavy frame and flipped him over, relieved to see that the blond with the long, deeply seamed, blood-less face was still alive, relieved to see his mouth move as he breathed in short gasps.

"I can't . . . I can't move my legs," he whispered, quivering lips displaying the fear of a shattered spine.

The former Stasi operative holstered her automatic and cupped his face. "The Kardinal betrayed you," she said in a voice without inflection, looking deep into the owllike stare of this frightened middle-aged man who suspected he had been paralyzed. "He sent another team to terminate you."

"No . . . impossible . . ."

"I speak the truth. I saw them. Two men in gray overcoats. One shot you and the other went after Fischer. I can help you get even, avenge your death. But I need information. I need to find the Kardinal."

"You . . . you lie!" He coughed bloody foam before taking a deep breath through his flaring nostrils.

"Tell me where the Kardinal is. Tell me and I'll kill you quickly. Resist and my people will force it out of you with a blowtorch and a pair of pliers."

"My legs . . ." the man whispered, blood oozing out of his mouth. "I can't feel . . . them. I—"

Sonya slapped him, reaching down and pulling a stiletto from a nylon leg holster under her jeans. "Tell me!" she demanded, bringing the dagger up to his right eyeball, the steel edge glistening in the night. "Tell me or I'll carve your eyes out of your face!"

The man died a few minutes later, but not before the seasoned operative had extracted the information her government needed. Her plan had worked. Titov's men had been monitoring Jake Fischer's home phone, and they had come after him—just as Sonya had hoped.

Sonya Wüttenberg left the blond there, to be found by some morning jogger or a paper boy. But it would not matter, for the professional killer carried no identification, only his weapon and two thousand dollars in cash, money Sonya confiscated not out of greed, but to make the police believe he had been robbed. She also took the blond's stainless-steel Rolex and the Smith & Wesson .45-caliber automatic that had fallen on the grass after she had shot him in the back, just as he'd taken aim at Jake Fischer while the scientist ran into the woods.

Standing up and wiping her eyes and cheeks, her soaked blond hair stuck to her forehead, Sonya shook her head at the naive Fischer, feeling terrible about the way she had had to treat him in order to force him to run away from the car and draw the assassin, who had followed them from the Fish Market, away from Sonya. She knew, though, that Fischer would be safer running from the assassin, whom she could intercept, than staying with her when she would be forced to confront the killer.

The Fed briefly considered going after him in the woods and explaining what had really taken place, but chose against it. She would order a team to go looking for the scientist, but only after she conveyed the information Titov's gunman had released with his dying breath. Sonya remembered what she had been told, realized that the value of the information hinged on timing.

Perfect timing.

Every second now counted for the FBI agent. She rushed back to the Sable, which she had left in the business park. She ignored her throbbing wound, the stitches pulling on tender flesh, her priorities clear in her mind in spite of the heavy, sodden dullness that had descended over her.

What is the matter with you? You're a professional, dammit! Jake Fischer means nothing! Start acting like the seasoned operative you are!

Her disciplined mind resetting her priorities, Sonya reached her car, got in, and drove away while dialing the phone. The assassin had to be intercepted. The Kardinal could not reach his destination, could not be allowed to fulfill his contract—regardless of the consequences.

NATIONAL PHOTOGRAPHIC
INTERPRETATION CENTER,
WASHINGTON, D.C.
Friday, July 21, 11:30 P.M.

The telephone rang once, twice. Sitting alone at the head of the metal conference table, CIA Deputy Director for Operations Donald Bane reached for one of the phones crowding the table, accidentally tipping his coffee mug with his right elbow. Steaming brown liquid splashed the surveillance file spread out across the dark laminate surface.

"Dammit!" he barked, lifting his heavyset frame as he stood, catapulting his chair against the rear wall of the operations room.

Shoving papers and high-altitude photos out of the way with one hand, Bane grabbed the phone with the other and pressed it to his ear, silently cursing the assassin who'd kept him awake for the past thirty-six hours.

"Bane," he said in a hoarse voice tinged with exasperation while shaking coffee droplets off the glossy surface of an eleven-by-fourteen photo he had printed just ten minutes ago.

"Paris, sir," came the distant voice of Sonya Wüttenberg through the secured line. "I have one source claiming the Kardinal and the cargo are heading for Paris."

Paris! The data collected by the U-2R flying over the coast of Spain while tracking the Gulfstream jet forty thousand feet below told Bane that Paris was definitely within the realm of possible destinations of the assassin and his stolen cargo.

"What about Fischer? He is still in danger."

"I'll order a team to go after him as soon as I hang up. . . . Where is the director?"

"Went home to shower. He'll be back in an hour."

"I'm getting on a plane to Paris," Sonya said. "Please let him know. My legats need me over there."

"All right," Bane said. "I'll pass that along."

Hanging up and redialing, Bane started to bark orders to his subordinates in Langley, who immediately alerted the Paris station. Then he called Roman Palenski, who'd just come out of the shower.

The Kardinal was coming.

BERLIN, GERMANY
Saturday, July 22, 5:00 A.M.

The phone rang once, twice. Johann von Hunsinger, German minister of industry and commerce, reached over the warm body of a female assistant he'd hired only the week before and grabbed the telephone.

"Yes?"

"We're on our way," came the distant voice of Hans Bölling. "The package will be delivered to us in a little over an hour."

"Will you be attending personally?" asked von Hunsinger, his eyes on the exposed breasts of the sleeping blonde, whose name he couldn't quite recall at this hour.

"No. But my son will. He is leading the operations department."

The German minister smiled. "All in the family, Hans?"

"Yes, Herr Minister. He is already a better spy than his old man."

"Good," von Hunsinger said, his mind clearing. "Call me when it's over."

"Yes, sir."

The line went dead. Johann von Hunsinger replaced the phone on its cradle and tried to go back to sleep but couldn't, not when he was so close to delivering his Deutschland the technology of tomorrow. Today.

8

OLD WISDOM

Learning acquired in youth arrests the evil of old age;
and if you understand that old age has wisdom for its
food, you will not so conduct yourself in youth
that your old age will lack for nourishment.

—*Leonardo da Vinci*

PARIS, FRANCE

Saturday, July 22, 6:17 A.M.

The rising sun stained the City of Lights with orange and yellow, swallowing the glittering streetlamps illuminating the Champs Elysées. The legendary boulevard ran from the Arc de Triomphe to the Place de la Concorde, the open square where, in 1793, the Directorate of the French Revolution erected the famous guillotine, which beheaded 1,343 victims over a period of two years, including Louis XVI and Marie Antoinette. Beyond the pink-granite Egyptian obelisk, standing seventy-five feet tall in the center of the square, the lush gardens known as the Jardin des Tuileries led the way to the Louvre.

Far to the north was Montmartre, dominated by the Sacré Coeur Basilica. The monumental church, completed in 1910, with its many cupolas and center dome rising 262 feet, was very much a part of the Paris skyline.

A few blocks southwest of the white basilica, slowly making its way down the Boulevard de Clichy, a black Mercedes-Benz sedan with dark-tinted windows slowly cruised past the many restaurants, cinemas, theaters, and nightclubs that made this street the center of Parisian nightlife. The sails of the world-famous Moulin

Rouge still turned at this hour, long after patrons from all over the world had left the legendary French music hall and retired to the comfort of their hotels.

Paris slept at this hour. The deserted streets, damp with the night's dew, still wore the scars of the night before. Four-hour-old trash, debris from a night most tourists were unlikely to forget for years to come, mixed with dry leaves drifting down from the many trees lining the wide boulevard. The sight, however, presumably meant nothing but work to the crew of a garbage truck slowly coming in the opposite direction from the Mercedes.

Three garbagemen, armed with wide shovels and dressed in gray jumpsuits, gloves, and black boots, hung off the sides of the truck. Quickly springing to life and leaping to the street, they began scooping up plastic cups, paper plates, beer and soda cans, crumpled cigarette packs, and everything else the lazy tourists had failed to deposit in the ornate garbage bins located every twenty feet along the boulevard.

From the front passenger seat of the Mercedes, the oversized hood of his navy-blue nylon windbreaker hiding his bearded face, the Kardinal took a deep breath of cool morning air, made the sign of the cross, and put his rosary away, ending his morning prayers, which today he dedicated to the uneventful completion of his noble cause against the American infidels.

Wearily, he studied the street, the clubs, and the cleanup crew before lowering his bloodshot eyes to the Omega watch half covered by the windbreaker's sleeve. The exchange had been set up for twenty past the hour, just thirty seconds away.

Yolanda Vasquez drove the sedan that had been waiting for them at Charles de Gaulle Airport when their transatlantic flight arrived.

The Kardinal shoved the archive tape into a small, padded manila envelope and sealed it, then turned around and glanced at the two operatives escorting him this cool and breezy morning, who were flanking Sergei Iyevenski.

"Uncuff the infidel, put this package in his pocket, and put a gun to his head."

One of the guards, wearing a pair of khaki pants and a yellow long-sleeved shirt and sporting muscles worthy of a championship bodybuilder, nodded, took the envelope, and shoved it into one of the large Russian's coat pockets. He then removed the cuffs. Sergei's blue eyes, mere slits of resentful rage, scorched his captors. His sailor hands, at the end of his grizzly-bear forearms, slowly rubbed the purplish lines encircling both wrists. The scientist gave the large pistol pointed at his head a disdainful glance before lowering his gaze to his lap.

Turning back around, the Kardinal looked at the oncoming garbage truck, now about fifty feet away, slowly making its way up the street, its crew hurrying to keep up with it while shoveling junk into its open side.

They're two minutes late, thought the Kardinal, his eyes following the second hand on the white faceplate of a watch he'd purchased a few years ago at one of the many luxury shops along the Rue Royale.

Titov-Escobar wondered what had gone wrong. Just ninety minutes ago, while flying over the Pyrenees Mountains separating Spain from France, the former Stasi boss had spoken with Hans Bölling, the director of the German BND, and confirmed the time and the place for the exchange. The Kardinal always conducted exchanges on common ground, which, as long as he was not dealing with the French intelligence service, usually meant Paris, where the assassin also happened to have many disciples.

He reached for the small two-way radio shoved in one of two cup holders between the bucket seats, brought it to his lips, and set the switch to Talk.

"Team check," he said into the black unit, ordering the four snipers set up on the rooftops on both sides of the street and the four armed men in a BMW parked three blocks away to check in. The team in the BMW responded first, followed by three of the snipers. The fourth sniper failed to report. A second check brought identical results.

Titov glanced at Yolanda, who winced slightly as if her flesh had been nipped. As the sunshine broke across her light-olive face, catching her jet-black eyes, the former Cuban air force pilot gave him a slight shake of the head. "Doesn't look good, *mi amor*. It could be a trap."

The assassin, staring back at the street with a combination of concern and defiance, said, "Appearances, my dear child, could be deceiving. It could also be a bad radio. We still have three men up there plus four more three blocks away. Do not forget that impulsiveness is the companion of ignorance. Do not also forget that the Lord is on our side, helping us battle the infidels, the wicked that corrupt the land." Titov's hands, however, instinctively reached for the Heckler & Koch MP5 submachine gun lying on the tan floor mat by his feet. He held his breath and seriously considered calling the exchange off. He could contact Bölling in a few hours and set up another meeting.

As he thought it over, the Kardinal watched the threesome shoveling trash into the moving truck, their lack of team coordination catching his professional eye. The crew seemed out of rhythm, lacked the fluid motions of a well-coordinated team. As the truck slowly moved down the deserted boulevard, the workers, instead of taking turns scooping up trash and unloading it into the side opening one at a time, tried to do it in parallel, constantly getting in one another's way.

At that moment, a blue Volkswagen van turned the corner and began to accelerate down the boulevard. It passed the garbage truck and then parked across the street, on the other side of the ten-foot-wide median separating the eastbound and westbound sides of the boulevard.

The Kardinal, although still apprehensive about the one sniper and the garbagemen's ineptness, released the breath he'd been holding, but not the automatic weapon. His hand had already flipped the submachine gun's safety while holding it between his legs, an action that prompted an already weary Yolanda Vasquez to pull out her own MP5.

Walking the fine line between useless paranoia and life-saving caution, he brought the slim radio to his lips and simply said, "Careful," then set it back in the cup holder.

The van's side door slid back, and a tall and slender dark-haired man in a gray business suit, wearing a pair of tortoiseshell glasses, emerged hauling a thick black leather case, exactly as Hans Bölling had described during their short conversation.

He looked at Yolanda once more. Her fingers fiddled with the weapon's fire-selection lever, her black eyes trained on the van, the point of her tongue slowly moistening her underlip. The Kardinal's gaze drifted to the MP5 in his hands, to the garbage truck, and finally to the slim, well-dressed figure walking toward the median.

Motioning to the two guards in the rear to move out, the Kardinal said, "It is time."

The bodybuilder opened the door, got out, looked up and down the boulevard, and, weapon pointed at Iyevenski, ordered the Russian out of the Mercedes. The second bodyguard followed, leaving Titov alone with the former pilot, who gave the Kardinal a sideways glance of concern. Titov kept his gaze on the departing trio as they crossed the street and reached the median, just as the man in the gray suit also reached the lawn-covered divider.

His mouth suddenly drying, his pulse rising in spite of decades of field work and years of reflection in a monastery, the Kardinal observed the cleanup crew going about their business without as much as a look at the four men on the lawn before he returned his attention to—

"Mira! Mira!" screamed Yolanda, pointing to the obvious.

The bodybuilder was down, rolling on the ground, and the second man escorting the Russian suddenly dropped to his knees, his chest ripped open by a marksman's silent bullet. A sniper from some vantage point, following tactics Titov-Escobar had used for years, had been waiting for them.

"Mierda! I knew it!" barked Yolanda as Titov reached for the radio and calmly ordered his team to jump into action.

Someone had crossed them, someone close to his network. Perhaps a leak in the BND. *Maybe in my own network?* he thought.

Operating on instinct, refusing to accept the possibility of betrayal by one of his trusted followers, the Kardinal pushed the door open and rolled away from the car, hugging the MP5. He stopped by the concrete steps leading up to a restaurant, iron-gray eyes searching the rooftops, finding his own men sweeping the area with their high-powered rifles, looking for a break in the pattern, for a disturbance in the rhythm of the skyline.

At that moment, the cleanup crew dropped their shovels and pulled out automatic weapons from underneath their bulky jumpsuits.

A trap!

A BMW raced down the street, a blurry, silvery shape rushing past the truck before coming to a screeching halt near the men in jumpsuits, inky smoke coiling behind the tires. Doors swung open and men with automatic weapons rolled onto the damp street, instantly engaging the fake garbagemen, who had sought cover behind parked vehicles. Multiple reports thundered down the street.

Titov's seasoned mind told him to eliminate the sniper first, and he began to pray. *Guide me, my Lord. Show me the way to defeat the infidel sniper. . . .*

As Yolanda Vasquez viciously kicked the door open and used it as shield, crouching behind it and firing at the fake garbagemen, a stray round punched a hole in the Mercedes's roof. At the same second one of Titov's men fell to his death from a three-story building across the street, next to·the Moulin Rouge.

"Thank you, Lord," the Kardinal whispered. The glint of glass reflecting the sun's wan light atop the Moulin Rouge across the boulevard marked the scope of the sniper. A man, dressed in black, hid behind one the sails of the famous music hall. His weapon pointed toward where Titov's sniper had been.

The conviction of his noble cause reinforced by another heavenly sign, the Kardinal took careful aim, lining the dark silhouette between the fixed forward sights and the rear adjustable sights of his German-made weapon, already set in single-shot mode. He fired three times. A man fell from the rooftop, still holding a large rifle in his hands. In the same instant, however, another of the Kardinal's own snipers also dropped from a rooftop.

Sergei Konstantinovich Iyevenski froze the moment the two brutes escorting him dropped to the ground, followed by the pandemonium of an exchange going bad. From his position in the middle of the boulevard, the large Russian saw armed men in jumpsuits huddled behind vehicles, exchanging fire with the pair in the Mercedes and the foursome behind the BMW. Men fell from rooftops.

Professionals against professionals. And I'm caught in the middle of it.

Iyevenski saw the businessman holding the briefcase stare back at him through the tortoiseshell glasses, eyes narrowed in a mix of fear and anger. Using his free hand, the well-dressed figure reached inside his coat.

Reflexes Iyevenski had not used in two decades resurfaced with shocking force. The Russian lunged, striking the man's abdomen with his right shoulder, hearing a large expulsion of air while hefting the man's slender frame off the ground with the energy of an angered bear. Letting go of him, Iyevenski catapulted him off the median, just as two men wearing black suits and hoods jumped out of the van bearing automatic weapons. The businessman landed headfirst, blood spurting over his face from a cracked skull, his hand clutching the pistol he never got a chance to fire.

Amazed at what he had just accomplished, the Russian scientist stared at his own hands, holding the black case he had unthinkingly wrested from the businessman, who now rolled away on the pavement, unconscious or dead.

As he tried to run away from this madness, Iyevenski saw the Hispanic woman, an assault weapon in her hands, take aim in his direction. The woman was trying to kill him!

Using the thick black leather case as a shield, Iyevenski clenched his jaws and closed his eyes. The report whipped through the morning sky, the hollow-point round piercing the case but not going through. The energy transfer shoved the attaché case against his groin, abdomen, and lower chest, pushing him off the median and against one of the black-hooded operatives racing away from the van. Iyevenski's larger mass was the clear winner over the slender operative. The Russian used the man to cushion his fall, ramming him against the pavement.

Groaning from the pain in his ribs and groin, the attaché case still in his hands, Iyevenski staggered off the crushed figure in black, who now lay next to the bleeding businessman. The second man in black turned his weapon to the Russian but did not get a chance to fire. A round in the face snapped his head back, sending him crashing against the side of the van.

Attaché case still in hand, Iyevenski reached for the unconscious businessman's automatic, fingers naturally curling around the handle of the Sig Sauer 9mm, then began running away from the small battle.

Multiple reports filled the boulevard, a few rounds shaving clumps of grass on either side of him while the former KGB operative zigzagged over the median, the sharp smell of gunpowder mixing with the stench of warm beer, urine, and mounds of litter. Old training, however, dictated he not turn around, not look at anything but his getaway route. His legs, following instincts long dormant but suddenly awakened, showed amazing elasticity. They would not stop running, would not stop carrying him away from a crossfire he had been lucky enough to survive once.

Smothering a groan, the bearlike man shoved the Sig Sauer into the small of his back, beneath the coat jacket that flapped in the wind, as he dashed past the Moulin Rouge. He got off the median, raced across the street, reached the entrance to the music hall, and continued east up the boulevard, quickly running out of breath but refusing to slow down.

Reaching the corner, panting, his blue eyes barely reading the street sign as he cut left, Iyevenski faced a cobblestone street flanked by one- and two-story masonry houses and fed by many alleys.

Rue Lepic, the sign had said. He ran up it, sweat pouring down his face and neck, his right shoulder beginning to ache. He allowed himself one brief, downward glance and realized he still clutched the black attaché case, the one that had saved his life, the one he suspected was to be traded for him. Opting to hang on to it for the time being, the Russian scientist continued to run up the street, ignoring his burning legs, his hammering heart, his exploding lungs, anxious to escape the pursuers he felt certain

would soon come after him. He needed a place to hide, tempo-
rary shelter where he could analyze his situation, figure out what
to do next.

Iyevenski lost himself in the maze of narrow cobblestone streets
making up the heart of Montmartre, his only reference point the
tall white dome of the Sacré Coeur, which he kept in sight, using
it as a beacon to avoid moving in a circle and getting caught by
the same men who continued to fill the Parisian morning with
gunfire.

The Kardinal silently prayed for strength and understanding.
*Why are you testing me, Lord? I'm just trying to be your instru-
ment of justice against the infidels.*

*The Lord God works in mysterious ways. Thou shalt not ques-
tion the ways of thy Lord.*

Accepting the will of his one true Master, the Kardinal caught
sight of the Russian disappearing around the corner as Yolanda
Vasquez and he returned the fire from one of the three garbagemen, the other two keeping the men behind the BMW at bay.
Angry eyes watched his last sniper fall, victim to a wicked enemy
who still controlled the scene from a secret vantage point. Next
would be the men by the BMW, one of whom was already bent
over the hood of the silver car.

Then he finally understood. The Kardinal was the instrument
of God. He had been spared the flames in Croatia to handle
God's work on earth *himself*. He could not depend on his followers to do it. He had to act as the leader of his flock, as the shepherd. The Kardinal was the hammer of God and the infidels the
anvil. Only he could pound the wicked into hell.

"The rooftops!" the Kardinal shouted with renewed strength
at Yolanda over the noise of the gunfire. "Watch them! I'm going
to draw his fire!"

"You're crazy!" she responded, black eyes briefly shooting Titov an admonishing glare. "He'll kill you!"

"Have no fear, my child! The Lord is my Shepherd!"

Blinded by his faith, gambling on the notion that snipers are superb shots at stationary targets but lousy on moving ones—particularly one as fast as Titov-Escobar—the hooded figure in the dark windbreaker lunged away from the protection of the Mercedes, firing the Heckler & Koch MP5 at chest level, racing up the street in a slight zigzagging motion, directing his fire at the men hiding behind parked vehicles on his side of the boulevard.

A round shaved the bark off a tree to his left, another ricocheted off the sidewalk. The Kardinal dove toward a large garbage bin, hiding behind the protection of an ornate green-painted iron pot, watching in satisfaction as Yolanda pointed her weapon at a brick building halfway down the block, letting go a half-dozen rounds. An unnerving shriek followed a man hanging from his waist out of an open third-story window, a rifle falling from his dead hands to the street below.

The Lord is by my side. Have no fear, Vladimir Titov-Escobar. The Lord is by your side.

Suspecting additional snipers, the Kardinal rushed ahead once more, charging toward the infidels who had dared interfere with his holy mission, mowing down one of them with marksman accuracy, flushing the other two into motion, giving his remaining men the opportunity to pick them off.

He silently gave thanks to the Almighty as his tactic worked. The two men raced for the cover of the large garbage truck but never made it, falling to the fusillade of rounds fired with deadly accuracy by the surviving members of the BMW team, and also by Yolanda Vasquez. The tall and slim Cuban remained in a crouch behind the sedan's driver side door, firing through the rolled-down window, gray smoke streaming out of the muzzle of her MP5.

Replacing a spent magazine with a fresh one, Titov-Escobar turned the sights of his weapon on the garbage truck, his gray, sharklike eyes misted with rage against the nonbelievers.

The Volkswagen van accelerated up the boulevard, disappearing around the corner. Titov, Yolanda, and the survivors from the BMW covered its escape by firing dozens of rounds at the garbage truck, flattening two tires, hitting the driver, spraying the inside of the windshield and side windows with blood.

The truck came to a stop just twenty feet from the Mercedes, flames spewing inky smoke that spiraled into the clear skies over the Boulevard de Clichy.

"Let's go," the Kardinal calmly said to the Cuban woman as he returned to the German sedan. A dozen people in robes or night-gowns ventured out of their homes and peered down the boulevard. "The Russian infidel. We shall find the Russian."

"I will kill the *puto* for trying to escape!" Yolanda shouted.

"No! You shall not! We need him alive!" the Kardinal shouted. He got behind the wheel, barely giving Yolanda enough time to jump into the car before he swung the large Mercedes around, the passenger-side wheels jumping the median, gouging furrows in the grass, driving Yolanda's head into the ceiling. Strengthening his grip on the steering wheel while flooring it, Titov-Escobar kept the vehicle from skidding as it came back down off the grass.

Rocketing down the boulevard, the Kardinal took his foot off the gas and wrenched the wheel sharply to the left the moment he reached Rue Lepic, the Mercedes fishtailing, threatening to go into a spin. Flooring it again, Titov straightened the rear, forcing the vehicle forward, feeling his stomach press against his spine.

Steel-belted radials spun furiously over the slick cobblestones, the vehicle racing up the street until Titov reached the middle of the block, where he pressed the brakes hard, the antilock mechanism safely halting the dark sedan without skidding.

Pulling down the windbreaker's hood, his sandy hair swirling in the light breeze sweeping down the narrow street, the Kardinal gazed at the many alleys, at the garbage bins lining the murky, narrow spaces between houses. The place was deserted, save for the few locals curious enough to venture into the street, who quickly retreated to the safety of their homes when the Kardinal jumped out of the car carrying his automatic weapon.

"He can't be far," he said to Yolanda Vasquez, who was inserting a fresh clip into her MP5. "Go that way," he ordered, using his MP5's muzzle to point into a deserted alley. "I'll drive around the block and try to cut him off. He shall not escape us."

The agile operative obeyed immediately, racing into the alley as the Kardinal got back in the Mercedes and floored it. The vehicle fishtailed until the tires gripped, gaining the traction required to propel it forward. Turning right at the next street, Rue des Abbesses, Titov stopped halfway down that block and got out, inspecting both sides of the street, looking, searching, *praying* to find someone he didn't think could be found in this neighborhood. Montmartre, with its many alleyways and rundown hotels separating the touristy Boulevard de Clichy from the Sacré Cœur Basilica, would make the perfect place for the Russian to seek shelter, especially after he opened the briefcase containing the BND's final donation, the balance he always received upon completing a mission.

Now he had lost the money and the merchandise!

The Kardinal closed his eyes when he spotted the tanned silhouette of Yolanda Vasquez emerging empty-handed from the alley, his mind searching for the divine words his imperfect soul demanded to remain in control.

Whom the Lord loveth He chasteneth.

The phrase repeated in his head over and over, again and again. He believed in it, gained strength from it; it renewed his faith in his cause. He had lost today but had lived to fight another day.

"The *puto* is gone!" shouted Yolanda as she reached the sedan.

The Kardinal simply said, "The end is not yet, my dear Yolanda. And only he that endureth to the end might be saved. We *shall* endure to the end. We *shall* complete our noble mission in spite of the obstacles erected by the infidels. The evil ways of the enemy have allowed the Russian to escape . . . for the moment."

The Kardinal looked away, in the direction of the distant sirens of the French police. The large Russian would eventually have to come out, attempt to leave Paris, and when he did, eyes would be on the lookout everywhere, including Métro stations, hotels, car-rental agencies, and airports.

No one escaped the Kardinal.

No one.

Except for her.

Vladimir Titov-Escobar used the discipline developed through years of isolation, prayer, and fasting to fling aside the sudden memory of Sonya Wüttenberg as he jumped back into the sedan. He reached for the two-way radio and ordered his surviving men to leave the area immediately. Then Titov and Yolanda, slowly, casually, drove toward a nearby safehouse.

Hiding in a deep crouch between two large garbage bins, Sergei Iyevenski, exhausted, his bruised ribs aching, turned the thick attaché case over, inspecting for the first time the inch-diameter hole in it. He rubbed a sternum that would have been shattered by the round absorbed by his handy shield, then flipped the latches and looked inside.

His eyes grew wide in astonishment. There appeared to be hundreds of thousands of deutsche marks in large denominations, and stock certificates for a variety of American, German, and French corporations. There were thick stacks of shares—Siemens, Dupont, IBM, Shell Oil, and Telekom, Germany's equivalent of AT&T. There were also various government bonds.

Quickly closing the case as well as his eyes, he leaned against a brick wall and took a deep breath stained with decomposed food, urine, and other odors he couldn't identify. Iyevenski wondered who had been willing to pay such a fortune for him. A fortune the magnitude of which he could not really calculate until he could inventory the securities and check stock prices.

Who did this?

The Komitet Gosudarstvennoi Bezopasnosti, had said the leader with the peculiar eyes.

But the KGB had died with the Soviet Union. It couldn't possibly be them, unless his old superiors now operated under a different name. Perhaps they were now integrated with the *mafiya,* the Russian Mafia, which, in addition to running the classic rings of prostitution and drugs, also capitalized on the proliferation of nuclear technology leaving Russia. But that argument didn't make sense, because the *mafiya*'s customers were not Russians, but wealthy foreigners, particularly those from the Middle East and South America. The mysterious man with the iron-gray eyes had indicated that Russia itself might be interested in the technology of the F1 chip—something Iyevenski found quite difficult to believe, because Russia simply didn't possess the infrastructure necessary to bring it into the world high-tech marketplace, as the United States could.

Frowning, as he heard the sirens of police cars converging at the crime scene and smelled the stench oozing from the garbage bins, Iyevenski realized that his former captor had not said that Russia actually *wanted* the technology, but merely that members of the KGB, probably now working for a third party, had been contracted to steal it for the benefit of someone who had yet to surface. And that someone could very well be a nation with the means to take advantage of FTI's invention. Nations like Japan, Germany, France, and even South Korea had the high-tech infrastructure in place to become world economic leaders in the twenty-first century with such technology.

While he considered the possibilities, Sergei Iyevenski also wondered what had actually happened to him. The last thing he remembered was going over a manufacturing report on the most recent batch of F1 disks that had come out of the helifurnace ten minutes before. The disks were on their way to a final cleaning bath prior to delivery to the test floor across the glass partition.

Then nothing. Not a damned thing until waking up on that plane.

Other sirens echoed across Montmartre, causing a commotion that brought a smile to his lined face. The streets were getting crowded, and a crowd was just what Iyevenski needed to escape, perhaps find the nearest Métro station and get himself to the other side of Paris, away from this madness. But first he had to find a place to change marks into francs. He also lacked identification, passport, driver's license, credit card—

"Chort voz'mi," he hissed in the darkness of the alley. *The money, you stupid Russian! You have the money!*

Iyevenski's smile widened. He had managed to escape the claws of the KGB right here in Paris, many years ago, with far less in financial resources than the currency inside that attaché case. This was Paris, where money could buy *anything.* He knew the city from his multiple trips to represent Russia at international conferences. He also knew the language from his KGB multilingual training. A surge of confidence told him he would prevail.

But he had to be cautious. Iyevenski's former captor and his client—the owner of the deutsche marks and stock certificates inside the leather case—would not give up easily. Iyevenski not only had the money, but also the archive tape in his pocket. He basically had it all, the buyer's money and the seller's merchandise. Iyevenski would have to depend on the training acquired from years working under the umbrella of the KGB, formulating a strategy not just to survive, but to win. In the KGB he had been trained to win, regardless of the consequences. And Sergei Konstantinovich Iyevenski, scientist, former KGB agent, and currently a hunted man, silently planned to win.

THIRTY THOUSAND FEET OVER THE ATLANTIC OCEAN
Saturday, July 22, 11:00 A.M.

Sonya Wüttenberg, sitting alone in one of twelve leather seats of the small cabin section of a leased Learjet she had boarded in San Jose, courtesy of Roman Palenski, stretched her slender frame. The droning hum of the turbines that had lulled her into sleep after the refueling stop in Boston now woke her up. She checked her watch and saw that she still had three more hours before reaching Paris.

Yawning and running fingers through her short, ash-blond hair, gently massaging her scalp, Sonya licked her palate, her mouth feeling dry and pasty. She reached for the half-empty can of soda on the seat's armrest, took a few sips, and set it back down. She yawned again, her green eyes scanning the spotless interior of the Learjet, decorated in a eye-soothing combination of pastels.

Briefly raising the shade of her small oval window, Sonya squinted at blue ocean and clear sky. Pulling it back down and rubbing her eyes, she stretched once again. Tired, nauseated, and with a side wound that refused to stop throbbing in spite of the mild painkillers and antibiotics she had religiously taken for the past forty-eight hours, the seasoned Fed closed her eyes, discouraged. This operation was not progressing well. In fact, so far she would call it an utter failure. Not only had the FBI failed to prevent the deaths of twenty-two Americans, the destruction of a corporation, and the robbery of precious technology, but her team in California had failed to find Fischer.

And on top of all that the operation in Paris to recover the lost technology—and with luck to eliminate Titov-Escobar—had not gone as planned. A CIA observer, posted on a rooftop two blocks away, had recorded the event, which had resulted in the deaths of three CIA officers and three FBI special agents from the Paris station. In a peculiar turn of events, however, Sergei Iyevenski had managed not only to escape his captors, but to do so with what appeared to be the payment for his delivery to a third party, the German BND. A hooded man, believed to be the legendary Kardinal, and a woman with an olive complexion had also escaped unharmed and were probably on the trail of the Russian. The BND was probably also in on the chase, for obvious reasons. Between the two pursuing parties, Iyevenski stood little chance of surviving without help.

And this was where Sonya Wüttenberg came in. Her new mission: to work in conjunction with what was left of the CIA Paris station and the FBI legat to rescue the Russian and use him as bait to draw the Kardinal into an inescapable trap, a trap Sonya feared the seasoned Titov-Escobar could easily reverse.

Icy dread twisted around her heart at the thought of confronting Titov-Escobar. The apprehension squeezing her throat gnawed at her confidence. Many years had passed since the fall of the Berlin Wall, since Titov-Escobar had escaped her trap in southern Germany. She was not the same operative, did not have the stamina of her younger days. Her body demanded more rest than the mission allowed. And the thought of facing her old instructor while not functioning at her best only added to her anxiety.

But mixed with the anxiety, flickering through it, Sonya also felt a mounting rage that hardened her pearly features every time Titov-Escobar entered her mind. Her lips thinned with anger at the thought of the assassin, the man responsible for the death of Ludwig Wüttenberg, her younger brother.

Sonya remembered the sidewalk café in East Berlin, recalled

the sunny autumn afternoon just outside the one-story red-brick building where her teenage brother had asked her to meet him during his frantic call the night before. Ludwig had mumbled something about getting a girl in his high school pregnant. Sonya had rushed to her brother's aid. She had walked across the cobblestone street, listened to the rock music piping through the outdoor speakers of the café, heard the noise of the afternoon traffic and the steady hum of dinner conversation from the patrons sitting at two dozen outdoor tables, watched slim waiters in dark uniforms negotiate the narrow spaces between tables as they served the thirsty and hungry crowd. And she had spotted Ludwig, alone, by the sidewalk, concern on the boyish face framed by ash-blond hair like her own. He wore loose blue jeans, polo shirt, and sneakers. She approached, wearing a sisterly smile. After all, what were siblings for if not to support each other in times like this?

But then came the shout, Ludwig's ear-piercing scream warning Sonya of the trap she was about to walk into, the trap set by Vladimir Titov-Escobar, sitting two tables behind the doomed teenager. In a blur, in the time that it took Sonya to realize the danger, Ludwig's chest exploded in a cloud of blood, propelling him forward, onto the street, right into the path of an accelerating sedan. She stiffened at the shocking sight, at the screams and the noise of screeching tires over slick cobblestones, at the rag-doll body of her brother bouncing over the hood, the windshield, the roof and trunk, finally landing on the street, head and limbs turned at grotesque angles. Abruptly shielded from Titov-Escobar by a surging wall of people, Sonya felt vomit reach her gorge, shook with impotent rage, anger lighting up her eyes as they met Titov's iron-gray stare the moment the assassin broke through the crowd, a silencer-fitted weapon in his hand. A cobblestone exploded by her feet with the sound of a hammer cracking stone as a round missed its mark. The professional in her quickly damming a torrent of emotions as wild as the stampeding crowd, Sonya used the crowd to escape, to run away from her slain brother, whom Titov-Escobar had used as bait, and who had sacrificed himself to warn her.

Ludwig.

Sonya breathed deeply as her jade-green eyes aimlessly gazed about the interior of the cabin, her hand reaching for the can of soda once more. Every time she thought about Ludwig, the face of Karla Valentinovna Naidenova also entered her mind.

A wife for a brother.

That had been the price Titov-Escobar had to pay for the death of her brother. Sonya remembered the fugitive couple racing through the woods of the Schwarzwald, Germany's Black Forest, after a CIA team she led had ambushed them on Route 317, just three miles from the Swiss border. The couple had shot their way out of the roadblock and raced into the woods, followed by Sonya and her team. Sonya remembered the chase, remembered the pleasant surprise of intercepting them a short mile from the border, could still see their shocked faces over the sights of her pistol as she stood in front of them, alone, her companions searching other sections of the large forest. Sonya had seconds to choose, a brief moment to decide whom she would kill first, and whom she might risk losing.

A wife for a brother.

And Sonya Wüttenberg had chosen Karla Valentinovna Naidenova, a woman who had joined the Stasi within a month of her. They both had been trained by Vladimir Titov-Escobar. They both had been assigned to West Berlin at roughly the same time.

Sonya remembered pointing her pistol at her former friend and classmate and pulling the trigger—in the process giving Titov-Escobar the precious seconds he had needed to vanish.

It had been an emotional choice, not a logical one. Her training had told her to eliminate Titov-Escobar first. But Sonya had wanted to *punish* Titov, make him feel the pain of losing a loved one, or loved *ones,* as Karla's autopsy later revealed.

A wife for a brother.

Seething with rancor, slender hands clamping the armrests of the tan leather seat, the turbine noise once again fading in the background, Sonya Wüttenberg slowly, icily, began to formulate a plan of attack, one she prayed the resourceful assassin would not be able to reverse.

CIA HEADQUARTERS, LANGLEY, VIRGINIA
Saturday, July 22, 9:19 A.M.

Roman Palenski, director of the Federal Bureau of Investigation, slapped the smooth mahogany surface of Donald Bane's desk.

"Dammit, Don! What in the fuck are we supposed to do now?"

The bald-headed director, his large frame elegantly dressed in a three-piece suit, pulled out a new cigar from his shirt pocket and bit off the end, spitting it into a wastebasket before sitting across the desk from the CIA's deputy director for operations and pulling out a silver lighter.

"Doesn't look good, Roman," said Bane, inspecting his fingernails, keeping a cool head in spite of the anger he felt at the loss of so many American intelligence officers. "Not only did the son of a bitch get away, but the Russian escaped, and we lost six men in the process, including the Paris station chief, whom I knew personally. Now I have to contact their families with the terrible news."

Crossing and uncrossing his legs while chewing on the end of the cigar, his fingers fumbling with the lighter, Palenski tilted his large head at Bane. "I also have the unenviable job of having to go back to my office and call the families of three agents. Damn, Don. What went wrong?"

"Simply put, Roman, we underestimated the Kardinal again," Bane responded with a straight face. "This one's going to be tough to explain. You'd figure we would have learned our lesson in California."

The seasoned men measured each other for several seconds be-fore Palenski said, "Sonya should be in Paris shortly."

Leaning back in his chair and looking over Palenski's head with a pensive stare, Bane said, "Yep. And she'll be our most ex-perienced operative. We lost our veterans this morning." Bane felt a headache coming and rubbed the tips of his fingers against his temples. Losing officers was the hardest pill to swallow in his po-sition, but one that over time Bane had learned to cope with. One way he dealt with such losses was by focusing on a plan to fix the problem that had caused the loss in the first place.

"I'm pulling some veteran agents out of London today," said Palenski. "How long before we can get them some experienced CIA help?"

Bane shared Palenski's concern. Those rookies needed local di-rection, and though the veteran female officer had what it took to turn havoc into order, she still would need some senior oper-atives to help her run the show smoothly. Bane had already con-tacted three offices, London, Berlin, and Rome, and ordered them to dispatch all available senior officers to Paris. Unfortu-nately, diverting field operatives without jeopardizing ongoing operations took time.

"I'm already working on it. We should have them in place in less than thirty-six hours," said Bane. "What about Fischer?"

Palenski shook his head. "Still no sign of—

The phone rang.

Bane saw that it was a call coming in through his superior's private line, forwarded to him as acting director of central intelligence. Bane closed his eyes. Very few people in the United States knew the number.

Picking up the phone and pressing a red button on the black unit, Bane said, "CIA. Donald Bane."

"Bane, this is the President of the United States. Do you recognize my voice?"

A shrinking feeling descended over him. He had dealt with a few presidents in his long career, but there was something about getting a call directly from the current commander in chief, the most powerful man in the world, that affected anyone, regardless of position and experience.

"Yes, Mr. President," responded Bane.

Roman Palenski leaned forward and made a face.

"Bane, I understand that the old man's still recuperating from surgery, which means you're still filling in for him."

"Yes, sir."

"Then I suggest you get yourself over to my office ASAP. I've just got a very disturbing call from the U.S. ambassador in France . . . something about a shoot-out in Paris that we might have been involved in."

Bane shook his head. *The damned ambassador!* Bane had planned to inform the president through the President's Daily Brief, which would also have included the recovery plan and current options. "I think I need to get over there right away, sir."

"One hour, Bane. I've also called Palenski and left him a message."

"He's right here, sir."

"Good. In that case I expect you both."

"Yes, Mr. President."

The line went dead, and Donald Bane suddenly got the urge to vomit.

BERLIN, GERMANY
Saturday, July 22, 2:30 P.M.

On the top floor of the Detlev-Rohwedder-Haus, Minister of Industry and Commerce Johann von Hunsinger, dressed in a pinstripe suit, sat behind his desk while browsing through a copy of the daily *Frankfurter Rundschau,* one of a dozen German papers he read every afternoon.

Leaning forward, he tried to kill the time before Bölling's call came through by reading about a failed third round of negotiations between the eighty-five thousand workers in the chemical industry of Rhineland-Palatine and their employers. The union of chemical workers was demanding an 8 percent pay increase to help offset the rising cost of living. The employers, however, struggling to remain competitive in a soft global market, could only go as high as 5.5 percent, an offer that was met by a large riot at one of the chemical plants. Local police had to intervene. Three rioters were killed and dozens more were wounded when someone opened fire on the police and the officers fired back to defend themselves.

Von Hunsinger sighed, his eyes reading the adjacent front-page story, about a large workforce reduction in Stuttgart. Mercedes-Benz and Porsche, faced with fierce competition from Japan and the United States, were cutting back the number of automobile exports this year. Over four thousand skilled workers would be unemployed before the end of the month.

Tossing the newspaper aside and standing, von Hunsinger paced the length of his spacious office in anger, chin up, hands behind his back. The German economy was at its lowest point in thirty years, and so far he had been unable to do a damn thing to alleviate the problem. And what was worse, not only was his department out fifty million deutsche marks in cash and securities, but he had nothing to show for it. The famed contract assassin who Bölling had promised would perform flawlessly had indeed shown a flaw: he had failed to do the job for which he had already been paid handsomely. In von Hunsinger's eyes the payment had been delivered to the Kardinal, who was supposed to have handled security during the exchange.

The phone rang. Checking his watch, the secretary walked to his desk, sat down, and picked it up on the third ring.

"Yes?"

"Herr Minister?"

"It is me. Any news?"

"Yes. We have been contacted by the Kardinal. A meeting has been set up," responded the distant voice of Germany's top spook.

"When and where?"

"In about thirty minutes at a nearby church. I'm supposed to come alone."

"I'm assuming you will remind this contractor of his responsibilities."

Silence, then, "Certainly, Herr Minister. It will be handled properly."

"I shouldn't have to remind you that we've already lost a fortune between the advance and the final payment."

"Do not forget the lives, sir. I lost my son because one of our organizations has a leak and someone tipped a third party."

"Then I suggest you plug it," von Hunsinger responded, without extending his condolences to the seasoned spy, figuring that those who signed up for that kind of work knew the risks involved. "And call me back after the meeting."

"Yes, sir."

"Good. Remember our priorities. We *must* recover the biotechnology, but without damaging our country's reputation. Our nation needs that chip, but we cannot allow this problem to be traced back to us. Understood?"

"Yes, sir."

Von Hunsinger hung up the phone, fuming at the thought of losing the perfect opportunity to jump-start the German economy. It would actually be far more than just a jump-start. Protein memory chips would propel Germany to the very top of the economic food chain.

But fear slowly mixed with his anger, fear of anyone higher than himself in the German government learning about the problem.

It has to be contained, he thought. *One way or another, it has to be contained.*

9 JUDGMENT

Judge not, that ye be not judged.
—*Matthew 7:1*

The midafternoon sun cast a glow through the stained-glass windows of the Saint-Germain-des-Prés church on the Left Bank, just two blocks from the Université René Descartes and across the street from the Café des Deux Magots.

Dozens of tourists in shorts and T-shirts soaked in the sun at the café's sidewalk tables. Waiters in black stood by tables tending to their customers, many of whom, unable to speak a word of French, simply pointed to the laminated menus in their hands as the waiters nodded and scribbled in tiny notepads. Soft music streamed from unseen speakers.

An emaciated man with thinning white hair, a white mustache, and a face scored with fierce, deep wrinkles, wearing a tan suit that hung from his coat-hanger shoulders, slowly made his way through the crowded streets, where tourists snapped pictures of one of the oldest churches in Paris, some sections of which dated back to the tenth century.

BND Director Hans Bölling steeled himself for another meeting with the Kardinal.

From across the street, hiding behind the bushes beside the church, Yolanda Vasquez slowly parted two shrubs and watched the old man cross the street, reach the curb, and wait as instructed. Next to her, quietly sitting on the dry ground while waiting to perform a job that would earn him a glassine bag of heroin, a junkie she'd found an hour ago in Montmartre turned his young, anxious eyes toward the smooth face of the former Cuban pilot.

Yolanda, who had already given the junkie a taste of what was to come—and a slap across the face when the young man had tried to grab her breasts shortly after their meeting in a dark alley— slowly brought a slim finger to her lips. The junky nodded, eyes filled with anticipation.

Kneeling on the soft soil, her blue jeans stretching as she sat on her ankles, Yolanda smiled inwardly. She knew how to handle men. She had been doing that for fifteen years in over a dozen countries, many of them, like Nicaragua and El Salvador, ruled by macho politicians and chauvinistic army officers. It never took long for a man to respect Yolanda Vasquez, particularly after taking a severe beating at the hands of a woman who belonged on a pin-up calendar instead of in a guerrilla camp or a backstreet alley. And it had not taken her long to gain absolute control of the junkie next to her.

Yolanda leaned forward again and inspected the street, watching Bölling slowly move up the side of the church and approach the steps. Turning to the junkie, she gave him a nod.

Like someone leaping away from a nest of scorpions, the twenty-year-old junkie sprang to life with a swiftness that surprised her. Kicking bits of mud as his sneakers sank in the soil, he darted from the bushes and rushed toward the unsuspecting Bölling, who was looking the other way.

The Cuban woman held her breath as the jackal-like figure reached the old man, frisked him, and shoved a note into his hand before rushing off to the reward waiting for him three blocks away.

No alarms followed. No sudden eruption of shadows or gunfire, no hastening footsteps from across the street, no accelerating vehicles turning the corner. Just a few tourists turning to point at the departing figure and his victim, who read the brief note, shoved it in a side pocket, and walked the twenty feet separating him from the steps at the front of the church.

The meeting rules had not been violated. Yolanda reached for her two-way radio and clicked the Talk button three times. After a few seconds she received three clicks in return.

Hans Bölling struggled to control his trembling hands, his racing pulse. He was too old to be doing this, but he found himself out of choices. Secrecy within the BND was in question. A leak had compromised the initial exchange, and he couldn't afford to send a subordinate to do this job for him, even when his heart was stricken with the grief of losing his only son. Bölling's only consolation was that his wife had died of cancer five years before. Otherwise this would certainly have killed her.

Briefly pausing to look both ways as the tourists turned back to their sightseeing, the old man went up the slate steps and pushed one of the two heavy wooden doors.

Inside, the air was much cooler than in the street, insulated from the scorching sun by four-foot-thick walls of stone. Two rows of wooden pews ran down the nave as far as the transept, where a large stone altar stood under the Gothic vaulted ceiling decorated with frescoes depicting the life of Jesus. The glazed limestone floor, alive at this hour of the day with the sunlight forking through the stained-glass windows along the walls of the nave and the transept, met sixty-foot-tall marble-inlaid stone columns supporting the thousand-year-old structure.

Hans Bölling made the sign of the cross, not because he was a Christian, but because he had been ordered to do so by the Kardinal, signaling that he wished to continue the meeting, and further confirming that he was alone and that, as far as the BND was concerned, the meeting had not been compromised in any way.

Slowly, keeping his head bowed as ordered by the words scribbled on the piece of paper now crumpled inside his pocket, the chief of the Bundesnachrichtendienst, Germany's federal intelligence service, made his way to the right side of the church, where five wooden confessionals lined a granite wall erected five centuries before Columbus first traveled to America.

The first two confessionals, themselves marvelous works of woodcarving, had a dimmed red light above them, meaning a priest sat in each waiting to hear confessions. The last three were empty.

Hans Bölling passed the first three and went inside the fourth one at exactly 3:20 P.M.

The Kardinal heard someone enter the confessional just as his Omega's second hand marked the twentieth minute past three in the afternoon. Exactly ninety seconds before, he had received confirmation from Yolanda Vasquez that Bölling had indeed come alone. So far no rules had been broken.

The Kardinal, wearing a dark robe and hood that cloaked his tanned face, continued to say the rosary as he moved the thick curtain separating the holy man from the common sinner, leaving only a translucent veil covering the foot-square opening at face level.

"*Angelus Domini,*" murmured the Kardinal, a Mauser 9mm pistol with a silencer screwed on its barrel clutched in his right hand, the rosary in his left.

"*Angelus Domini,*" responded the aging intelligence officer. "Forgive me, father, for I have sinned. It's been three years and twenty days since my last confession."

The code was completed.

"I apologize for the impromptu check outside, but I had to be certain," whispered the Kardinal.

"I understand. What I *don't* understand is how it can be that my country has already spent fifty million deutsche marks and not received anything in return," replied the old man, visibly shaken, in a tone of voice that made Titov-Escobar's eyelids drop halfway over the iron-gray eyes studying the quivering, wrinkled face from the darkness of the hood.

"It is my duty to give you results in return for your generous donations. I have no excuses," said the Kardinal, keeping his voice low and monotone. "But today—"

"Today you lost your credibility with our country!" Hans Bölling snapped, his rheumy voice rising above the level allowed by the implicit rules of this encounter.

"I may have lost my credibility with you, Herr Bölling, but if you do not respect the sanctity of this place, the sanctity of this meeting, you will lose your *life,*" the Kardinal hissed, pocketing the rosary before reaching for the hood. If he removed it, exposing his face to the aging BND spy, Hans Bölling would never see another face. He pointed the silenced Mauser at the man's heart.

"Nein—nein, Bitte. No, please. I beg you," replied Bölling, quickly lowering his eyes, not wishing to see the forbidden face. "I'm getting too impulsive and emotional in my old age. Forgive me. My only son was killed on the Boulevard de Clichy this morning. He was the one in the business suit. And I won't even get the chance to bury him next to his mother."

The Kardinal eased back on his seat, leaving the hood in place and lowering the automatic. He felt sudden sympathy for the aging spy. "My most sincere condolences on the loss of your child. We now have a common enemy, one who has caused us great pain. Some of my most trusted disciples also perished in the exchange."

Silence, broken by the church's bells announcing the half hour.

"What do we do now? My country still needs the package," Bölling said as the sound of the bells receded.

"The Russian infidel will be found. He is hiding in this city, and I have many eyes looking."

"The BND can help," said Bölling. "We have many resources inside—"

"No. Remember the leak—the reason we are having this con-

versation in the first place. I suggest you start looking for a trai-
tor in your agency. I'm certainly looking in mine. Right now I trust
only my inner circle of followers, whom I'm using to look for the
mole and also for the Russian."

"Very well," responded Bölling. "Do as you think is best, Herr
Kardinal, but also do remember our contract. Shoot me if you
wish, but I must tell you, with the utmost respect, that if the Russian is not delivered to the BND within forty-eight hours, you will
go delinquent on a contract for which you have already been paid
. . . *in full.* And even then, the European intelligence community
may never touch you again for fear of another Montmartre. In our
short-term minds, you're only as good as your last contract. And
your last contract is stained with the blood of my only son."

The Kardinal tightened his grip on the Mauser. He had killed
for far lesser insults, yet he felt a rare wave of compassion sweeping through him when staring at the BND officer in front of him,
old, wrinkled, quivering, already a widower, and now mourning
the loss of a son.

"And I shall live and die by the rules of our agreement," said
the Kardinal. "An agreement I intend to honor in spite of the unexpected difficulties. Now go, old man. Go in peace."

WASHINGTON, D.C.

Saturday, July 22, 10:30 A.M.

Although this wasn't Donald Bane's first visit to the Oval Office, the experience was still a humbling one. Everything about
the White House had been designed to intimidate its visitors. In
fact, the entire downtown Washington area had been built with
the purpose of impressing and humbling foreign dignitaries with
the power that resided within the boundaries of this city.

Donald Bane felt that White House energy working through
his nervous system, creeping into his gut, making him wish he

could go to the nearest rest room and vomit again. But the seasoned spy wouldn't dare move a hair until told to do so by the
president, who had not said a word since Bane arrived at the office ten minutes ago—aside from a brief greeting when shaking
hands, a courtesy the commander in chief also extended to Roman
Palenski, who now sat next to Bane.

The president remained behind his desk reading over some
documents, a pair of rimless spectacles hanging off the end of his
nose. Donald Bane glanced at the impeccably dressed Palenski,
who had been told to put out his cigar by a White House aide five
minutes ago.

Palenski gave him a shrug.

Sitting in one of two cream leather sofas flanking the fireplace
opposite the presidential desk, Bane discreetly looked around
the room, taking in the history of the place, his eyes finally returning to the president, still hunched over the documents in his
wrinkled hands.

An old president, observed Donald Bane, who'd actually voted
for the astute but aging politician two years ago, when the country had elected him over his far younger adversary.

The short, white-haired president, dressed in a fine silk suit and
maroon tie, stood and looked at Bane, inspecting the large acting
DCI with the determined stare of narrowed brown eyes which
he'd used to dominate his party. He then shifted his silent probe
to Roman Palenski, before checking his watch.

Looking worried, the president walked around his desk and sat
across from the intelligence officers.

"Do you gentlemen feel we did everything possible to protect
those men?" the commander in chief asked in a grave tone.

Palenski grimaced and looked away. Bane bit his lip in sorrow
while nodding ever so slightly. "It's a risky business, this intelligence profession, sir," the acting DCI said, feeling a sourness in

the pit of his stomach. "We never thought the party we were going to ambush would be as formidably armed as it was."

"The level of hardware brought to the exchange was a call made by the FBI agent in charge of the Paris legat, Mr. President," added Palenski. "He was among the victims. In retrospect, I probably wouldn't have changed his approach. Our men were well armed, and—"

The president raised his right hand, a look of sadness passing over his tired features. He stared at the presidential seal embroidered on the light blue carpet in the center of the room. "If you gentlemen tell me you did everything possible to protect those men, that's good enough for me. I'm just disappointed that we lost a number of American lives and still have not recovered the stolen technology."

Clearing his throat, fingers tensing in his lap, Bane said as confidently as he could manage, "We're still on it, sir. Our best field operative, a former CIA officer and currently the head of the FBI's legats, is on her way to Paris right now."

"Her?" the president asked.

"Yes, sir. She's one of my finest."

Palenski leaned forward. "In addition, we have the cream of our people in Europe—CIA and FBI—converging in Paris to join forces and get back what's rightfully ours, sir."

The president checked his watch. "I've asked our ambassador in Paris to deny all involvement. I gather that proper rules were followed by your men in Paris and that there isn't any way the French can track this back to us?"

Bane nodded, straightening his posture with dignity. "That's correct, Mr. President. Our people in Paris went strictly by the book, down to the labels on their clothing."

"Are you handling the family issues?"

Both Palenski and Bane nodded.

The president patted Bane's shoulder, shaking his head regretfully. "A most unpleasant job, I'm afraid, but one which both of you must handle as warmly as possible. Today there will be six American families who'll never see their loved ones again—not even to bury them. That's a hard one to swallow."

"Yes, Mr. President," they replied in unison.

"Now," the president continued, rubbing his hands together while standing. "I must attend to other issues. Please keep me informed of any developments. In addition to your individual reports, gentlemen, I also got a chance to chat with the secretary of commerce and the director at Los Alamos, and they both educated me on the importance of this technology. Do not let it fall into someone else's hands. Understood?"

"Yes, sir." Bane's gaze met the brown eyes of his commander in chief. Now more than ever he had to do everything within his power to recover those tapes. Losing the technology meant losing an edge America could not afford to lose if it wanted to remain competitive in the twenty-first century.

PARIS, FRANCE
Saturday, July 22, 4:30 P.M.

The afternoon sun splashed the city with vivid hues of yellow as traffic thinned on all major thoroughfares, from the huge business park of La Défense to the Place de la Concorde, from the Invalides and Eiffel Tower to the Jardin des Plantes.

Paris was relaxing.

Singles, couples, families with kids, and even tourists enjoyed the beautiful afternoon at dozens of parks and gardens across the city. From the Jardins du Trocadéro, the gardens sloping down from the Palais de Chaillot, to the Bois de Vincennes, an English-style park with lakes and rose gardens, locals and visitors took in the warm sun. At the Jardin du Luxembourg an army of swimsuit wearers, their exposed torsos and legs soaking in the rays, lay around the huge octagonal lake in the center of the park, under the watchful eyes of century-old statues. Beyond the Jardin du Luxembourg, across the Seine, north of Notre Dame Cathedral and the Louvre, camera-bearing tourists lined up for a chance to go inside the famous Opéra of Paris. Many of them had stood there for as long as an hour.

A clean-cut, husky man in his mid-fifties, dressed in a dark-gray Ralph Lauren silk suit, Gucci soft leather shoes, and a hand-painted Pavone tie hanging from a perfect knot over a starched white shirt, slowly walked past the long line of tourists as he made his way to the Boulevard de la Madeleine.

His right hand holding a Louis Vuitton leather attaché case and his left a matching overnight bag, Sergei Iyevenski reached a taxi stand.

Three dark Renault sedans hugged the curb, their drivers smoking by a sidewalk café. Peering at the trio from behind his dark Ray-Ban sunglasses, Iyevenski said, *"Êtes-vous libre?"*

One of the three, a short, middle-aged man with five-o'clock shadow and hints of silver in his dense black hair, ran up to the Russian scientist, a half-smoked cigarette hanging off the corner of his mouth. *"Oui, monsieur."*

"A l'Hôtel de Crillon, s'il vous plaît," replied Iyevenski, casually naming one of the city's most luxurious hotels, just off the Place de la Concorde.

Anticipating a good tip, the Parisian taxi driver's eyes widened as he snapped to attention, quickly opening the rear door and ushering Iyevenski in while chattering obsequiously.

Iyevenski sighed. Paris. The City of Love, the City of Lights—as long as he had the francs to pay for it, francs he had received after converting deutsche marks at six different money-exchange bureaus within a three-block radius of the crowded Place de l'Opéra.

Anything could be bought in Paris; the energetic taxi driver; the gaunt female clerk at the elegant clothing store on the Rue de Rivoli; the hostile-suddenly-turned-friendly barber across from the Louvre. Smiles had cracked their contemptuous facades the moment they saw the francs inside the Louis Vuitton wallet that matched the elegant leather luggage set he had purchased at yet another exclusive store by the Place de la Bastille.

"Voyage d'affaires, monsieur?" asked the curious driver, eyes glancing at Iyevenski in the rearview mirror as he put the Renault in gear and merged with the traffic rushing down the Boulevard de la Madeleine.

"Oui," responded Iyevenski, forcing a hint of annoyance into his voice. "I'm here on very special business."

"Special business, monsieur?"

Iyevenski inspected his fingernails as he said, "The kind that can be very rewarding to those who choose to accommodate my requests without asking needless questions."

His eyes returning to the road, the driver said, "That just about qualifies anyone in Paris, monsieur, including myself."

"What's your name?" asked Iyevenski after a few moments of silence, a plan coming together in his mind.

"Jacques d'Anjou," responded the driver, his eyes once again venturing to the rearview mirror to inspect his peculiar passenger.

"How many francs do you earn in one day of work, friend?"

Curious brown eyes briefly returned to the road before bouncing back to Iyevenski. "About three hundred."

"Three hundred?" Iyevenski repeated, almost to himself while displaying feigned surprise. "Well, Jacques d'Anjou, how would you like this fare to bring you more francs than the next *thousand* fares?"

Wide-eyed, the Frenchman shifted his gaze back and forth between the road and his eccentric passenger. "I think I would like that very much, monsieur."

"There will be risks," warned Iyevenski, his tone suddenly hoarse. "But you will not be committing any crimes, only observing and reporting."

"Paris has many eyes, monsieur. There are many people observing and reporting," answered d'Anjou, both hands on the wheel as he abruptly changed lanes, earning a horn blast from an angered driver.

"Do you live alone?"

"I live any way monsieur wishes me to live."

Iyevenski smiled. *Paris.*

Ten minutes later, the large Russian reached the entrance to the elegant Crillon, a massive four-story structure overlooking the slow-flowing Seine, the Place de la Concorde, and the lush Jardin des Tuileries.

Iyevenski, with a mixed air of elegance and arrogance, approached the ornate doors of the hotel, which was often used by foreign statesmen on official visits. A doorman in a bright red-and-gold uniform solemnly bowed as he let him in.

The marble floors of the spacious lobby were warmed by black and cream leather sofas, Oriental rugs, and large trees in deep brass pots. Mozart flowed from unseen speakers. Elegant men and women lounged or walked about with their noses pointed at the vaulted ceiling.

Iyevenski smiled again. Paris had not changed since the last time he had been here, and he doubted it would ever change.

He approached the front counter, and a gray-haired clerk, impeccably dressed, slowly walked up to him, obviously not impressed by the expensive suit and attaché case, or the solid-gold Rolex President hugging Iyevenski's left wrist.

"Bonjour, monsieur," he said indifferently. The name Henri Peletier was embroidered on the right breast of his coat.

"Bonjour," responded Iyevenski, reaching for his wallet and removing not francs, but several one-thousand-deutsche-mark notes. "I do not have a . . . reservation," he added in French he purposely gave a heavier than normal Slavic accent, "but I would like a room."

Peletier's expression remained unchanged as he said, "I'm afraid we have no rooms available, monsieur."

Iyevenski sighed. Adding a few more bills to the stack, he folded them, covered them with a hairy hand, and slowly moved them over the counter to the clerk. "I would like to have a room, and I'm willing not only to pay in advance for it, but also to reward those who accommodate my humble request."

The Frenchman remained impassive, although his brown eyes did drop to the Russian's hand for a fraction of a second.

The Russian calmly added three more thousand-mark notes, bringing the total to about six thousand dollars. Iyevenski could see the Frenchman doing the conversion to francs in his mind while lightly wetting his lips with the tip of his tongue. A brief glance to either side, and Henri Peletier reached for the money, but the Russian quickly pulled his hand back on the marble counter. "A room and a key first, monsieur."

Breathing deeply as he swallowed his indignation, the clerk brought the tip of his right hand to his forehead before reaching under the counter, spending a minute typing on a keyboard, and finally producing a computerized key and a registry form.

Iyevenski looked down at the hand hiding what was probably three months' wages and said, "You fill it out."

Peletier's eyes went from the hand to the form, which he pulled down below the counter. He passed the key to Iyevenski, who slid the bribe money over to the clerk. Peletier, looking both ways, again touched the side of his perfectly combed grayish hair before pocketing the money.

"Room four zero five, monsieur. The key is good for two nights."

Iyevenski nodded. "That money was for your consideration, my friend. How much for the room?"

The Frenchman dropped his eyelids and warily said, "Four thousand . . . four thousand francs per night, monsieur."

Again, Iyevenski reached into his designer wallet, this time pulling out two five-thousand-franc notes and handing them to Peletier. "Here is the room fee plus an extra two thousand to cover any additional expenses . . . discreetly, of course. I want no one to know I'm here. Understood?"

The Frenchman winked and waved over a bellboy, who took the overnight bag from Iyevenski. "Of course, monsieur."

Sergei Iyevenski, key in hand, followed the bellboy to the elevators.

In a warehouse two blocks from the Boulevard de Clichy, Vladimir Titov-Escobar, wearing nothing but a towel around his waist, finished shaving over a sink in the private bathroom of the office area of one of his front companies, a construction equipment distributor. Yolanda stood behind him, naked, her soaked hair wrapped in a white towel, her hands massaging the back muscles of her leader, the large brown nipples of her firm breasts pressed against him as she hugged him from behind in appreciation for having spent thirty minutes of his busy schedule loving her while they showered together.

"I must be alone now, child," the Kardinal said, grateful to the beautiful Cuban for allowing him to release his stress, but unwilling to show an ounce of that gratitude. "Go and get ready in case there is a breakthrough."

A final kiss to the back of his neck, and she was gone.

His bare feet on the cold ceramic tile, the Kardinal turned on the faucet, cupped both hands, and softly splashed water on his face. Straightening and grabbing a small red towel hanging next to the sink, he breathed deeply as he pressed it against his sharp Slavic features.

Putting down the towel and staring at his own reflection on the round mirror above the sink, the Kardinal grimaced. The swarthy skin, once as smooth as silk, now showed not only the wrinkles of age, but the marks of a life filled with hardship, with hatred, with sorrow, with the loss of . . . *Karla.*

Tears suddenly blinded his iron-gray eyes, and a suffocating sensation tightened his throat. It was only during private moments like this that Vladimir Titov-Escobar allowed his unrestrained feelings to surface.

Alone.

Titov-Escobar had been alone for a very long time. Even when loving Yolanda he felt alone, wishing the light olive body beneath his were silky white, wishing the brown eyes were hazel, wishing the black hair were cinnamon, wishing her passionate whispering were in Russian and not in Spanish.

Leaning toward the mirror, his face only an inch away from his reflection, the Kardinal stared deep into his own eyes and saw the face of Sonya Wüttenberg, the woman responsible for his loneliness. Titov had planned to retire with Karla, lose himself in South America, buy enough land to keep all visitors away, focus on being a husband and a father. He had been willing to give it all up for his wife and unborn child.

His nostrils flared with fury, and his hands clasped the edges of the sink until his knuckles turned white. Titov-Escobar would have succeeded in vanishing with Karla had it not been for Wüttenberg. Had he not missed his mark outside the café, Titov's life might have taken an entirely different turn. There would have been no Croatian monastery, no isolation, no fasting, no Kardinal. But fate had dealt Vladimir Titov-Escobar a hand different from the one he'd hoped for.

Fate.

The Kardinal had spent many nights during his isolation years in Croatia wondering about fate, about his failed attempt to escape with his family, about the few seconds that had defined the rest of his life, while Sonya Wüttenberg pointed her pistol at him and then at Karla, before coldly pressing the trigger, before killing Titov-Escobar's only reason for living.

The Kardinal gave the reflection in the mirror one final look before turning around and leaving the bathroom. He walked into the office area, where there were four desks and a dozen chairs. A coffee machine by the door leading to the warehouse was brewing, and the aroma filled the tiled room. Yolanda, already wearing a tight green dress, sat against the edge of one of the desks and put on dark stockings. She gave him a slow female wink.

Ignoring her, he reached for a set of clean underwear, a starched white shirt, and a freshly pressed suit hanging on the wall next to the desk where Yolanda sat. He dressed in silence, his mind still flashing visions of the forests of southern Germany, of Croatian nights, of—

The phone suddenly rang, and Yolanda picked it up on the second ring. She listened intently for fifteen seconds and then hung up.

"We've found him," she said, raising her brown-eyed gaze to her leader, who was putting on a pair of dress pants.

Calmly looking at the beautiful Cuban, the Kardinal asked, "Where?"

Dressed in a pair of Levi's, sneakers, and a light white cotton jacket over a black T-shirt, the Sig Sauer pistol shoved in the small of his back under the jacket, Sergei Iyevenski walked out of the hotel with a brown nylon backpack hanging off his left shoulder.

Slipping on a pair of oval-shaped Ray-Bans while crossing the street under the warm late-afternoon sun, Iyevenski reached the Place de la Concorde. The large plaza with its towering obelisk gave the Russian a terrific view of the hotel across the Quai des Tuileries.

He checked his new Rolex. It and the Louis Vuitton wallet were the only luxury items from his Paris shopping spree left on his person. It had been exactly thirteen minutes since he had walked away from the hotel's front desk. He reached into his backpack, which held not only a portion of the stolen German currency—he had hidden the rest of the cash and the archive tape in a locker at the Gare du Nord train station—but also a Nikon camera and the most powerful telescopic lens he could find at a camera shop on the Rue de Rivoli. A second locker at the same train station housed the stocks and bonds, which the Russian, after consulting the London *Times* and the international edition of the *New York Times,* had been able to calculate at a current worth of about twenty-four million deutsche marks.

Sergei Iyevenski adjusted the foot-long telescopic lens, bringing the front of the Hôtel de Crillon into focus.

Eight minutes later, a white Mercedes-Benz drove up to the entrance and came to a smooth stop, and an elegantly dressed couple got out, a controlled urgency in their movements. Smiling, Iyevenski recognized the tall female who had accompanied the bearded, hooded leader. He began to snap pictures of the woman and her companion, who had Slavic features but a dark complexion. Noticing the way the man moved, and that the woman opened the door for him, Iyevenski concluded that he had just photographed the face of the man leading this terrorist group. The automatic camera advanced the film to the next frame, allowing

Iyevenski to take two more shots—fifteen in all—before the elegant couple disappeared through the front doors.

Keeping his Mauser automatic in its chest holster, the Kardinal walked up to the elevators, stopping by a large ficus tree, almost fifteen feet in height, planted in a wide brass pot. The clicking of Yolanda Vasquez's stiletto heels on the marble floor stopped as her companion briefly paused by the ficus, reached beneath the mulch by the trunk, and silently thanked his Creator when he found a hotel key, placed there by the manager himself, one of many disciples loyal to the Kardinal in Paris today.

The phone call had been sudden but somewhat expected. The Russian *had* to surface sooner or later. Titov-Escobar had been quite surprised that Iyevenski had managed to get past the many observation points he had set up between Montmartre and central Paris.

"Soon, *mi amor,*" Yolanda said, pushing the elevator button with the tip of a scarlet fingernail. The Kardinal ran a hand over his coat pocket, iron-gray eyes coolly staring at the floor.

The elevator doors opened and the couple entered. They reached the fourth floor thirty seconds later and fast-walked down the champagne wall-to-wall carpet under the soft-white lights of small chandeliers evenly spaced down the long hall.

Room 405. A Do Not Disturb sign hung from the brass doorknob on the tall wooden door. The Kardinal glanced to both sides of the hallway.

Empty.

Yolanda reached inside her small purse, removed a Walther PPK automatic, and screwed a silencer to the muzzle. The Kardinal unholstered his Mauser, reached into a pocket, and also attached a small silencer. Then he slowly inserted the key in the slot above the doorknob.

Swiftly but quietly, with a smoothness that could only be ac-

quired through years of fieldwork, the Kardinal, closely followed
by the Cuban woman, burst inside the room, the pistol leading
the way.

Empty! The room is empty!

Perplexed, an unaccustomed feeling of lack of control sweeping through him, the Kardinal glanced back at Yolanda, who automatically went inside the bathroom, coming back out a moment
later wearing the same expression of concern that had cracked the
Kardinal's poker face.

"The room," she whispered. "Did we get the wrong room?"

Just as Titov-Escobar was about to answer, he noticed something on the bed, an envelope.

Angry eyes darting from the envelope to the coal-black stare
of his subordinate, the Kardinal took a deep breath and tucked
the silencer-fitted Mauser into the small of his back, his suit coat
hanging over it. He walked to the bed and picked up the envelope. It was sealed.

Tearing it open, he pulled out a ten-mark bill and a note on
hotel stationery, hand-printed in capitals.

YOU CALL YOURSELF A PROFESSIONAL? YOU DARE STEAL OUR
SECRETS AND THREATEN MY FRIENDS? THIS BILL IS WORTH
MORE THAN YOUR SERVICES SO FAR, THIEF! JACKAL! YOU WILL
PAY, MY FRIEND! YOU WILL PAY DEARLY FOR WHAT YOU HAVE
DONE!

Calmly handing the note to Yolanda as he crumpled the bill and
threw it to the carpeted floor, the Kardinal closed his eyes and inhaled deeply. His right hand automatically thrust into a side
pocket, fingers reaching for his rosary.

Patience, he thought, praying for the strength to keep calm, to
absorb this slap in the face. *Patience is the companion of wisdom,
one of life's most coveted virtues. Patience is a weapon.*

Lord, please grant me the patience to accept Your wishes. Let Thy will be done on earth as it is in heaven.

Opening his eyes, acid eating away his stomach's lining, the Kardinal confidently walked out of the room with Yolanda Vasquez in tow. The rules had just been changed. The tables had been turned on a man who was not used to not being in control. In a strange way a part of him admired the Russian for doing what he'd done. It wasn't every day that the Kardinal encountered a man who could outwit him. But the more essential question was, why just leave a note? Why go through the whole effort of setting a trap just to leave a simple message? Why not have the room booby-trapped?

Iyevenski's behavior bothered Titov-Escobar more than the note itself, for the Russian was not abiding by the usual rules of the game. Titov and Yolanda should never have left that room alive. Yet they did, and that fact sent a wave of fear through the body of a man who had not known fear since Karla died at the hands of Sonya Wüttenberg. The possibility certainly existed that the Russian scientist could be just an amateur who got lucky this once, who didn't know how to get the most out of this opportunity. But the Kardinal couldn't think of Iyevenski as an amateur. His professional side told him he was dealing with a powerful opponent, one who deserved respect, one whom he should fear. The Russian was like an old volcano, dormant for many years after leaving the KGB and immersing himself in the scientific world. That volcano had now awakened, and its molten lava threatened to drown those who had disturbed its long sleep.

But the Kardinal also realized that once more, he had escaped with his life. Just as in Germany and Croatia, he had walked out of a situation in which he should have died. He had not. He had been spared. The Lord had judged Vladimir Titov-Escobar and continued to spare his life so that the Kardinal could continue to do His work.

Thou art always at my side with Thy rod and Thy staff that give me courage.

"The Russian wishes to play the game," the Kardinal whispered to himself, a surge of confidence battling his fear. He had fallen into a trap but still lived. But he could not fail God again. He could not let the overconfidence of strength and numbers over the Russian cloud his judgment again. He had a duty on earth. He was the hammer of God, the dispenser of divine justice. He would have to tune his senses, pray for wisdom, use his experience to outwit the man who had just outwitted him.

"Let him play the game," the Kardinal said, begining to formulate a counterattack. "The Russian infidel dares challenge me? He dares oppose the wishes of my Master? He dares interfere with my holy cause against the Americans? Let him come."

Yolanda pocketed the note and followed Titov-Escobar into the elevator. "He got lucky, *mi amor.* We will get him next—"

"My dear child, you do not understand," said the Kardinal, putting a hand to her smooth face, running a finger over her pursed lips. "He did *not* get *lucky* today. He set a brilliant trap to draw us in, and we fell in it. He *allowed* us to walk away with our lives. This man is after us for what we did to him, and he not only wishes to destroy us, but to humiliate us, to torture us. He will not stop until he has achieved retribution. He is an evil prophet, my naive child, perhaps the devil himself. We must destroy him first."

"But we *can't* destroy him," Yolanda said, keeping up with Titov's accelerating pace. "The BND needs him alive. That was part of the contract."

The Kardinal smiled as he strode to the elevators. "A paradox, my young Yolanda. Life is full of them. But there is always a solution . . . if one is willing to think through it carefully. You see, they're only interested in his *mind,* not his *body.* First we must capture him alive, then we will decide on the best way to deliver his intellect and the technology to our generous clients."

"I'm—I'm confused," said Yolanda.

"Confusion is merely a state of mind, my child, not a reality in our lives," the Kardinal said, entering the empty elevator.

"I do not understand you when you speak this way. How is it that we are going to both kill and deliver the Russian?"

The Kardinal smiled.

Sergei Iyevenski watched the couple exit the hotel, under obvious forced calm. As their Mercedes accelerated down the Quai des Tuileries—a mere thirty feet from where Iyevenski stood, indistinguishable among a dozen tourists snapping pictures of a beautiful Parisian afternoon—the Russian scientist finished the twenty-four-exposure roll and waved.

He waved not at the Mercedes, but at the black Renault following the German car through the heavy afternoon traffic. Jacques d'Anjou waved back.

Iyevenski put his photographic equipment away. He had a phone call to make.

LOS PADRES NATIONAL FOREST,
NORTHERN CALIFORNIA

Saturday, July 22, 8:15 P.M.

The mobile phone made an electronic chirp inside the Ford Bronco parked in a large forest sixty miles south of San Jose, where Jake Fischer had been hiding since his multiple, nearly fatal encounters the night before.

Jerking in his sleep, quickly sitting up in the rear seat and bumping his head against the padded ceiling, Jake blinked rapidly, his eyes wildly scanning the dark interior of the truck, his mind replaying the last few seconds of a nightmare that had been reality less than forty-eight hours ago.

He instinctively reached for the phone but quickly pulled back, hesitating. Few people had this number. Very few, actually . . . and they had all been killed during the explosion. Maybe it was the district attorney's high-tech crime unit. Or maybe the FBI had tracked this number down. Or maybe it was PCA, or . . .

Quickly realizing he couldn't possibly remain isolated from the world forever, Jake reached for the console between the leather bucket seats and picked up the phone.

"Yeah?" he grumbled, forcing his voice to sound deeper than normal, figuring that if he didn't want to speak with the party at the other end, he'd pretend to be a wrong number and hang up.

"It is about time someone answered the blasted phone! I have been trying to find you since yesterday evening, my friend!"

Jake became instantly wide awake, momentarily speechless in his surprise, his breath caught in his lungs, fingers frozen around the small portable unit.

"*Sergei?*"

"Yes, of course! Who did you expect? Saint Nicholas?"

The vigor in Iyevenski's voice hitting him full force, Jake gasped, stunned, not sure what to expect. Right now a call from Sergei Iyevenski ranked at about the same level of insanity as one from Saint Nick.

"My friend? Are you still there?"

"I . . . well, yes, *yes!*" responded Jake, snapping out of the trance. "Of course I'm here. The question is, where are *you?* I thought that you—"

"I'm in Paris, my friend. Paris, France. Eating truffles and drinking Dom Pérignon courtesy of the bastards who kidnapped me."

Paris? The large Russian sounded as if he were next door. "Paris? Kidnapped? What the *fuck* are you talking about?" Jake asked in dazed exasperation.

"Thursday night, after you left the plant to go find Katherina, I blacked out . . . somehow. When I woke up I was on a plane to Mexico in the company of a contractor."

"A *contractor?*"

"Yes, a contractor . . . someone hired by someone else to kidnap me, yes? Anyway, after we crossed the border, I was transferred to a jet, which took me to Paris, and next thing I knew, I was standing in front of the blasted Moulin Rouge! Wild, yes?"

Wild? Everything was once again moving too fast for Jake Fischer. Just when he thought he was beginning to get a handle on his situation, to get a chance to think it through, the roller coaster took an unanticipated turn. Sergei Iyevenski had survived the blast and was now calling him from Paris!

Goose bumps crawling up his forearms. Jake heard his own intake of breath through his open mouth and managed to say in a voice threatening to crack, "But . . . but how did you escape?"

"I cannot tell you anything else on your mobile phone. Anyone can pick up the conversation. Rush to a pay phone, my friend. I'll call you in thirty minutes."

"Pay phone? What are you—"

"We are operating in a different world from the one you are used to, my friend. We must abide by its rules or perish. Now, trust me, go find a pay phone and get the number. I will call you again in fifteen minutes. Have the number ready."

The line went dead.

Torn by conflicting emotions, a scream of frustration caught in the back of his throat, Jake stared at the small Motorola unit in his hands, blinking in bafflement, many questions drilling his mind. *Different world? New rules? What does it mean?*

Shaking his head, Jake crawled into the front seat and turned the ignition. The Bronco came alive, its headlights slicing through the night. He put the truck in gear and pressed the gas, driving to a nearby Texaco station in a daze, his brain in tumult, his mind spinning with bewilderment.

A single pay phone stood under a small wooden porch. A bulb

hanging at the end of a black coiled wire cast a dim light on the porch and the gravel driveway leading to the pumps.

Taking the cellular phone with him, Jake got out and slowly walked to the service station, closed at this time of the night. Standing next to the pay phone, he checked his watch. Fifteen minutes. The cellular phone rang. He answered on the first ring.

"Yeah?"

"The number of the pay phone?"

Forcing the shock out of his voice, Jake gave it to him, and a minute later the pay phone rang. Jake picked it up immediately, cradling it against his right ear with both hands. "Sergei, for crying out loud! What's going—"

"Listen carefully, my friend," the Slavic voice came from the other end, but not nearly as clearly as on the cellular phone. "We are dealing with professional operatives, possibly ex-KGB, who have been contracted by someone, who still remains unseen, to steal our F1 chip's technology. But apparently there is a third party involved. Someone who interrupted the exchange."

"What exchange?"

"The one that took place outside the Moulin Rouge this morning. One of Katherina's archive tapes and I were going to be traded for twenty-five million deutsche marks. But the third party ruined it for the other two. They began shooting right in front of the Moulin Rouge, giving me a chance to escape. In the commotion I grabbed the briefcase with the money and . . . like you say, *bailed* while I had the opportunity. I also have the archive tape."

Jake struggled to absorb and digest all of the information, which told him that Sonya Wüttenberg had been right in her assessment of high-tech bandits stealing his secrets. "So what are you doing now? Are you hiding from them? Are you trying to escape? Head back home?"

"I am not planning to leave . . . yet."

Jake frowned at the unexpected answer. But then again, everything about this conversation had been highly unexpected. "What do you mean?"

"I am not trying to escape, friend. I am trying to catch them."

Jake pressed the phone hard against his ear, his eyes gazing at the empty gas station, at the uneven gravel driveway, at the red paint peeling off the sides of the weathered pumps—all under a partly cloudy sky fighting a moon in its first quarter. "*Catch* them? You want to *catch* them? Are you *insane?* You yourself said we're dealing with trained killers. You'd better get the hell out of there while you can and go to the embassy, get help from the CIA."

"Listen, my friend," the hoarse voice of the Russian scientist came out of the old telephone. "Listen very carefully. There are things you do not know about me. I have skills I learned long ago, the skills I used to fool the KGB here in Paris in 1990. Remember?"

Jake exhaled, remembering the heart-stopping episode several years ago. "How can I forget?"

"Just like I fooled them back then, I will fool them again," Sergei said. "I have not only the money, but also the archive tape . . . the one those imbeciles stole when they kidnapped me. Did they touch anything else in the factory aside from the archive tape?"

Taking a deep breath, realizing that Iyevenski simply didn't know, Jake Fischer said, "I'm afraid so, Sergei. They did far more than just kidnap you and steal that archive tape. They also . . . destroyed the factory."

Silence. Followed by, *"Destroyed?"*

"Yes . . . by fire. There was a chemical fire that night, shortly after I left. Everything was destroyed."

"Everything?"

"Nothing's left. FTI is a pile of smoking rubble," Jake said, tensing, waiting for the obvious question. It was another few seconds before the Russian asked it.

"Was anyone in the team hurt?"

A sudden shrinking feeling descending over him, Jake Fischer felt tears welling in his dark blue eyes as visions of body bags flashed in the night, shielding the distant stars, the quarter moon. "Everyone died in the fire, Sergei . . . *everyone*. And up to a few minutes ago, I thought that you too had perished in it."

Sergei Iyevenski's heavy sigh came through clearly from a third of the way around the globe. "No survivors?"

Jake forced back the tears, his muscles tensing until they hurt, his trembling hands gripping the phone. "None."

"And . . . and Katherina? Did she . . . ?"

Jake Fischer momentarily lost control of the river of emotions eroding his self-control, and the tears flowed freely down the angular features of his tanned face. "Kathy also died, Sergei. I lost her. Those bastards killed her . . . they killed everyone."

More silenced, followed by, "But . . . but how? She was not in the building when you left."

Quickly regaining his composure, rubbing his eyes against the shoulders of his shirt, Jake took a couple of deep breaths and said, "I know . . . it's very strange, but according to the computer entry log, she arrived shortly after I left, minutes before the place caught fire. She apparently went straight for the vault . . . for some reason left it open before she entered the test floor, and then the whole place went up in flames."

More silence, until the voice of Sergei Iyevenski broke it. "They will pay, my friend! I promise you they will pay! Now, tell me everything that you know. I need to know *everything* that has happened to you since we last saw each other."

For the next ten minutes, Jake told his Russian partner everything up to the point when the Motorola phone had waked him up half an hour ago.

"So, Sergei," Jake finished, "what in the hell do we do now?"

"There is only one way to win . . . only one way. And that is to *fight* these people . . . to fight them *my way,* the way I was taught many years ago, before I joined the Shemyakin Institute."

Curiosity forced Jake's brows down over his indigo eyes. "The way you were *taught?* What are you talking about? *Who* taught you *what?*" Jake asked.

"The KGB. I was one of them, my friend."

Jake held his breath, felt his stomach cramping, his forehead throbbing. *Just when you think you know someone!*

"Jake? Are you there, friend?"

"Barely," he whispered. "Just *fucking* barely. Do you have any more . . . *surprises* for me?"

"Hang in there, friend. You are not alone."

A few more seconds to swallow that last revelation, then Jake asked, "Should we get help, Sergei?"

"From whom?"

Jake shrugged. "I don't know. What about the U.S. government, or maybe the FBI or the CIA?"

Silence, followed by, "In time, friend. In time, and not until we can get them to help us under my rules, not theirs."

Jake shook his head. "I . . . I don't understand."

"You will. Now, this is what I want you to do," started Iyevenski, getting down to business, taking twenty minutes to explain his strategy to a perplexed Jake Fischer, who slowly realized the brilliant way Iyevenski intended to exact revenge on those who had slaughtered their team, destroyed their factory, and attempted to steal their invention.

10

THE AMATEUR

Every step by which men add to their knowledge and skills is a step also by which they can control other men.

—Max Lerner

Gray moonlight, soft and dramatic, accentuated the jagged pine trees lining the suburb outside San Jose where Sergei Iyevenski rented a two-bedroom house. Quiet, deserted, punctuated by a few porch lights, the street curved, following the contour of a hill overlooking Silicon Valley.

Jake Fischer noticed the top-of-the-line BMW parked outside Iyevenski's house, dark with tinted windows, cigarette smoke curling out of a crack on the passenger's side window. Jake figured there were at least two men stalking the house, waiting, probably with instructions to shoot to kill. Or could they be FBI? Not likely; not in that car.

Do not take any chances, my friend. Assume the worst.

Jake, in a crouch behind a pine tree, the Bronco safely parked a few blocks away, swallowed hard and dialed Iyevenski's home number on the Motorola unit in his hands. Three rings later, the Russian's answering machine came on.

Struggling to control the hammering of his heart, his eyes on the BMW at the other end of the block, Jake patiently waited for the long beep at the end of the greeting, the adrenaline salvos fired into his bloodstream rocketing his pulse rate.

"Sergei, Jake," he said, struggling to keep his voice from cracking. "I'm on my way to San Jose International. By the time you check this message, I'll be in the air, heading for a meeting with the FBI. Hang in there, guy. Keep on distracting them. The cavalry's on its way."

Shutting off the small unit and shoving it in a rear pocket, Jake stood, a bit frightened by what he was doing, feeling way out of his league, but willing to trust his friend over the strangers at the DA's high-tech crime unit and especially the FBI. The mere thought of associating himself with an agency that had known about the imminent threat FTI faced and had done nothing made him angry.

A figure emerged out of the shadows of the house and raced to the BMW, reaching the rear door on the driver's side and getting in. A few seconds later the vehicle sprang to life, rear wheels chirping on the asphalt, headlights almost catching Jake Fischer as he peeked from behind the pine.

Dropping to the ground, Jake let the wide evergreen shield him as the BMW cruised by, disappearing around the corner and accelerating toward the highway several blocks away.

Damn! Just like that! thought Jake, quickly understanding what Sergei Iyevenski had meant by turning the tables, by using your enemy's own weapons to your advantage.

The same confidence that had filled him the night before, after he'd managed to escape two assassination attempts, now swept through him like the light breeze caressing the evergreens.

Careful, my friend. Overconfidence will get you killed.

Jake remembered the words. Sergei had estimated no more than thirty minutes before their enemies realized the trick and returned to their posts at both houses, Jake's and Iyevenski's. He had to hurry.

Running down the street, he reached the front of the house, breathing heavily, walked up to the front door, and leaned down to retrieve a key hidden under a few rocks next to the knee-high bushes hugging the house.

He found it exactly where Iyevenski had said it would be. Going inside, he went straight for the alarm keypad in the foyer and entered the disarming code. Then he rushed through the small hallway separating a neat living room from the master bedroom. Jake had been here many times in the past years, mostly nights and weekends spent strategizing, working out the thousands of small details that had made their venture a success. The level of planning that had gone into FTI was mind-numbing, and those bastards had come and simply—

Concentrate! Behind the dresser, a small fireproof box. Get it! And get out!

Jake silently reprimanded himself for his loss of focus as he took the box in his hands and sat on the water bed, dialing the combination Iyevenski had given him. Inside, he found ten thousand dollars in cash, Iyevenski's passports—Russian and American—and a pistol. A Russian Makarov.

Jake, never having handled a gun before, remembered what he had been told. Iyevenski had been perfectly clear. *Flip the safety lever on the right while pointing the weapon away from you. Press the rear of the weapon and release the magazine. Make sure it is full before reinserting it into the gun's handle. To cock it, hold the gun by the grip with the right hand and pull the slide back. It will pull the hammer back and chamber a round, and you are on business, my friend.*

"*In* business, Sergei. We're *in* business," Jake whispered.

Leaving the house just three short minutes after he had gone inside, Jake Fischer rushed to his Bronco. He still had another appointment tonight before he drove to Los Angeles.

Although it was uncomfortable, Jake kept the weapon shoved

in the small of his back as he drove to his own house, not at all surprised to find it clean, without surveillance, after the message he'd left on Iyevenski's answering machine.

He passed the house and parked around the corner, got out, and slowly approached his house from the opposite side of the street.

Then Jake saw him, a stocky figure lurking in the shadow of a tree on the side of his house.

Beware when you approach either house. They might leave some-one behind just in case. Shoot first and ask questions later, my friend. They will not hesitate to shoot you.

His pulse rate rocketing, Jake hid behind a large rose bush in full blossom two houses down and across from his own. Moon-light showed him his enemy, calmly leaning against the brick side of his house . . . smoking. Jake could see the steady glow splash-ing his face with deep hues of red and orange.

Jake slowly crept away from the bush, trying to think of a way to draw the figure into the light, where he could see him, maybe get a clear shot. Iyevenski had warned him that firing straight re-quired many hours of practice, and he recommended not firing at a target more than fifteen feet away. He also encouraged Jake not to fire at moving targets.

One shot, my friend. One shot, maybe two, is probably all you will get, unless you catch him unprepared. And remember, don't yank the trigger. Squeeze it gently.

Looking around him, Jake picked up a stone roughly the size of a walnut. Drawing the Makarov, which he cocked as had been explained to him, chambering a round, the amateur threw the stone down the street, his dark blue eyes on the figure in black.

Moving forward, the cigarette falling to the ground, the glow-ing extinguished under a shoe, the figure slowly walked down the lawn, his face turned away from the light. He was a muscular man, much wider than Jake, certainly trained in the art of killing, someone who would not hesitate to shoot Jake the moment he spotted him.

But what if he was FBI? What if he was one of Sonya's agents sent to protect—

The Asian assassin!

Jake momentarily froze, his breath caught in his throat when he recognized the stocky Asian with the ponytail, the one who had tried to kill him at the Fish Market.

Regaining control, elbows on the manicured lawn, hands gripping the Russian weapon, feeling the weight, defining the balance point, Jake Fischer kept both eyes open and the front and rear sights lined up with the assassin, who was stopping in the middle of the street to pick up the stone Jake had just thrown.

A stationary target.

Twenty . . . maybe twenty-five feet away.

Keep it under fifteen or risk missing.

What if I can't?

Then fire repeatedly. Increase your odds of hitting before he can reach for his own weapon. Go for the chest.

The Asian had a powerful chest.

But could he shoot another human being?

Think of Katherina when you aim, my friend. Think of our team, slaughtered by this animal in your sights!

Think of Kathy! Think of the life that will never be for you and her! Think of her face, her smile, her eyes!

For Kathy, Jake! For Kathy and the others! The butchers that killed them are all the same. They must be fought with fire, my friend, with FIRE!

Jake Fischer kept the still figure lined up with the Makarov's sights for five seconds, his eyes focused not on the sights but on the target, exactly as Iyevenski had instructed. His mind replayed visions of his slaughtered team, most burned to a cinder, brought out one by one by the firemen. Those bastards had not hesitated before lighting the fuse. Neither would he!

Jake, firmly planted on the ground, his muscles hard with tension, fired quickly, three times. The multiple reports was deafening, the scream that followed unnerving. The massive figure in black stumbled frantically on the street, hands reaching for his chest, tearing his black shirt, falling to the ground, momentarily thrashing before finally going limp.

Four minutes, friend! After you shoot you will have just under four minutes, the average time an average person lets pass before venturing into the street. Thirty seconds before someone dials nine-one-one. Ten minutes before the police arrive. Hurry!

Emptying his mind of all emotion, Jake sprinted across the street, following Iyevenski's strict order not to look at his victim, and reached his doorstep. Quivering hands tried to unlock the door, but the door was already unlocked. Turning the knob, Jake went inside, the rotting smell assaulting him, nauseating him. Jake fought it. He didn't have much time to—

He froze when he saw the bodies of two large men in business suits sprawled on the foyer facedown, pools of blood around their chests.

What in the hell?

Regaining control, Jake dropped to one knee and frisked the closest one, reaching under his coat, pulling out an ID card. He refused to believe his eyes.

FBI. Damn!

Jake stood, the badge in his trembling hands. The FBI had sent two agents to guard the house in the hope that Jake would show. But instead they had been killed by the Asian.

You don't have much time, friend!

Forcing his mind to ignore this unexpected sight, Jake rushed into his bedroom, glancing at the ghostly operative on the bed, who was still clutching his weapon. The overpowering stench nauseated him. He reached his nightstand and grabbed his passport. Then he got a small towel from the bathroom and dashed past the dead Feds and out of the house, not bothering to close the door.

Down the street he ran, keeping his head covered with the white cloth—just as Iyevenski had instructed him. He reached his Bronco two minutes later. The street was still deserted. He drove out of the neighborhood with the lights off. At the entrance ramp to Highway 101 he switched them on. He headed south, toward Los Angeles.

The problem has to be solved at the root, my friend. When shooting at the enemy, you must aim for the body of the beast, not its tentacles, and the body is here, in Paris.

PARIS, FRANCE
Sunday, July 23, 6:45 A.M.

The bells of the Notre Dame Cathedral pierced through the fog shrouding the Ile de la Cité, the slow-flowing Seine, and its surrounding quays. Its sounds, heard across Paris since the fourteenth century, propagated up the Boulevard Saint Michel, to the Rue de Cujas.

On the third floor of a century-old house, Sergei Iyevenski cleaned his Sig Sauer 9mm pistol. He used fine engine oil soaked into a soft cloth to rub the barrel and the firing mechanism, then a dry cotton rag to wipe it clean. Trained fingers had disassembled and reassembled the weapon automatically, amazing Jacques d'Anjou, the taxi driver, who had not said much since arriving at the flat thirty minutes before, after following the Mercedes for an hour and keeping watch on a warehouse on the outskirts of Montmartre.

"Tell me again who this woman is," asked Iyevenski in an admonishing tone. D'Anjou had called a close associate to take over the surveillance of the warehouse for the past few hours without checking with Iyevenski first.

"Nicole Rochereau," responded d'Anjou. "Another taxi driver. I have known her for fifteen years. Very trustworthy, monsieur."

Sliding the barrel back into its metal base, Iyevenski eyed d'Anjou sternly. "Listen, friend, from now on you concentrate *only* on the job I give you and leave it up to me to decide who is and is not trustworthy. Do we understand each other?"

"Pardon, monsieur. I do not wish to do anything that might jeopardize the monsieur's business. It will not happen again."

Iyevenski waited a few seconds of silent reprimand.

"Tell me more about this warehouse," the Russian said, completing the assembly and inserting a clip filled with 9mm hollowpoint rounds into the gun's handle. Shoving it in the small of his back, he let his white cotton jacket fall over it.

"It's about a kilometer from the Sacré Coeur. The warehouse is used to store construction equipment . . . wire, tools, steel beams, concrete. There is an ideal observation spot for taxi drivers at a café at the corner of the Boulevard de Clichy and Rue des Martyrs, not far from the Moulin Rouge."

"I know the place," said Iyevenski, the bloody gunfight of just twenty-four hours ago still alive in his mind.

"Would the monsieur like me to take him there?"

"Oui, but first you must make a delivery and a purchase," Iyevenski said, scribbling some notes on a piece of paper and shoving it inside a brown manila envelope, already containing six of the pictures he had shot the previous afternoon, the best ones of the female terrorist and her companion at the hotel, the man Iyevenski suspected was the leader. He'd had the film developed and printed at a one-hour-processing lab off the Rue de Rivoli.

"A delivery and a purchase, monsieur?"

"Yes, a delivery near the Place de la Concorde. You must deliver this to a friend," Iyevenski said, sealing the envelope and standing. "Then I need you to purchase something for me, for us. Let's go, d'Anjou. We must not waste time."

LOS ANGELES, CALIFORNIA
Sunday, July 23, 5:00 A.M.

Sometime after Sergei Iyevenski had Jacques d'Anjou deliver his package, Jake Fischer boarded an American Airlines Boeing 747 at LAX with direct service to Charles de Gaulle Airport in Paris.

Having reached the airport uneventfully, Jake left the weapon under the seat of his Bronco before checking with every airline and finding the next flight to Paris. As an American citizen, Jake did not need a visa to travel through most of Europe, France included. All he needed was an airline ticket and a valid U.S. passport.

Tired, nauseated from lack of sleep, a two-day stubble covering his tanned face, Jake Fischer slowly made his way through the jet's first-class section, the only class with available seats in the midst of the tourist season.

Jake sank into a window seat with a view of a ramp packed with airliners. Pulling down the shade, he adjusted the overhead vent, then leaned his head back and closed his eyes. Too much had happened too quickly for the events to really sink into Jake's exhausted mind. But the long high-speed drive from San Jose had given him time alone to reflect on his situation enough to realize that Iyevenski was right. Going to the police or the FBI would probably be useless—a judgment that was reinforced by the sight of two dead FBI agents at his house. But how were he and Iyevenski supposed to beat an enemy who could kill FBI agents with such ease?

Leave that to me, my friend. You just leave that to me.

Exhaling in frustration, but also giving Iyevenski credit for having managed to keep him alive—without FBI protection—

Jake pinched the bridge of his nose as the jet pulled away from the gate. Flight attendants sprang to action, automatically going through their routines. A young blonde, squeezed into an incredibly small uniform, stood in the center aisle toying with a seatbelt buckle and an oxygen mask. His mind, however, flashed the slim silhouette of Kathy Bennett approaching him, embracing him, taking him to faraway places. He saw her eyes gleaming at him as their bodies melted together in a rapture that removed them from clean rooms and high-tech testers, from helifurnaces and biochemical lattices. He heard her soft moans, felt her hands pressing his back as she pulled him closer to her, sensed her body heat radiating around him, enveloping him, absorbing him. He sensed the heat and suddenly saw Kathy Bennett disappearing behind a sheet of orange-and-red fire. Jake saw the line of body bags, saw the personalized license plate, felt the world collapse around him, burying him, changing him, turning him into a man capable of killing another.

The jet taxied to the runway. Jake ordered a double scotch on the rocks despite the early-morning hour, his logical side telling him the alcohol would relax him, allow him to absorb the impact of his actions, help him justify the cold-blooded murder.

Jake knew he would not be able to rest until he had destroyed those who had tried to destroy him. Only then would he be able to avenge the deaths of his beloved Kathy and the rest of his team, only then would he be able to rebuild their dream from the ashes.

But can I really start all over?

Jake had not had the time to think through that one, but he did know that at this moment Iyevenski possessed one copy of the biorecipes and Jake the other. No one else had a copy. In spite of all the hardship, Jake and Iyevenski were still in control of the technology. Perhaps there was a way after all.

The blond flight attendant brought him the scotch, which Jake drank in seconds, letting the liquor warm his core. The drone of the engines slowly pulled him away from the reality of his situation, lulling him into sleep.

Sitting in the last row of the first-class section, just six rows behind Jake Fischer, a muscular man in his early forties pretended to read a Tom Clancy novel he'd purchased at the gift shop by the gate. Although his dark eyes currently scanned the pages of the thick paperback, they had tracked the scientist as he appeared in the aisle after boarding, checking the row numbers against the airline stub in his hand. It had taken the muscular man a few moments to match the ragged-looking face in line at the American Airlines ticket counter to the four-by-six shot of a clean-cut Jake Fischer on the FTI brochure Titov-Escobar had faxed to him—and twenty other agents operating in California alone—thirty-six hours before.

But it *was* him. The muscular man was certain, and he had confirmed that when he managed to overhear the airline clerk addressing him by name as he returned his passport.

Have a pleasant flight, Mr. Fischer. Enjoy Paris.

The muscular man smiled.

And you shall enjoy Paris, Mr. Fischer, he thought. A message was already on its way to the Kardinal.

PARIS, FRANCE

Sunday, July 23, 3:45 P.M.

"When did you say this arrived?" said Sonya Wüttenberg to the others in the office of the former CIA station chief at the American embassy. She waved the handwritten note at them, three rookie CIA officers and two junior FBI agents—all that remained after the bloodbath of the day before, when the CIA station chief, his deputy chief, and the FBI agent in charge had been among the dead.

The shoot-out in Montmartre had been in the news since yesterday morning. The French police, however, had not released any details about the dead, none of whom had carried identification.

"I already told you, mademoiselle. It was delivered to the front desk early this morning along with the mail," answered one of the clerks, a Parisian woman working the lobby of the American embassy building, situated just north of the Place de la Concorde, at the east end of the Champs Elysées. The clerk, a brunette with a beauty mark in the middle of her right cheek, was unimpressed by Sonya, who could not believe that this information had sat in an in-basket since this morning.

This morning! Sonya tried to control her rage.

"Was he American?" asked Sonya, the current top-ranking U.S. intelligence officer in Paris.

The weekend clerk, dressed in a skin-tight gray frock and stiletto hills, crossed her arms and legs while Sonya paced the small second-floor office where they had been since word got to Sonya about the mystery envelope addressed to "The CIA" from "A friend."

"Non, he was French," she replied indifferently, covering a yawn with a manicured hand.

Irked by her aloof manner, Sonya, unable to control her flaring tamper, snapped, *"Think!* Are you *certain?"*

Standing, a hand on her hip, the index finger of her other hand cocked at the female FBI agent, the brunette retorted, *"Pardon,* mademoiselle, but I do believe I can differentiate between an . . . an *américain* and one of my own."

The five male rookies surrounding them exchanged glances before looking at Sonya, whose lips puckered in annoyance. She motioned the brunette to sit back down.

"Mon Dieu!" the petite clerk blurted, shooting Sonya a resentful look before folding her pencil-thin arms, breathing deeply, and pointedly looking away. She hesitated for a few seconds before complying.

"Please, describe him to me," Sonya asked as politely as she could. The jet lag, the side wound that would not stop throbbing, the disaster in California, the failed mission by the Moulin Rouge, and now this strange envelope delivered to her many hours late were trying her patience.

Looking in the distance for a few moments, the brunette said, "Short, about my height, a medium build, dark hair with a little gray, brown eyes, fair skin. He spoke perfect Parisian French. *That's* how I know he was not *américain."*

Shifting her gaze from the woman to the rookies, then back to her, Sonya said, "Thank you for your cooperation. I had to ask you these questions because the ambassador finds it offensive for any-one—French or any other nationality—to insinuate that this build-ing houses officers of the Central Intelligence Agency. This is a diplomatic institution with a clear charter. As a member of the am-bassador's staff, I find this envelope quite insulting, and I'll see to it that it reaches the right level of attention." Smiling, Sonya added, "Again, we thank you for your cooperation and for the outstand-ing job you have done at our embassy. And I apologize for the in-convenience. These gentlemen will escort you back to your desk."

The brunette stood and nodded, arms still crossed. *"Merci, mademoiselle."*

As the rookies left with the brunette, Sonya fell into the leather chair behind the desk of the dead agent in charge of the Paris legat, planted both elbows on the smooth surface, and buried her face in her hands.

She was exhausted, tired, on the edge. Screams of frustration reached the back of her throat. This bad day was getting worse by the minute. But as she opened her eyes and stared at a framed eight-by-ten of an attractive woman in her early forties flanked by two teenage boys, Sonya decided that "bad day" was a rela-tive term.

Picking up the gold-framed photo and looking into the smiling faces of the agent's family, Sonya began to wonder how long it would be before Roman Palenski broke the news to them. What kind of story would the FBI director fabricate about the fate of the husband and father? The United States government would vehemently deny any involvement in the shoot-out. That was standard U.S. policy. The bodies would remain in France, probably would be cremated in another week or so, after the investigation finally stonewalled. His family would not even have the right to bury him.

Sonya felt a shudder of sorrow for Jake Fischer, a man who'd also lost his family, his girlfriend, everything he'd held dear to him.

Her stare hardened at the thought of her former Stasi controller.

Sonya reached for the manila envelope on the desk and extracted the photos she'd studied carefully before summoning the brunette to her office.

Vladimir Titov-Escobar. The assassin. The jackal!

Sonya didn't recognize the woman, but seeing a woman with the man known as the Kardinal immediately triggered the memory of Karla Valentinovna Naidenova. And the vision of the pale Russian woman with the cinnamon hair inexorably brought back the painful memory of Ludwig.

A wife for a—

No time for that now!

Imposing an iron control over her emotions, Sonya fought hard the tears, refused to let them fall. She was a professional, dedicated to her mission, to her adopted country, to catching the man who had already caused so much death and destruction, a man Sonya had missed the opportunity of killing once.

But next time . . .

Shoving the color photos back in the envelope, Sonya Wüttenberg headed for Montmartre.

She went alone. All the personnel left in the Paris station were rookies. Roman Palenski and Donald Bane had promised her seasoned officers were on their way, but until they arrived, she would feel more confident by herself.

Hiding behind an open newspaper at a sidewalk café at the corner of the Boulevard de Clichy and the Rue des Martyrs, Sergei Iyevenski warily inspected the large warehouse in the distance through his green Ray-Bans. The large building was almost out of sight from the wide boulevard, at the other end of the narrow Rue des Martyrs.

In front of him, next to the half-drunk plastic cup of café au lait, was one of two small mobile phones d'Anjou had purchased after delivering the package to the American embassy. The price to obtain the phones immediately, fully charged, and with backup batteries, had been exorbitant, but Iyevenski had very deep pockets these days.

"How long have they been in there?" the Russian asked the mature but quite attractive Nicole Rochereau, who sat with a slim cigarette—so strong that even in an open café it almost brought tears to Sergei's eyes—wedged between her lips. The woman had actually turned out to be a blessing for Iyevenski, who felt much more comfortable surveying the warehouse from this spot while in the company of a presentable woman.

The eyes of Paris would be looking for a large man with unkempt salt-and-pepper hair walking the streets or hiding alone. They would miss the casually dressed Iyevenski who, in addition to the sunglasses and the stubble, had most of his grizzly hair hidden under a black beret he'd borrowed from d'Anjou. If there was trouble, of course, Iyevenski could rely on the well-oiled Sig Sauer shoved into his belt at the back and covered by his white cotton jacket.

Nicole, dressed in stonewashed jeans and a T-shirt, brought the unfiltered cigarette to her lips, her large round eyes, emphasized

by heavy purple mascara on a well-tanned but bony face, turning
to Iyevenski. "All day, monsieur," she said, her purple lips barely
moving. "I have been watching since last night."

Keeping most of his face hidden behind the paper, the Russian
reached for the café au lait and took a sip. It had been several
hours now since d'Anjou had delivered the package to the American embassy, and as of yet he had not seen a sign of the mighty
CIA, which Iyevenski expected to strike in full force.

"Do you live nearby?" asked Iyevenski without looking at the
redheaded woman.

A suspicious line forming at the corner of her mouth, Nicole
asked, "Why does monsieur wish to know this?"

"Because I must know how many safe houses I have available
and where they are."

Obviously uncomfortable, Nicole said, "I worry that—"

"No worries." Iyevenski pulled out a roll of thousand-franc
notes and peeled off a dozen. "In case there is . . . trouble, and
you have to move. And if anything should happen to your Renault,
I'll buy you a new one."

Drawing on the cigarette, Nicole's large eyes grew wider on her
slim face as she slowly shook her head, a thin hand patting Iyevenski's sailor hand holding the bills.

"The monsieur has already been *much* too generous with his
francs. I am just concerned about my health."

Iyevenski nodded and gave her a brief smile. "Take them anyway, Nicole. For a rainy day."

Nicole Rochereau returned the smile, took the money, and
shoved it into a small purse. Leaning toward him, her face only
inches from his, she whispered, *"Merci beaucoup."*

"Je vous en prie," responded Iyevenski, pleased with the sudden intimacy of her nearness, his gaze momentarily dropping
from her dark and somewhat insolent eyes to the olive expanse
of her neck.

"I have a house a few kilometers from here, north of Montmartre. Small but clean," she added hesitantly, obviously uncomfortable about disclosing such personal information to a stranger.

"Alone?"

She stirred her light frame uneasily in the chair, a pensive shimmer veiling her eyes as she thought about it for a moment. "Sometimes."

Suspecting what she might mean, Iyevenski decided to take no chances and pulled out more bills. "Would this make sure you will cancel your . . . appointments for the evening? Just in case we need to use your place. I don't want any . . . surprise visitors."

Nicole Rochereau's countenance turned hostile at his insinuation. "I am not a whore, monsieur!" she hissed, tossing the cigarette to the sidewalk. "I have a daughter. She goes to the Université René Descartes! She sleeps at my home on some weekends!"

Feeling surprisingly weak and vulnerable in the face of her anger, Iyevenski removed his glasses, feeling color coming to his cheeks as Nicole Rochereau, shaking her head, dropped her gaze to her bony hands, fingers interlaced.

Placing a hand over hers, the Russian said, "I owe you the *biggest* apology, Nicole. I am an idiot, one who is much too preoccupied with matters that, if not properly handled, could result in the death of a close friend—and maybe my own. I never meant to insult you. *Never.* You are a fine lady, earning a decent living to put your daughter through school. Please, forgive me. I beg you."

The thin, attractive face slowly softened at his words, and she nodded once. *"Oui, monsieur."*

"Sergei, please," Iyevenski said, regretting the words the instant they came out of his mouth. *Never disclose your real name to anyone. Never get personally involved with anyone in a mission.*

"Apologies accepted, Sergei," Nicole said.

"What is she studying?" asked the Russian, a warm glow of relief flowing through him.

"Julianna?"

"Is that your daughter's name?"

"*Oui*. She is studying to become a doctor," the woman responded, her braless chest suddenly expanding as she leaned forward and took a big breath, small nipples pressed against the cotton of her T-shirt. "One more year before she begins her practice. She is good with medicine, like her father."

"Father? Are you . . ."

"Divorced. Five years ago he left me for a Belgian woman just a little older than Julianna. We have not heard from him since. I work now to make sure Julianna gets a good education and never has to depend on a husband to support her."

Grimacing while putting his glasses back on, Iyevenski handed her a few extra bills. "For books and tuition. I'm sure the universities in Paris are every bit as expensive as the ones in—" He stopped abruptly, catching himself before he let her know he lived in the United States. His Slavic-accented French and his Russian first name were at least nonconflicting and served as a reasonable cover. Putting a hand to his chest, the Russian looked in the distance while breathing through his mouth.

"Sergei?" she asked, now placing a hand over his. "Are you all right?"

"It will pass, my dear," Iyevenski said, feigning a chest pain. "I'm afraid I am no longer the powerful man I was in my youth."

"I think you are more than powerful enough," she said, obviously quite conscious of his virile appeal. "You are also *too* kind." She gave him a light kiss on the cheek.

Color returned to Iyevenski's lined face. He felt electrified by her touch, her smell, her eyes. "You have no idea," he responded, his body feeling heavy and warm. "And I think you are not just the epitome of a good mother, but also . . . *belle*."

Nicole Rochereau tilted her head to the side and smiling broadly, softly punching him in the shoulder.

As he kept up the small talk with the French woman, while Jacques d'Anjou guarded the taxis a half block away, Sergei Iyevenski forced himself to scan not just the warehouse, but the crowded Boulevard de Clichy, which, as the sun began to sink below the horizon, became noisier.

At this moment, while flirting and softly laughing with the taxi driver, Sergei Iyevenski noticed a woman walking down the wide boulevard. What had caught his attention was not the model-like physique of the blonde. There were many such women crossing his field of view at the moment. Instead, Sergei Iyevenski noticed the eyes. They were not simply looking at the crowd to help her navigate without colliding against a tourist. Her eyes were *studying* the boulevard, analyzing it, surveying the street leading to the warehouse.

Keeping the conversation at a good pace, something the Russian was enjoying more than his training told him he should, he discreetly kept a close watch on the new arrival.

At dusk, Sonya Wüttenberg inspected the Boulevard de Clichy, which was alive with tourists on their way to an unforgettable Parisian night. The wide boulevard burst with a camera-bearing crowd reading maps and speaking a dozen languages.

Her Glock automatic shoved in the small of her back and covered with her long-sleeved black shirt, and a small Walther PPK strapped to her left calf under a pair of Levi's, the Fed casually made her way up the street, past the taxi stand at the intersection with the Rue des Martyrs, her green eyes finding the warehouse at the other end of the block.

An ocean of neon lights came alive, humming along the long boulevard as she stood at the intersection inspecting the distant three-story stone building, tourists passing her in both directions, some apologizing when accidentally bumping into her.

A purse hanging loosely from a skinny shoulder struck her side wound and she winced in pain, instinctively dropping her elbow to protect her left side from another careless pedestrian, furious eyes watching the slim figure in a black miniskirt and blouse walking away while looking at a travel brochure, the culprit black leather purse swinging behind her.

Tears momentarily blinding her, Sonya swallowed hard and let only one escape. The hot tear trickling down her cheek reminded Sonya of her vulnerability. The purse had merely bumped into her side. One hard blow by an opponent would cripple her long enough to get her killed.

Leaving the crowd behind, her wound protesting, Sonya made her way up the long street, remaining on the left-hand side, opposite the warehouse at the other end.

You will find them inside, the scribble on the piece of paper enclosed with the photographs had said. Sonya considered her choices, none of which appealed to the seasoned operative. She noticed two men standing in a recess by the warehouse's main entrance, partly cloaked by the shadows between streetlights. One of the men smoked while the other leaned against the doorway with both hands shoved in his side pockets. Flanking the small entrance, Sonya saw two wide garage doors, probably used for deliveries. Her eyes returned to the men, now looking in her direction.

Guards, probably armed.

Without breaking her casual stride, Sonya weighed her options. If the message was genuine, it presented her with a unique opportunity to catch the Kardinal off guard, giving her a second chance at killing him. If the message was not genuine, she felt she would have been shot by now. The flat roof of the warehouse made a perfect vantage spot for a sniper. The fact that she was still alive, as she walked right in front of the building, probably meant the message had been real. It also meant Titov-Escobar would not be expecting her.

Outnumbered and probably outgunned, Sonya needed an edge, and she instinctively decided to bank on the element of surprise. Her hand reaching behind her back, she pulled out a French phrase book and a map. Casually, she crossed the street, walking directly toward the pair looking in her direction, both bulky, hard, and as tall as she. As she got closer, leading the way with her opened phrase book, ignoring her aching wound, Sonya noticed a substantial age difference between the two men. One was in his mid-twenties, a stocky blond with curly hair down to his shoulders. He pulled his hands from his pockets and crossed his bare arms, biceps bulging under his bronze skin. The other, much older, totally bald, and apparently in charge, wore a shirt that revealed the firm contour of his powerful pectorals. He brought a palm to his pockmarked face, taking a drag from the half-smoked cigarette wedged between his index and middle fingers.

"Ah . . . *bon* . . . *bonsoir?*" Sonya asked, an embarrassed smile on her pale face, noticing the bulge under the pockmarked man's open shirt. *A chest holster.* She also noticed the automatic rifle standing against the door, by the feet of the blond.

The pockmarked man glanced at the blond and smiled, taking another drag and shifting his gaze back to the slender figure already pivoting on her left foot while bringing the right one up, striking him across the left temple. The cigarette flew to the side as the edge of her boot ruptured the nerves and arteries close to the skin, inducing internal bleeding that made him collapse immediately, his body briefly jerking in seizures.

Before her first victim had dropped to his knees, Sonya had extended her left leg against the blond, heel striking the solar plexus.

His body instantly curled into a ball of agony. She thrust the palm of her right hand against the blond's right shoulder.

Cartilage cracked. His shoulder dislocated, the blond fell, groaning, gasping for air, right arm hanging by his side, useless, left hand reaching for the rifle by his feet.

Grabbing a clump of curly blond hair with both hands, Sonya crashed her right knee against his face, driving the nose into the cranial bone, gray cerebrospinal fluid jetting through his nostrils as she pushed him toward his limp companion.

Silence.

Sonya took a deep breath, steadying herself, the side wound screaming obscenities the operative didn't care to hear. Adrenaline would soon soothe the throbbing, numb the burning stabs of pain.

Clenching her teeth while scanning the deserted street that led to the cemetery, Sonya felt a trickle of disappointment at the quality of help guarding Titov-Escobar. These two brutes would never have gotten past the Stasi officer review board after the initial seven-week training period, the equivalent of an American boot camp.

Quickly searching the bodies, she found pistols on both. Then she dragged them into the shadows of the recess—an action that threatened to rip her homemade stitches.

Reaching for the weathered wooden door's knob, she turned it as she drew her Glock. Another deep breath and she stepped inside, her right hand holding the weapon over her right shoulder, muzzle pointed at the thirty-foot ceiling of the vast room.

Three yellow forklifts stood to the side, near a two-story-high pile of wooden crates covering many square feet of stained concrete floor. A white Mercedes-Benz parked in front of the forklifts told Sonya someone important hid here. Beyond the crates, she made out what looked like offices, yellow light outlining the distant silhouette of a person behind a frosted-glass window.

Under the dim grayish glow of a few scattered fluorescents hanging from long black cables dropping from the corrugated-metal ceiling, Sonya distinguished a dozen rows of floor-to-ceiling freestanding equipment shelves, similar to those in supermarkets, but taller and running the length of the cavernous room. Four-foot-wide platforms spaced by six-foot-wide aisles, starting at the floor and going all the way to the ceiling, housed everything from bags of concrete to steel beams, lumber, hardware, and other construction equipment.

A noise!

A door closing to her right, her far right. Sonya lunged, reaching an aisle between the towering equipment shelves, hiding behind white bags of concrete mix.

Urgent footsteps neared, the clicking sound not of soft-soled working shoes but of dress shoes.

Tightening the grip on the Glock 19 pistol, Sonya licked her dry lips as a husky, medium-height man with gray hair, dressed in a business suit, walked rapidly toward the front door, a sense of urgency in his moves. He went outside and came back a moment later, locking the door from the inside.

"Achtung! Achtung!" he screamed into a small radio he retrieved from a coat pocket. "The guards are dead! *Machen Sie schnell!"*

German. Vladimir has to be near.

"What is going on?" shouted a familiar voice in flawless German as more steps echoed down the warehouse. The gray-haired man was joined by the bulky figures of two men bearing automatic weapons, behind them Vladimir Titov-Escobar and his female companion—the same woman Sonya had seen in the color pictures.

Five against one. Two of them clutched assault rifles, hopelessly outclassing her Glock automatic, which Sonya still aimed at the man who had shot her brother many years before, the man she had not seen since their brief encounter in Germany's Black Forest, the man she had sworn to kill.

But shoot you cannot, Sonya.

Doing so while trapped inside this warehouse would be suicidal. Besides, Vladimir Titov-Escobar was more than fifty feet away from her. She felt she might be able to hit him, but if she missed the first round, the two assault rifles would not allow her to fire a second time.

For a moment—a very brief moment—Sonya flashed back to the woods of southern Germany, racing in the Black Forest, following her prey, her former trainer, Ludwig's assassin. She remembered the smell of pine trees, heard the crunch of their feet on the leaf-covered terrain, heard their groaning as they struggled to reach the border, cross into Switzerland. But she had intercepted them, held them at gunpoint, leveled her weapon at him, at her,

A wife for a brother. Karla for Ludwig.

Wishing to inflict more pain on the assassin by killing his wife, Sonya had pointed the weapon at Karla and—

The loud report shattered the silence, the round splintering a wooden crate a foot to the left of Vladimir Titov-Escobar, who dove behind a forklift, followed by the tall woman. The three guards swung their weapons toward where the single shot had originated, toward Sonya Wüttenberg.

Instinct overcoming surprise, Sonya dropped to the floor, rolling away from the cloud of white dust created by the deafening rounds impacting the bags of ready-mix concrete.

The gunfire suddenly ceased, followed by hasty footsteps.

Scrambling across the floor, sneaking her way into a shelf half-packed with planks of lumber, skinning her elbows, Sonya painfully emerged on the other side and raced toward the back of the warehouse, hoping for a rear door—praying for one.

She found none. The aisle ended in a corridor that ran the entire width of the rear of the warehouse, a towering stone wall blocking her way out. Cutting left, her lungs burning, her arms caked with the white powder of the torn concrete bags, Sonya lurched six aisles over and headed back up to the front, pausing halfway to listen for footsteps.

A bullet ricocheted off the steel beam to her left. Trained reflexes assumed control, movement became automatic. Sonya sprang forward, lunging directly toward an opening in the lower equipment shelf to her left, landing on her right side, gasping as her slim frame absorbed the blow, trying to protect her wound.

A shot walloped the wooden shelf above her, splinters showering her. Another bullet thundered inside the warehouse as Sonya, Glock held in her right hand, wiggled her body farther onto the shelf while bringing her weapon around, aiming it at the oncoming figure thirty feet away, and firing just as the gunman also fired.

The reports cracked inside the warehouse like a whip. The guard arched back, his head blown apart the same instant that a bullet nipped the collar of Sonya's black shirt. She heard it—*felt* it—zoom past her, crashing into a box of nails behind her.

One down.

Silence, followed by an engine being gunned at the front of the warehouse.

The Mercedes!

The engine noise mixed with that of an electric motor and the sound of a garage door. Panic rose within her.

He can't get away! Not again!

The screeching sound of spinning tires over concrete marked the escape of the Kardinal while his guards hunted her down.

Sonya forced down the impulse to run after the vehicle, her logical side telling her it could be a trap, urging her to follow the priorities dictated by her professional training.

Survive first. Live to fight another day.

Squeezing through a narrow opening between the canvas sacks, Sonya heard the automatic garage door closing. The Mercedes must have left. She crossed over the next aisle, peering up and down the long space between the tall equipment shelves. She saw nothing, but above the noise of her beating heart drumming against her temples, she heard footsteps, then saw the well-dressed man, the one armed only with a handgun, running away from her, obviously not knowing her position.

Lining him up, Sonya pressed the trigger just as a shot from behind her grazed her left temple, ricocheting off the barrel of her gun, stinging her, making her drop the automatic, sending a trembling ache through her forearm.

The echo of her scream merged with the sound of another gunshot.

Feeling warm liquid on the side of her face, knowing she'd been shot, the FBI agent retreated back to the safety of the nail sacks as a bullet split a corner of the wooden shelf where her torso had been a second before. A splinter sliced the back of her hand as she groped for the small Walther PPK strapped to her left calf, bleeding fingers curling around the alloy handle, sliding the barrel back, chambering a round, aiming it.

A bullet came from the opposite direction, screaming in her ears, imbedding itself in a bag of nails. The well-dressed man had doubled back and joined the hunt.

Sonya had seconds to live if she remained in the crossfire of the guards. Crawling backward, skinned elbows leaving narrow bloody tracks on the white lumber, the Walther PPK pointed at the opening in the shelf covering her hasty retreat, Sonya jumped off the wooden plank, rolling over the cold concrete of the adjacent aisle. Having lost the element of surprise, the operative needed a new edge, a new equalizer against the killers hunting her down.

Desperate eyes panned to the guard she had killed, shifting to the weapon. Firm leg muscles sprang to life. She raced toward the weapon, reaching it in seconds. Shoving the bloody PPK in her jeans and gripping the Heckler & Koch MP5 submachine gun, the operative wiped the bloody side of her face against her shoulder and raced toward the front of the building, running parallel to the guards, four feet of shelved equipment separating them inside the murky room.

Murky room!

She'd found her equalizer, her new edge, a way to turn the tables.

Glancing upward, she fired at the fluorescents ahead of and behind her. The fast rattle of the automatic weapon thundered inside the enclosed structure. Shattered glass showered down on her, lacerating the forearms she used to shield her head, her face.

Sprinting ahead once again, boots crushing the broken glass layering the stained concrete floor, Sonya reached the front of the warehouse, where the aisles met the delivery area by the forklifts. Lifting her weapon once more, she took out two more sets of overheads before dropping to a deep crouch and waiting, listening for the footsteps of her enemy.

A dark figure dashed past her field of view, like a black ghost, gone before Sonya could turn the heavy weapon in his direction.

Damn!

Now she had one guard on either side of her. Wary of being sandwiched, Sonya raced back to the rear of the warehouse, cut right at the end, and carefully moved up the back, taking out three sets of fluorescents in a burst of deafening fire. More glass fell on her, adding injury to injury, and she was giving out her position every time she used the MP5—not to mention depleting her limited supply of ammunition. But creating darkness was worth it.

At the corner, she made another right, moving up to the front, reaching the side of the main office, in front of the forklifts.

Silence.

Controlling her breathing, the operative slowly removed her boots, one at a time. Then her white socks, using one like a bandanna to wrap the superficial head wound and another to wipe the blood off her cut forearms and cover the gash on her hand.

Barefoot, careful not to step on broken glass, she moved toward the forklifts while sweeping the dark surroundings with her weapon, not certain where the two operatives had—

A blow to her side sent her crashing against the cold concrete.

Dazed, confused, not understanding how the guard had managed to sneak up on her, Sonya tried to roll away as the kick came, missing the wound but striking her abdomen, making her gasp for air.

"Weibsstück! Bitch! You will pay for your intrusion!"

Sonya heard the words as another set of footsteps reached her and a swinging dress shoe kicked her from the opposite direction, a direct hit on her side wound.

Trembling, the agonizing pain making her bladder release, Sonya's bursting lungs wrenched out a howl of raw pain. She saw the translucent image of the concrete floor, men's legs, and the metal roof swap places as she rolled back to the first guard, like a pain-maddened animal, her back arched like a bent bow, the searing pain from the torn stitches of her reopened wound making her wish for a quick death.

Another kick to her bleeding torso made her want to cry out in despair again, but the savage pain clamped the words in her throat.

The stench of her own urine soiling her jeans reached her flaring nostrils, mixing with the coppery smell of her blood, now flowing out of her face, hand, and torso. Light-headed, pain-crazed, gasping for air, Sonya watched through her tears the dark figures of the two guards as they raised their assault weapons, butts falling in her direction.

But instead of the deathblows she anticipated, several gunshots came, multiple reports thundering inside the stone-and-steel structure. She watched the figures fall back, their heads exploding in clouds of human debris.

Silence, followed by footsteps.

Confused, dizzy, the world around her spinning with overwhelming intensity, Sonya Wüttenberg raised her bruised face to the dark silhouette approaching, reaching her side, carefully inspecting her side wound, then walking to one of the dead guards, tearing off his shirt with bearlike strength, and silently returning to her side.

"Who . . . who . . ." Her side, her face, her everything hurt too much to talk, forcing Sonya to accept in silence the field dressing the large man, whose face was still cloaked by the darkness engulfing them, expertly applied.

Lifting her light frame off the concrete with amazing ease, the powerful man carried her out of the warehouse and into the cool night air.

"Who . . . who are you?" Sonya whispered through the pain. "Who . . . are . . . ?"

As her eyes closed, as her head leaned to the side, landing on the stranger's chest, Sonya heard the English words spoken with a heavy Slavic accent.

"A friend. I am a friend."

11

UNCERTAINTY

We sail within a vast sphere, ever drifting in uncertainty, driven from end to end.

—*Pascal*

Sunday, July 23, 11:00 P.M.

Thick rain pounded against the sidewalk as Jake Fischer ran from his pursuers, two bulky figures in gray overcoats. Lightning flashed, the thundering sound of a gunshot mixing with the natural sounds of the storm, as Jake reached FTI's parking lot.

Dodging parked cars, Jake ran toward the front entrance as one bullet ricocheted off the asphalt, another shattered the windshield of a car, sprinkling him with broken glass. But Jake could not stop, would not stop. He had to warn them, had to sound the alarm, make them evacuate the building, try to save them. *Do* something!

Jake screamed as he reached the building, screamed at the guard to let him in, to unlock the glass doors. *They're not supposed to be locked! Let me in! Sound the alarm! Get everyone out of here! Kathy, my team, my life! PLEASE!*

A thundering explosion turned the night into day, catapulting Jake away from the building, dropping him like a rag doll in the parking lot, where he could only watch helplessly all over again as the building, his team, Kathy, were consumed by fire. He had failed them . . . he had—

Jake Fischer woke up soaked in perspiration as the jet landed at Charles de Gaulle International Airport. Wiping the sweat off his face, he looked around the first-class section of the Boeing 747, noticing the blond flight attendant smiling at him.

"Bad dream," he said with an embarrassed shrug.

"Welcome to Paris," she responded, patting his shoulder as she turned around and walked to the front of the plane.

Jake checked his Seiko and noticed that the trip from LAX had taken twenty minutes less than anticipated. He now remembered the pilot saying something about a tailwind.

The only one sitting in his row, Jake moved over from his window seat to the aisle and waited for the jet to reach the terminal.

Once inside the terminal, Jake Fischer cruised through immigration and security without a problem. Flashing an American passport usually made life easier when traveling in Europe.

Wearing a clean pair of jeans and T-shirt, Jake walked into the arrivals hall, where a mob of tourists waited for their luggage before proceeding to customs and then to the buses, taxis, and trains that would take them to final destinations.

Jake made his way through the crowded place, remembering Iyevenski's instructions. He scanned the faces around him, never staring at anyone in particular, but always looking long enough to register facial expressions, looking for a pair of eyes that might stare back at him with an intensity absent in the average jet-lagged traveler.

The eyes, Jake, Iyevenski had told him when Jake called him from the phone built into the armrest of his seat in the 747. *Look at the eyes. Discard vacant stares but beware of a flash of recognition. Constantly check for tails without drawing attention.*

Pushing a glass door, Jake walked onto the concrete sidewalk bordering the long arrivals and departures ramp, where Iyevenski had told him he would meet him, but he saw no sign of the large Russian.

Turning around, Jake verified that he had exited the terminal by the American Airlines sign.

Where are you, Sergei?

At that moment, Jake Fischer felt the muzzle of a gun pressed against his back. Just as a white Mercedes pulled up to the curb, the muzzle lightly tapped his back, pushing him forward as a voice behind him commanded, "Get in."

"Step on it, Nicole!" barked Iyevenski. The slim French woman was doing her best to maneuver her Renault through the Sunday-night traffic on the expressway leading to the airport. Iyevenski silently fumed, angry at himself for having lost track of time while saving the FBI woman.

The Russian checked his gold Rolex. Jake's plane was due to arrive in minutes, and, given their current predicament, he didn't want to leave his friend exposed at a crowded airport terminal. The eyes of Paris were looking for a Russian, but Iyevenski felt it likely that the mysterious assassin would no doubt have also passed pictures of Jake to his soldiers just in case.

Iyevenski had carried the FBI woman into Nicole's Renault and gone to her house. Julianna Rochereau had arrived within fifteen minutes and relieved Iyevenski in his efforts to minimize the blood flow. She had then removed the old stitches, cleaned the lesions, and sewn up the hand and the torso. The cuts on her head and forearms only needed disinfectant and Band-Aids. Two broken fingers had required splints. After injecting the FBI woman with antibiotics and painkillers, Julianna had kissed her mother, said, *"Au revoir, Mama,"* and headed back to school. She lived on campus and came home only when her studies allowed it.

But the whole episode had taken several hours. *Too long,* thought Iyevenski, who had to carry the unconscious woman back to the Renault before they drove off. A glance into the back-seat confirmed that she still slept.

The traffic headed for Charles de Gaulle thickened as the large airport neared. At least he'd had the presence of mind to have

Jacques d'Anjou follow the white Mercedes as it had left the warehouse and accelerated down the Rue des Martyrs. He could only hope word had not reached the assassins about Jake's spur-of-the-moment trip. Based on the level of surveillance at Jake's home and his own—which Jake had described during an in-flight phone call—Iyevenski felt it likely that his friend could very well fall into the hands of the enemy if left stranded at the airport for too long.

Reaching down for the phone strapped to his jeans, the Russian dialed an eight-digit number. A moment later, d'Anjou's raspy voice came on the line.

"Oui?"

"Where are you, friend?

"On the expressway, monsieur. Going back to the city from the airport."

Anguish, like a steel weight, nearly crushed his self-control when he heard the word "airport." It could mean only one thing.

His throat aching with anxiety, Iyevenski cleared it before barking, "The *airport?* What did you observe at the airport?"

Nicole gave him a sideways glance before turning back to the traffic flowing down the four-lane expressway. A large sign on the side on the median depicting a road with a red line going diagonally through it told the Russian the expressway would end in another kilometer. He could see the outer edges of the airport on the right.

"They picked up two passengers by the American Airlines terminal and drove off."

Damn! "Turn around, Nicole! We need to head back to the city!"

The muscular man who had forced him into the Mercedes was driving. Jake Fischer sat in the backseat, next to a peculiar-looking man who had the olive skin of a Hispanic or Italian but the strong features of a Russian. It was the eyes, however, that had really caught his attention. They were dark gray and almost lifeless, like those of a shark. And those eyes were on Jake Fischer at this moment, burning him with an anger Jake found it easy to return in full force. This one looked and behaved like a leader. He had ordered the musclehead to drive and the beautiful Hispanic woman in the front to keep a gun on Jake while he browsed through Jake's personal effects.

Jake turned his attention to the barrel pointed at his face, to the narrowed onyx-black eyes of a woman who belonged in a beauty pageant.

"Where is he?" the man suddenly asked in a chilling voice with a heavy accent. He waved Sergei's Russian and American passports in Jake's face.

"What makes you think I'll tell you assholes anything?"

The blow from the woman came before he knew it, hard, the barrel of the gun striking his left cheek. Momentarily dazed but quickly regaining his composure, Jake wiped at a trickle of blood with the sleeve of his T-shirt.

"Where is the Russian, *puto?*" she asked in a Hispanic accent.

"It is not wise to resist the ways of our Lord," the Slavic man said in a low, even tone of voice. "Tell us where is the Russian infidel."

Jake gazed into those iron-gray eyes and found he had little fear. "Fuck you," he replied defiantly. Instantly a fine hand armed with five red fingernails reached his throat, squeezing with a pressure he would have thought impossible for a woman.

Gasping, his face rapidly turning deep red, eyes bulging, Jake brought both hands to his throat, struggling to peel off the viselike hand, but it only squeezed harder, threatening to break his windpipe. Clawlike fingernails broke the skin, digging deep into the flesh, bringing tears to his eyes.

"Enough," the leader ordered.

Releasing the grip and smiling contemptuously, the Hispanic woman made a fist with her hand, ebony eyes drilling him. "Next time, *cabrón*. Next time I'll crush it."

Jake coughed and swallowed, his throat in flames, blood tricking down from five half-moon-shaped cuts. Massaging his larynx with the tips of his fingers, shuddering, blinking rapidly to clear his eyes, Jake gasped, filling his lungs, a cry choked in his gorge as he slowly exhaled.

The woman slapped him with the same hand. "Speak up, *puto*. Where is the Russian?"

The powerful blow shoved the side of his head against the glass window, stunning him. Dark spots danced in the two feet of space between the woman and Jake.

"I said that is enough, my dear child," the Slav repeated. He cupped Jake's chin, swiftly turning it in his direction. "I ask you again. Where is the Russian? Do not resist me, infidel. It is the will of our Lord that you yield to His way."

Stunned by the odd words as well as the physical punishment, Jake asked, "The way of our *Lord?* You *kill* people for a living, mister. You inflict pain on others for *money*. That's hardly the way of *my* Lord."

"I stand as a force against the current. I am the hammer of God. I represent His wrath against the wicked, and in the end I shall prevail, for God is at my side."

What a nutcase! Jake rolled his eyes and turned away from this character.

"He asked you where is the Russian, *pendejo*," the woman said, her hand turning into a fist.

"He is *stalking* you," Jake found himself responding in an icy tone, a smile flashing on his boyish face. "And *he* is the one who will prevail in the end, because he is *smarter* than all of you." He wasn't sure why he'd responded like that. Perhaps it was that he had little else to lose—aside from his life.

"*Hijo de puta,*" hissed the gorgeous woman from the front seat. "I will cut off your *cojones* for this."

"Pain is a weapon," said the leader, turning to Jake with dark amusement in his eyes. "You *will* tell us where he is. After you get a taste of her skills, you will tell us *everything* we wish to know."

"You're wasting your time," replied Jake. "He was supposed to pick me up at the airport, but you beat him to it. I couldn't tell you where he is even if I wanted to."

"We shall see, *puto,*" said the woman. "We shall see."

Wiping the blood off his neck, Jake looked at the woman's cat-like, inky eyes, but they were looking past him, at the traffic behind them.

"*Hijo de puta,*" she murmured again after another minute. This time, however, the comment was not directed at Jake, but at the traffic beyond the rear window. "Someone is following us, *mi amor.*"

"I know," the Slav said, his eyes looking straight ahead. "He has been following us since we left the warehouse."

"How did you know?" she asked.

"The Lord speaks to me, my dear child."

Jake almost chuckled at that one but decided not to risk another slap.

"Do you want me to lose him before we reach the Left Bank safehouse?" asked the muscular driver, peering into the backseat through the rearview mirror.

"No," the Slav said, without taking his eyes off the traffic flowing into the French capital, showing no sign of alarm. "Let the infidel come," he said, reaching for the mobile phone built into the seat. "He is not the only one who knows how to turn the tables."

The woman smiled a captivating smile, her jet-black eyes focusing on Jake Fischer. *"Carnada,"* she said, the pearly smile widening. *"Tu eres la carnada."*

Carnada. Jake had heard the word before, a few years back, when Sergei and he had taken a break from the planning of FTI and had gone fishing off a pier in San Francisco. He remembered a group of Mexicans fishing next to them. They had used the word repeatedly when hooking worms at the ends of their fishing lines. They had pointed at the worms but had referred to them not as *gusanos,* their proper Spanish name, but as *carnada.*

Bait.

"Speak up, d'Anjou! I'm losing you!" Iyevenski shouted into his portable unit, icy fear twisting in his gut at the thought of losing Jake, who would not be able to defend himself against those professionals.

"They're crossing the Place de la République going south toward the Place de la Bastille," came the Frenchman's voice mixed with static.

Iyevenski relayed the information to Nicole Rochereau, who sped down Boulevard de Magenta, directly toward Place de la République.

"Were you serious about buying me a new car, Sergei?" Nicole asked, swinging the steering wheel left to avoid hitting a pedestrian, the dark sedan fishtailing when she straightened the wheel and floored it, nearly ramming a parked Fiat.

"I always mean what I say," he replied, a hand on the dashboard and another on the handhold above the side window, which he'd rolled all the way down to let out the smoke from her cigarette.

Paris rushed by, the cool evening air whipping his face, swirling his long hair, the multiple horns of angered drivers blasting every time Nicole pulled a new stunt. Place de la République came and went. They now accelerated toward Place de la Bastille. Iyevenski estimated that they were no more than a few blocks behind d'Anjou.

"Then put on your seat belt," she replied, hands clutching the black steering wheel. She leaned forward, dark eyes on the narrow street. "I don't want you dying on me if we get in an accident."

Iyevenski sank into his seat as the Renault rocketed down the right lane for two blocks before Nicole forced the car into a sharp turn, the vehicle skidding over the asphalt, barely missing a streetlight post, jouncing over the curb. A clattering told Iyevenski they had just lost a hubcap.

She expertly kept her foot on the gas, steering it back on the asphalt, and the vehicle regained speed, shooting down the narrow street. Iyevenski reached for the seat belt and strapped it across his broad chest.

They had to hurry. This was the best time to rescue Jake, shortly after his kidnapping, before the enemy reached a safe house, before they got a chance to regroup, to set up a defense. Nameless streets darted past, one after another. Restaurants, clubs, churches, century-old buildings, all under a twilight that blended with that of a thousand neon signs. But the former KGB officer concentrated on conveying directions to Nicole as d'Anjou followed the white Mercedes to the Left Bank, down the Boulevard Saint Michel, past the Luxembourg Gardens, and into Avenue Denfert Rochereau. He could now see d'Anjou's cab less than a block away. He also spotted the white Mercedes.

The Mercedes turned right into Rue Froidevaux, which ran alongside the large Cimetière du Montparnasse. The traffic lessened.

"Can you get a couple of blocks ahead of them?" Iyevenski asked. "I want to cut them off."

Nicole cut sharply left at the next street and then right at the end of the block, pushing the Renault as fast as it would go. After five blocks, she turned back toward Rue Froidevaux.

Strike at the most unexpected moment without hesitation, with full force.

Hang in there, my friend. Hang in there.

Traffic had been reduced to a half-dozen cars as the German sedan left the city's main boulevards and now drove on secondary streets. Jake watched the endless rows of crosses as they drove at the posted speed limit through a cemetery on the Left Bank. Everyone had remained quiet, and that had suited him just fine. Not only did he not feel like listening to another morbid litany from the dark crusader, but no questions meant no pain, especially at the hand of that woman.

The beauty of a model and the skills—and the strength—of a professional assassin. This world never ceased to amaze Jake Fischer.

A glance at his watch caused the Hispanic woman to jerk the gun back toward him. Jake grimaced and shook his head. *Shot in the face for checking the time.* He found dark amusement in that thought.

Nothing was funny after that.

"Ram it!" Iyevenski commanded as they came to a screeching halt at the intersection of Rue Froidevaux and Rue Amie. As expected, the Mercedes was coming towards them from the right about two blocks away.

"What?" Nicole Rochereau asked, barely able to control her gasp of surprise.

"You heard me," Iyevenski said, his wrinkled features hardening. "It's the only way!" The Russian used an index finger to stab a switch on the dashboard, cutting off the headlights.

"You're insane, Sergei! You can't pay me enough to kill myself," Nicole shouted back.

"Fine! Get out and I'll ram it myself!" Iyevenski said curtly, glancing down Rue Froidevaux while unbuckling, the headlights of the oncoming Mercedes still a block and a half away. In considerably less than a minute it would reach the intersection and cross directly in front of them.

"One hundred thousand francs and you can do as you wish to this car," she said coldly, crossing her arms.

"Deal! Now get out!"

"The money, Sergei," she said, sticking an open palm at the Russian. "If you kill yourself I might not be able to collect."

"Damn!" The Mercedes was only a block away. Iycvenski shoved a hand in his pocket and handed her the roll of cash. "Count it outside. Now, move . . . *please!"*

Nicole opened the door, extending a thumb toward the backseat. "What about her?"

"No time! There might be some shooting, so find some cover! Now, out, *out!"*

"Crazy Russian!" she said, leaping out of the car as he scooted over to her seat.

Closing the door and buckling up, Iyevenski put the car in gear and waited, hands gripping the steering wheel. The Mercedes continued toward him in the right-hand lane, its headlights cutting through the dusk.

Iyevenski waited, black fright sweeping through him, his stomach clenched tight, his heart feeling as if it would beat its way out of his chest.

Forty feet.

The Russian breathed in shallow, quick gasps, nerves tensed, hands loosening and tightening their grip on the steering wheel.

Twenty feet.

The muscles of his forearms tightened, his biceps trembled, his hands melted with the steering wheel.

Ten feet.

Five.

Imposing savage control on himself, Iyevenski shoved his foot against the accelerator and released the clutch.

Rubber burned on asphalt as the black sedan fishtailed for a second and then rocketed forward, almost as if being released from a slingshot. The Russian sank into the seat, felt the acceleration shoving him back, fought for control of the car, struggled to keep the nose aimed toward the Mercedes.

The driver saw him at the last second and tried to steer away from him, but Iyevenski made one final adjustment without releasing the pressure on the accelerator.

The impact jerked him forward, against the seat belt, compressing his rib cage, as the Renault pinned the Mercedes to the wrought-iron fence surrounding the cemetery, a shower of sparks engulfing the vehicles. The Renault's front grill locked with the torn driver's door of the Mercedes. The vehicles' independent momentums suddenly became one, throwing their combined mass into an uncontrollable spin.

The fence gave, a section falling over the Renault, another crashing through the windshield of the Mercedes as the vehicles skidded onto the grass. The Renault's radiator hissed, a veil of vapor suddenly blocking the view of the Mercedes as Iyevenski fought for control, his foot still on the gas, the engine wheezing, losing compression, the tires slowing over the lawn.

Jake saw the oncoming car a fraction of a second before it hit, giving him the time to brace himself against the side door, a hand gripping the handle.

The collision shoved his right shoulder hard against the door, and the leader against him. He lost track of the woman and the driver in the spinning nightmare that followed the initial crash.

Then came a second impact, as sudden as the first, this one against the wrought-iron fence, which the car blasted through in a shower of sparks. The door suddenly gave and Jake found himself rolling on the grass.

The night, the lawn, the spinning wrecks filled his eyes as he rolled away from the vehicles, away from his captors, stopping by a gray mausoleum.

His chest and head ached, his ears buzzed, his shoulder burned from the impact, but his mind was clear, telling him to get out of sight, to seek shelter. And Jake did, crawling over the damp grass, going around the six-foot-high mausoleum, painfully rising to a deep crouch, back pressed against the cold slate layering the ancient memorial, his face running into spiderwebs spun between the rear of the mausoleum and the low branches of an oak. Rubbing a palm over his face and head, he wiped it clean, feeling a lump swelling over his left temple. Like most of his recent bruises, he didn't remember getting it.

Abrupt silence descended over the cemetery.

The cars had stopped. Jake looked over his left shoulder, saw the rising steam boiling up to the sky, smelled the burning rubber mixing with the fetid dankness of mold on the slate. He saw no movement from either vehicle.

Who had rammed them?

Then Jake saw that it was a taxi. As he thanked his lucky stars, Jake Fischer suddenly smelled—

Gasoline!

The thought had just entered his mind when the hood of the Mercedes burst into flames.

In the same instant, through the flickering light, he saw the Slav roll out of the car and pry the front door open, dragging the Hispanic woman out. She appeared hurt but could walk with help. The two frantically looked around, obviously searching for him, but probably more concerned about escaping with their lives to live to fight another day.

Jake inched his head back and dropped all the way to the ground, feeling the cool grass against his face, keeping them in full view as the flames spread to the Mercedes's midsection. Without bothering to help their own driver or the driver of the taxi, the couple staggered away from the wreck, reaching the street through the missing section of fence. In another thirty seconds they were out of sight.

The flames reached the hood of the Renault, growing brighter and illuminating a dozen wooden crosses listing from decay. Two thoughts swept through Jake's mind with equal force.

The taxi driver!

The passports!

As much as he hated the idea of the passports burning inside the Mercedes, Jake couldn't possibly risk letting the driver of that taxi burn to death for some pieces of paper. He had to get him out first. Only then could he go and look for the passports. If he had time after that, he would try to save the bastard who had driven the Mercedes.

He raced for the taxi and reached the driver's door, but the door was already open, the front seat empty. Through the flickering light, Jake looked in the rear seat, saw a slim figure sprawled over the gray upholstery.

Had the impact thrown the driver into the back?

Deciding not to worry about what laws of physics might have made that possible, Jake jerked the door open, the heat of the nearing flames, which now fully enveloped the Mercedes, making him cringe. He had to hurry, had to get away from the wreckage before it—

He heard a groan. It was a woman, unconscious, stirring, unaware of the grave danger she was in.

As the intense heat bubbled up the paint on the Renault's hood, as inky smoke began to fill the compartment, Jake momentarily froze when he recognized the face.

The FBI woman! Sonya Wüttenberg!
Impossible!

Eyes watering from the acrid smoke swirling thickly around him, Jake Fischer, choking, his bruised body protesting the strain of shouldering the unconscious woman, raced toward the wrought-iron fence, snorting, coughing to clear his airway from the choking smoke he'd inhaled.

Then he froze, seeing the dark figure of a large man holding a pistol.

Not again!

Cursing his luck, Jake was about to cut left, take his chances in the cemetery while hauling this stranger, when he heard a familiar voice.

"Welcome to Paris, my friend!"

Jacques d'Anjou tried his best to find the missing pair Sergei had asked him to follow, but they had vanished. He spent thirty more minutes crisscrossing the area, without success.

Lighting a cigarette, taking a drag, and reaching for the mobile phone, the Frenchman dialed Sergei's number.

"Talk to me, d'Anjou!"

"Monsieur, I'm calling to report that I have lost them."

Silence, followed by, "You did your best, d'Anjou. What about papers, documents? Did you find your friend?"

D'Anjou nodded. *"Oui, monsieur.* I will go to him next. His name is Pierre. He will be the broker between us and the seller. I will stipulate to him our requirements. Pierre will contact the seller, and if there is a matching interest, Pierre will contact us."

"Good. Have him call me directly."

"Oui, oui, monsieur."

"Say, d'Anjou, when was the last time you slept?"

The Frenchman stared at his own bloodshot eyes in the rearview mirror. "Two days ago."

"Make the arrangement with Pierre and have him call me directly. The code will be as follows. He will say, 'Paris in springtime.' I will respond, 'New York in the fall.' Got that?"

Having seen enough American espionage movies, d'Anjou asked no questions, just jotted down the strange combinations of words on a small notepad clipped to the dashboard. "I got it."

"Arrange it and go rest, my friend. I'll contact you in another day."

"*Merci, monsieur.*"

The line went dead as d'Anjou stopped at a traffic light just two blocks away from the accident. The lights of a police patrol car and a tow truck flashed in the distance.

He rolled down the window and drew on the cigarette, waiting for the light to turn. A figure crossed his path. A woman.

The woman!

Fear squeezed his throat, cramped his gut. Before he could react, Jacques d'Anjou felt the muzzle of a gun pressed against his left temple. Someone had walked up to the side of his car and now pointed a weapon at his head through the rolled-down window.

"*Mon Dieu!*" he said, suddenly frozen in terror as the woman walked to the passenger side, got in, and also pointed a weapon at him. A trickle of blood ran from a purplish cut on the forehead of the beautiful, angry stranger.

The rear door also opened and closed, and a gun was then pressed against the back of his head.

"Drive," said a male voice in German-accented French.

"Where . . . where to, monsieur?" Jacques d'Anjou found himself saying, barely able to keep his voice from cracking, fighting his weakening bladder muscles.

"Just drive, infidel. You've been following us for a while now. I think it's time we had a little chat."

Sunday, July 23, 9:05 P.M.

Alone in his office, Donald Bane wondered why this shit all had to happen on his watch. Sonya Wüttenberg had left the embassy to check up on a mysterious message and photos delivered to the front desk that morning, Paris time. The photos, which had clearly shown the man known as Vladimir Titov-Escobar, merited Sonya's immediate response, even if she had to go without backup.

But something had gone wrong. Sonya had failed to report as planned. Several hours had gone by and the rookies at the Paris Station had not heard from the seasoned operative. A call to Roman Palenski minutes before also indicated no word.

Donald Bane cursed his predicament. If she was compromised, Sonya would bring the running total to seven American officers.

Closing his eyes and pinching the bridge of his nose, Bane prayed that Sonya would somehow reappear and return to the Paris station, where the stressed Roman Palenski and Donald Bane planned to hold a video conference call with the arriving troops from the other European stations.

12   QUESTIONS AND ANSWERS

Pain will force even the truthful to speak falsely.
—Publilius Syrus

Yolanda Vasquez knew how to break a man. She had been doing it since the day she'd joined the revolutionary party in Havana at the age of eighteen. The slim Cuban with the glistening honey skin approached the shivering, pale man tied naked to a long table in the basement of an old mansion south of Paris, an estate purchased by the same front company that owned the warehouse in Montmartre.

Yolanda approached the terrorized taxi driver from the side. She remembered the many times she had done this, remembered the formidable warriors she had broken like children. She remembered the trips to Nicaragua as a member of Castro's envoy to assist the Sandinistas in the final days of the revolution that toppled the government of Anastasio Somoza during the Carter years, before she earned the visibility that helped her join the elite Cuban air force.

Yolanda had become a specialist in the art of inflicting very high levels of sustained pain without causing death on the toughest of soldiers for the benefit of the revolution. *La Doctora,* they had called Yolanda, for her interest in unusual methods of administering pain without leaving a mark on her victims.

She approached the horrified Jacques d'Anjou, who had already confessed freely, but the Kardinal wanted him tortured to corroborate his original information.

Yolanda Vasquez almost felt sorry for him. The Frenchman would not last five minutes, the time it took her just to set the instrument in place.

As she picked up an inch-and-a-half-diameter brass ring, Yolanda suddenly realized she had not done this for some time ... for almost six years. She suddenly realized that she had missed the savage intimacy of the process, the brief closeness she felt with her victims—the closeness that drew her to her subject. She slid the ring down d'Anjou's flaccid member, hanging loosely between his hairy upper thighs, before taking it in her hands and stroking it.

The uncircumcised D'Anjou mumbled through the rag shoved in his mouth, closing his eyes, leaning his head back, hardening quickly, growing to a size that Yolanda would have thought impossible from its unexcited state. The brass ring, firmly held in place now by the throbbing member, would maintain the erection long after the pleasure of the moment was contradicted by savage pain.

The Cuban had seen it many times before, had heard the screams as she inserted the flexible electrode down the urinary tract, until she felt the tip curve toward the bladder. She remembered the slight resistance telling her she had gone deep enough for the treatment.

As countless times before, the moan had turned into a muffled cry that preceded the familiar twisting, the tight fists, the supplicating eyes, the quivering legs, but the erection remained firm thanks to the brass ring. She needed the stiff member to maximize the effect of the treatment, every nerve end attuned to the most minute of inputs. That had been the secret of Yolanda's treatments, the reason for her ability to break her victims in a fraction of the time taken by other "Cuban field intelligence officers" assisting Central American rebels. She used the male body's natural ability to focus all energy on an erection to her advantage, by maintaining the erection during the treatment and amplifying the effects tenfold, making it impossible for any human being to resist, regardless of their pain-tolerance level. This went far beyond pulling fingernails or driving needles into eyeballs. That was the work of amateurs, who seldom got results before inadvertently killing their subjects.

Before connecting the wires soldered to the end of the electrode to the small generator resting on one corner of the table, Yolanda reached for the gag and pulled it free, saying in heavily accented French, "Where is the Russian?"

Just as many times before, an awful cry followed the sudden removal of the cloth, a desperate cry from a desperate man. She'd heard such cries twenty years before, in the jungles of Guatemala and on a boat off the coast of Haiti. She'd heard the awful sobs as she broke a Somoza strongman and an American military adviser. And she heard it now from the helpless Frenchman, who turned the sobs into information at her simple request, who confirmed what he had already told her time and again about the location of the Russian with the unlimited budget, about the house of a woman named Nicole Rochereau, about d'Anjou's own second-floor flat on the Left Bank.

But Yolanda had to be certain, had to connect the electrodes and crank the handle of the manual generator. This she did without shoving the cloth back into the Frenchman's mouth, a part of her longing for the shriek that would soon follow, the cry that would bring back memories of simpler times, of nights when the crazed howls told her she was making a difference, contributing to the revolution.

She quickly turned the generator handle three times, sending a burst of current through the electrodes, scourging the Frenchman with the power of a thousand kidney stones. His back bent like a bow, his bulging eyes threatening to pop out of his contorted face.

The information came without her asking for it, just as in the old days. This time, instead of coordinates on a map, instead of number of soldiers, ammunitions depots, or communications centers, the trembling voice filling the basement spoke of street addresses, of phone numbers, of the secretive Russian, of the message delivered to the American embassy.

Slowly, with a care that she had not forgotten in spite of the years since she had done this, Yolanda Vasquez collected the information that the Kardinal would need to complete the contract.

PARIS, FRANCE
Monday, July 24, 4:30 A.M.

Jake Fischer sat across the small kitchen table in the two-story brownstone belonging to the French woman Iyevenski had introduced as Nicole Rochereau. In one of the upstairs bedrooms slept Sonya Wüttenberg, who looked as if she had been just as mistreated as Jake since their brief meeting in San Jose last Friday evening:

Not much more than two days. So much has happened!

Jake sipped the Perrier Nicole had handed him ten minutes before, shortly after the foursome had arrived at the house. Still unseen was another French accomplice of his Russian friend, a man Iyevenski referred to as d'Anjou.

Nicole prepared coffee in the cream-tiled kitchen, which consisted of a couple of eggshell-colored cabinets flanking a two-burner stove. The modest counterspace was supplemented by the top of a waist-high walnut refrigerator, from which Nicole, leaning down, removed a small bottle of milk.

As the French woman prepared café au lait, Jake softly rubbed the facial bruises and neck cuts the woman with the black-pearl eyes had inflicted on him.

"You get used to them after a while," Iyevenski said, patting Jake on the shoulder.

"I don't intend to get used to them, Sergei. I intend to get the bastards who did this to us and then get the hell back home and start rebuilding our company."

"Our dream . . . yes," Iyevenski said, his words trailing off as he gazed in the distance. "There is something I have not told you, yes?"

Jake leaned toward him. "What, Sergei?"

"You know about the cash and the tape in the locker at the train station, yes?"

Jake nodded. "You already told me. You keep the key inside your underwear."

"There is also another locker, friend."

"Yeah?"

"It has the rest of the stolen payment."

Crossing his arms, briefly eyeing Nicole still working in the small kitchen, Jake asked, "How much is it, Sergei?"

"It's a large number of stocks and bonds worth around twenty-four million deutsche marks."

Jake leaned back on the chair, stunned. "That's . . . that's . . ."

"About fifteen million dollars, yes?"

"Damn," Jake said, staring into Iyevenski's amused eyes, his voice dropping several decibels as he whispered. *"Fuck,* Sergei. Are you thinking what I'm thinking?"

The Russian smiled. "There is no need to whisper, friend. And I *am* thinking the same, yes."

Jake also smiled. "Poetic justice, Sergei."

The Russian gave him a puzzled stare. "What?"

"Never mind. Where is the key to this locker?"

"Taped to the ceiling of the first locker."

"Who else knows about it?"

"No one else. Not even Nicole or d'Anjou."

"Where is d'Anjou?" asked Jake as Iyevenski took a cup of hot coffee from the attractive woman.

"He is running an errand for us," replied the Russian, setting his nose over the steaming mug and inhaling while closing his eyes, then taking a sip and setting the cup on the rust-colored table.

Aside from this last revelation, Jake and Sergei had gotten a chance to catch up during their multiple Métro trips, which not only Iyevenski but also Nicole had insisted on to make sure no one followed them here. According to Iyevenski, Nicole, whose car he had trashed, didn't feel like also losing her house on the same night—regardless how much the Russian was willing to pay.

Nicole now sat next to Iyevenski, her lavender lips parting as she took a sip of his coffee before setting it back down in front of the large Russian and lighting a long brown cigarette. She took a drag and, keeping her chin up, blew the smoke toward the small brass chandelier over the table.

The powerful, borderline-nauseating smell attacked Jake's nostrils. How or where Iyevenski had met such a woman, Jake didn't know—and didn't want to ask, figuring he'd just go with the flow. If Jake had learned something in the past few days it was the lack of control he had over his own destiny. The more he tried to bring matters under his control, the more they spun out of his reach. He had not been in Paris for more than forty-five minutes before he'd been kidnapped, beaten, nearly choked, and rescued by a deliberate automobile crash. Now, after getting a thorough tour of the Métro system and Montmartre, he drank Perrier in the home of a stranger. For a man who'd always been in control of his life, Jake found it quite difficult to get used to his new situation.

After the joy of the reunion faded, the problem of the burned passports had settled in. Now both Jake and Iyevenski were stuck, unable to go back home unless they involved the FBI, namely the severely beaten woman in the bedroom.

"There is another way," Iyevenski said, glancing at the model-thin Nicole Rochereau and whispering a few words in French. Unlike Iyevenski, Jake was not fluent in French.

The woman took another drag before giving Iyevenski a frown and a shake of the head.

"She is not very happy about d'Anjou's suggestion. She thinks it is much too dangerous," said Iyevenski, winking at Nicole and leaning over and whispering a few more French words.

"Quel imbécile!" she let out with a blast of smoke. "You stupid . . . stupid . . ."

"Russian?"

"Oui!" she punched him in the shoulder and, flustered, got up and stomped out of the kitchen and into the small downstairs bathroom, slamming the door while cursing in French.

"A beauty, isn't she?" asked Iyevenski, blowing a kiss toward the bathroom door. "I think she really likes me, yes?"

"I think she likes your money, Sergei."

"At first, yes? But now . . . she is a good woman, my friend. Good heart, good mother, hard worker, does not ask many questions, understands that I must do what I must do."

Jake took in the large Russian, who, dressed in a T-shirt and white cotton jacket, looked as if he'd just stepped out of a *Miami Vice* episode. "How do you do it, Sergei? How do you . . . Never mind, I really don't want to know. Let's go back to this d'Anjou person. What's his story?" Jake heard a toilet flushing.

The Russian shrugged. "He knows someone who knows someone who might get us passports . . . for the right price."

"A friend of a friend of a friend? I don't know, Sergei. I tend to agree with Nicole on this one. That sounds like a good way to get yourself in trouble."

"Ha, ha!" the Russian exclaimed, slapping his thigh with mirth, and then the table, startling not only Jake, but also Nicole, who'd just come out of the bathroom. "You make me laugh, friend! You are concerned about getting yourself in *trouble?*" The lined face under the moussed salt-and-pepper hair suddenly turned as stern as the cold blue eyes under his bushy eyebrows. "What do you call twenty-two dead at our plant? What do you call having assassins shooting at you all over Palo Alto? What do you think it means to have dead men in your own house, and another in front of your house—that last one killed by you? You barely stepped out of the plane and someone forced you into a car! Face it, my friend, you—*we*—are in trouble above our necks."

Jake nodded. *"Up to* our necks, Sergei. It's *up to,* not *above.* And you're right. We're already in pretty deep waters."

"We are out of choices, yes? We need the mobility that those passports provide. Without them we are sitting pigeons."

Jake got the message and realized why Sergei Iyevenski was willing to take a risk like that—the same reason he had rammed the Mercedes using Nicole's Renault: it was an all-or-nothing game now, if one could call it a game. In order to win against an enemy like the one who'd killed their team, Jake and Iyevenski had to become something worse than the enemy. They had to become their enemy's ultimate nightmare.

"We must make them *fear* us, force them to play according to our rules," Iyevenski said, sipping coffee.

"Which is why we simply can't go to the FBI, right?"

"We go to the FBI or the CIA, or any other government agency, and we will be killed . . . just like those poor bastards in front of the Moulin Rouge, just like the two federal agents in your house—"

"Or Sonya," Jake interrupted, pointing at the upstairs bedroom, where she now slept. "She would also be dead if you hadn't rescued her. I get the message."

Iyevenski just shrugged and sipped more coffee.

Fatigue settling in pockets under his eyes, Jake sank back in his chair, his mind trying to size up the power of an enemy skilled enough to kill American intelligence officers as if they were kids in a playground.

"So, what do we do?"

"We continue playing *my* game, friend. The game that has kept us alive, the game that keeps weakening our enemy, forcing it to retreat, to regroup. *That* is what we do, yes? We use agencies like the FBI and the CIA to help, but *we* are in command, not them."

"And when does the game end? When do we get to go back home and start over?"

"We will know when it is time."

Crossing his arms, Jake asked, "How?"

"I do not know how," Iyevenski responded. "We just will know it is over."

Nicole sat back down next to Iyevenski, stole his coffee, and began to sip it between drags of the same cigarette she'd taken to the bathroom. The smoke reached Jake's eyes, which instantly began to burn.

What in the world is she smoking?

The mobile phone rang, and Iyevenski picked it up on the second ring, listened for thirty seconds, said something in French, and hung up.

"Was that d'Anjou?" asked Jake, blinking rapidly, rubbing his eyes.

"No."

"No? Who then?"

"A new friend."

"A new friend?"

"Yes."

His mouth pulling into a sour grin, Jake asked, "Do you even *know* his name?"

Iyevenski nodded while grinning mischievously. "Pierre."

"Pierre?" Jake repeated.

"Yes, friend. His name is Pierre."

Jake exhaled while half laughing and threw his hands in the air. "Is this d'Anjou's friend of a friend?"

"No, just the friend, the broker."

"And . . . what did he tell you?"

"That he wants to meet to define the elements of the trade."

"Trade?"

"Cash for passports."

Jake shook his head disapprovingly. "I don't know, Sergei. Sounds too dangerous. We know nothing about this Pierre, much less *his* friend."

Iyevenski looked at Jake, irritation on his face. "See her?"

Jake shifted his gaze to the gaunt Nicole, her scarecrow shoulders raised above her chin as she planted her elbows on the table and worked a plastic lighter, a new cigarette in her mouth.

"What about her?"

"She *trusts* me. Never asks questions, because she knows that I know what I am doing."

Jake felt color coming to his cheeks as he looked away and crossed his arms.

"In corporate America you were the boss, yes?"

Jake nodded without looking at Iyevenski, knowing exactly where this was headed.

"And many times you did not bother explaining business details, yes?"

Another nod.

"I simply trusted your good business sense and concentrated on making the technology work. You selected the customer base. You selected the terms of our financing, our building, our staff, our schedules—as you *should* have, being our CEO, yes?"

Jake's gaze returned to the Russian. "I think I get the point, Serg—"

"My friend, this is another world, and in it *I* am the CEO. You must learn to trust me without question if you want to remain alive, just like her . . . just like d'Anjou. Now, do you trust me, Jake Thomas Fischer?"

Tilting his head back, dark blue eyes wavering at the Russian's uncompromising stare, Jake Fischer said, "Yes, Sergei . . . of course I trust you."

The beginning of a smile tipped the corners of Iyevenski's mouth. He looked at Jake, the warmth of his smile echoing in his voice as he patted Jake's back. "Good. Very good. You trust me now, and when this is over and we go back home with our . . . *new funding,* I shall trust you. Now, I must go, but you cannot come, friend."

Jake jerked to his feet. "What do you mean, I can't—"

The Russian also stood, a large palm facing Jake. "Trust, my friend. Remember? I need you to stay behind in case something goes wrong. I need her with me for cover," he said, pointing at Nicole, who stood and finished Iyevenski's coffee.

"You mean she gets to go and I"—Jake pressed an index against his sternum—"get stuck here?"

His face taking an unpleasant twist that also caused his bushy brows to fall over his eyes, Iyevenski said, "You begin to sound like a spoiled child, my friend. I fear I might have to start treating you like one."

Breathing heavily, Jake put both hands on his waist and silently stared at Iyevenski. He simply couldn't stand not being in command. Since he was a teenager in Los Angeles, Jake had been forced to make his own decisions, lead his own life, and he had grown used to it. He had become a leader. In academics, during his wrestling days, at FTI. Now he had to follow, and he was having a difficult time swallowing that pill.

"Here," Iyevenski said, sliding the mobile phone over the wooden surface of the square table toward Jake. "I will be in touch, and you can always reach me if you need to. It is fully charged. . . . One more thing." He went to the bedroom and came out a moment later with a red backpack, which he had retrieved hours before from the trunk of Nicole's burning Renault.

Unzipping a few inches, he put in a hand and fished out a two-inch-thick stack of deutsche marks. "For a rainy afternoon," the Russian said, handing them to Jake.

"Rainy *day*, Sergei."

Iyevenski's lined face rearranged itself into a broad smile. "Yes?"

Jake also smiled and shook his head. "You're incorrigible, Sergei."

"Inco—what?"

"Never mind. Go do what you must. I'll keep an eye on my old friend up there."

Iyevenski winked and headed for the door with Nicole in tow, but suddenly stopped, the French woman bouncing against him and landing on her butt on the hardwood floor.

"Zut alors!"

"Pardon," he said, helping her up and patting her buttocks once before turning to Jake. "I almost forgot." He went into the living room and came out a few seconds later with a small gun. "For you," he said to Jake. "It works the same way as the Makarov."

Jake took the gun in his hands, his mind instantly replaying the vision of gunshots, of the Asian man falling in the middle of the street. Looking up at Iyevenski, Jake said, "I don't know if I can do it again, Sergei."

Iyevenski put a hand on Jake's left shoulder and gave him a soft squeeze. "You will kill again if you have to, my friend. The first time is the most difficult. After that it is a slice of cake."

Iyevenski and Nicole left Jake standing in the doorway to the kitchen, one hand holding enough money to purchase a Mercedes, the other clutching a pistol, the name WALTHER PPK .308 ACP stamped along the shiny stainless-steel slide.

As the door closed, Jake felt the weight of the gun in his right hand, fingers curling around the checkered plastic stock. Setting the cash on the kitchen table, he released the magazine and counted only six shots. The bullets looked larger than the ones the Makarov held. Shoving the magazine back into the butt and sliding the barrel back, chambering a round, Jake took a deep breath and stared at the weapon long and hard, Iyevenski's words echoing in his mind.

You will kill again if you have to.

A block away from the entrance to Nicole Rochereau's two-story house on the outskirts of the city, a black-garbed man lay flat on the roof of another stone house. A powerful nightscope was attached to his Heckler & Koch PSG1 sniper rifle.

The man watched the large Russian leave the brownstone accompanied by a slim woman. The couple were certainly within the range of his weapon, but the man had not been ordered to fire, only to observe and report.

And he did, using a mobile phone to convey the information to the Kardinal.

Having done as ordered, the black figure resumed the surveillance of an address that had been learned from a brutal interrogation at a safe house south of Paris.

As he pressed his right eye to the rubber end of the scope, changing the night into shades of green, the figure in black concluded that his second report of the evening had been as important as his first, when four people, two men and two women, had arrived at the house. He had been able to identify the two men as Jake Fischer and Sergei Iyevenski. One of the women was Nicole Rochereau, who, according to the information extracted during the interrogation, owned the house. The identity of the second woman, however, was unknown.

13 UNLIKELY ALLIES

The firmest friendships have been formed in mutual adversity, as iron is most strongly united by the fiercest flame.

—*Charles Caleb Colton*

PARIS, FRANCE

Monday, July 24, 5:25 A.M.

Jake Fischer heard a noise from the bedroom upstairs and jumped to his feet. He had dozed off while sitting at the kitchen table with the cash and the Walther PPK.

Half asleep, he thought perhaps he had just been dreaming, but the moan came again. It was Sonya Wüttenberg.

Running up the stairs and into the small bedroom, Jake stared down at the slender figure, wearing one of Nicole's nightgowns, sprawled on the small bed, which was flanked by antique wooden nightstands. A dresser stood to the right, next to the only window, which led to a spring-loaded fire stair. Jake recognized it as the type used in old buildings in San Francisco, which lowered to the street under the weight of the evacuating party.

Jake walked to the side of the bed and pressed a hand on her pale forehead. No fever. Still, she was in far worse shape than he'd thought when he'd shouldered her after the crash. In addition to the wounds on her left hand, head, and torso, she had a variety of bruises on her face, lips, neck, and arms. Some, Iyevenski had explained during their long Métro trips, while Jake and the Russian had held her up to avoid drawing attention to themselves, had been from a beating she'd taken from two guards at a warehouse a mile away. The rest probably were from the crash on the Left Bank.

"Nein . . . nein . . . Hilfe . . . nein . . ."

Jake stared at her in the dawn light filtering through the open window, a soft breeze gently swirling white lace curtains. She had kicked the cotton sheets down to her knees and her nightgown had inched up, exposing firm, pale thighs with scattered purple blotches. The German muttering that had started a half hour ago, lasting for a few minutes before she faded back into a deep sleep, now returned.

"NEIN!"

The woman suddenly sat up, shaking, bracing herself, blinking rapidly at the stranger staring down at her, the forest-green eyes gazing wildly around the room.

"Who . . . where . . ." she mumbled, trying to get up, licking her lips nervously.

Jake sat at the edge of the bed and put his hands on her shoulders. "Hey, hey, take it easy. You've been—"

In a single swift and fluid move, her good hand reached up to her shoulder and grabbed Jake's hand, twisting it sideways and down, forcing Jake to flip his body in midair to avoid breaking his wrist, the jolt bringing back memories of lost wrestling matches. Before he knew it he was flat on his back, looking up at a woman who was as deadly as she was lovely, even with the bruises and the knotted, bloody hair. Jake also had the strange thought that this woman could have done wonders coaching the UC Berkeley wrestling team.

Rolling away from her, Jake stood and was about to run for the Walther PPK in the kitchen downstairs when she collapsed back on the bed, dazed, still trying to figure out where she was, obviously having acted entirely on instinct when she'd attacked him.

He got the gun anyway and returned to the bedroom. The FBI agent was in the middle of her second attempt to get up.

"You need to rest," Jake said from a safe distance.

The narrow face turned to Jake Fischer, her eyes suddenly glinting recognition as she succeeded in sitting up. *"You?* What . . . are you doing in . . . Oh, my head," the Fed mumbled as she fell back against the pillow, hands pressed against the sides of her head, eyes closed. "It feels like it is going to explode."

"I want to help you, but you're going to have to stop the karate crap," he warned.

"Where am I?" she asked, propping a pillow under her head and discovering her bandaged hand. "How did I get here?"

"My friend rescued you from a warehouse."

Sonya looked into the distance, "Yes . . . the warehouse." She ran a hand over her left torso. "Did you do this?"

"No," Jake responded. "The daughter of a friend of my friend." Jake suddenly realized he was beginning to sound like Iyevenski.

Sonya shook her head. "I don't—."

"It's okay. You're with friends." He gave her a slight smile.

"Where?"

"In a house just outside Montmartre, backing on some woods north of the city."

"How long have I been out?" She went to check her watch but saw the white bandages covering her left wrist and hand.

"About twelve hours, I think."

"I need to call and report—" Again she tried to get up and failed.

"You're in no shape to do anything but lie there and rest. Besides, no phone calls until my friend gets back."

"Who is that?"

"The guy who rescued you from the bastards kicking your face in."

Sonya brought a hand to her face.

"Don't worry. You're not disfigured. Just a couple of bruises. The big damage was done to your chest, abdomen, legs . . . and the nice job on your hand, of course. Looks like you really pissed somebody off."

The green, catlike eyes dropping from his face to the Walther PPK, the woman said, "Jake . . . please stop pointing my own gun at me."

He looked at the gun in his hands. "I thought you FBI types carried heavier artillery."

She smiled without humor. "Backup weapon."

Jake put on the safety and slipped it into the small of his back, letting his blue T-shirt cover it.

"I'll take it that your friend is the missing Sergei Iyevenski?"

Jake nodded once.

"Where is he?" she asked, turning sideways, noticing her exposed thighs and quickly using her right hand to lower the nightgown to her knees.

"He'll be back shortly."

"Who owns this place?"

"A friend of Sergei's."

"Who is that?"

"Why do you need a name?"

"I see," she said, frowning. "You still don't trust me, do you?"

"Why should I? You won't level with me. And besides, I'm still pretty pissed at you for not doing anything to prevent the butchering of my entire team, not to mention the destruction of my company."

Sonya gloomily shook her head, scarlet appearing on her cheeks. "I am truly—*truly*—sorry, Jake. I really mean it."

Jake crossed his arms. "You didn't seem that sorry the other night in Palo Alto."

"Oh . . . that." She exhaled heavily, looked in the distance for a moment, frowned, and then returned her gaze to Jake. "Look, I had no choice but to take that attitude with you, Jake. You see, we were being followed, and I knew they were after you, not me, so I had to make you want to run away."

Jake closed his eyes in disbelief. Every time he turned around, someone else was trying to use him as bait. "So . . . let me get this straight. You saw armed assassins following us in the car and you behaved like that so that I would run away . . . so that they would go after me, and then you could go after them and capture one alive?"

She nodded, her eyes filled with regret. "I had no—"

"And you still want me to trust you?"

"You have to believe me when I tell you that I am truly sorry, Jake. But the FBI, the CIA, *and* the U.S. government are still on your side, and we can help you."

His voice rising, Jake snapped, "Help *me?* Help me do *what?* Get *killed?* Like the team outside the Moulin Rouge? Or yourself, had it not been for Sergei's intervention? Face it, lady, your track record so far leaves a lot to be desired. Sergei's record, on the other hand, is very good."

"Do you trust he has the necessary skills and resources to see this through all the way? This is not a movie, Jake. This is the real thing. We are fighting the most feared independent contractor in the world, someone with unimaginable resources and intelligence."

"Sounds like you admire the bastard. To me he's nothing but a butcher, and I told him so to his face."

"I do *not* admire, him, Jake," she sputtered, bristling with indignation. "I do, however, respect and fear him, for I have seen firsthand what he's capable of."

"And so have I. Don't forget I saw those firemen drag out the burned corpses, one at a time. As far as intelligence goes, Sergei so far has outsmarted this Titov person at every turn. He's even outsmarted you."

After a moment of silence, Sonya leaned forward. "I . . . I need to use the bathroom."

Leaning down, Jake ran an arm under her shoulders, helping her stand, feeling her firm back muscles as she flexed them getting up.

"Aghh . . ." She closed her eyes, wincing in pain the moment she tried taking a step. Her face was a mask of agony. "Let me sit, please. I need to massage my knee for a moment. It is very stiff."

Jake momentarily enjoyed watching her suffer, but quickly felt ashamed of it. Although he resented her failure to protect his team, he helped her sit at the edge of the bed. She tried to lean down and reach for her bruised knee but quickly shot back up, her one good hand grabbing her side instead, a slight moan escaping her before she mumbled, *"Bastards."* Her fine features drew into a mask of pain as Jake stood in front of her.

"The ones at the warehouse?"

She nodded.

Jake hesitated before saying, "May I?" and pointing to her knee. Without waiting for a response, he kneeled in front of her, reached for her knee, and slowly began to rub it, just as his old wrestling coach had done many times between matches to loosen bruised joints, hands conforming to the shape of her lower thigh, thumbs pressing the flesh as he lowered his hands over the slightly swollen knee and onto her upper calf.

She didn't respond, but didn't pull away either.

"How long have you been a spy?" Jake asked to break the silence, fingers trying to work out a kink on the left side of her knee.

"Too long. And on days like today I wonder why I ever became one in the first place."

Jake sighed. "Why did you?" he asked, trying to remain professional, uncomfortable with the sudden intimacy, feeling as if he were cheating on Kathy Bennett.

"I was orphaned at the age of nineteen," she replied, keeping her eyes closed. "I never knew my father, and my mother died in an auto accident. I had the talent and the physical strength to become a female agent for the Stasi. The pay was far beyond anything I could have earned otherwise, and I had a young brother to support. At the time, I was naive enough to think that I could do this just for a few years and then get out."

Placing a hand under her knee, Jake said, "Try bending it now."

Slowly, a hand on his shoulder, Sonya succeeded in bending her knee.

"Let's try this again," she said.

This time, with Jake's help, Sonya was able to take a few painful steps and reach the bathroom door. Jake opened it for her and helped her make it to the toilet.

Turning around, Sonya said, "I will call you when I am finished. Thank you."

Jake gave her a slight nod and walked out, closing the door behind him.

Jake began to pace the small bedroom, his sneakers thudding lightly on the pine floors, eyes drifting from the closed bathroom door to the open door leading to the stairs and finally landing on the window. Outside, he could see a large wooded area behind the house.

"What am I supposed to do with her now, Sergei?" Jake mumbled to himself. He had hoped that the Russian would return before she awakened.

Sonya took a few minutes longer than Jake had expected, but when she finally came out, her hair was wet and brushed straight back. Her face was clean and alive.

He opted not to comment on her physical appearance and just politely helped her back to the bed, where she sat on the edge. Jake remained standing, keeping his distance, reminding himself what she was capable of.

"How did you get to Paris?" she asked.

Jake decided that was a harmless enough question. "Long story. Sergei coached me long-distance. But they must have followed me, because the moment I stepped out of the airport I was kidnapped by the same people who'd kidnapped Sergei."

"How did you escape?"

He told her.

A hint of astonishment touched her ivory face. "He just *rammed* the Mercedes?"

Jake couldn't help a slight grin. "Amazing, isn't he?"

Disapproval gleamed in her compelling eyes as she slowly shook her head. "Suicidal is more the term, I think."

The grin vanished. "Call it whatever you like. The fact of the matter is that it worked. He hit them hard when they least expected it and rescued me."

"Where was I?"

"In the rear of the Renault."

"When he rammed it against the Mercedes?"

"Yep."

"Then what happened?"

"The cars caught on fire after the collision. I pulled you out of the wreck just in time."

Looking deeply at him, she said, "You . . . you saved my life, Jake. Thanks."

Jake shook his head and walked to the dresser, wondering if she would have done the same for him. Maybe he should have let her burn, just as she had let his team burn at FTI. Deciding to keep it civilized for now, Jake remained silent and handed her a pair of jeans and one of Nicole's shirts. "Here, we washed your jeans for you. Your shirt got trashed."

He turned around, and she dressed in a silence occasionally broken by a soft groan. Dawn light from the window projecting her blurred shadow on the wall. Jake stared at it for the two minutes it took the operative to change.

"I'm finished," she said.

Jake turned. The jeans fit tight around the waist and thighs. The rough cotton shirt hung loose over her torso.

"Here," he said, handing her a pair of sneakers that belonged to Nicole. "I hope they fit. You were barefoot when Iyevenski found you."

She tried to lean down to put them on but jerked up in pain, tears welling in her eyes. "Damn."

"Hold on," he said with a heavy sigh, kneeling down by her feet while she sat on the edge of the bed. Jake guided her left foot into the tennis shoe and tied the laces, then did the same to the other foot.

Sonya's eyes narrowed at him. "Thanks. I—"

A heavy knock came from downstairs.

"Expecting anyone?" she asked.

Jake shook his head, his pulse rising. "No one that needs to knock to get in."

"Look out of that window," she said, pointing to the one next to the dresser. "Tell me what you see, but be careful. There might be a sniper out there."

Struggling to control the fear inundating his system once again, suddenly glad that he had rescued her from the burning taxi after all, Jake used the off-white curtain as a veil as he peeked down at the alley behind the row of houses. "Just an alley bordering some woods. A few garbage cans. No sign of life . . . wait. I see a man hiding behind a garbage bin."

Three more knocks rumbled inside the house. Jake felt the adrenaline rush cramping his throat. It was happening again. He could feel it, could smell it, could sense it.

"Are you a good shot?" she asked.

"Lousy," he admitted, concerned eyes meeting hers.

"Let me have that gun and carry me to the window."

Jake hesitated for a moment before reaching behind his back

and handing her the weapon. Picking her up with both arms while she flipped the safety and cocked the PPK, her face inches from his, Jake carried her to the edge of the window.

Slowly, his heart hammering his chest, his stomach cramping, Jake dropped to his knees and set her on the floor, her hands resting on the windowsill as she sat up and winced, obviously in pain but temporarily pushing it aside.

Keeping one arm around her back to provide stability while she aimed, Jake decided not to look, waiting apprehensibly for—

The report blasted inside the house, rattling the mirror above the dresser, further unsettling Jake Fischer. The smell of gunpowder hung in the air, reminded him of the Fish Market, of the Asian man, of—

"Got him, Jake! Now go! Go and get help!"

The knocking downstairs turned into multiple gunshots, followed by the splintering and cracking of wood and steps in the foyer.

It took Jake a second to digest her words. "Go?"

"Yes! Now!"

"What about you?"

"I'll hold them back."

Jake looked toward the stairs, saw shadows on the wall, heard foreign words shouted in anger, understood what would happen to either one of them if captured. Despite his contempt for her and the FBI, Jake couldn't possibly abandon her.

Without warning he lifted her slender frame, hugging it tight against his chest while going through the window, landing on the narrow iron platform of the fire escape.

"Idiot! You'll get us both killed!" she shouted, admonishing eyes shifting from Jake to the interior of the house.

Setting her down, pulse rushing, panic squeezing his chest, Jake barked in a mix of fear and anger, "No time to argue, Sonya! Get on my back! We're going down!"

Shouts and the noise of broken glass filled the house. Jake turned around and pressed his back against Sonya Wüttenberg, who hopped on, legs wrapped around his waist, arms around his neck. Feeling her warm breath on the back of his neck, Jake Fischer reached for the fire ladder and jumped on it, their combined weight overcoming the spring mechanism. As he began to climb down the ladder, the ladder itself lowered to the street, setting them on the cobblestone alley between the back of the row of houses and the woods.

A shot ripped through the gray dawn sky. Sunrise was just around the corner.

Without hesitation, his heart doing a backflip, Jake Fischer raced past the limp body of the man Sonya had shot and through the knee-high grass to the trees, reaching a towering pine, filling his lungs with its resin fragrance, his shoulders and legs beginning to burn.

"You can't . . . carry me all the way, Jake," she whispered as the woods engulfed them, as his feet sank in an ocean of spongy leaves layering the forest floor, as the sound of a near miss buzzed in his ear long after the bullet cracked a branch from a tree. "Leave me. I'll hold them back. You cannot outrun them . . . not with me on your back."

Jake didn't answer. He simply kept rushing ahead, perspiration already running down his forehead, automatic fire turning the trees behind them into a cloud of mulch and splinters that momentarily covered them as he dashed through it.

Jake didn't look back, couldn't afford to. His eyes concentrated on the woods ahead as he ran through the scraggly underbrush, each frantic step raising clouds of leaves. He had to increase the gap, increase the width of the shield. He heard footsteps behind, crushing leaves and fallen branches.

"Drop me off. Save yourself," she whispered in his ear through the thundering gunshots that followed, her face pressed against the side of his head, arms taut around his shoulders, legs around his waist.

"No . . . no," he muttered through clenched teeth, the stress on his legs agonizing as he kept up the pace, running a straight line for about fifty feet of uneven terrain, rapidly blinking to adjust his eyes to the murky woods, suddenly cutting left, thicker underbrush thrashing at his jeans, low branches slashing his face. Sonya realized what was happening and began to use her good hand to swat branches aside, clearing a path for them as they moved for a few hundred feet parallel to the long row of houses, before Jake stopped, drenched in sweat, arms trembling, back muscles tingling, legs beginning to cramp.

Gently, he set her down behind a pine tree surrounded by thick bushes, tangled and dense enough to give them cover. Their faces inches apart, her eyes glinting in the dim sunlight beginning to filter through the thick canopy, Jake listened for the crunch of footsteps, and he heard them, distant, temporarily nonthreatening.

Shaking his limbs, relieving their soreness while taking deep breaths, Jake tried to relax, to still his pounding heart, the exercise reminding him of breaks between wrestling matches. They had managed to get away, but it was not over. Full daylight would open up the woods, make them a poor hiding place. Sonya extended her good hand toward him and massaged his right shoulder and arm, working the throbbing biceps and triceps. Then she switched to the other arm, and again massaged his aching muscles, fine fingers digging into his flesh, a look of concentration on her pale face.

"I'm—"

She put an index finger over his lips and leaned forward, pressing her lips against his ear, softly whispering, "Sound travels very easily in the woods. They might pick up a whisper as far as two hundred feet away."

Taking in a lungful of air through his mouth and slowly letting it out through his flaring nostrils, Jake felt his strength returning. Nodding and slowly turning around as the sounds of their pursuers neared, he motioned her to get back in the saddle.

He felt her on his back, thin but firm arms around his shoulders, her legs once more clamped to his waist.

"They're tracking us," came another whisper of warm air, tickling his cheek. "They're following your footsteps on the leaves."

Nervousness worming into his stomach, Jake cut left and went deeper into the woods for another fifty feet, beams of sunlight sporadically breaking through the canopy, painting brown leaves with live red-and-gold light. But for Jake and Sonya, light meant exposure, meant death from a marksman's hollow-point round.

Stumbling on a boulder as the terrain sloped upward, Jake fell, instinctively twisting his body to cushion her fall. Sonya's frame, albeit light, still felt crushing as she pinned him over the leaf-covered terrain.

"Are you okay?" she whispered, her body pressed against his side in sudden intimacy.

"I'll live," he responded.

They remained like that for a few seconds, her face only inches from his, listening to the nearing footsteps, to the rustling of leaves that made Jake jump to his feet, hitch Sonya onto his back, and take off just as gunfire once again whipped through the woods. He heard the thud of rounds pounding a pine to his right, peeling off the bark.

Grunting, her weight taking a toll on his speed, the staccato gunfire ringing in his ears, Jake Fischer invoked the last of his strength to make it up a small incline, breathing in the resinous scent of trees, kicking the boulders as he followed the sloping terrain for another minute before cutting left, going deeper into the woods.

Turning around after another minute, he saw the futility of their situation.

"Tracks," he whispered, nearly out of breath, hot air exploding through his mouth. "Those bastards . . . are just following my tracks."

He set her down on the ground, took in the musky odor of acrid loam beneath his sneakers, stared into her eyes.

"We cannot escape together," she said, her chest expanding, her eyes displaying a fear absent until now. "We will both be shot in minutes."

Jake shook his head. "I can't leave you here."

Sonya removed the PPK from her jeans and handed it to him. "Go, Jake. Please. Save yourself."

"What about you?" he asked, amazed at her willingness to sacrifice herself for him.

"It is the risk of my profession."

Jake stood still, right hand clutching the small automatic.

"But before you leave," Sonya said, her jade-green eyes finding his in the darkness, "please, kill me."

Startled by her request, Jake stared at her wordlessly, the sound of his pounding heart fading as the sounds of the gunmen became more discernible. Slowly, Jake managed a slight shake of his head as he said, "You're nuts."

"Think about it. They *cannot* capture me alive," she implored, cupping his face, bringing it to within inches of hers, peering deep into his soul. *"Please,* I beg you. Go, but don't leave me here alive."

The rustling of leaves in the distance told Jake his hunters were closing in. But through the fear stabbing his gut, the spine-freezing reality of facing death, his engineering mind suddenly thought of another possibility, of a way to turn the tables, just as Sergei Iyevenski had done. Those men belonged to Titov, who had not killed Jake but kidnapped him. The contract assassin had wanted Jake alive, which meant those men also wanted him alive. They might shoot Sonya on sight, but not Jake.

"I've got it," he said. "You have four rounds in the PPK, right?"

"Yes."

"Do you trust me?" he asked.

Breathing through her mouth while meeting his gaze, she said, "Yes, but—"

"Then, this is what we have to do."

A minute later, Jake Fischer collapsed on the cushion of leaves, screaming once, holding on to his ankle, his face smeared with the blood from a small cut in the palm of his right hand.

Sonya sat a dozen feet to his right, out of sight from the small clearing, hiding behind the thick undergrowth.

Jake waited, the silence of the woods descending on him, making him reconsider his decision of becoming . . .

Carnada. Bait.

He remembered her words: *Tu eres carnada.*

Lying sideways, his head half buried in the leaves, right eye anxiously watching a cluster of trees twenty feet away, Jake swallowed hard, remembering the olive-skinned woman's hand, like a vise, choking him; remembering her midnight eyes scourging him, drilling him.

Carnada.

Damn, Jake. Here you go again.

A minute went by. Then another.

Jake waited apprehensively, ears tuned to the natural sounds of the woods, waiting for a break in the pattern, for the snap of a dry branch.

Feigning pain, breathing heavily, struggling to get up and falling again, Jake suddenly saw a shadow detach itself from a clump of trees to his far left. Then another, moving toward the first. The crunching footsteps resumed, slowly, the hunters checking the wounded prey, looking for signs of a trap, but seeing none, even after waiting for what had been at least five minutes, while Jake struggled to get away.

The shadows solidified into the shapes of men bearing automatic weapons. Two of them, muzzles pointed at Jake Fischer, who wondered how in the hell he could have been so stupid as to come up with this idea.

The men got closer, lowered their weapons as Jake made one final attempt to get up and landed on his face, to the laughter of the two men in black.

On the ground, Jake turned to face his pursuers, genuine fear shrouding his eyes, dread filling his gut. Both young, blond, muscular, the operatives grinned at Jake Fischer. A single thought flashed in his mind.

Shoot, Sonya!

Jake waited, praying for the shots to come, his mind anxiously longing for the multiple reports that would stop the nearing figures, slowly closing in, until they were just a couple of feet away. One of them swiftly, abruptly took a step forward, swung his foot back, and kicked Jake in the lower abdomen.

He cried out as the boot pumped hot breath out of him, the loud hiss of a deflating balloon drowning his howl. Arms bracing his gut, rolling on the whirling blanket of leaves, his mind exploding in colors, his ears picking up laughter and shouts in German, a scream reached Jake Fischer's throat, clamped by the harrowing pain, unable to let pass the words he longed to shout out loud.

Shoot, dammit! What are you waiting—

Another boot found its way into his crotch, and Jake Fischer finally learned the meaning of pain, savage, raw, inconceivable pain. The kind that made Jake wish he had never been born, had never started FTI, listened to Iyevenski, come to Paris, put himself in this predicament. The fire streaking up his body from his aching testicles scourged him. His hunters were barely visible beyond his convulsively twitching lids. Jake felt bile rising in his gorge, felt his bowels loosening.

Praying for death but instead getting kicked in the solar plexus, Jake trembled, heaving in pain, vomiting, gasping for air, but somehow unable to breath, to see, to hear, except for the cracks of a firearm.

One, two, three.

Facedown in the leaves, he simply lay there, shattered, physically incapable of making the slightest move, paralyzed in pain, his mind growing cloudy, hazy, his collapsed diaphragm unable to force air back into his lungs.

Then he felt a hand on him, turning him over, caressing his chest, his abdomen. Jake saw her as if in a dream, hovering over him, at the end of a tunnel, whispering words he could not hear. He saw her distant face . . . the face of Kathy Bennett, her lips parting, pressing against his own, forcing warm air into him, and then moving back.

Breathe!

He did not hear the words but saw her lips move.

Breathe, Jake! Breathe!

But the face was not Kathy's, it was Sonya's, and she came down on him once again, her lips tight over his, his lungs once more expanding.

Breathe!

Jake Fischer coughed bile and blood before taking a deep breath on his own, quickly followed by another, his body responding to the oxygen, his limbs once again coming alive, his eyes clearing, the tunnel vanishing, sound returning to his world.

In the gloomy woods, a single beam of sunshine reflected off her ash-blond hair as her pale face remained inches from his. Jake Fischer smiled.

14

THE TRAP

We are never so easily deceived as when we imagine we are deceiving others.

—*La Rochefoucauld*

Sergei Iyevenski and Nicole Rochereau walked under the Arc de Triomphe, at the west end of the Champs Élysées, the long avenue connecting the legendary monument to the Place de la Concorde and the gardens leading to the Louvre. Twelve avenues in total radiated from the arch, built during the nineteenth century to commemorate Napoleon's victories.

In the early-morning mist, Iyevenski walked under the towering arch, a cool breeze swirling his long hair and that of Nicole Rochereau. He dropped his gaze to the fire burning over the Tomb of the Unknown Soldier while holding her hand.

Glancing at the magnificent landmark and its surroundings, Iyevenski breathed deeply before turning to Nicole. Her face had once been as smooth as silk, but now showed the fine lines around the eyes that came with age and a hard life.

A strong woman.

In the hour or so they had spent wandering through the streets of Paris, killing time and shaking any possible tails before the meeting Jacques d'Anjou had set up for them, the Russian had learned much more about the attractive taxi driver. Abandoned by her husband, saving every franc to purchase the used Renault Iyevenski had wrecked, making a hard living driving tourists through her city to earn the money for Julianna's studies, Nicole Rochereau represented everything the Russian had always wanted, respected, and admired in a woman.

"You'd better wait here," he said, glancing at three other couples walking around the monument, as well as two police officers drinking coffee by the side of the arch facing the Champs Élysées. "It might be dangerous."

She smiled, putting a hand to his face. "If that's what you want me to do."

"You have a daughter, someone who depends on you. I should be back in half an hour."

Without looking back, Sergei Iyevenski left her there, leaning against the wall of the passage under the arch. He continued by foot up the Avenue Foch for nearly half a mile until he reached the Bois de Boulogne, a large park on the west side of the city with a large children's amusement area covering its northern section.

Sergei Iyevenski walked around the back of the amusement park to the employees' entrance, checking his gold Rolex. Over three hours before opening time.

Pushing the heavy metal door in the middle of a two-story-high brick wall at the end of a gravel path connecting the park with the employee parking lot, Iyevenski remembered the instructions from the man who'd called himself Pierre, d'Anjou's friend, whom the taxi driver claimed would negotiate the terms of an agreement between Iyevenski and one of France's best counterfeiters. Pierre had mentioned a fee over the phone. This healthy fee Iyevenski carried in his coat pocket, money he had retrieved from one of the lockers at the train station an hour ago. Over three quarters of a million deutsche marks still remained inside the red backpack, along with the archive tape. The second locker, housing the stocks and bonds, Iyevenski had left alone. As an added precaution, the Russian had given Nicole the key, which the streetwise woman had inconspicuously hidden in a place where only a lover could find it.

Iyevenski grunted in a half-laugh at the thought and at her words: *Maybe you can retrieve it yourself later.*

Focus! Concentrate!

His KGB training admonished him for allowing such personal thoughts into his mind at this moment. He looked for the monkey cage he had been instructed to find. Grabbing the Ray-Bans he had not needed until now, he slipped them on and carefully scanned his surroundings, finding the cage, roughly two hundred feet to his left, bordered on the south side by a stream that flowed into a goldfish pond to his immediate left, next to a cage with an assortment of parrots and macaws.

The park seemed deserted. Iyevenski saw no workers, no cleanup crews, no security guards.

Frowning and shaking his head, the large Russian walked down the gravel path leading to the monkey cage. Small black shapes began to climb and howl the moment he reached the steel mesh enveloping the four-story-high habitat, housing what looked like at least two dozen animals.

Turning around, his back to the noisy primates, the former KGB operative spotted a man in a two-piece business suit entering the park. Tall, of medium build, sandy hair, dark sunglasses, facial features covered by a thick beard, the man stopped by the goldfish pond, roughly a hundred feet from Iyevenski. He abruptly reached inside his coat and pulled out a handgun.

Dropping to a low crouch, the Russian unholstered the Sig Sauer and leveled it at the assassin.

The sound of a gunshot thundered across the amusement park. Birds squawked, monkeys howled, rattling their cages. A marksman's bullet struck the side of the Sig Sauer, just above the stock, narrowingly missing Iyevenski's thumb. The stinging vibration reached his elbow, and he helplessly let go of the weapon, watched it land on the gravel.

Another shot, and the gravel by his feet exploded in a cloud of white debris that covered his feet.

No time to get the weapon.

Trained reflexes made him ignore the fear in his gut, propelled him into motion, making him turn right and drop again to a crouch as he raced for the other side of the cage, his ears waiting for follow-up shots that never came. Breathing heavily, wondering how the shooter had missed in plain daylight and relatively close range, Sergei Iyevenski heard the noise of a footstep over wet leaves behind him.

Turning around while bringing both arms in front, making an X with his forearms, the Russian blocked a kick aimed for his solar plexus, delivered by a compact man with blond hair and muscular arms. Iyevenski countered with a backfist to the nose. The man's legs gave, and before he hit the ground Iyevenski had crashed his left knee against his chest, sending him flying over the neatly trimmed bushes bordering the rear of the cage, under the ear-piercing shrieks of the monkey audience.

The compact man had not reached the ground when two more operatives, a man and a woman, approached the Russian, one from each end of the cage. Iyevenski recognized the Hispanic woman and silently chastised himself for falling into the trap.

Both figures stopped a few feet from Iyevenski and began to circle him, slowly, neither of them sporting weapons other than their limbs. While the man lunged, striking the Russian in the abdomen with a knuckle punch, the woman swung her right leg at knee level, sweeping Iyevenski's feet from under him.

The Russian landed on the ground, flat on his back, the impact taking the wind out of him, momentarily stunning him, giving his enemies the vital seconds required to control him. By the time he came around, three muzzles were pointed at him.

"You are becoming a nuisance," said the bearded man dressed in a business suit, a pair of charcoal eyes regarding Iyevenski with contempt.

The Russian recognized the voice. *The leader.*

"And I'm just getting warmed up," responded Iyevenski, sitting up and brushing the dirt off his white jacket. "I plan to bring you down, butcher."

"Shut up, *puto!*" the woman screamed, slapping the Russian with the back of her left hand.

Hands in his pockets, the assassin said, "You call me a butcher, but I ask you this: are you without sin?"

Iyevenski narrowed his gaze at the man's odd words. "What?"

"He who lives by the sword shall perish by the sword. You have chosen to raise your sword at me, the instrument of justice of our Lord God Jehovah, leaving me no choice but to strike back with all His might."

"I believe it is actually the other way around, jackal. You drew first blood."

"Ah," said the assassin. "So it is vengeance that you seek."

Iyevenski grinned. "With a passion."

Raising both hands high in the air, the assassin said, "Vengeance is mine, saith the Lord! And I am the hammer of God, sent forth to pound on the wicked anvil of infidels like you, like the Americans."

"And I am the hammer of true justice who is not going to stop until I pay you back for what you did to my friends."

The assassin measured Iyevenski for a few seconds before replying, "Not very convincing words when coming from a man with three weapons pointed at him."

"Kill me then," the Russian challenged, a hand rubbing the red mark on his cheek. "Kill me, or by God I will kill *you.*" Eyes shimmering with hate, Iyevenski stared at the barrel of the gun the assassin held.

"Death comes to us all, Sergei Konstantinovich. But your time has not yet arrived," said the assassin. "Now . . . you have something that belongs to me."

"I burned everything."

The assassin looked into the distance with a vacant stare. "Only the truth shall set you free, Sergei. Only the truth." Looking at the Hispanic woman, the assassin nodded once.

Instead of administering the expected beating, the woman turned around and came back thirty seconds later with another guard. The two of them flanked a visibly shaken Nicole Rochereau.

Iyevenski felt a burst of anger scourging his gut, a twisting fury spinning out of the darkest corner of his mind. "You bastards! You filthy—"

The blow came now, a steel slap with the muzzle of the gun the Hispanic woman held.

"There is no sense in resisting, infidel. The Lord is by my side, not yours," the assassin said as the Hispanic woman pointed the gun at Nicole's face.

Iyevenski locked eyes with the man. *Insanity! Madness!* This could not be happening to him! Not with the precautions he had . . . *D'Anjou!*

"Where is Jacques d'Anjou?" Iyevenski asked.

The assassin looked up at the clear skies over Paris. "At peace with himself."

Nearly out of choices, but willing to play the game to the end, Iyevenski decided to buy himself some time and said, "Jake Fischer. The tape and the money are with Jake Fischer."

After taking almost twenty minutes to recover from the beating and his near-death, Jake Fischer finally sat up, a bit light-headed, the throbbing stabbing his abdomen and groin slowly eased by the thrill of being alive, of having outsmarted the professionals sent after them.

"That was close. Thanks," he said, carefully getting to his feet before helping her up.

"We need to move away from them," she said in a low voice. They could hear the sounds of police sirens in the distance. "We've spent too much time here."

Staggering side by side, Jake and Sonya left the small clearing and put several hundred feet of woods between themselves and the dead operatives, finally collapsing on a moist blanket of leaves, hidden from sight by a large boulder and surrounding bushes.

Helping Sonya sit with her back against the slippery surface of the rock, his insides still protesting the multiple blows, Jake collapsed in front of her. In the twilight of the forest, his eyes found hers. They were glistening with tears.

"Are you all right?" he asked.

Sonya slightly shook her head. "Rarely in my life has someone cared enough to risk his life for me. Thank you."

"What did you expect me to do? Actually shoot you? That might be what they taught you in spy school, but I'm not capable of taking innocent lives, or sitting idly by while innocents are killed."

His words stung Sonya. She knew he still blamed her for the deaths of his team.

"Just as you didn't leave me to burn in that taxi."

Jake shrugged.

Sonya leaned forward, close enough for Jake to see the fine lines around her eyes. "Jake, you seem to be a sensitive, brave, and reasonable man. I'm trying to appeal to your sense of reason and ask you to *please* trust the FBI. We can help you. Look at what just happened. With all of Iyevenski's precautions, Titov still found your safe house. Sooner or later they will catch up with you."

Jake looked away and crossed his arms.

"Look," Sonya said, putting a hand over Jake's shoulder. "I *know* what you are going through—"

Jake Fischer jerked back, shocked at her words. "How can you say a thing like that, Sonya? That bastard killed my girlfriend, the only woman I've ever loved! The asshole blew up my entire company, murdered my team, destroyed my dream! And you . . . you have the . . . the *boldness* to tell me that you know what I'm going through?"

Sonya glared at him with reproachful eyes, glistening with tears. "Vladimir Titov-Escobar and I go back to the Cold War days, Jake. He trained me in the Stasi to spy in West Berlin during the eighties. Eventually I realized what a mistake Communism was, and I turned to the CIA. I became what some people call a double agent. Titov somehow figured out what I had done, and he used my younger brother, Ludwig, to set a trap for me. I escaped the trap, but Titov shot my brother in cold blood. I never even got the chance to bury him. That day I had to walk away from everything I held dear in my life."

Sonya gulped hard and bit back the tears as Jake Fischer's face grew hot with embarrassment. "So when I tell you that I know what you are going through, Jake Fischer, I *do* know. I *have* been there. I also lost everything to that butcher."

A deep sense of shame enveloping him, Jake just stared at Sonya. A tear slowly slid down her cheek. "I . . . I didn't know . . ."

Her color and her strength slowly returning, Sonya nodded. "It does not matter. It happened a long time ago, and you did not know. Just remember that you cannot do this alone, Jake," she added. "Not against Titov."

Silent, Jake and Sonya stared at each other for a moment.

"About your brother," he said. "How long ago was that?"

Sonya lowered her gaze, her right hand absently inspecting the bandage over her left. "Shortly before the fall of the Wall."

"Oh man, so close to when you both could have been free."

She nodded, her lips pursed in bitter remembrance. "It took me a long time to get over it. But in the end I avenged him," she said, lifting her chin, her voice hardening.

Jake gave her a puzzled look. "How so?"

She told him about Titov and Karla, about the chase, the interception, the kill, the escape.

"That's . . . that's some story," Jake said, amazed. "Too bad he got away."

"Yes," she said, her gaze still on her bandaged hand. "Too bad. Had I succeeded, this whole episode would never have happened."

"You can't blame yourself for that," Jake said. "If it hadn't been Titov, then it would have been someone else. I'm sure he's not the only assassin out there. But he's not getting away with what he—"

A high-pitched ring made Jake jump.

The phone!

Reaching into his back pocket, while a look of curiosity crossed Sonya's face, Jake brought the unit to his face, surprised that it still worked after everything they'd been through, and said, "Yes?"

"Jake, Iyevenski. It's over. We won. I need you to bring the tape and all of the money to the Parc de Monceau in three hours."

Jake Fischer remained silent for a few seconds, eyes on Sonya, who gave him an inquisitive glance.

"How do I get there?"

"Take the Métro and get off at the Monceau exit. The park is not very large. Follow the signs to the Corinthian colonnade and wait for me."

"So . . . it's really over?"

"Yes, old pal. Finally. Three hours, Jake."

"Got it."

The line went dead, and Jake shoved the phone back into his rear pocket.

"What was that all about?" she asked.

"It was Sergei. He said that it was over, that we've won. He asked me to meet him at a park in three hours. . . . Something's seriously wrong, Sonya."

"Why?"

"Because he also asked me to bring the archive tape and the money. I have neither—aside from these." Jake extracted a wad of deutsche marks from another pocket. "Sergei told me late last night that the rest of the money—and the archive tape—were in a locker at the Gare du Nord train station, and he has the key," Jake said, deciding not to mention the existence of a second locker. "Why would he ask me to bring him something he already has? And why did he call me 'old pal'? He always refers to me as 'friend.' "

Sonya looked off in the distance. "They captured him, Jake. Titov is doing the exact same thing he did with Ludwig: he has captured Iyevenski and is trying to set up a trap for you as well. This is how he operates."

"What are we going to do?" Jake asked. "I have no idea how to get hold of that tape or the money."

Sonya smiled. "Are you ready to trust us, Jake? Are you ready to trust the U.S. government?"

Reluctantly, Jake nodded.

"Then let me use that phone and I'll have a diplomatic car pick us up and take us to the embassy in less than twenty minutes. Titov thinks that you are alone. He is in for a big surprise."

15 POLITICS

Politics is the art of preventing people from taking part in affairs which properly concern them.
—Paul Valéry

The CIA Paris station's operations center was a bug-free, sound-proof and bulletproof room on the second floor of the American embassy building. Shielded with alternating layers of Kevlar and copper and fitted with multiple dedicated and secured voice, data, and video links with Langley, the center housed some of the most sophisticated communications equipment in the world. Its electronics hardware and software underwent yearly upgrades that coincided with the beginning of each yearly budget cycle.

FBI Special Agent Sonya Wüttenberg sat at one end of the large conference table in the middle of the carpeted room. Jake sat to her right, his eyes on the two projection screens at the end of the room, each currently displaying the seal of the Central Intelligence Agency.

The head of the table had a built-in keyboard and a small monitor, enabling its user to configure the video and sound in the room.

Jake just sat back and watched Sonya work, amazed that the embassy actually had such technology at its disposal. What he had seen today—something he had already been sworn to keep secret or risk getting slapped with the charge of treason against the United States of America—destroyed the myth in the computer industry about government agencies using dated technology. The

Space Shuttle and the F-15 Eagle might be filled with components designed and manufactured a decade ago, but the software and hardware in this room were pure state-of-the-art.

Three intelligence officers sat around the table, one next to Jake and two across the table. All three men wore stereotypical poker faces, eyes glued to the color screens. Jake didn't know if they were FBI or CIA, and he actually didn't care. He simply wanted to get his friend out of harm's way, take the money, and head on home to start over.

One screen abruptly changed to a full-motion video of another conference room, where a large man, almost as big as Iyevenski, sat at the head of a long conference table working the keyboard, just like Sonya. He wore a red polo shirt. Sitting next to him was another bulky man, bald, wearing a dress shirt, tie, and suspenders. The second screen then showed a video of the embassy operations center. Jake saw himself sitting behind the table, and suddenly realized he needed to get some rest. The purple bags under his bloodshot eyes and his messy hair testified to the stress he had experienced in the past few days. He also needed to shave.

The first screen zoomed in, showing a close-up of the large man in the red shirt. His rugged features would look perfect on a retired boxer. The camera then zoomed back out to frame them both.

"Good morning," Sonya said, the bruises on her pale face standing out starkly on the video monitor.

"Morning," the two at the other end replied. "You look like you had a rough night," added the bald man.

"Yes, sir. I did. Actually, *we* did. This is Jake Fischer," Sonya said in her German-accented English. "Jake, meet Roman Palenski, director of the FBI, and Donald Bane, deputy director for operations of the CIA and acting director of central intelligence."

"A pleasure, Dr. Fischer," came the booming voice of Roman Palenski through the Sony speakers above the large screens.

"I'm glad you've decided to cooperate with us," added Bane.

"I didn't have any option."

Bane's pugilist face hardened at the remark. Palenski briefly looked away. Sonya Wüttenberg winced at the tactless remark, while the stone-faced rookies simply exchanged glances.

"Indeed, Dr. Fischer. You—and we—are out of options on this one," said Donald Bane.

"The classic case of two unlikely allies joining forces to defeat a larger, common enemy," said Jake, crossing his arms while staring at the video screen.

"Dr. Fischer," Palenski said, leaning forward, his voice coming from the speakers a fraction of a second after the lips moved, comically reminding Jake of cheaply dubbed martial arts movies. "We're faced with a number of facts that must be dealt with on a priority basis. You, as a businessman, understand priorities."

Jake uncrossed his arms, planted his elbows on the padded arms of the swivel chair, and interlaced his fingers. "You may have a priority list in mind, gentlemen, but the first thing on *my* list is rescuing my friend, even if it means giving up the tape."

"We must have those files," replied Bane.

"That's right," added Palenski. "We simply can't afford to lose—"

"Excuse me, gentlemen, but you're acting as if this involves some top-secret government project. While I appreciate your concern and desire to help, the tape and its contents are the property of FTI, and if I feel we need to trade it for the life of my friend, I expect your full cooperation."

Leaning forward, a grin on his weathered face, Roman Palenski said in a deep voice, *"Correction,* Dr. Fischer. Yesterday, Preston, Colton & Associates filed a motion to take control of all remaining assets of Fischer Technologies, Inc. A district judge, under the recommendation of the Supreme Court of the State of California, granted the motion in light of the recent incidents.

PCA, at the request of the U.S. secretary of commerce—and the FBI—has agreed to transfer all available information salvaged from the fire, including partially damaged backup tapes and equipment—and, of course, the biotechnology patents in PCA's legal department—to the Los Alamos National Laboratory in New Mexico, where it can be properly protected."

"Bastards," said Jake under his breath, playing along. He knew the small value those damaged goods and old patents had without Iyevenski's and his own know-how—and the secret backup of the biorecipes and other data. Jake had chosen to keep that one to himself for now, as well as the contents of the second locker at the train station. Now he was glad he had. If Uncle Sam wanted to play hardball, so would Jake Fischer. "How dare you? You have no right to—"

"Yes, we do, Jake," said a familiar voice through the speakers.

Jake leaned forward, puzzled at not seeing anyone else in the room with Bane and Palenski. Then the elegantly dressed William Preston, his athletic body well packed inside a dark suit, entered the picture, taking a seat to Donald Bane's left.

"Hi, *Bill*," Jake said, after the few seconds it took him to recover from the unexpected addition to the video conference, no longer caring to conceal his lack of respect for the venture capitalist. The incidents of the past two days had changed the way Jake Fischer viewed the world.

"It's all over, Jake," said William Preston, a trace of annoyance at Jake's disrespectful tone flashing across his aristocratic face. "PCA, on my recommendation, has agreed to cooperate with the federal government in transferring anything that can be salvaged to Los Alamos. We're also releasing control of all existing patents in our files."

Smiling at the irony, Jake blurted, "And how much did PCA get for whoring itself to Uncle Sam, *Bill?*"

Red-faced with indignation, William Preston replied matter-of-factly, "That's not your concern. You lost control of the invention the moment you defaulted on your contract by failing to protect my investment."

"With all due respect, *Bill,* you'd better take a look at the guys next to you. They're the ones who failed to protect FTI, not me."

"The way the press sees it, Jake—which is the way the fire marshal reported it—you failed to provide proper safety measures for the dangerous chemicals used in the biolab. That is the official statement. I also believe the DA is considering charging you with involuntary manslaughter."

"That's a bunch of horseshit, Bill. And you know it. FTI was attacked, dammit! And neither the FBI nor anyone else in the government did squat to protect it!"

"That's not the way we're reporting it, Dr. Fischer," said Palenski as Donald Bane sat back. "It's not in the best interest of the current administration to admit such a thing when the press has already bought the chemical accident story."

"You're nothing but a bunch of liars! *You* fucked up. *You* failed to protect my company against some assassin, and now *you* are trying to pin the blame on *me!* This is blackmail!" protested Jake, pounding a fist on the table, angry and frustrated. "Damn you, Bill! Damn all of you!"

"Gentlemen! Please!" interjected Sonya, kicking Jake under the table. "There is no need for insults. The situation is what it is, and there is nothing we can do to change the past. However, there's much that can be done to limit any future damage, particularly by recovering the lost technology and helping Jake Fischer get his friend back. But we won't be able to accomplish that unless we all work together."

Jake glared at Sonya and pointed at the screen. "I told you I couldn't trust the U.S. government."

Sonya pressed the mute button on the keyboard and whispered, "I didn't know they were going to take this approach to force you to cooperate, Jake. I swear it."

Crossing his arms, Jake sank back into his chair. "Somehow I don't believe that."

Reactivating the audio, Sonya said, "With all due respect, gentlemen, I strongly disagree with any position that suggests that Jake Fischer was responsible for what happened at—"

"Sonya," Palenski said. "The current position of—"

"I was there, sir. I ran the surveillance for months, listened to his conversations at home and at Iyevenski's. I also monitored all phone conversations and intercepted all of his e-mails to PCA."

Jake snapped forward. "You *did?*"

Sonya nodded. "We had known about the Germans' interest in you for a few months, Jake. And I wasn't going to bring it up, but they have left me no choice. You're a victim, and my agency is trying to take advantage of that to blackmail you."

Bane leaned forward and calmly said, "Sonya, you're out of line."

Glancing at Jake, who seemed surprised at her taking a stand for him, Sonya replied, "I'm sorry, sir, but you know quite well that I left the Stasi because they were a bunch of lying, cheating bastards who took advantage of innocent civilians. I was told from the beginning that the CIA and the FBI were government agencies created to *protect* the interests of innocent Americans. Right now we're doing the exact opposite. I refuse to sit by quietly while you further abuse the rights of someone who has been abused enough already. My official position on this is that I will not agree to blaming the fire on Jake Fischer. All of us know that he is not responsible. The only reason he is here right now is that I made a deal with him to help him get Sergei Iyevenski back if he cooperated with us."

Bane and Palenski exchanged glances. Then Palenski addressed his subordinate, who, like Jake Fischer, now sat leaning back with her arms crossed.

"Sonya, I admire your integrity, and I thank you for reminding us of our oaths. However, the situation here is critical. We must—"

"And I am telling you, sir, with the utmost respect, that you are not going to get far by making threats."

Palenski was going to reply when Donald Bane raised a hand. "Look, Dr. Fischer," said Donald Bane, placing his arms on the table. "We're all on edge here, especially you. I realize that this has not been easy for you. You have seen your own team killed by a terrorist group, which was contracted by a foreign country. You have seen your company destroyed, and now you're being told that PCA has acquired all rights to all surviving assets and inventions and given them to Los Alamos. And on top of all that we come right out with threats to force you to cooperate."

Jake shrugged. "Tell me something I don't already know."

"Dr. Fischer," Bane continued, "I urge you to be reasonable. The technology you have created is far too dangerous to exist anywhere outside the protection of Los Alamos. The temptation from competition, foreign or domestic, to steal it would be immense, as you have seen firsthand. We have to protect it for the benefit of the United States of America. But we can't guard it against enemies like the ones who attacked you if it's not entirely within our control."

"So," Jake said, his engineering mind helping him refocus and think logically, "*you* are stealing the technology instead of the bastards who blew up my company. That puts you both in the same category."

"There is a difference," responded Palenski, rubbing a hand over his bald head. "Biotechnology is the way of the future, and we intend to handle it responsibly, slowly phasing it into the commercial, industrial, and military markets starting in about a decade

from now, *not* right away, when it would irreversibly damage the
thriving semiconductor industry, which is still at the peak of its
lifetime. Right now we have trillions of dollars invested in semiconductor technology. From university curriculums and R&D
labs, to multibillion-dollar fabrication areas and design centers
around the world, the investment in silicon-based integrated cir-
cuits represents our immediate future. That entire infrastructure
can't change overnight."

"In other words," said Jake, his full attention on the screen, "I
have created the ultimate memory system using a technology that
was not supposed to be available for another ten or fifteen years.
Therefore, you're telling me it cannot be released or it would collapse the semiconductor market? Doesn't sound like the capital-
istic society I grew up in. I would venture to say that what you're
doing would be the equivalent of the U.S. government telling Edison back in 1880 that his carbon-filament electric bulb couldn't
go to market because it would crash the thriving gaslight industry of the time."

William Preston shook his head and leaned forward, his voice
carrying a condescending edge. "We live in different times, Jake.
The downfall of the gaslight industry at the turn of the century
was well offset by the emerging electric light bulb, and both industries were tiny compared to the high-tech industry of today.
Besides, even though Edison did invent the electric bulb in 1880,
its use did not become widespread until ten years later, when the
infrastructure of electric generators and distribution systems came
into existence. Like Edison, you did invent something quite revolutionary here. Hell, I backed you up from the day you walked
into my office four years ago. But now I've seen the light and come
to terms with the realization that the infrastructure is simply not
there to support it now. The infrastructure of our country—and
the world—is not ready to transition from semiconductors to
biotechnology. Cutting loose the F1 RAM—and all of the bio-

products that would quickly follow it—in the open market today would be suicidal.

"We must *control* this technology," he continued. "We must keep it in a safe place until the right time, when we will trickle it out to a selected group of American corporations to give them all an equal sporting chance to bring their initial products to market at around the year 2015, close to the end of the life cycle of the silicon chip. That way we reap the benefits of our current investment, the high-tech industry continues at its current pace, Wall Street doesn't crash, millions of Americans get to keep their jobs and their homes and send their kids to college, where they get exposed to emerging biotech courses. When those kids graduate they will witness a healthy and exciting industry transition into biotechnology—just as Americans at the turn of the century witnessed the light bulb replacing gaslight."

"And *that,* Dr. Fischer," added Donald Bane, "is why we must recover the technology and then keep it under lock and key until the right time. This is more valuable than all the diamonds or gold in the world. Remember what the Japanese did to the memory industry in the mid-eighties? They began dumping DRAM chips into the world marketplace at a fraction of their manufacturing cost, forcing everyone else with far less capital out of the memory business. Many corporations in America went bankrupt because of that. And what did they do after they drove the competition out of business?"

Jake nodded. "They jacked up the prices."

"DRAM became one of the most expensive components in personal computers, right up there with microprocessors. Now can you imagine what the Japanese would do with the F1? Can you imagine what they would do if they also applied that biotechnology to microprocessor design? Or video controllers? Or modems?"

Jake sighed. It would be a disaster.

"And the problem is that those bastards would use it as an economic weapon, as a negotiating tool to get an edge on every trade agreement. They would get the best end of the stick on everything from agricultural products to airliners. They would use biotechnology as a hammer to kill our auto industry by forcing us to cut back on import tariffs and price their vehicles below the manufacturing cost of American automobile manufacturers. The same would apply to any other import that competes with American corporations. And the Germans, the Koreans, and even the Chinese wouldn't be any different. Biotechnology is the future, Dr. Fischer, our children's future, and it's our responsibility to guard it and protect it."

His eyes briefly locking with Sonya's before returning to the screen, Jake Fischer accepted the fact that he simply could not move forward with his invention at this time, but also realizing that he—not the U.S. government—had the right to control how his invention made it into the marketplace, he decided to play along for now so that he could get the full backing of the FBI and the CIA to rescue Sergei Iyevenski—and, of course, avoid a felony charge.

"Thanks for siding with me, Sonya, but I'm afraid that this is far bigger than the two of us," Jake said, giving Sonya a wink before turning his attention to the screen. "All right, gentlemen. You win. You'll have my full cooperation, but you must give me your word that a priority will be placed on saving the life of Sergei Iyevenski, and that no felony charges will be pressed against me."

"Agreed," said Palenski.

"Furthermore," added Jake, "I want no reprisals taken against Sonya for her comments in this meeting."

"We train our operatives to balance following orders with independent thinking," replied the FBI director. "Sonya's reputation is in the clear."

"Finally," Jake said, "I want the U.S. government to authorize the disbursement of twenty million dollars—tax-free—to the families of the victims at FTI. I'll spare you any payments to Iyevenski, myself, or Kathy Bennett, who didn't have any surviving relatives."

"A million bucks a head?" asked Palenski.

"Nonnegotiable," said Jake. "You want my help in getting that backup tape to Los Alamos, it's going to cost you."

"That's quite a sum," said Bane.

"A small price to pay to get access to the data in that archive tape, Mr. Bane," said Jake. "Everything that was FTI is contained in that tape and in whatever you were able to salvage from the fire."

Bane grinned and gave Jake a single nod. "All right. You have my word."

Jake also grinned. "Sorry. I'm afraid that's not good enough."

Palenski frowned. "What would you like us to do, Dr. Fischer?"

"I'll hand over the tape after Sergei is safe, and after I get confirmation from my lawyer in California that the appropriate amount of money has been transferred to an escrow account for my former employees. I'll contact him immediately to get you the bank account numbers."

Bane breathed heavily and set both elbows on the table. "Is there anyone you *do* trust, Dr. Fischer?"

"Yes," Jake replied. "And now you're going to help me get him back."

16

FINAL CONFRONTATION

> *Victory at all costs, victory in spite of all terror, victory however long and hard the road may be; for without victory, there is no survival.*
> —*Winston Churchill*

Monday, July 24, 9:20 A.M.

A red backpack filled with fifty thousand deutsche marks' worth of CIA and FBI money hanging off his left shoulder, Jake Fischer walked up the narrow cobblestone path that led to the moss-covered Corinthian colonnade bordering the edge of a small lake in the center of the Parc de Monceau. The charm of the place, the water lilies layering the smooth lake, the blue skies, the towering trees isolating the eighteenth-century park from the busy streets of Paris, the sounds from the mountain cascade at the other end of the long lake, were all lost on Jake Fischer, whose tired blue eyes warily scanned the faces of the two dozen men and women visiting the picturesque park. Some snapped pictures of the round colonnade, others sat at the water's edge. An old lady fed bits of bread to a group of pigeons. Three college kids, wearing T-shirts advertising the University of Paris, skipped stones on the water's surface.

Jake Fischer had a difficult time breathing, his nerves on the verge of collapsing from the relentless stress that not only refused to go away, but was now increasing with every step he took toward the long, curving Corinthian structure. He couldn't understand how Sonya Wüttenberg coped with the insanity of her profession, with the madness of living in a world where nothing was as it seemed, where people had the power to decide who would and would not get charged with manslaughter based on a level of cooperation.

Jake shook his head and briefly closed his lids, focusing his mind on his mission, then opened them wide, feeling a trickle of perspiration running down his back.

He was actually beyond nervous. He was downright terrified, and the reason for his fear was the thought of losing Sergei Iyevenski, his only friend left. Jake also dreaded the idea of being captured alive by that sadistic couple, especially by the Hispanic woman, who'd nearly choked him with such amazing ease.

Jake gritted his teeth, deciding, as he walked the entire length of the colonnade, that he definitely didn't belong in this shadowy, deceitful world. Not only was he still playing this insane game, but for the fourth time in the past few days he was being used as bait. *Carnada.*

The word brought back images of the woman, of the fire in her ebony eyes, of the—

Jake froze when he saw her. For a second, no more, he doubted his own eyes. But the slender figure, the tight jeans, the bony face framed by the jet-black hair told Jake Fischer that the bell had rung and this round had definitely started.

Following Sonya's strict instructions, Jake ran a hand through his hair, an action that made the old lady with the white hair and long, blue dress, fifteen feet to his right, briefly turn away from the hungry pigeons she had been feeding for the past ten minutes before resuming her work.

We will remain put until someone spots Iyevenski and Nicole Rochereau.

Those had been Sonya's words shortly after the video conference with Palenski and Bane. To Sonya's displeasure, however, this meeting had been scheduled to take place before the arrival of the seasoned CIA and FBI troops due later on this morning, forcing Sonya to go with what she had. She chose to take three rookies along, all FBI, all trained for this type of ambush.

Neither Sergei Iyevenski nor Nicole Rochereau was in sight, only the Hispanic woman, who continued walking in Jake's direction, flashing him the same grin that had preceded her gripping his throat the day before.

She stopped a few feet from him, a stern glare in her green eyes, her honey-colored skin glistening in the sunlight, except for a purplish bruise on her forehead, perhaps the result of the auto crash.

"The tape and the money, *puto*. Hand them over," she said, extending an open palm in his direction, then slowly making a tight fist. "Give them to me or I will finish what I started in the car."

Jake put a hand to his throat, felt the half-moon-shaped scars while studying her. "Not until you show me Sergei and Nicole."

"There is a gun pointed at your head at this moment," the woman said, flashing Jake another smile. "Do not be a fool. All I have to do is give the signal."

"And you'll never find what you seek," he responded, returning the smile, his heart racing, his palms sweaty, his mouth suddenly dry. But he couldn't afford to let his fear show. He had to hold his ground.

The woman's gaze shifted from his face to the red backpack, and back to Jake.

"You didn't think I would be foolish enough to actually bring the tape and all of the money here, did you?"

"What's in the bag?"

"Just part of the money . . . to show you that I have it." Jake tossed the bag at the woman, who unzipped the top and pulled out a couple of inch-thick stacks of deutsche marks.

"Where is the rest? Where is my tape?" she asked, waving a stack of bills at Jake Fischer.

"*Your* tape?" Jake asked, rising both brows. "Did I hear you say *your* tape?"

Breathing heavily now, the woman slapped the bag and shouted, "Where, *puto?* Where is the fucking tape and the money?"

"I thought you were a professional. Control your temper. You're drawing unnecessary attraction with your amateurish shouting," Jake admonished. A few heads had indeed turned in their direction.

"The tape and the money," she repeated, this time in a low voice. "You must deliver them to us immediately. Now, for the last time, where are they?"

"In a safe place."

"Safe place?" the woman said, eyes burning Jake.

"Is there an echo around here?" Jake remarked, not believing his own words. This woman was a trained assassin who could probably kill him with a single strike, and he was taunting her.

"Only a fool takes unnecessary risks, infidel," came a male voice from behind.

Turning around, Jake stared at the man Sonya had called Vladimir Titov-Escobar, also known as the Kardinal. His Slavic features were hidden under a beard. Calm charcoal-gray eyes returned Jake's harsh stare.

"Where are Sergei Iyevenski and Nicole Rochereau?" Jake asked the legendary assassin.

"Nearby."

"I want to see them."

The Kardinal sighed. "Blessed are those who believe and yet have not seen." He nodded at the Hispanic woman, who turned around, walked to the other side of the colonnade, and disappeared behind a cluster of trees. She reappeared moments later with Sergei Iyevenski, Nicole Rochereau, and two men who kept their hands hidden inside their overcoats, no doubt clutching weapons. The two bodyguards remained a few feet behind their prisoners.

Jake felt a deep sense of relief when he spotted his large friend, whose angry, lined face turned to Jake Fischer.

"I am sorry, my friend," Iyevenski said in his heavy Slavic accent. "I had to trick you. They threatened to kill Nicole if I did not cooperate."

"Don't worry about it, pal. They won't get away with it."

In the middle of the clearing, surrounded by a few tourists, the Kardinal moved next to the Hispanic woman while the two gunmen flanked Jake and Iyevenski from several feet away. Nicole Rochereau stood to the side, and Titov took her hand and pulled her to him, a reminder to Iyevenski.

The gaunt French woman flashed a frightened glance at Jake Fischer before bracing herself and dropping her gaze to the ground. Jake simply nodded and turned to Iyevenski, whose blue eyes were already on Jake.

"You brought the money and the tape, yes?"

"Ah . . . not exactly, Sergei."

"No?"

Keep playing along, Jake. Sergei knows you don't have the key to the locker at the train station.

"Nope."

"Where is it?"

"In a safe place until—"

"Until you had the opportunity to see your friends, Dr. Fischer," interrupted the Kardinal, his eyebrows slanting in a frown. "Now you must live up to your promise so that I may complete my noble mission."

"Not so fast. First let the woman go," said Iyevenski. "This doesn't concern her."

The Kardinal thought about it for a moment, then said, "I have made my request. If you choose not to comply, her blood will be on your hands."

Jake knew Titov-Escobar was not bluffing. Right now Nicole Rochereau was expendable to the assassin, but obviously not to the large Russian, who took a step toward the Kardinal.

The assassin, one hand grabbing Nicole around the neck from behind and positioning her as shield, pulled out a gun and leveled it at Iyevenski.

"Back, infidel!" he commanded. "Get back or you will lose her forever. I am the hammer of God, His instrument of—"

In the same instance, gunfire erupted. One of the bodyguards was shooting at a young FBI agent, who'd made the mistake of prematurely drawing his weapon and dropping to one knee.

Havoc. A dozen tourists ran away screaming in a multitude of languages. Once again everything moved too fast for Jake Fischer. The old lady feeding the pigeons, Sonya Wüttenberg, pivoted on her left leg just as the first FBI agent went down, his abdomen ripped open by a marksman's bullet. The other two rolled away while drawing their weapons and firing back at the bodyguards. Two tourists fell when caught by the crossfire, their chests exploding in clouds of blood and foam.

Iyevenski's large body rushed past Jake, wedging himself between the assassin and Nicole, separating them.

Jake also reacted quickly, ramming his left elbow against the Hispanic woman's chest, sending her crashing against a nearby concrete bench.

The bearlike man collided with the Kardinal with locomotive force.

A single shot cracked from Titov-Escobar's pistol, followed by Iyevenski's painful cry as the Russian smothered Titov with his large mass and both men fell to the ground. The pistol in Titov's hand flew to the side, landing by Jake's feet.

"Sergei!" Jake shouted when he realized he'd been shot.

"Mon Dieu! Mon Dieu!" exclaimed Nicole, a hand cupping her face.

"Nicole! Jake! Run away!" Sergei Iyevenski commanded while holding down the assassin, dark liquid spurting freely from his right shoulder, where the bullet had ripped a hole the size of a golf ball. "Run away!"

Staccato gunfire ricocheted off the cobblestones, splashed the calm water's surface, shaved the bark of a large pine. Screams filled the air. The smell of gunpowder suffocated Jake as the FBI agents and Titov's bodyguards exchanged fire.

Kneeling by Iyevenski's side as the Russian pinned the momentarily stunned assassin to the ground, Jake Fischer picked up the pistol and aimed it at one of the bodyguards, who was busy firing his assault rifle at Sonya and a rookie agent hidden behind an oak by the water's edge.

It will be easier the second time.

Jake remembered the words, recalled what he had been told. The bodyguard stood still, less than twenty feet away. Visibility was perfect, the target was large, and Jake Fischer, both hands on the weapon while keeping both eyes open and focused not on the sights but on the target, fired once, the gun's recoil jolting the barrel upward. Jake fired again, and again.

The man in the overcoat dropped his weapon, both hands clutching his chest as he fell to his knees. He froze for a few seconds, then collapsed on the ground.

Sonya and the two rookies, standing roughly fifty feet from Jake, forced Titov's surviving bodyguard back, until he finally fled, disappearing up a cobblestone pathway. The two FBI rookies pursued him.

Shouts and cries came from everywhere. Jake pointed the pistol at Titov-Escobar, who'd managed to push the weakened Russian aside and get to his feet.

"Stay where you are," Jake said, keeping a respectful distance from the assassin, before turning his attention to the Hispanic woman, who was racing away from them down the curved colonnade.

"Sonya!" Jake shouted, pointing at the getaway terrorist.

Sonya Wüttenberg went after the Hispanic woman, the throbbing of her side wound damped by the adrenaline flooding her veins. Taking in lungfuls of cool morning air, the seasoned FBI agent dashed over the manicured lawn past the Corinthian columns, running the entire length of the colonnade, emerald-green eyes focused like a laser beam on the tall figure in front of her.

Twenty feet.

Sonya noticed the Hispanic woman was limping slightly, possibly from the fall she had suffered when Jake hit her.

A weakness.

Tired, wounded, nauseated from lack of sleep, her left hand bandaged, her right knee throbbing from last night's beating, Sonya Wüttenberg needed an edge, a way to best her opponent. Like a predator selecting its prey, hungry eyes searching for the weakling in the herd, the former Stasi operative took advantage of the leg wound slowing down the Hispanic woman as she left the colonnade behind and darted across a small clearing bordered by knee-high bushes and flowers. The clearing, like the rest of the park, was now deserted, except for Sonya's prey, whom the seasoned operative could already have shot if she had so chosen. But she needed her alive, wanted to squeeze every ounce of information from her.

The gap closed to ten feet, the limp working to Sonya's advantage. The federal agent pressed harder, pointed her weapon at the sky, pressed the trigger once as a warning.

Nothing. Her weapon, a Glock 19 she had found in the office of the former CIA station chief, had jammed!

Five feet.

Cursing her luck, not having enough time to reach for the Walther PPK strapped to her ankle, Sonya Wüttenberg took four final steps and jumped forward, tackling the Hispanic woman from behind, wrapping her arms around her legs, tripping her, in the process further aggravating her own wounds. Her broken hand, abdominal stab wound, and bruised knee screamed obscenities at her.

The women rolled on the damp grass, got to their feet at the same time, and began circling each other. Sonya quickly reached down and unholstered the Walther PPK but never got a chance to fire it. The Hispanic woman, in a lightning-fast move that surprised Sonya, pivoted on her left leg while bringing her right leg up, slashing Sonya's right hand with a black sneaker.

The weapon flew over the grass, landing several feet from the women, who locked eyes and continued circling each other. Sonya's right hand throbbed as much as her side, but at least it was not broken, like her left one.

"I'm going to kill you, *puta!*" the Hispanic woman shouted, jet-black eyes shimmering with anger as she faked Sonya with her left hand while turning and extending her left leg toward the FBI agent, heel up, toes pointed down.

At the same instant, Sonya turned sideways, narrowingly missing the powerful sidekick, stepping closer to the Hispanic woman and striking her face with her left elbow. The woman fell to her knees, hands on her bleeding nose, giving Sonya the precious seconds she needed to dive for the PPK and grab it. She rolled once on the grass under the protest of her ribs, then stood up and pointed it at the other woman's face.

"Up!" Sonya commanded, ignoring the pain. "Get up and start walking!"

Slowly, her face, neck, and white T-shirt smeared with blood, the Hispanic woman obeyed, silently walking back toward the colonnade. Sonya remained five feet behind. Checking her watch, she noticed that exactly five minutes had elapsed since the shooting began. The French police would arrive soon. They had to hurry.

Jake Fischer saw Sonya returning with the Hispanic woman.

"We need to get Sergei to a hospital!" he shouted as the two women joined the group.

Jake stood next to Nicole, who kneeled, sobbing, next to Iyevenski. While Sonya was catching the Hispanic terrorist and Jake had kept the automatic trained on Titov-Escobar, Nicole had rushed to the bleeding Iyevenski, quickly removed his shirt, and used it to field-dress the wound and stop the blood loss until the Russian could get proper medical help. Then she had punched him on his good shoulder. *"Quel imbécile!"*

"And I love you too," Iyevenski had replied, a smile cracking his heavily lined face as he looked at Jake Fischer, who simply shook his head.

Joined by the two surviving FBI agents, who returned empty-handed from their chase, Sonya commanded one to keep an eye on the bleeding Hispanic terrorist. She approached the Kardinal.

"It's been a long time, Vladimir," she said in English, letting the assassin finally take a good look at her.

"You?" Titov-Escobar shouted, removing the beard, the Slavic features on his tanned face hardening, iron-gray eyes shimmering with a mix of surprise and raw anger. "Sonya . . . it—it can not be! *Impossible!*"

"It's been a long time, Vladimir. We have much to talk about. This time around, as you can see, I don't have to chose between you and your whore," she said, her head tilting to the FBI agent guarding the Hispanic woman. "There is no escape this time. I'm taking you both in. Put both hands behind your back and start walking," she added. She reached for her radio and called in a van standing by two blocks away.

The group, led by Nicole and the wounded Russian, crossed the cobblestone path and reached the street, where a curious mob had gathered. Sirens were audible in the distance. Ten minutes had gone by since the shooting started.

The FBI agents handcuffed the terrorist pair and shoved them into the rear of a van with tinted windows and muddy license plates. Sergei got in the front, Jake in the center seat flanked by Sonya and Nicole. The blond FBI rookie officer sat next to Titov in the rear, a gun pressed against the side of the terrorist. The other operative drove. Nicole, who sat behind Iyevenski, leaned forward and hugged his neck from behind, her dark mascara leaving tracks down her gaunt face, her quivering lips mumbling something in French.

"To the embassy! Quickly!" commanded Sonya as the driver pulled away from the curb, leaving the crowd of onlookers behind. The van had not even driven a couple of blocks when the first police patrol car, a white Renault with green stripes and flashing red and blue lights, its sirens blaring, sped in the opposite direction, followed by three others.

Jake watched them pass before looking at Sonya. "Is it over?" he asked, his body pressed against her as she turned around to face the terrorists in the rear seat, pointing a gun at their heads.

"No, Jake. It is not over yet. We have merely captured the hounds. We have yet to find their masters."

"Their masters?"

"Yes," she responded, eyes locked with Vladimir Titov-Escobar's scourging stare. "The ones who hired this trash to steal the secrets of FTI."

"How are you going to find them?"

"Titov-Escobar and I go back a long way. I'm quite certain he will not mind sharing some of his secrets with me. Isn't that right, Vladimir?"

"The Lord is my Shepherd; I shall not want. Even though I

walk in the dark valley I fear no evil; for You are at my side with Your rod and Your staff that give me courage," the Kardinal responded, his harsh stare on the green eyes of Sonya Wüttenberg, who simply nodded.

She smiled, shaking her head. "Have you forgotten the Staatssicherheit's medieval methods of extracting information, Vladimir? *Überlegen Sie sich's mal.* Before the day is over you and your whore will tell me everything I need to know. *Everything.*"

The van reached the Arc de Triomphe, drove around it, and continued down the Champs Élysées. Jake looked out with a vacant stare, glad he didn't belong to this world of deception. This was in essence over for him, but not for the FBI and the CIA. The intelligence agencies had found their criminals and they were apparently going to dig deeper to catch the big fish, those who had started it all. And when they did, Palenski and Bane would dispose of the terrorists in a way Jake Fischer did not care to imagine.

The van turned left a block from the Place de la Concorde and reached the front gates of the American embassy. A Marine passed them through and they drove onto U.S. soil.

The resident doctor and his nurse rushed to the van's side the moment it came to a full stop in front of the main building and helped Iyevenski to a wheelchair. Jake got out and took a deep breath, stretching his limbs while four U.S. Marines bearing automatic rifles escorted the terrorists inside, followed by Sonya and the two rookie operatives.

Jake followed Sonya. "What about the FBI agent who was killed in the park?"

Sonya turned her pale face to Jake Fischer. "He was dead, Jake. We left him behind."

"Just like *that?*" he asked, the cold realities of this business never ceasing to amaze him.

"Rules, Jake. The priority in this type of mission is to avoid getting caught by the local police, avoid embarrassing your government. Taking him with us would have slowed us down. He has no ID with him—there's no way he can be traced back to us. He knew the risks associated with the job when he signed up for it."

They went through a side entrance, Jake and Sonya remaining behind while the Marines took the prisoners to a basement holding cell and the doctor and nurse rushed Iyevenski to the embassy clinic, with Nicole Rochereau close behind.

"I think he is going to be all right," said Sonya, nodding toward the disappearing wheelchair.

"It's going to take much more than a bullet in the shoulder to kill Sergei," Jake replied with a smile, a smile that faded at the thought of what he had been through, at the thought of being alone, without Kathy Bennett. At least Sergei Iyevenski had managed to find himself some company. Jake wouldn't be at all surprised if Iyevenski remained in Paris, living off some of the money they had stolen from Vladimir Titov-Escobar. The rest Jake intended to use to start over again, using the backup he'd made a few days ago in Palo Alto. Jake's agreement with Donald Bane was to turn over the archive tape, nothing else. And he intended to keep every penny of the Kardinal's confiscated fee.

"What happens next?" Jake asked Sonya.

"We interrogate them, find out what they know. If we get lucky we might get the name of the BND officials behind this."

Jake Fischer looked into the eyes of a woman he had initially hated, then grown to like and even admire, though he still despised the FBI and CIA for what they had done to him. "How do you know it was the BND that's behind this?"

"We have our connections."

Jake smiled. "I should have known."

"You also must give us the tape, Jake. That was part of the deal."

"I'll get it from Sergei as soon as I get confirmation from my lawyer that the funds have been transferred to the escrow account for the victims. I want their families taken care of for life. That was part of the deal too."

"You know how to get the tape, though?"

Jake nodded. "Sergei's got a locker key hidden somewhere. When I asked him about it on the way over from the park, he told me that only he could retrieve it. He was smiling, and knowing Sergei, who knows what *that* meant. But I'll hold to my end of the deal. The archive tape will be in your hands before the end of the day—again, assuming the funds are transferred."

In spite of the way he had been treated, Jake felt sorry for them, for thinking that just an archive tape, which they wouldn't even be able to read without a decoder, would give them any real head start in the development of a protein-based memory chip. The folks at Los Alamos were in for a big surprise. They didn't realize that Jake Fischer was still very much in control of his technology, of his own destiny.

"Thanks. I have work to do," she said, extending a thumb toward the other end of the hallway. "Will I see you later?"

The smile broadened on Jake's boyish face. "Sure. How about a cup of coffee on the Rue de Rivoli?"

"You are on, Dr. Fischer," she said, giving Jake a slow wink before turning and walking off.

Jake watched the slim blonde pacing down the hall, and he suddenly didn't feel all that alone. But then another thought struck him. Sonya was headed to a room where she would employ interrogation techniques, methods she had called medieval, to extract the desired information from those terrorists.

Disturbed by his conflicting feelings for Sonya Wüttenberg, by the memory of Kathy Bennett, and by his anger at the U.S. government for trying to blackmail him, Jake headed back outside, toward the large courtyard formed by the embassy building on one side and a ten-foot-tall wrought-iron fence on the other three.

The skies were blue over Paris today, and Jake Fischer filled his lungs with the renewed hope that came from repeatedly facing, defying, and defeating death. He wasn't certain what the future might bring. The millions in those lockers would certainly be enough to get a new company rolling. Of course, there would be a great deal of rehiring, retraining, and rebuilding involved, not to mention writing and filing the new patents that reflected the biorecipes in his personal backup hidden in Palo Alto, but as long as he could count on Sergei Iyevenski to lend him a helping hand, Jake felt he could handle just about anything.

Through the ornate fence surrounding the American embassy, Jake Thomas Fischer watched the traffic on the Champs Elysées, felt the cool morning breeze caress his face.

It felt good to be alive, to have prevailed against the most dangerous assassin in the world, to be about to use the actual payment due that assassin to rebuild FTI under a new name. It would require a lot of work and dedication, but he felt it would be easier the second time around, and this time he would be financing his own operation. No more dealing with venture capitalists.

Jake Fischer decided at that moment that having been able to survive the past week, he could handle anything the future might bring. He had no doubt about that.

EPILOGUE

Jake Thomas Fischer never had that coffee with Sonya Wütten-berg, at least not in Paris. Whatever methods the slender FBI agent used on the terrorists in that basement cell generated enough information that same afternoon to send Sonya, and a team composed of the arriving senior intelligence officers from other European stations, off to Berlin.

There hadn't been any explanations, just a rushed "I must go away, Jake. I'll contact you when this is over," and she had vanished from his life as abruptly as she had entered it.

That evening, Sergei Iyevenski underwent surgery at the St. Vincent de Paul hospital in Paris. He was ordered to rest for two months before resuming a normal life. Sergei chose to spend his recovery time in Paris, under the care of Nicole Rochereau.

"Are you sure you want to stay, Sergei?" Jake asked three days after the surgery, as he pushed Iyevenski in a wheelchair along the east fence of the American embassy, which had a great view of the Place de la Concorde.

"She'll look after my needs, friend. After that I will return to California and start over, yes?" responded the Russian. His shoulder and arm were bandaged.

"I don't know about Sunnyvale. Too many bad memories, plus a bad reputation, if you know what I mean." Although FBI intervention had prevented the DA from filing charges against Jake, the scientist couldn't avoid his notoriety in Silicon Valley, mostly thanks to the rumors created by William Preston and Jacob Colton.

"I know," Iyevenski replied. "Where then?"

"What about Austin?"

"Texas?" the Russian asked.

"Sure. Why not?"

Iyevenski nodded. "I have always wanted to see Texas, yes?"

"I've been there a few times. Great place. Hills, lakes, rivers—"

"Texas? I thought it was a desert and . . . what do you call them . . . timberweeds?"

Jake smiled. *"Tumbleweeds,* Sergei. And much of west Texas is desert, but not central Texas, where Austin is located. You'll love the place. It kind of looks like California, but with hills instead of mountains, and a whole lot fewer people. There are also a few top-ranked universities nearby for future employees of . . . what are we going to call ourselves now? PCA owns the name FTI."

"I am sure you will think of something appropriate."

"With the amount of money we wired to Zurich this morning, it doesn't matter *what* we're called. We're going to kick ass."

Three days ago, following Iyevenski's strict instructions, Jake Fischer had retrieved the tape at the train station in the company of a pair of CIA officers. Jake had taken the bag containing the tape and the cash and handed it to the officers, who quickly opened it and began to inspect its contents. Jake had taken advantage of the diversion to stick his hand back in the locker and pull free the key taped to the top. Jake had used that second key this morning to access the second locker and retrieve a large blue backpack. He had gone directly to an office of the Bank of Zurich in Paris, where Swiss bank officials, for a substantial fee based on the face value of the stock certificates, opened a new account under Jake's name with a starting balance in the low eight digits.

"Kick ass, yes?" Iyevenski said. "When are you leaving?"

"Tomorrow morning. I'm flying straight to Sunnyvale. I have to meet with my lawyer and the families of the victims and go over the disbursement of the funds from the FBI. After that, I'll take care of moving your junk along with mine to Austin. By the time you show up in a couple of months I'll have us a nice place to live and some leased floorspace to start getting the ball rolling."

"Just make sure that the place is large enough for Nicole also."

"Nicole?"

"She is coming back with me, yes?"

"Does she know this?"

Iyevenski shook his head, laughed, and slapped his thigh. "Do not worry, friend. She will come. Her daughter is graduating this fall and will be moving to the south of France to work. Nicole will be left in Paris all alone. I don't think it will be difficult to convince her. She is a . . . handful, but she has a good heart. What happened to the blond beauty?"

Jake shrugged. "Kathy's still up here, Sergei," he said, touching his temple with an index finger. "Besides, Sonya lives in different circles from mine."

The traffic around the Place de la Concorde flowed slowly, engines idling and horns blaring, the sounds mixing with the mellow tunes of a saxophone player giving a solo performance on a street corner, in front of an empty hat. Above, the radiant, clear skies showed the promise of a new beginning for Jake Fischer.

Two days later, as Jake returned to the United States of America, another jet crossed the Atlantic in the opposite direction, carrying Acting Director of Central Intelligence Donald Bane to Berlin.

A dark limousine was waiting for the seasoned intelligence officer when he arrived. It took him from the airport to the Grand Hotel Esplanade. On the way, Sonya Wüttenberg briefed him on

the latest intelligence collected by a team of twenty-five officers—
the largest American intelligence operation in Berlin since the
Cold War days.

When the limousine pulled up to the elegant hotel, Bane, carrying a thick manila folder given to him by Sonya, got out and
went straight to the Harlekin, one of the finest restaurants in
Berlin, adjacent to the hotel's lobby.

Sonya and a dozen other intelligence officers, both CIA and
FBI, guarded the meeting grounds with enough concealed firepower to start a small revolution.

Bane reached a table in the rear of the crowded restaurant, near
the windows facing a traffic-jammed street. Two men in business
suits sat at the table. They gave the large American puzzled looks
when they saw him approach. The puzzled looks changed to
masks of fear when they noticed their three bodyguards, a few tables away, also in the company of strangers.

"Afternoon, gentlemen. Mind if I join you?"

The oldest one, a lanky, frail man wearing a green bow tie and
starched white shirt, slowly shook his head while telling his companion, "CIA, Herr Minister."

Bane pulled up a chair between the two Germans and set the
thick manila envelope on the tablecloth.

"Proof, gentlemen," he said, patting the package. "This envelope contains undeniable proof of your dealings with a terrorist
who used to call himself the Kardinal."

"Preposterous," hissed Johann von Hunsinger, elegantly
dressed in a dark gray suit. "How dare you—"

"The Kardinal fingered you," Bane said, interrupting the German minister of industry and commerce. "The rest was easy. I'd
say you two gentlemen shouldn't meet in public places such as this
to discuss your terrible behavior, as you've done in the past two
days. Doing so makes it quite easy for another intelligence agency
to videotape the meetings, creating the kind of evidence that

would get you both incarcerated after a short trial, not to mention the shame it would bring to your families."

Von Hunsinger opened his mouth to say something, but Bane didn't care to hear it. "Look at the enclosed video and imagine what it would do to your careers if released to the television networks."

"This is *blackmail*," complained von Hunsinger, a finger running over his silk tie.

"Call it whatever you like, asshole. But, as they say in my country, I've got you both by the balls, and I'm going to start squeezing. You have forty-eight hours to make your decision."

"Decision?" asked von Hunsinger. "What kind of decision?"

Bane turned to the other man, Hans Bölling, who sighed and nodded. "And I thank you for giving us a choice, Mr. Bane," he said in his rheumy voice.

"Choice? What are you talking about, Hans?"

Ignoring the well-groomed minister, Bane kept his gaze on Bölling, who said, "Thank you for your discretion in this matter, sir. I will explain the options to my colleague. We will act within the allotted time."

While von Hunsinger protested, Bane turned around and left the restaurant. The Central Intelligence Agency had just recruited two agents in Germany.

Eight months later, Jake Thomas Fischer, dressed in blue jeans, a black long-sleeved shirt, a tweed jacket, and loafers, no socks, left his leased building in the Arboretum, a large business park in the hills of north Austin. It was lunchtime and he was starving.

Adjusting to the life of the self-financed entrepreneur had been easy for Jake Fisher. He had quickly grown to enjoy and appreciate not having to deal with venture capitalists. His private company, Third Coast Technology, had liquid assets worth more than fifteen million dollars, enough capital to support TCT's current charter as a think tank. With fifteen employees, including Sergei Iyevenski and himself, TCT's end product would not be actual biomemory chips, like FTI's F1, but the biotechnology itself, the core of the future high-tech platform, which Jake planned to license to major corporations starting in about five years. In the meantime, Jake would have his hands full training his recently hired college graduates, a healthy mix of computer science majors, chemical engineers, and biochemists. Jake also had one full-time patent lawyer on his staff.

It would take Jake and Iyevenski a few years to train the young engineers to the level of FTI's employees at the time of the explosion. But when he was done with them, those kids would be the first biotech scientists in the world specialized in the manufacturing of protein-based computer chips. In addition, Jake had been in contact with the deans of engineering at the University of Texas in Austin, Texas A&M University in nearby College Station, Rice University in Houston, and SMU in Dallas. Private meetings had already been set up with key representatives from those schools. Jake wanted to begin the long and arduous transition from silicon to bacterial protein as soon as possible. University curriculums were the first step.

In four years, letters would be sent to major corporations, and Jake Fischer would begin licensing his technology to the world—for the right price. By then, Jake also planned to have process recipes, equipment specifications, and installation modules ready for those corporations willing to start making the transition and leaving their competitors behind. Jake just had to achieve critical mass in the marketplace to trigger the chain reaction that would dwarf the silicon revolution of the sixties and seventies.

As he reached a busy intersection and waited for the pedestrian light to turn green, the notes that would eventually become another biotech patent tucked under his right arm, Jake heard a familiar voice behind him.

"Good afternoon, Dr. Fischer."

Stunned, Jake turned, dropping the notes on the sidewalk, staring in surprise at a tall, pale woman with emerald-green eyes dressed in a denim skirt and a UT Austin T-shirt.

"Sonya?"

"You look as if you just saw a ghost," she said in the German accent Jake Fischer had actually missed since Paris.

Sonya Wüttenberg leaned down, picked up the sheets of paper, and handed them to the nearly frozen entrepreneur.

"What . . . how . . . when did you . . . you never called, and . . ."

She put a finger to his lips. "I wanted to call but couldn't. Not until my release from . . . my former employer was approved."

"You mean you're no longer with—"

She made a face and shook her head. "Do not mention the name. Let's just say that I am temporarily unemployed."

Jake took her hand and pulled her away from the crowded corner, finding privacy in the shade of a nearby oak.

"What *happened* to you? You just disappeared."

"We caught the ones responsible for the attack," Sonya said, sitting down on the lawn. Jake sat in front of her, feeling as if he were in some sort of dream.

"And?"

"And we made sure they will not get the chance to do such a thing again."

"How?"

"You don't really want to know, Jake. . . . But how have you been?"

Jake tilted his head. "Well . . . I haven't been used as bait for the past eight months, so I'd say things are going quite well."

She nodded and smiled.

Jake placed a hand over hers and said, "It's good to see you again, even if it reminds me of a period in my life I'm trying to leave behind."

The former FBI agent shrugged. "You are not the only one trying to leave a previous life behind. . . . Speaking of which," she added, patting Jake on the shoulder, "good job. Los Alamos was never able to do anything with that tape of yours. All they got when they tried to read it was electronic junk."

Jake tilted his head and shrugged. "Your people saw me take it out of the locker. Maybe it got damaged in all the commotion."

Sonya's generous mouth gave Jake a smile. "Right."

"What about the equipment they salvaged from FTI? Was that any good to them?"

"Jake . . ." she said with a heavy sigh. "You know as well as I do that neither the hardware nor the patents are any good without the people who created them."

Jake simply looked away.

"What about Third Coast? What is its charter?" she asked after a few moments of silence.

"We're a think tank. Sergei and I lead a team of scientists to create new patents in biotechnology and other advanced sciences."

"How is Sergei doing?" she asked, pointing to her shoulder.

"Fine. He's on a three-month sabbatical with Nicole. Just got a postcard last week from Australia."

"Good for him," she replied, dropping her gaze to the lawn by her feet.

"It's really great seeing you again," Jake said, losing himself in her green eyes. "What brings you to Austin?"

"Figured you could use some help."

"Yeah?" Jake's eyes brightened.

"This think tank of yours is developing biotechnology recipes, right?"

"Yes?"

"How are you handling security?"

Jake crossed his arms and gave her an amused look. "Why do you ask?"

"Thought I might be of . . . some help."

"Hmm. . . . And exactly what do you have in mind?"

"Twenty years of experience in the intelligence business protecting your investment . . . for a reasonable salary plus benefits."

Jake first smiled, then frowned and crossed his arms. "How do I know you're not just on some government assignment to penetrate my company?"

Her face slowly drew tight. "I am *out,* Jake. There are no tricks. I just . . . I would like to . . . help you be successful this time around."

Jake smiled again, put a hand to her face, and leaned forward to kiss her. Sonya met him halfway. This was the first time he'd kissed a woman since Kathy Bennett, and he welcomed it, running a hand through the closely cropped hair before slowly pulling away, keeping his face a few inches from hers, memories of an intimate moment in the woods north of Paris flashing in his mind.

"This could be complicated, you know," he said, the hand caressing her pearly skin. "I would be your boss."

Cupping his face and kissing him once more, Sonya said, "Jake . . . *nothing* can be as complicated as my previous life."

Attracted by her perilous proposition, Jake Fischer said, "Well, Sonya, I know this little coffee shop down the street. Best croissant sandwiches and cappuccinos in Austin. Why don't we negotiate your proposal over lunch?"

Available by mail from

TOR/ FORGE